HOT BLOOD BEGETS HOT THOUGHTS...

A ponytail-clad woman with gorgeously slender long legs in a blue tank and matching short shorts looked over her shoulder and grinned at him. It was that Summer Sunshine chick.

She was as pretty as a picture, all slender and sweet as she ran past him. Man, she was fast!

He thought about turning around and following her, but when he looked over his shoulder she hadn't slowed. If she had, she would have been signaling she was interested, right? God, he was clearly out of practice with women. She was amused by him. She might even be having fun with him. She was a mystery. A challenge.

"Okay, that's kind of hot," he muttered to himself.

He could see her in the distance on the beach, doing that whole lunging warrior thing and other seamless moves that suggested she was not only fast but flexible. Again, really hot. He thought about asking her out for a drink with adult conversation. Would it be such a bad idea?

Yeah—yeah, it would.

PRAISE FOR AVA MILES' NOVELS

See what all the buzz is about...

"Ava's story is witty and charming."

— BARBARA FREETHY #1 *NYT*
BESTSELLING AUTHOR

"If you like Nora Roberts type books, this is a must-read."

— READERS' FAVORITE

"If ever there was a contemporary romance that rated a 10 on a scale of 1 to 5 for me, this one is it!"

— THE ROMANCE REVIEWS

"I could not stop flipping the pages. I can't wait to read the next book in this series."

— FRESH FICTION

"I've read Susan Mallery and Debbie Macomber... but never have I been so moved as by the books Ava Miles writes."

— BOOKTALK WITH EILEEN

"Ava Miles is fast becoming one of my favorite light contemporary romance writers."

— TOME TENDER

"One word for Ava Miles is WOW."

— MY BOOK CRAVINGS

"Her engaging story and characters kept me turning the pages."

— BOOKFAN

"On par with Nicholas Sparks' love stories."

— JENNIFER'S CORNER BLOG

"The constant love, and the tasteful sexual interludes, bring a sensual, dynamic tension to this appealing story."

— PUBLISHER'S WEEKLY

"Miles' story savvy, sense of humor, respect for her readers and empathy for her characters shine through..."

— USA TODAY

OTHER AVA TITLES TO BINGE

The Paris Roommates

Your dreams are around the corner...

The Paris Roommates: Thea

The Paris Roommates: Dean

The Paris Roommates: Brooke

The Unexpected Prince Charming Series

Love with a kiss of the Irish...

Beside Golden Irish Fields

Beneath Pearly Irish Skies

Through Crimson Irish Light

After Indigo Irish Nights

Beyond Rosy Irish Twilight

Over Verdant Irish Hills

Against Ebony Irish Seas

The Merriams Series

Chock full of family and happily ever afters...

Wild Irish Rose

Love Among Lavender

Valley of Stars

Sunflower Alley

A Forever of Orange Blossoms

A Breath of Jasmine

———

The Love Letter Series

The Merriams grandparents' epic love affair...

Letters Across An Open Sea

Along Waters of Sunshine and Shadow

———

The Friends & Neighbors Novels

A feast for all the senses...

The House of Hope & Chocolate

The Dreamer's Flower Shoppe

———

The Dare River Series

Filled with down-home charm...

Country Heaven

The Chocolate Garden

Fireflies and Magnolias

The Promise of Rainbows

The Fountain Of Infinite Wishes

The Patchwork Quilt Of Happiness

Country Heaven Cookbook

The Chocolate Garden: A Magical Tale (Children's Book)

———

The Dare Valley Series

Awash in small town fabulousness...

Nora Roberts Land

French Roast

The Grand Opening

The Holiday Serenade

The Town Square

The Park of Sunset Dreams

The Perfect Ingredient

The Bridge to a Better Life

The Calendar of New Beginnings

Home Sweet Love

The Moonlight Serenade

The Sky of Endless Blue

Daring Brides

Daring Declarations

———

Dare Valley Meets Paris Billionaire Mini-Series

Small town charm meets big city romance...

The Billionaire's Gamble

The Billionaire's Secret

The Billionaire's Courtship

The Billionaire's Return

Dare Valley Meets Paris Compilation

———

The Once Upon a Dare Series

Falling in love is a contact sport...

The Gate to Everything

———

Non-Fiction

The Happiness Corner: Reflections So Far

The Post-Covid Wellness Playbook

———

Cookbooks

Home Baked Happiness Cookbook

Country Heaven Cookbook

———

The Lost Guides to Living Your Best Life Series

Reclaim Your Superpowers

Courage Is Your Superpower

Expression Is Your Superpower

Peace Is Your Superpower

Confidence Is Your Superpower

Happiness Is Your Superpower

––––––

Children's Books

The Chocolate Garden: A Magical Tale

A VERY UN-SHAKESPEARE ROMANCE

AVA MILES

www.avamiles.com
Ava Miles

To all of those who protect children,
and to the children who need protecting.

ACKNOWLEDGMENTS

A special thank you to an old friend from the FBI who happily answered my questions and helped me with the more technical aspects of this story. He didn't want any thanks, but when I think of everything he's done for me, especially in my old career, there was no way I wasn't going to say something. The quiet heroes never want our gratitude, and that's what makes them heroes. So thank you, Mr. Anonymous.

CHAPTER ONE

SLAMMING THE CASE FILE ON A BAD GUY WAS AS GOOD as sex.

Had he really just thought that? Robbie O'Connor filed the paperwork sitting on his messy desk and then picked up his shitty precinct coffee to wash the taste of that sorry realization out of his mouth. Sure, the criminal who was now serving twenty years had hurt his wife and kids like it was his daily right. Robbie lived for getting scumbags like that thrown into the slammer. Work had always been his mission. His source of pride. He loved making a difference in people's lives.

But had he really gotten to a point where he thought putting someone away was as good as a roll in the sheets with a hot-blooded woman?

Okay, he knew he worked a lot. He'd gotten into the habit of taking on extra cases to help out other cops with families since there was no reason for him to go home. He was patted on the back all the time for it. But this notion? His brothers —all six of them—would likely say he'd become a pathetic excuse for a man. Okay, maybe not Tim. The youngest

1

O'Connor male was the most sensitive one. He'd be more inclined to point out Robbie had become overly cynical since his divorce. Not so far from the truth.

"O'Connor!" his intercom blasted from reception. "The UPS guy needs your pretty signature."

Shoving out of his creaky office chair, he strolled down the hallway, wondering if his sister Kathleen had sent him something from Ireland. She liked to pop the odd stuffed sheep or eerie leprechaun into the post, but those packages usually came in around birthdays or holidays. It was late August, but maybe she'd sent him a *Just Because* present. He was her favorite brother, after all—not that his other brothers would agree, the idiots.

They all adored their one and only sister, and God knew she'd put up with a lot having seven older brothers. But she'd turned out okay. In fact, she was the only O'Connor kid who was happily married with a baby on the way. He was smiling at the thought of his first niece or nephew when he reached the man in the brown uniform beside the reception desk. The guy was belly-laughing with Patty Fitzgerald, both men huddled over the latter's phone.

"Hey, O'Connor!" Patty smacked him on the back. "I was just showing Al here your latest stupid criminal video. I still can't believe that murderer thought he could erase all the evidence by sticking the body in a vat of vanilla ice cream. I about died laughing when the local reporter quoted the suspect as saying the victim loved having his cherry pie à la mode, so he figured he'd appreciate the gesture of burying him in it."

Robbie puffed out his chest, taking pride in spreading his sick version of law enforcement cheer. His family, friends, and fellow co-workers all loved it. "It might be a top ten, given the suspect dropped his cell phone in the vat along with the body. Forensics found the sim card and recovered everything from his threatening texts to his murder shopping list at Home Depot. Idiot thought the ice cream would cure all his troubles."

"A pint of chocolate chip usually cures mine when my old lady gives me fits," the UPS guy said with a snort. "You O'Connor?"

"Didn't you hear me call him that?" Patty walked back behind the reception desk. "What? You got lime sherbet in your ears?"

Robbie shot Patty an amused look before pulling out his ID, tucked beside his badge inside the wrinkled tan sports jacket he really needed to get to the dry cleaners. "Don't mind him, Al. Patty hasn't had his donut quotient for the morning. Thanks."

"No problem," the man answered as Robbie signed for the package.

He immediately noted it wasn't from Ireland as the UPS man took off. Just a simple Next Day Delivery envelope with an illegible return address in Boston. His instincts revved. He hadn't been sent anonymous evidence through the mail in a while, but maybe today was the day. The thought excited him more than it probably should. He needed an interesting new case. Something to hold his focus. The run-of-the-mill breaking and entering was like stale bread.

"That from your sweet little sister?" Patty asked, slurping coffee from his carefully guarded *I'm Too Sexy* cup, an outrageous lie his fellow police officers knee-slapped themselves silly laughing over. Patty had the kind of unmemorable face that had made him great for blend-in-anywhere undercover work. Now, with only a few years to go until retirement, he was proud of his weekly donut intake.

"Doesn't look like it's from sis." Robbie casually rested against the desk and snagged an apple crumb donut from Patty's box. "Maybe I won the lottery. Wait, I just did."

"Hey! Donut stealing is a serious offense. Don't make me cuff you."

"I'm good for it," he called over his shoulder, moving quickly to his office and then dramatically slamming the door. Only one other officer had ever cuffed him—Patty, back when Robbie had been a hotshot rookie. The older officer had taken it upon himself to give him a lesson in police hierarchy after he'd solved one of Patty's cases in a day—a case that had been open for six months. So the big lug had cuffed him to one of his cousin's garbage trucks for revenge.

Robbie had taken the hint to shut up and done his job, letting people come to him if they wanted his help. He'd risen through the ranks faster that way, not that promotion had been his focus. But to this day, he'd never been recreational with handcuffs in the bedroom.

God, here he was again, thinking about sex—or his current dry spell. To be fair, it was of his own choosing. He was turning forty this year, and he was tired. Tired of dating apps that brought strange messages to his inbox, and even more so of the bar hookup scene, including at his brother's Irish pub, O'Connor's.

He didn't want to get married again just for the sake of it, and he wasn't even sure he wanted kids of his own. They were great and all, but they asked so many questions and needed so many things. He'd practically helped raise seven siblings, being the oldest. He was good with living life as a single man. Or so he was telling himself...

He carefully opened the envelope, checking the interior with the eraser end of a pencil from his desk. It only nudged a half sheet of paper. When he withdrew the note inside, he froze.

Robbie,
I need you to get into a taxi right now and go to the Beacon Hill

Gym. My babies are there. You have to pretend to be their father and pick them up. Don't try and call me. More information will be waiting for you there. Don't leave this note at your office and don't tell anyone where you're going. Make sure you aren't followed. I haven't been kidnapped, fyi.

Love,

The one who helped you out of Carson Bay after that lion's mane jellyfish stung you.

TARA!

Robbie read his first cousin's cryptic note over again, rubbing the back of his neck as he tried to make sense of it. Jesus, she hadn't even signed it. Just given a detail only he would remember, much more cloak-and-dagger than he was comfortable with. And why the fuck had she thrown in the haven't-been-kidnapped part? His blood pressure was soaring already.

He looked at the UPS envelope, noting she'd sent the letter yesterday. Yesterday...

Why not call or text him? He knew she'd caught her worthless husband, Scotty, cheating with one of her nail salon technicians a few days ago and thrown him out of the house, saying they were done. His brother Danny had spread the news after Tara had stormed into O'Connor's wanting a fully loaded Rueben and a Cosmo.

Why were Tara's two girls at some gym way up in Beacon Hill? Tara didn't belong to a gym as far as he knew, and neither did Scotty. Certainly they didn't hang out in that chichi neighborhood. And what was with the bit about not telling anyone or being followed? Had Scotty hired an investigator for divorce proceedings?

Shit. Divorces sucked. He'd left his cousin a voicemail the moment he'd heard about the O'Connor's incident, saying he was sorry Scotty was such a worthless jerk and asking if she needed anything. Her parents had both passed and she was an only child, so Robbie felt a sort of responsibility toward her. She was almost like another sibling to him and his brothers and sister. But he hadn't worried too much when he hadn't heard back from Tara. He'd figured she had her hands full. Obviously, she did. But with what?

He eyed his gun. He didn't love the idea of picking up kids while he had his service revolver. Technically, he was on duty, however, so he was required to be armed. Shrugging out of his jacket, he refastened his shoulder holster and tugged the garment back on, grabbing his cell phone. He was out the door moments later, walking past Patty with a brief wave. Finding a taxi was always challenging, but he walked up the road until he hit a main intersection and hailed one there.

The ride was over twenty minutes with lunch-hour traffic, giving him time to stew and put extra wrinkles in his pants as he gripped his knees. Tara was a smart, independent woman who handled her own shit like the rest of the O'Connors. Something was wrong. Bad wrong. His gut was flip-flopping like a largemouth bass hooked at Hammond Pond. He was sweating by the time the cab dropped him off in front of the gym, but he was ready for anything. Tara could count on him. She'd always known that. He'd made her that promise when he'd held her after arriving with the police to inform her of the tragic car accident that killed her parents.

The electric double doors of the gym whooshed open as he approached, the blast of the air-conditioning welcome. He approached reception with his best attempt at a smile.

"Hello, I'm Robbie O'Connor." He masked a shaky breath. "I'm here to pick up Reagan and Cassidy."

"Oh, Mr. O'Connor." The woman whose gold nameplate read Brenda gave him a blooming smile. "I'm so glad you made it. Your wife was so worried."

Wife? He compressed a shudder. "Do you need to see my ID?" he asked, already reaching into his back pocket.

Brenda rolled her eyes. "Yes, I do even though your wife showed me your photo. She's never left the kids with us before, so she was a little nervous. Then her boss made it worse when he called her back to work only ten minutes after she'd started her workout. What a jerk. Poor thing was beside herself having to leave them here for longer and asking you to take off work early to pick them up. I felt so bad for her."

He heard this story with more than a little shock. His cousin didn't have a boss; she was the boss, of three nail salons. The lies were clearly necessary in Tara's mind, but why? He made himself nod as he quickly flashed his ID and then signed the kids out, not feeling exactly comfortable with being on record for something he didn't yet understand. He was the guy who put liars away when they took things too far. Impersonating a child's father to remove them from gym daycare was skirting the line, but he knew Tara must have a damn good reason.

"I'll just call and have your kids come out since you don't know where the daycare is," Brenda said helpfully.

Moments later, he heard *"Daddy!"* echo throughout reception.

Robbie's muscles locked hard. The girls were in on it? He swung his head to the right as a young girl ran into him and wrapped her little arms around his leg, gripping it with all her strength.

"Da-da," another childlike voice sounded as a soft lump knocked into his other side, tiny fingers tickling his kneecap.

He hoped the gym attendant hadn't seen his ripple of shock as he automatically put his hands on the girls' heads. What the hell was going on? The smells of workout sweat and pool chlorine kicked up his mounting nausea. Tara had said more information would be at the gym. It had better be.

Because now he was super freaked. And he dealt with life-and-death situations daily.

This was family, though, and that made the stakes so much higher.

"Hey, Cassidy and Reagan," he managed to say through a dry mouth as he looked down at the little girls.

Big matching blue eyes in unsmiling china-doll faces filled his vision. He knew Tara's girls, of course. But man, had they grown since he'd seen them at the annual O'Connor July Fourth BBQ over a month ago. Reagan looked inches taller. Was that possible for a six-year-old? And Cassidy's short, curly hair was a darker brown. He tried to smile despite the tension in his jaw. This had to be weird for them too, right?

Cassidy gave him a drool-drenched grin as she clutched the girliest teddy bear in history, decked out in a pink gingham dress with a huge matching bow between her fuzzy white ears. Miss Rosie, if his memory served.

He studied the girls for any signs of further distress as he would on a 911 domestic call. They both had bright bows in their hair, which added to the girly ensembles of flowery sundresses and glittering sandals, Reagan's open-toed and Cassidy's closed. They were dressed just like Tara, who loved her bright colors and bling. The kids didn't have any bruises, thank God. Not even a scratch. He tried to suck in some oxygen in relief, but he caught the worry in their eyes. You could always tell what someone was really feeling by looking there.

This had to be about their father. Robbie hadn't liked Scotty Flanagan from the time they'd shared a playground at St. Stephens Catholic School. He was a weak excuse for a man, but Tara had fallen for him and said he both supported and helped her business aspirations, so Robbie had kept his lips zipped and been pleasant to him at family events.

If Scotty had done something to hurt Tara and her babies,

as she called them, they were going to have one hell of a serious talk.

"*Hi,*" Cassidy drew out, hugging his leg harder. He felt something wet touch his knee through his pants and cringed. She was a drool factory, which is why her nickname was Drool Baby while her sister's was Miss Pixie.

"Mr. O'Connor, I'll just grab the diaper bag. Your wife said to make sure you didn't forget it since it's not your fave."

Diaper bag? His balls shriveled, and he immediately looked down at Cassidy. Yeah, she had the puffy outline under her dress that indicated she was still in diapers. His brain shorted. Man, he hadn't changed a diaper since Kathleen was little, and it wasn't something he missed. Then he realized the bag might contain the information his cousin had mentioned was waiting for him, and his palms started to sweat again.

"Thanks, Brenda. I'll just wait here with the girls."

Kneeling to their level as the woman took off, he laid a hand on Reagan's shoulder. Cassidy cuddled into his body with Miss Rosie and laid her head against his chest, smelling of sour orange juice she must have spilled on her dress. "You guys okay?"

Reagan bit her lip but bravely nodded. "Mom said you need to read her letter."

"Is it in the diaper bag?"

"Yes." Reagan curved into him so she could say something into his ear. "Mom said you would take care of us until she came back."

Came back? Where the fuck had Tara gone? His stomach dropped to the floor at that pronouncement, but he hugged them both. They had to be scared, and Tara had to be terrified to have taken off and left her babies. "You know I will. We O'Connors stick together. We'll figure it out." He patted their little backs with assurance. God, they were so tiny compared to his large hands.

Brenda returned with a large bedazzled bag, which said BOSS on the side in white rhinestones. He lurched forward to help her with it as she was straining with effort.

"Your wife is like I used to be," Brenda commented as he gently slid the heavy bag off her shoulder. "Ready for every emergency. I had three boys. My husband joked that hefting around the kids and the diaper bag was like lifting dumbbells."

He tested the heaviness, estimating it weighed about thirty pounds. Did Tara's diaper bag usually weigh this much? Brenda didn't seem to consider it strange.

"It keeps Tara fit too," he said, keeping the conversation normal as Cassidy hugged his leg again. "I told her she didn't need to join a gym. She looks great just as she is."

"Oh, that's so sweet," Brenda said with a breathy sigh. "I wish my husband thought that. Even so, your wife wanted to join today, but she didn't have time to finish the gym membership paperwork. She said you could bring it with you for her to fill out. I know she wanted to get back here tomorrow to continue her workout."

Robbie doubted she'd be back, but only nodded. "I'm happy to take the papers, Brenda."

"Are you interested in joining too? Your wife said you loved to work out, but not in gyms. That's pretty obvious. What do you bench?"

Her appreciative nod at his impressive build had him shrugging with a little embarrassment. "If there were any gyms I'd consider, it would be this one, but I'm more the outdoor workout type. Well, girls..."

They were staring up at him with their hearts in their eyes. He nearly gulped at the trust there.

"Let's get this show on the road." He made sure to flash Brenda a smile. "Thanks again for your help."

Hefting the diaper bag up higher on his shoulder, he

glanced down at Cassidy. How far could a two-year-old walk? Screw it. He swung her into his arms and felt Reagan grab his other hand as they left.

"Mom parked in a garage," Reagan told him the moment the doors whooshed closed behind them. "She helped me memorize the directions."

Tara had left a car? How had she gotten home? But that wasn't a question fit for the kids, so he just said, "All right. Lead the way."

The girls were quiet as Reagan navigated them to a garage three blocks from the gym. He was impatient to reach the letter, but he had to walk like a snail so the young girl could keep up with him. Tara had chosen a parking deck loaded with top-model, freshly washed cars and parked in the corner on the second floor by an exit. When they reached the shiny black Cadillac SUV with dealer's plates—not Tara's—Reagan dug into the diaper bag's front pocket and pulled out a key fob.

"Mom told me to keep the diaper bag safe and I did. When Cassidy needed a change, I got the diaper out and everything."

Her smile exhibited a certain pride, and it made him wonder at the little triumphs that helped build a kid's self-confidence. "You did a bang-up job, Reagan. Did your mom get a new car?"

"No, she got it from someone after all our tires got nails in them." She blew an exasperated breath toward her short bangs, a move she'd clearly copied from her mother. "Mom was so mad, but she said this was the bright side. We got two new cars for our adventure. One for Mom. And one for us."

Battery acid pooled in his stomach. Being in law enforcement, he knew parents used "adventure talk" to dress up bad shit. He popped the trunk and startled at the three suitcases, two girly ones and another in a dark black, along with cardboard boxes loaded with family-size snacks and beverages. He even noticed his favorite beer. Then he saw the giant bag of diapers and winced.

"You're packed for that adventure, it seems." What was the adult-sized case for if Tara wasn't coming?

"Mom went shopping for our trip before we came to the gym." Reagan stood on her tiptoes and pointed to the beer. "She wanted us all to have our favorites."

The beer was a downright bribe. "That was nice of her."

"She brought you some clothes too," Reagan added shyly, ducking her head. "We hope you like them."

"Mine," Cassidy said, pointing to the purple suitcase with the smiling unicorn on the front, decked out with rainbows that made him think of Ireland.

Then he heard an angry meow and looked down at the girls in horror. "Did you bring your cat?"

"Mom said we *had* to take Miss Purrfect with us." Reagan looked at her sister, who nodded, wide-eyed. "She's part of our family, and Mom said we could have her so we wouldn't miss her so much."

How could they not miss their mother? He fought a curse when they both studied their feet. Just how long did Tara plan to be gone—and why? It was time for answers.

"Okay, Reagan. Where's this letter of your mom's?"

She pointed to the diaper bag again. "There's a zipper part on the bottom. Mom said everything you need to know is in there."

He dropped the diaper bag on top of the other suitcases and unzipped the bottom one-handed while balancing Cassidy against his chest. Sure enough, inside the clever compartment was a manila envelope with his name scrawled across it in a hurried cursive.

He pulled out the envelope, hoisted the bag back over his

shoulder, and slammed the trunk shut. "Let's get you guys in the car."

"We have our car seats," Reagan informed him as he opened the back passenger door, kicking off another angry meow. "Mom said Miss Purrfect wouldn't be happy being caged in the car, but she couldn't bring her to the gym. Can we let her out now?"

"Sure." Why not add a snarly cat to the party?

She gave him a beaming smile as she leaned down and opened the cage, her hair bow flopping to the right. The animal's pointed white face snarled at him like he was the reason it had been in feline jail, its green eyes staring at him with as much menace as the serial killer he'd busted ten years ago. Great. He was already on this cat's shit list.

"Look, Robbie! Mom made Miss Purrfect a new collar." Reagan fingered the bedazzled band that had probably been inspired by that Marilyn Monroe song she loved, "Diamonds Are a Girl's Best Friend." Tara had the movie poster of *Gentlemen Prefer Blondes* in her main nail salon, and it seemed like the song had been playing every time he'd swung by to say hello and check up on her.

An image of Tara and his little sister Kathleen doing art projects on the kitchen table in his childhood home rose up in his mind. "Your mother has been gluing sparkles to everything she could get her hands on since she was a kid."

"That's how we make things prettier," Reagan told him matter-of-factly while the cat tugged at the collar with its paw as if it understood their conversation. "I can hold Miss Purrfect on my lap after I help buckle Cassidy into her car seat. Mom says you might not know how to do it."

What did Tara think he was? An idiot? But he was sensitive to Reagan's pride. "She might be right. How about we buckle in after I read your mom's letter?" His fingers were itching for information.

The SUV was designed for comfort, he noticed, as he settled Cassidy in the left captain's seat and then helped Reagan into the right one before fitting himself into the spacious rear middle seat with the diaper bag at his feet. Next, he was going through that. Unsealing the envelope, he pulled out the pages and began to read.

Dear Robbie,

I'm in trouble. I didn't dare call you on your phone because they told me they would find out and hurt my babies.

Let me back up. Scotty has taken off—with that skank nail girl Janice Brewster he screwed at my new location. I know Danny told you that I'd caught them together in the office doing the business on my desk four days ago. I fired Janice and kicked Scotty's sorry ass out of the house, changed the locks, and took him off all the bank accounts, telling him I was getting a divorce. Like my lawyer advised.

Later that day, two of Branigan Kelly's tough guys showed up at my main nail salon. They said they expected things to be business as usual with me even though I'd kicked Scotty out. I didn't know what in the hell they were talking about and told them that they could go fuck themselves.

But the moment I closed for the day, I locked the door and searched every corner of the salon. I found over three hundred thousand dollars, which was like getting hit in the face by a two-by-four. I was sick with worry by the time I finished searching the other two salons. Robbie, I found over three hundred thousand dollars hidden in each nail salon—almost a million dollars total! I gathered it all up in a black suitcase and then put it in my BOSS bag under Cassidy's diapers when I got home—the last place I thought anyone would look. The one I left at the gym for you.

Scotty was laundering money for the Kellys. He's called my phone a million times begging me to let him pick up a few things he left behind at the nail salons. Personal mementos and his precious computer. What bullshit! He showed up when I was out, but my girls told him to buzz off. When he came by the house, I told him I'd call the police if he stuck around. What was he thinking? Doing that in my place of business and risking everything I've worked so hard for? I want to tear him apart.

He had to stop reading. His heart was pounding in his ears. The Kellys? Jesus, he hadn't thought Scotty was that stupid. Everyone knew Branigan Kelly's reputation in South Boston. He was a low-level monster who'd risen to the top by forming alliances with the Russians and the Albanians.

"Daddy really messed up, didn't he?" Reagan said in the quiet of the car.

He looked over to see her holding Miss Purrfect tightly against her chest, her little chin resting in the fur. "What else did your mom tell you?"

"Mom is so mad at Daddy for being a moron and hurting our nail salons by being a bad businessman. She kicked him out of the house when he said he wasn't sorry and wouldn't make it right. Then she told us he left town and might not be coming back and good riddance. We girls are better off."

"Yeah," Cassidy echoed in baby-like support, her tiny fist banging the side of her car seat. "Good riddant."

He tried to give them a smile. As a story, it was a solid one for kids. Believable details. Enough of the truth to make it passable. As a cop, he knew how critical it was for kids to have a story for their minds to hold on to. Otherwise, they might make up a story ten times worse than the truth, which would leave them in a fearful place of confusion and uncertainty. Never a good space for any person, least of all a child.

"I'm sorry this happened, but your mom is correct, and now we're going to fix things." He leaned forward with the letter in his hand and touched both girls' arms, making sure to look them both straight in the eye. He knew how important such a look was. They had to know he could take care of them.

God, this situation was a heavy load for kids to carry. He knew the work it took for kids to keep positive in the face of major family changes and tragedy. He and his family had gone through the wringer when they'd lost their mom to breast cancer. Kathleen had only been five, the youngest of a whole bunch of pissed-off kids who'd done their best to tell her everything would be okay.

But it hadn't been.

Their mother's absence had left a hole in them all. He wondered if Scotty would leave such a hole, asshole that he was.

What the hell was the right thing to say here? "We O'Connors stick together."

"And we're as tough as they come," Reagan added, echoing what she'd heard their family say over and over again. His mother used to say that if you repeated a sentiment often enough, you'd truly feel it, and Robbie believed that. It was the only way he'd gotten over his mother's death.

"You bet we are." He held out his hand for a fist bump, which Reagan gave with a surprising force.

"Me too," Cassidy cried, holding out her little fist as well as her teddy bear's.

His mouth twitched as he included them in the gesture. Tara was tough, and it was clear she was raising strong, independent girls. "I'm going to keep reading, and then we'll...get going."

Not that he knew what his next steps would be yet. He sat back with the letter.

Robbie, the Kellys slashed my tires in front of my townhouse yesterday, and I freaked. Then a man called my cell, said Scotty had taken off with Janice, and that if I knew where he was, I'd better tell them.

I said I didn't and that I was divorcing his sorry ass. He said Mr. Kelly expected me to change my mind about continuing Scotty's business arrangement with them or they would hurt my babies. They even told me the name and address of their daycare and said accidents happen and children disappear or fall into the Mystic all the time. At the end, he told me not to go to you or the cops because they had people on the inside and would know.

I lost it. All I could think about was getting my girls to safety. But then what? My businesses have obviously been laundering money for the Kellys, and I have their cash. I think they believe Scotty ran off with it. But if and when they find him, they'll know he doesn't have it. So I'm turning the money in to you as an officer of the law and telling you Scotty is the criminal here. Not me.

But me and the girls are still in trouble. I knew the Kellys would start looking for us the moment I left town. They're already looking for Scotty and Janice. I realized I couldn't get far with two girls their age. Or protect them against Branigan Kelly's guys.

So I'm asking you to take my girls and protect them with everything you've got. But not with the cops. Like family does. Because I won't bet my girls' lives that Kelly's guys were lying about having people on the force.

Robbie tipped his head to the ceiling as tension gathered at the base of his skull. He couldn't be one hundred percent sure either. The Kellys were legendary for throwing money at people until they caved or, if that didn't work, threatening their families or setting them up for blackmail. They'd already caught one cop working on the Kelly payroll in the last year. But it would be a pain in the ass to handle this without doing it by the book. He didn't want to lose his job by going rogue or become a suspect in this fiasco. Shit.

"Want Miss Rosie?"

He glanced over to see Cassidy holding out her bear. Shaking his head, he let out an uneasy breath when her lower lip wobbled. God, was she going to cry? "Nah, she looks pretty happy with you."

"Mom said to tell you that she trusted you and that she knew it was going to freak you out a little bit to have this adventure with us while she worked things out with the business." Reagan was suddenly pushing Miss Purrfect off her lap and jumping out of her seat, coming to stand in front of him in the short aisle, gripping his forearm. "Me and Cassidy promised Mom we would be really good and make things easy for you."

God, that crushed him. He pulled her to his chest. "You two have always been as sweet as angels. That's not my worry. I'm only worried a little about your mom. Going off on her own adventure like this." Okay, so now he was stretching the truth too. "But don't you guys worry. We're going to get her back here really quick. I'm going to help make that happen. I promise."

"I sure hope so." Reagan tunneled into him. "I already miss her."

"Me too," Cassidy half wailed, eyes full of those tears he feared as she clutched her bear.

This sucked. All of it. "Let me finish your mom's letter."

Reagan pushed away and picked up the cat again. He turned the next page and started reading where he'd left off.

You always say stupid criminals get caught using their own car and their cell phone, so I made other arrangements. I borrowed this car from a client who said I could use it for as long as I need to while I'm getting new tires. He's a dealer and won't miss it. Another client just talked about her vacation in the Outer Banks and how family-friendly it is. I figured it would be the perfect cover for you and the girls if you pretend to be a single dad on a final summer vacation with his girls before school starts. I secured a house through my client's property owners in the Outer Banks. You can pay cash on-site.

I told them you were my ex-husband but that I still make reservations for you with the kids because I'm choosier, even though you're a good father.

A good father? He was supposed to continue this charade? He fell back against the seat. Holy shit. As an officer of the law, he couldn't take off with these kids and pretend to be their father. Especially across state lines. That could be called kidnapping if someone like their real father chose to make a stink. Jesus. He gritted his teeth and kept reading.

I know you're going to want to do this like a cop, <u>but you can't.</u> I believe the Kellys when they say they have people on the inside. I can't take the chance with my babies, and neither can you. I'm begging you on your mother's grave to protect them, and I'm telling you that my aunt—your mother—would agree with me.

I'm only asking for two weeks. You've always said the first two weeks after any crime-related incident are the most critical in the way things play out. Plus, you always joke about all your unused vacation time. Something will give. Either Scotty will confess everything to the cops when he realizes he can't outrun the Kellys, which will make it easier for all of us to return to Boston and you to make the case airtight so the inside guys on the police force can't fuck it up... Or the Kellys will find Scotty and deal with him. Hell, Janice might turn Scotty in to save her skin or because she'll hate being on the run.

If and when the Kellys realize I'm gone and so is the cash, I can't imagine how many guys they're going to send out. They might suspect me, but they're more likely to think Scotty is behind it.

I'm disappearing too, although it's going to kill me to be away from my babies, but I know you can do a better job of keeping them safe. Right now, you're the only person I trust. I know you'll know what to do with the cash. And because this vacation is going to put you out, I took out some of my savings and stuffed it into the black suitcase for you to use. Don't get mad. You know we O'Connors pay our way.

Plus, you'll need to pay everything in cash like you always say is mandatory for people on the run. I did some early shopping since it's a long drive—directions are in the envelope. Also, there's a burner phone in the diaper bag. You know you can't use your regular phone while you're hiding, so I got new ones for both of us. Even though I want to call my babies and check in every single day, I won't. You always say phones are the surest way of getting caught. So when something gives, I'll call you and we'll meet up. If it doesn't—God help us—at the end of two weeks, then we'll meet and make a new plan.

I've written down everything imaginable for you about the girls and put it in this envelope, from their favorite foods to how Cassidy needs to sleep with her feet out of the blanket because they get hot and she starts fussing. I know it's a lot, and I swear I'll make it up to you somehow, but Reagan is a good helper, and Cassidy is as sweet a baby as God has ever made and put here on earth.

Take care of my babies for me, Robbie. I'm trusting you with their lives—and mine.

Your loving cousin,

Tara

His heart was like a jackhammer as he stuffed the letter back into the envelope. He fingered the paper, one zinger repeating in his head. *I'm telling you that my aunt—your mother—would agree with me.* That was like a burr sticking to him.

His chest tightened as he realized what he was going to do—what he had to do. Sitting back, he planted his hands on his knees like he did when he was trying to figure out his next steps on a big case. Closing his eyes, he let the details swirl like dust coughed up from a strong wind off the Bay. He watched them all flash in his mind, fixing his gaze on one and then another, until they all settled to the floor. He could see the pitfalls now, the details that might hurt or injure. He waited for his mind to work out the things he could do now to offset those problems.

The next steps came to him, just as they always did. He was calm on the inside, a signature feeling for him when he was working something out in his mind. Still, when he opened his eyes to find both girls and the cat staring at him, practically holding their breath, pressure returned to his chest.

He could not make a wrong move here.

Pulling his cell phone out of his pocket, he turned it off and took out the sim card. He wasn't going to help the Kellys by letting them track him through his cell phone. Tara had clearly paid attention all these years when he'd talked about cases, way more than he'd ever imagined.

When he looked up, her little girls were staring at every move he made, as still as small china doll statues. The cat looked like a stuffed animal. "Girls, are you hungry? Thirsty? Because I need to make a few calls on this new phone your mom bought me before we take off. But good news. You remember my brothers, Billie and Tim, don't you? Billie's the big giant of the O'Connor clan, the one no one messes with, and Tim's the really nice guy who helps older people at the retirement home."

Poor things both nodded quickly, their eyes as wide as saucers.

"Good news. They're going on the adventure with us."

Because he was going to need some serious backup for this case.

CHAPTER TWO

HER HEART WAS GALLOPING LIKE A HERD OF WILD HORSES.

Lily Meadows shifted in her seat next to her partner, trying to ignore the feeling that the metal sides of their undercover vehicle were closing in on her. They'd lost their suspect.

How in the hell had Tara O'Connor given them the slip? When her boss found out, Lily's desire for the promotion to the FBI's Child Exploitation and Human Trafficking Task Force would be dead in the water.

She wanted to bang her head on the steering wheel in frustration, but that would be childish. Unprofessional. She might be the polar opposite of the stereotypical alpha, tough-guy FBI agent, but she was a seasoned field agent. She went undercover frequently. Faced down dangerous criminals. Prepared for every eventuality.

How had she blown it?

Lily had judged Tara O'Connor to be a good mother, but she'd just left her two children alone. *At a gym.* Those adorable little girls had been abandoned by the person who was supposed to love and cherish them the most. That kind of shit left scars. She knew from personal experience.

"Are you *wheezing*?" Sheila Morales was known for being one of the most wise-cracking, prank-playing agents in FBI circles, but when she put on her drill sergeant tone, people's spines straightened. "Pull it together, Sunshine. I know this looks bad, but don't make me get out a paper bag. I'd feel obligated to take a photo of you sucking in air on surveillance and pin it up in the break room."

That helped her get her breathing under control. She got enough ragging as it was for having a last name like Meadows and looking like the girl next door, an asset in undercover work. Add in the kernel of positivity she felt toward life despite everything in her past, and she'd been given the nickname Sunshine. Sheila had even given her a *You are my Sunshine* T-shirt for their softball games as well as a key chain, which she used for her apartment in Chelsea, an easy commute to FBI headquarters.

"You even think about telling anyone I wheezed, Sheila, and I'll tell everyone how you forgot to shave your girly parts on your last undercover gig when you were supposed to be a stripper."

"Almost blew my cover because of a bush." Her partner's rough laugh erupted in the hot car. "It was a last-minute assignment, and I still blame the head of the task force for forgetting to include that detail about my outfit in my undercover packet."

Lily couldn't even manage a smile as her gaze cut back to the parking garage they were surveilling. "We're so screwed, Sheila."

Sheila turned in her seat, and Lily focused on her grounding presence. Her black hair was pulled back in a ponytail, showing off dangling gold earrings. She wore minimal makeup and nude lipstick. Her pantsuit was all black with serviceable ankle boots she could run in. They'd been partners since Lily had been transferred to Boston six months ago. Sheila was the more senior agent, having been in the Bureau for ten years in comparison to Lily's five. Her experience in the field came through in moments like this, and Lily nodded to tell her she was ready to listen.

"We are not screwed." Sheila narrowed her brown eyes. "And you stop your rare Negative Nancy tirade. I'm the only person who gets to be Negative Nancy in this partnership. This case still has *golden ticket* written all over it. I'm going to say this slowly in case all the blood in your forebrain has up and left, but the Child Exploitation and Human Trafficking Task Force is going to be doing cartwheels to have you. When we nail Branigan Kelly and close down his operation, Lily, you'll get whatever you want. I'm going to miss you like hell when they put me with some other partner, but I tell myself we'll still work together on the odd case and hang out and talk shop. It's gonna happen. Listen to Mama on this."

God, she must be really freaking out to have Sheila put on her cheerleading outfit. "All right, Mama, dialing Negative Nancy back and putting my sunshine self back on," she tried to joke, flicking her wavy blond hair over her shoulder. "I'm going to miss you too, by the way."

"I know." Sheila lightly punched her in the shoulder. "Now, let's talk about where we are in this case. We know Tara is likely in the wind, which justifies the judge's decision to let us put a tracker on the car she was driving after we saw her bulk shopping at Costco this morning."

"But she didn't take her car, Sheila. Why didn't she—"

"Calm down, Sunshine. I'm telling you... We just watched her cousin, who's an officer in the precinct where we know Kelly has cops on his payroll, pick up the kids and bring them to the car we put the tracker on. That, my friend, is manna from heaven. Why? Because we happen to know there's fifty grand in that black suitcase. The same black suitcase Tara O'Connor was seen taking to and from her three nail salons."

That had been a day. But Lily still didn't believe Tara O'Connor was behind this mess. Otherwise, she wouldn't have removed the cash from the premises...and the Kellys wouldn't have slashed her tires. Sheila wasn't convinced— she'd argued that there'd been some kind of dispute, and Tara had moved the cash as a safeguard. Although fifty thousand seemed kinda light to her. With three nail salons, wouldn't there have been more?

"Your confidential informant told us that money is Branigan Kelly's dirty money," Sheila continued, although she didn't need the reminder. The informant had also told her that it had been laundered through Tara's nail salons. "We have confirmation that the cash is in Tara's new SUV in that garage, and Tara's husband and Janice Brewster disappeared. Enter the new actor today. One of Boston's finest. Lily, we could collar one of Kelly's dirty cops—"

"I don't think he's dirty, Sheila." Lily gripped the wheel. "We've looked at everyone in his precinct, and he didn't even make the third cut. Robbie O'Connor's from a squeaky-clean, toe-the-line proud Irish Catholic family that pays their taxes on time."

Sheila flicked her hand in the direction of the garage where Lieutenant O'Connor and Tara's two young children had entered over ten minutes ago. "And yet his cousin and her husband are suspected of laundering money for the mob."

Lily scanned the parking garage entrance. What was he doing in there with those girls? If the girls hadn't looked completely comfortable with him, she'd be sick with concern. Instead, he'd been holding Cassidy protectively and walking slowly so Reagan wouldn't have to run to keep up. Fact was, he'd look downright tender toward those two girls. Bad guys didn't do that.

"They've certainly been in there for a while," she said, fighting the urge to bite her short, unpainted nails. "You don't think the Kellys followed him, do you? I know we can see all the cars entering and leaving from this angle, but that doesn't mean they didn't go in on foot."

"I know you're worried about the kids," Sheila said, her eyes fixed like a laser to the garage. "I am too. Let's give it five more minutes before I walk in and look around."

When Tara hadn't reappeared through the main entrance, she and Sheila had gone in, pretending they were considering joining the gym. There'd been no sign of Tara, but Lily had managed to look around the corner into the daycare to confirm her girls were still there and okay. After watching them play duck, duck, goose with the daycare attendant, they'd headed back to the car. They'd barely made it inside before Lieutenant O'Connor had arrived in a cab—not his regular police-issue car—and strode inside with authority, only to exit with the girls minutes later, carrying the same bedazzled BOSS bag Tara had brought into the building. Damn, but she wanted to know if something important was in that bag, because it had looked heavy. More cash? But why split the cash into two pieces of luggage? And why risk it being discovered when Cassidy needed a diaper change? God, she had so many questions...

"He still might turn in the cash and put the kids into child protective services," Lily said with a glance at her partner.

Sheila only made a noncommittal sound in response.

Hating the waiting, Lily started tapping her fingers on her knees, chewing on what she knew of Robbie O'Connor from her file review of potential dirty cops. Thirty-nine. Six-four. Divorced. Residence in the Seaport District in South Boston. On the force for almost twenty years. He'd worked his way up, serving first as a patrol officer, then as leader of the department's tactical unit, and now as lieutenant with whispers that he might even be considered for captain. Impeccable record. Volunteered in the community. Heck, he'd even been a teen mentor for a few years before he'd been handed more responsibility in the department.

Basically, a stand-up guy.

Not a likely accomplice to Scotty Flanagan, whose bigmouthed girlfriend had led to his downfall. Janice Brewster had innocently shot her mouth off to one of Lily's confidential informants in a local casino, telling the CI that her new mink coat had come from the Kellys, whom Scotty was working for.

Brought down by a side piece.

Lily loved the poetic justice of that. Men were always thinking with their dicks. It happened everywhere, especially in law enforcement. "Sheila, I still think Tara kicking her husband out like she did and taking him off the bank accounts means something."

"That could have been because he was screwing the help and got caught. Just because she didn't want her man two-timing on her doesn't mean she wouldn't launder money."

This time she was the one who made the noncommittal sound.

"Tara wheeled that black suitcase out of her three nail salons, and she still hasn't called the cops."

"Maybe she just did by calling in her cousin."

"I know you think he's a Boy Scout..."

Lily wouldn't go that far. He was too rough-looking for that, what with his square jaw that could take a punch and probably had and his masculine, tough-as-nails demeanor. She wasn't going to lie—she liked the look of Robbie O'Connor. Sure, he was handsome enough, and that was part of it, but what affected her more was the sweetness with which he'd held Cassidy and led Reagan by the hand. Call her Sunshine as she was billed, but kids were good at telling you a lot about adults if you paid attention. Just like adults advertised a lot about themselves by how they treated kids.

"We'll know soon enough about Lieutenant O'Connor, don't worry." Sheila cracked open a trio of pistachios, her go-to for their waiting games, before tossing the shells on the floor and popping the kernels in her mouth.

"You know I hate it when you do that," Lily reminded her.

Sheila gave her a lopsided smile. "Yeah, but you'd take a bullet for me."

"Because you're my partner," she shot back, "and only a flesh wound."

"Not that me being your best friend has anything to do with it, of course." She cracked a few more nuts and extended them to Lily. "Come on. You need to eat something."

"You know I can't eat during surveillance." She clenched her knees. "God, what could he be doing?"

"He ain't changing no diaper." Sheila chortled. "That I can guarantee. Did you see that diaper bag? I can't believe an alpha dog like him would be caught dead carrying that. It looked like a bedazzler had thrown up all over it. I swear, I don't get why some women have an addiction to bling." She paused, considering, then said, "I guess maybe it's like men and toupees. But what are they trying to compensate for?"

"Maybe they just want to be more attractive. Some girls like to feel pretty." She thought of those poor kids. Feeling pretty would be little comfort to them if things continued to go south.

Their father was at large, and now that they'd seen the cash, there'd soon be a warrant out for his arrest. Mom was now at large as well, it appeared. A warrant might be in her future. Those two sweet girls couldn't be in a more vulnerable place. She knew. At one time, she'd been just like them.

Come on, you bastard. Don't let me be wrong. Don't be dirty.

"That's our SUV!"

Lily turned on the car, trying not to jump to conclusions. "Lieutenant O'Connor is driving. I think you should—"

"I'm calling Buck right this minute." Buck being their tough-as-nails boss. "It won't sound so bad that Tara snuck out a side entrance on us if we're following a possible dirty cop with mob money. Don't tail too close."

"What am I? An extra in a Hollywood movie?"

Her partner shot her a grin before taking on her *checking in* voice as their boss picked up. When Sheila winced, so did Lily. The FBI office in Boston was a large one with over four hundred agents. It was Lily's biggest office to date, her biggest opportunity too, and she didn't want her career to go down in flames because they'd assumed a mother wouldn't leave her kids in a gym.

From the irate response she could hear through the phone, their boss was chewing out Sheila royally. During her first meeting with Buck, he'd said she only had to remember one thing: don't fuck with Buck. He was going places, and if she didn't help him get there, he'd transfer her butt out so fast her pretty little head would spin. She'd managed to never make him repeat his famous motto since, but she wouldn't be surprised if he'd used it with Sheila today. Lily knew he had cause to be angry. She was upset with herself for the blunder.

Her partner was quiet for a long moment before clicking off the phone and saying, "We're to follow O'Connor and not blink our eyes once. So we won't lose him like we did our last suspect. Like a pathetic rookie who doesn't know his ass from the FBI handbook."

Lily swallowed thickly. "Terrific. If we mess this up, Buck will transfer us out, and we'll be lucky to land in an FBI office in Mobile—"

"Or El Paso." Sheila cranked up the air-conditioning and fanned herself. "You know how much I hate hot weather."

"I'll send you a fan," Lily remarked as she followed Robbie O'Connor onto I-93. "Where is he going, do you think?"

"This certainly isn't the way to his precinct." Sheila rubbed her hands together. "So I'm hopeful we're about to pull in a bigger fish for Buck."

"You're so pessimistic about people." Lily made sure to keep ten cars back, but she kept her eyes peeled.

"I know, and I love that about me. Better to be surprised than devastated. Or dead, for that matter."

Sheila had been shot at, but then again, she'd been in the FBI longer than Lily and had worked in Phoenix, Dallas, and Cleveland before Boston. Lily had only been in Sacramento and Tampa before.

"Okay, you win with the death card." Lily rolled her shoulders. "Do you think he's leaving the state?"

Sheila cracked her knuckles. "If he does, that shoots this whole thing to another level. Can you see your promotion papers in your hands now, Sunshine?"

"Are you going to sing the song? Because with your pipes, it makes me feel all special inside."

"Ah, that makes me want to sing real bad." Sheila stretched her feet out, kicking pistachio shells under her seat. "But I won't start singing the song until we take in Lieutenant O'Connor."

"I'm so hurt." Lily grabbed the volume dial for the stereo and turned it up, pleased Beyoncé was playing on one of their shared Spotify playlists. FBI agents got along best when they were in agreement about a number of things, music in the car being of top importance.

She followed as O'Connor took exit 7 for MA-3 S toward Cape Cod. Sheila cracked more pistachios, crunching as Sia sang about swinging from chandeliers. Lily had a practical side that always cringed from that one. She preferred rope if she was climbing.

They seemed to be on the MA-3 forever when he finally took the exit toward Smith Lane.

"Where is he going?" she mused aloud.

"No clue, but I'm glad you insisted we fill up the tank this morning."

"I always prefer having a full tank when we're conducting surveillance."

Sheila smirked. "Being Miss Prepared and all."

"No, my training officer told a story about running out of gas once when the suspect they were surveilling took off. They couldn't stop for gas, and he went farther than expected. They lost him when they ran out. It stuck with me."

"That sucks, but nice to know our fellow officers have their bad days. Like we did today. It happens."

"That error was probably why he was my training officer, Sheila," Lily reasoned. "Wait! He's turning."

"Slow down. You don't want him to spot you."

"He won't." She took her foot off the gas, slowing her speed rapidly, but then she spotted the sign, her insides pinging. "Oh my God! He's taking them to Maziply Toys."

"What's that? A fancy sex shop?"

She blew a raspberry. "New England's largest toy store, supposedly," she told her. "I heard one of the agents say he'd taken his kids there."

"So he's playing the part of a good cousin, huh?" Sheila threw more shells on the floor. "I don't buy it."

Lily parked well away from Lieutenant O'Connor but kept the engine running in case this was a ruse and he'd only stopped because he'd spotted her. Moments later, he was stepping out of the driver's seat, though, opening the back and plucking out Cassidy, who was still holding her adorable teddy bear. Then Reagan got out and took his hand, and they walked into the toy store like old friends.

"Hmm..." Sheila crossed her ankles. "Bribes for the kids for a long car trip?"

She shook her head. The endless speculation was part of being an FBI officer. She'd turned on some inner question fountain at Quantico, and since then, she'd asked more questions than any normal person alive. In fact, she was pretty sure that if she logged her annual questions number, she could go in the Guinness Book of World Records.

"Why don't you drink your fancy coconut water and turn off the car?" her partner continued. "We can pretend we're working on our phones. Do you remember when it was weird for people to stay in their cars? Now it's so common it makes me wonder what the world is coming to."

"But it makes surveillance easier." She grabbed her coconut water from her little cooler bag in the back. "I've given up trying to convince you how much better this is for hydration than all the Starbucks and Cokes you inhale. Not that I don't like caffeine, but six to ten a day is going to bite back someday, and I happen to like my partner."

"You're not too bad yourself—even if you do like pink water. Why it's pink and not white I still don't understand."

"I've told you it's the oxygenation of the sugars." She took a healthy swig and smacked her lips. "I can even taste the beach it was on. Man, I miss the beach sometimes." Even at her worst moments as a kid, she could find escape on the beach and then in the Pacific, first learning to swim and later surfing.

"We need a vacation." Sheila patted her belly, her pudge as she called it. "Not that I'm ever swimsuit ready. Doesn't matter if I run ten miles a day like I did when I was at Quantico. I'm always carrying the Morales extras around the bust, hips, and bootie, which I swear are from all the black beans, rice, and tortillas of my childhood."

"Your mother is the best cook I've ever met. If I were an

investor, I'd try to get her to quit the bench and open a restaurant."

"I'll tell Judge Morales about your offer when I call her next. Hey! Do you see that black car turning into the parking lot? It screams government issue."

She held up her phone, looking over her shoulder casually, as if she were on FaceTime. "Yeah. I agree. That pops your dirty cop theory."

"Not necessarily. They could be in on it."

When two men left the car with fuck-you strides and shabby suits, Lily straightened in her seat. "Hey, that's O'Connor's partner, Mickey Evans, and—"

"Roland Thomas from Internal Affairs. Dammit! It seems the jig is up. We're going to have to approach and tell them we're onto Scotty Flanagan and his wife for suspected money laundering."

"Not in the toy store," Lily pleaded, putting a hand on Sheila's arm. "There are kids in there, having fun, oblivious to how bad the world can be sometimes."

Sheila nodded crisply. "We can wait."

Fifteen minutes passed, and another car raced to the front of the parking lot. Lily gaped as a forest green Chevrolet Suburban arrived and parked close to O'Connor's car. Two men exited, the bulky one extremely tall with a shaved head, white T-shirt, and ripped jeans. The other was still a sizable height but with a more slender build. He had on a blue T-shirt and brown cargo pants. Lily studied faces for a living, and she caught the O'Connor resemblance in the jaw and brow line.

"Ladies and gentlemen, meet Boston's version of Vin Diesel and his sidekick," Sheila said with a laugh.

"They're his brothers," she said softly. "I'd bet you more pistachios."

Sheila lifted her phone and took a few photos. "You might be right, but I can put their photos in and check for sure."

"Later. Let's keep our eyes peeled."

The men quickly went inside. Sheila lowered her phone, her mouth twisting to one side. "Any ideas? Because I don't think they're here shopping for toys for their kids."

She turned the car on. "It has to be a meet, right? But if we go inside, we'll blow our cover. I say we wait here and see what their next play is."

"And hope they aren't going out the back," Sheila said wryly.

Right. Five minutes later, the tall bald guy exited the store with Cassidy in his arms while the other guy held Reagan's hand. Each girl was carrying a new toy, Cassidy's a furry brown rabbit and Reagan's a new Barbie of some sort. Both men were talking to the kids, and the girls were animated. Happy, even. "If they are Robbie's brothers, then it makes sense that the girls know them."

Sheila threw aside more pistachios and picked up her phone, surreptitiously taking photos. "They sure look chummy with the kiddies. I can't wait to see what happens next."

Lily watched as the brothers took the girls to the Suburban and proceeded to show them the inside of the vehicle. Robbie O'Connor appeared seconds later with the other two police officers. All were carrying gift bags from the toy store. Good cover that. At the car, Lieutenant O'Connor opened the side door, grabbed the diaper bag, and then disappeared around the back of the vehicle to unlock the trunk. The men huddled around it, obstructing their view.

"Dammit!" Sheila leaned closer to the dashboard. "I can't get a bead on what they're doing."

"Neither can I," Lily said. "Take some photos anyway. We'll see if our tech guys can work their magic."

Moments later, Robbie hefted out the black suitcase, handing it over to Roland Thomas, who shook his hand and took off toward his vehicle. Lily caught sight of the diaper bag resting in the back beside the girls' suitcases as Robbie turned to his partner. There was a tense moment when O'Connor laid his hand on Mickey Evans' shoulder.

"Whatever he's communicating is *serious*," she said.

Sheila gave a low whistle. "He's just gone to Internal Affairs and handed over the Kellys' mob money with his partner present. Smart to have a witness he trusts on the force. You're right about one thing. This likely blows my dirty cop theory. If they aren't dirty, O'Connor will be a target now, both from the inside leak on his own force and the Kellys. Because it doesn't look like he's going with them. Interesting..."

She watched as O'Connor and his partner man-hugged. "No, he isn't."

Then he tossed him the key fob and took out the remaining luggage.

"Oh, shit, he's changing vehicles!"

"Good thing you put a second tracker on the cat," Lily said as she watched his partner open the driver's side of the Cadillac and jump in.

"You're the one who said they wouldn't leave the cat if something changed, so that's a win for you. But I risked being clawed by the maniac cat for justice."

"You get major points," Lily said, watching as Robbie carted the luggage to the Suburban.

"You can buy me a drink when we finally get off our shift, Sunshine. My concern is that we have a police officer taking a car with an FBI tracking device on it to God knows where. We don't want the South Boston cops to know we're running this investigation."

Lily winced. "There's no reason to think anyone will find it."

"That's you being all sunshine again," Sheila said with an edge to her voice. "We'd better hope so or this case could go up in our faces."

Lily watched as the bald guy joined O'Connor. They stacked the girls' suitcases in the back of the Suburban, which already had three duffel bags inside. O'Connor dropped the diaper bag inside, and then the brothers crossed back to the Cadillac and lugged over the four boxes from Costco. The bald guy appeared carrying the car seats and the cat in her carrier.

"That pussy just saved our life," Sheila said with a wicked laugh.

Lily didn't appreciate that word, even though she worked around very rough-talking people, men and women included. "I won't have to follow so closely, which is good. Because God knows where they're headed now."

A loud meow tore through the parking lot, and the bald man's disparaging swear word carried, earning him a quick rebuke from O'Connor, who pointed at the kids in the Suburban. Lily rather appreciated his desire to protect the kids from foul language.

The bald guy made clawlike hands in O'Connor's direction before he disappeared from view into the green Suburban. Doors slammed on the passenger side. O'Connor stood alone by the driver's side, watching as his partner followed the officer from Internal Affairs slowly out of the parking lot.

"He looks like he's just lost his best friend," Sheila said with a sigh. "I kinda feel for him. But I'm still withholding judgment until we find out if Roland turns in the money...and where his partner takes Tara's new car."

"They're not dirty," Lily said in a steely tone as she watched Robbie O'Connor's hardened profile in the sunlight.

"He's turned the money over immediately and is taking off with some of his brothers to protect those sweet little girls—and his cousin, mind you."

"Don't make him into a knight yet," her own partner wisely pointed out. "We need more—"

"Call our boss and tell him what we saw." She put the car in drive. "Ask him for permission to follow the subject at a distance, even if they cross state lines. Tara O'Connor is going to reunite with her kids, and we want to be there to pick her up as a material witness when she does. She's the key to bringing down the Kellys. I know it."

She wasn't going to back down from the biggest case of her life, and if she could keep watch over those precious little girls, knowing the kind of heat coming for them, then all the better.

CHAPTER THREE

ROBBIE FLOPPED ONTO THE WAY TOO PRISTINE WHITE couch in the new rental house.

"I am *never* going on another car trip again."

He scrubbed his face as he thought of all the tough things he'd done today. Going to Internal Affairs for the first time in his life. Turning in Kelly mob money that had been in his favorite cousin's possession, along with his personal and professional cell phones so no one could track them. Involving his partner in the ordeal. Lying to his supervisor and fellow cops about being on vacation. Taking an encrypted IA computer so he could receive secret messages from either Roland or Mickey on any updates on the case that was now open with his cousin's name on it.

And he'd called his brother Danny and instructed him to buy their father an airplane ticket on the first flight out to Ireland so the Kellys couldn't put the squeeze on him. His brother had wanted to ask questions, of course, but he hadn't been able to provide details other than that Tara was in trouble, and he, Billie, and Tim were taking the girls to an undisclosed location. He'd also asked him to give the other

38

O'Connor brothers a heads-up so they could watch out for each other.

Danny was a hard sell, always had been, but that hadn't been the toughest part of his day. No siree. Try driving twelve hours to the Outer Banks until five o'clock in the morning with two babies, the children, and a pissed-off cat—the babies being his brothers. It had been enough to grind a man down to dust.

"Thank God the girls finally fell asleep and stayed that way through us carrying them inside," he muttered, wanting to plant himself face down on the nearest bed and sleep until the nightmarish day was gone from his mind.

"You said it, brother." Billie kicked at Robbie's feet before dropping down next to him on the couch. "That was the car trip from hell. I'm done with kiddie cartoons and potty breaks. Don't get me started on the diaper changing. Eight times is crazy. I still say Tim should change all the diapers since he does it in his regular job."

Robbie snorted with laughter along with Billie as Tim walked back in with beers despite the early hour. "I know I shouldn't be laughing since you both up and left everything when I called. Thanks, by the way."

"It's what family does," Billie said, fist-bumping him.

"What Billie said." Tim held out two opened beers. "And you really shouldn't talk about people in retirement homes like that. They can't help their incontinence. It hurts their pride."

Tim's response was exactly why Robbie had called him to come along, being a nurse and the only person in their family with a sensitive, caretaking streak. But Jesus, he must be tired, because when Billie started to laugh again, it kicked him off. "Tim, I know it's not right," Robbie said through laughter, "but I can't seem to stop laughing."

"You're stressed to the max, so you get a pass this time."

Tim sat across from them on the matching white leather ottoman. Robbie nearly winced at how *Architectural Digest* this place was, a magazine he'd only glanced at once in the dentist's office because all the others had been taken. He liked things clean and orderly, but the theme of this place fairly screamed two things: beach and family-friendly, from the boating and ocean subjects in the paintings and knick-knacks and inspirational sayings hanging from the walls like *Beach Life is Sunshine and Smiles, I Can See Clearly Now*, and his favorite, *Life is Better in Flip-Flops*. Kill him, right now.

"Also, you're going to have to clean your mouths up." Tim tipped his beer at them accusingly. "You can't be saying fuck and shit and everything else you string together around Reagan and Cassidy."

"But fuck is my go-to word," Billie complained. "If I stop using it, I won't have anything to say. I'll be a mute. Like in *Monty Python*."

That sent Robbie into even more laughter. "Come on, Tim. That was funny."

"Keep it down, will you?" Their baby brother jerked his head toward the stairs. "The girls might have been asleep when we tucked them in, but they won't be if you keep braying like hyenas."

"Mother hen is already doing her job." Billie slugged his beer and groaned. "God, I needed that. I never knew kids had so many questions or needed to play with something every f —reaking minute. Were we like that? Mom would have killed us. I mean, what the hell would I have played with—"

"Yourself," Robbie broke in.

"Right? Big Stallion does like to come out of the pasture."

This old dick joke led to more snorting laughter from him, but he was glad Tim joined in this time. Their youngest brother always had the hardest time feeling like he belonged.

Mostly because they were rough and sometimes crude, and Tim wasn't.

"I never asked so many questions," Billie continued on his rant. "What state are we in now? Why does that cloud look so weird? Don't you just love Miss Purrfect's collar?"

Robbie had to wipe tears leaking from his eyes as he guffawed at Billie's girlish impression. "Why in the world did Tara name that cat Miss Purrfect? That feline is the farthest thing from perfect. It's downright hostile."

Tim's lips twisted as he drank his beer. "That's because you've taken it out of its environment and keep glaring back at it. And Tara told me she named that cat perfect because she wanted her girls to know it's all right to snarl and scratch when they have to—and it doesn't make them bitches. Just independent women."

Billie slapped his forehead. "You're kidding! Wait. I thought dogs were the bitches. Not cats."

Robbie's shoulders shook with laughter. "You think Tara, who had no trouble telling Sister Mary Louis that she couldn't make her do something she didn't want because God gave her free will, would care about that little detail?"

"God, I forgot that story." Billie got a nostalgic smile on his face. "I can still see Sister's blank shock as she stood there in front of our class. That nun was never speechless. Mom laughed when Tara came home with me that day to do her homework."

"And Mom usually didn't laugh about discipline issues," Robbie said with fond remembrance. "But Sister was in the wrong for trying to make Tara stop wearing ribbons in her hair. From the minute she had hair, she wanted something pretty in it."

"Her girls are the same way," Billie said with a laugh. "Reagan asked if I could change the bow in her hair while you were driving. She said she wasn't feeling it anymore. Can you believe that?"

"You drive different cars depending on your mood," Tim pointed out, as if it wasn't a well-known fact that Billie had a collection of them, or near enough, because he liked renovating old cars in his spare time. "Tara—and now her girls—beautify. I think it's cute."

"Well, I think it's a little nutso, especially since Reagan asked me to make sure the bow was straight. The point is, I'm having Father O'Malley say a mass for our dear mother and all the others out there who put up with this crap. And I'm seriously considering snipping my you-know-what to make sure I don't end up having to raise any kids who ask ridiculous questions and want me to do things like adjust their glittery bows."

"You might give it a few months before making that kind of decision," Tim pointed out with an eyeroll. "But if you're already cracking after a car trip of barely thirteen hours, I can't wait to see how you are in three or four days."

Billie's response was to pick up a small seashell from the glass coffee table decorated with them and throw it at their brother.

He caught it deftly. "And you should stop throwing things. We need to set a good example for the girls."

"We roughhoused as kids," Robbie put in. He took another swig of his beer, mentally thanking Tara for thinking to pick it up. "With Kathleen, if you recall."

"Our baby sister is more like a guy thanks to all of your brotherly influencing." Tim stood and gently put the shell back on the coffee table. "Tara's girls are girly girls like her. We can't treat them the same way."

"You mean we can't take them to the salvage yard or give them a welding set for Christmas like we did with our sis?" Billie asked.

Kathleen had become a metal artist, so Robbie figured they'd done something right. But from the look Tim was giving Billie, he decided he'd better not say so.

"Baby bro," Billie continued, "if you start listing all of the things I can't do, you're going to find yourself pantsed and dumped in the ocean out there."

Billie's threats and imposing nature was the very reason Robbie had asked him to come along, but he knew it was time to intercede. "None of us are going to like refraining from cussing or throwing things at each other—"

"Basically not being ourselves," Billie added sullenly.

Robbie turned and gave him the *I'm the oldest brother* look. "Come on. You know he's right."

"You planning on putting away your grumpy OCD tendencies?" Billie's smile showed teeth. "Because if I have to stop saying fuck and throwing things, then you're going to have to quit your gruff and surly moods from not getting laid enough."

Hadn't he equated putting bad guys in jail with being as good as sex? But he wasn't going to let the other hit land. "Gruff and surly, my ass. I'm a cop in Southie. What the hell am I supposed to say when I go through the door to apprehend criminals? Oh, I'm so sorry your mother didn't love you, and I'm sure you didn't mean to beat up that old guy for his TV?"

"This is going nowhere," Tim said, cradling his beer between his hands. "All I'm trying to say is that we should each do our part to set a positive example for the girls. This is heavy stuff. Their dad getting kicked out and their mom taking off and leaving them with the three of us, two of whom are apes. Put yourself in their place."

Robbie gritted his teeth alongside Billie. "Fine," they both said at the same time.

"But what are we going to do about the cat?" Billie asked, his jaw knotted. "Because that pussy hates men."

"You're only upset because your wiles don't work on Miss Purrfect." Tim's lips twitched, and then they were all laughing.

Billie was the one who sobered first, possibly because Robbie had just toed his shoes off. "All right, do we talk about it now? What Tara's got herself into? And Robbie, for the love of God, put your shoes back on. Your feet are rank."

Robbie ignored him. Setting his beer on the glass table, he leaned back, closing his eyes. "Getting real is probably a good idea. I wish we could know for sure Pop made it to Ireland."

"No reason to think he wouldn't," Tim said with his usual gravity. "It scared me something bad when you said you thought he needed to get out of town because of the Kellys."

The earlier tightness in his diaphragm returned with a vengeance. "Pop is getting up in years. I was worried the Kellys might go by his house and maybe rough him up, ask him about Tara, me, or the girls. Everyone knows we're her main family." He'd go to his grave before admitting it, but he'd also worried about his little brother's safety. Tim wasn't a fighter, which was another reason he'd had him come along.

"Jesus, Tara's in a mess." Billie's feet landed on the coffee table. "I told her on her wedding day Scotty was no good."

"And she retaliated by not talking to you for six months." Robbie pressed his hands to his face, remembering having to intercede at Christmas and lock them in a room together to work out their issues, something their mother had resorted to when they were growing up.

"She's been so stubborn and independent, ever since we started kindergarten together." Billie's eyes narrowed, and for the first time Robbie could see the pinch of worry on his brow. "That's what I keep telling myself when I start going crazy about her being all alone out there. Any idea where she went?"

"No, and we don't want to." Robbie sighed. "Look, all I want to do is find her and wrap her up in my protection."

"Our protection," Billie said, flexing his massive guns.

"Right. But she was smart to pay attention to all my stupid criminal videos and what I always say about how people get tracked down."

"Who knew those gems would save the day?" Billie held up his hands. "Yay!"

"Oh, stop poking at Robbie," Tim broke in, setting his beer on his knee. "He's as upset as the rest of us, but Tara does know how to handle herself. I mean, look at the way she set things up. She even got you a burner phone, Robbie, and I imagine she got one for herself. That's smart."

"Right, but we're men. We're used to kicking bad guy ass when needed. Me at my car shop. Danny at the bar. And Robbie at the precinct. Tara shouldn't have to do that. Especially alone."

Billie's omission of Tim was like a stink bomb, so Robbie shot him a look before saying, "If Tara thought she had to separate herself from the girls to keep them safe, then we've got to respect her decision and support it." Even if he hated sitting in this saccharine beach rental until "something gave," as Tara called it.

"So we support her like we did when she married Scotty," Billie added. "That worthless sack of—"

"Leaving Reagan and Cassidy for two weeks—with us—is one hell of a gamble." Tim's heavy sigh carried across the low lamplight in the room. "It's going to eat her up, being away from her babies."

"Then we do everything we can to treat them like princesses and give them the time of their lives." Billie's feet landed on the floor then, like he'd come to a big decision.

"Dammit, I know I've been an ass, but taking care of these kids is nothing in comparison to what Tara is going through."

"On that we agree." Robbie sat up. "All right. So we're here in the Outer Banks for two weeks or until the case breaks and we can all go home."

"That fancy computer from Internal Affairs is our only window to the outside world," Tim said wistfully.

"Yes, and I plan on checking it every morning. I'm not even risking using the burner because—"

"Everything can be tapped," Billie finished for him. "I watch your stupid criminal videos too. Plus, some of the guys who work for me at the shop are ex-cons. A few of them got caught making stupid mistakes."

"We won't make any." He glanced at both of his brothers. "Tara deserves some credit. She picked the perfect place. It's the end of tourist season, so there are fewer people around us. We're just three brothers—"

"Correction," Billie pointed out. "A divorced dad with his two brothers along to help with his girls he has shared custody of. We need to get our story straight and stick to it."

"Oh, for the love of..." Robbie tipped his head back and regarded the ceiling. "I'm the cop in the family, remember?"

"But we do need a cover story," Billie pressed.

He gave up. "Yes. As close to the truth as we can get. Because God, I hate lying."

No legacy is so rich as honesty...

Robbie glanced at Billie before narrowing his eyes at Tim. "Have you finally lost it? What gibberish did you just spout off?"

"It's Shakespeare," their baby brother stated with a haughty brow lift. "His wisdom relates to all kinds of things."

Billie gave a snort. "Like in that old Gwyneth Paltrow movie Robbie used to watch, where she's practically naked—"

"Look, I was a horny teenager whose mother unearthed

every dirty magazine I smuggled into my room." He narrowed his gaze at their troubadour. "But that doesn't explain why Timmy here is quoting some dead guy. Explain."

Tim's smile widened in his angular face. "I seem to have struck a chord. Also, really gross about the Gwyneth Paltrow thing. She's a wicked successful businesswoman."

"And Kate Winslet's an Oscar winner," Billie broke in. "But that doesn't mean I don't enjoy that scene in *Titanic* when some chick forces me to watch it."

"You're both disgusting." Tim shook himself, fighting a smile. "If you must know—"

"We really must," Billie said with a laugh.

"I'm a new fan of the bard. One of the women in our retirement home is a former English teacher, and she's gone blind from diabetes. I read to her, and we discovered her roommate used to do off-Broadway Shakespeare shows. Her roommate and I started acting out the lines for her, and then the rest of our retirees thought it would be fun to do some productions. It's a great way to keep their memories active— better than crossword puzzles even."

"Or sudoku." Billie laughed. "I told Pop he needed to start doing it when he called me Danny the other day."

"He probably couldn't distinguish between you and Danny because you're both jackasses," Tim shot back. "Oh, and one more thing. The woman I'm seeing really loves Shakespeare's sonnets."

Was baby bro gloating? Robbie couldn't tell, so he elbowed Billie to signal that it wasn't time to rag on him about it. "Did we know you were seeing someone?"

Tim took a swig from his bottle. "Nope. It's going well, so why would I screw it up by having her meet my idiot brothers? You put Kathleen's husband in the police interrogation room."

Robbie winced. "That was *before* she and Declan got

married. I had to see what kind of man he was, didn't I? Plus, they'd had a huge fight."

"And the end justifies the means." Billie slapped him on the back. "Isn't that from Shakespeare, Timmy?"

"Not that I know of." He glared at him, likely because of his hated nickname, Timmy. "*All's well that ends well* seems more apt here."

"Terrific." Billie slapped Robbie's back again. "Glad we got that settled. Back to our cover story. We'll keep things light because that's in the kids' best interest."

"That's all that's important now," Tim said, taking a sip of his beer. "We need a united front of sensitivity and positivity."

"Oh, Jesus, here we go again," Billie complained.

"Stop saying Jesus," Tim cautioned. "Didn't you hear me about not cussing?"

"That's a cuss word?" Billie's chin jutted out. "He's a historical figure and the son—"

"You use it like a swear word, Billie." Judging by Tim's grin, he was clearly enjoying this. "Use something like holy cow or Jumpin' Jehoshaphat!"

"And what do you suggest, Shakespeare, for fuck and fucking?" Billie asked with an edge in his voice.

Robbie watched Billie pick up another shell as if weighing the merits of throwing it across the room despite their agreement not to roughhouse. He was ready to catch his brother's arm mid-throw if necessary.

Tim's eyes dipped to Billie's hand before he pursed his lips. "Fudge. Freaking. Frigging. Fecking—"

"We'll do our best to use alternate words, Tim." Robbie could see the smoke starting to come out of Billie's bald head, so he figured it was best to intervene. "On another note, I really am grateful you both came. I thought about taking off with the girls alone, but I figured it would be better to have more backup. Mickey offered to come along too, but I told him I needed him in Boston, working discreetly with IA to find those dirty cops. If for any crazy reason the Kellys find us, which I don't expect they will, given all our precautions, then I wanted to be with someone who could take the girls and run."

Billie extended his bottle in Tim's direction. "That's you, Shakespeare."

"Great, I have a new nickname," Tim said sarcastically. "How nice for me."

Robbie put his hand on Billie's arm before he could volley back. "We should get a few baseball bats, though. Couple easy window and door security devices. Just in case."

"You kept your gun, right?" Billie asked, shoving his hand off.

"Yeah, I told Roland I wanted to keep it with me even though I handed over my phone." He rubbed the back of his neck. "God...I've never gone to IA before."

But sitting in that garage, he'd known that was his best play. He couldn't very well take the dirty cash with him. So he'd turned it in to Internal Affairs along with Tara's letter, which both proclaimed her innocence and suggested there was someone dirty in the department. He'd brought his partner in for backup and as a witness, knowing he could trust Mickey Evans with his life as well as his reputation.

When questioned, Mickey would echo what Robbie had told his supervisor on the call he'd made from the burner phone while in the toy store—that he needed to take a sudden vacation to take care of a family matter. They could speculate to high heaven what that family matter was, but they wouldn't hear it from any of the O'Connors.

The good thing about going to IA was that they didn't have to share details with the rest of the department. This way they could start looking into who was on the Kellys' payroll without alerting the guilty parties. The Kellys would likely guess he was off helping Tara and the girls, but they might not know they'd gone separate ways. He hoped they would think twice about pursuing a cop and would instead use their resources to find Scotty and his new girlfriend, seeing as he was their point of contact.

"You were smart to ask Mickey to come along earlier." Billie pulled off his boots and tossed them to the side with a thunk. "Better to have a witness when you're turning in dirty money."

"That was the plan," he said, grimacing. "It made me feel sick, knowing Tara's going to have to be cleared of this."

Billie's face turned downright ferocious. "When I think about what Scotty's done—"

"We all have our thoughts on that," Tim said quietly, "but that's another thing you don't want to say in case the girls overhear you. They don't have the maturity to see things as they are."

"Tara gave them a good story," Robbie told them. "Enough believable details with a lot of girl power stuff. But Tim's right. We need to keep our thoughts to ourselves."

"So the plan is to lay low until something breaks and give the girls a good time." Billie slapped his knees.

"Billie, for the love of Pete," Tim moaned.

"Robbie, you are so going to owe me for all the hearts I'm breaking while I'm gone." He pushed off the couch. "Hey, maybe I'll get lucky down here. There have to be some single women looking to have a good time, right?"

"I'll make a list of fun things we can do with the kids in the area," Tim volunteered. "And I'm not sure this is your usual brotherly beer, boats, and babes kind of vacation."

"No, it's not." Robbie was going to make another list. They had to beef up their physical security. And they needed a boat. There were limited ways to leave the Outer

Banks. If something happened—and he hoped to God it didn't—they needed to be ready to take an alternate route out.

"Why are you guys still awake?"

He swung his head to the right. Reagan stood in the clothes she'd fallen asleep in, her new Barbie in her hand. Her second bow of the day lay like a flapjack against her right ear, and she had a pillow crease on her cute little face.

"We're night owls," Billie said, standing up. "Hoot hoot. Come on, let's tuck you back into bed."

"Can Robbie do it?" she asked softly.

He pushed Billie out of his way as he stood up, surprised. She wanted him? "Ah, sure thing."

"You want to change into your pajamas first, Miss Pixie?" Tim asked. Thank God, because it hadn't even occurred to Robbie.

"Yes, please, and brush my hair." She pulled the bow out and winced. "The tangles are going to be terrible."

Billie slapped him on the back. "Robbie's specialty. Untangling things. Shakespeare, let's head up too."

"I'll grab my bag and Robbie's," Tim said as Robbie shuffled forward in his socks. "We'll pick the rooms. Any dealbreakers?"

"A hole in the roof?" Billie bandied back.

Robbie ignored their antics and tried to smile at Reagan. She looked terribly small and tired.

"With this luxury four-bedroom, you're covered," Tim replied, heading to the front door where they'd dumped the bags. And the cat, who had disappeared the moment they'd arrived in the house, something he hoped would continue, especially since Tim thought the cat blamed him for its current predicament.

Reagan held out her little hand. Robbie awkwardly took it. Should he pick her up? He'd done that earlier, but only

51

because she'd been completely out. Heading up the stairs together, he noticed they hadn't taken her sandals off either.

When they reached the room she was sharing with her sister, he noted that Cassidy was still sleeping soundly in the pack and play that came with the house. Reagan sat on her twin bed, and he knelt on the floor to unbuckle her shoes.

God, her feet were tiny and decorated in sparkly nail polish. He hadn't registered that before, but it made sense, what with Tara being a nail person. God knew she'd tried to do the O'Connor brothers' nails from time to time, swearing a manicure would change their life. They'd always bandied back that they'd have to give up their man cards if they accepted.

He suddenly wanted to hang his head. *Jesus, Tara, please be safe.*

"I miss my mom," Reagan whispered. "I woke up and I didn't know where I was. Then I heard you guys talking."

"And you knew we were with you and not her." He set her sandals down beside the bed. "I know it's hard to miss your mom. My mom—ah..."

She was suddenly listening intently and he swallowed thickly. She probably already knew his mom had died, but he didn't want to remind her of it right now.

"My mom went away on a trip when I was a lot older than you—and it was really hard for me too. But Kathleen, my sister, whom you've met—"

"Yeah, she lives in Ireland now. Mom has shown me some photos. We went to her wedding when she came back to Boston."

Right. He rubbed the back of his neck again to wake himself up. "Anyway, she was five, and she missed my mother so much. That's normal when you love someone. But this is only going to be for a little while, and me and my brothers are going to make sure you and Cassidy have a lot of fun. Is there anything you'd like to do on vacation?"

She held up her doll, eerily perfect in the dim light through the cracked door of the bathroom. Tim had left that on, because there were no night-lights. "I want to build a sandcastle for my new Barbie."

A sandcastle. Huh. Had he ever done that as a kid? "We'll do it tomorrow. The best one possible. Now, do you want to get your pajamas?"

She nodded and headed over to her suitcase. Cassidy rolled over when the zipper sounded, and he froze like someone had just dropped a water bottle on a stakeout. God, is this what all parents went through? He breathed a sigh of relief when the little girl didn't stir again.

Dragging a long pink nightgown across the floor, Reagan returned and held it out. Pointing to the cartoon woman on the dress, she said, "My favorite Disney princess is Belle."

What was the appropriate response to *that*? "She looks...sturdy."

Reagan saved him from more awkward conversation by taking off her dress. Her complete trust pulverized him, and he remembered Kathleen being like this, all sweet, innocent, and little. She used to run around the house in her underwear, laughing as they tried to catch her and wrap her up in a nearby blanket or crocheted throw pulled off the couch. Good memories, he realized.

Reagan held up her arms, and then he realized he was supposed to put the nightgown on over her. He did so gently, and then she was throwing her arms around his neck. All of her fear and agony was in that hug, and he felt his throat getting thick with emotion in response. He remembered Kathleen had liked having her hair smoothed when she was missing their mom, so he lifted his hand and began an easy rhythm. When Reagan finally moved a little, he loosed her and they stood there looking at each other.

"Mom said you would take care of me and Cassidy like a fairy-tale prince." Then she smiled. "But you're not the Beast. I'll have to think about who you are. I'm going to brush my hair later so I won't wake Cassidy. But it's going to be awful."

Awful didn't sound good, so he was glad for the reprieve. He kissed the top of her head and helped her back into bed. She grabbed her Barbie and arranged the ever-smiling plastic doll against her chest.

"Thanks for my Barbie. I still don't know what her name is."

He tucked the flower covered sheet up over her. "You'll figure it out. Good night, Reagan."

"Good night, Robbie."

He gave a tired smile before turning to leave. But then he noticed that Tim had practically swaddled Cassidy in the blanket he'd thrown over her. He'd have to go through Tara's list of instructions with his brothers point by point, because this would not do.

He lifted the blanket until her tiny feet were peeking out, and for a moment, she smiled in her sleep, drool sliding down her sweet, round face. Something shifted in his chest. He walked out of the room feeling better equipped than he had all day.

With Tara's instructions, they'd have this parenting thing down tomorrow, Friday at the latest.

CHAPTER FOUR

A PIERCING SCREAM RENT THE AIR.

Lily winced, tying her blue and white-flowered sarong in place, as she headed to the patio door to look out at their new neighbors. The tourist season was waning, so they'd been able to rent out the place next to the O'Connors'.

Sure enough, Cassidy's arms were flailing in the air on the beach as she ran toward the ocean. Robbie had already pushed off the ground to give chase, barely missing the massive sandcastle he and his brothers were building with Reagan. Someone clearly had a flair for architecture, with the whimsical round towers and detailed turrets running between.

"It doesn't sound like all is going well in fake Daddydom." Sheila whistled. "This is the third time that munchkin's gone for the waves. Lieutenant O'Connor doesn't look too thrilled. I think you'd be the perfect treat to soothe his tangled nerves, Summer."

She crossed her arms as she regarded her partner. "You're seriously sticking with that name?"

Laughing, her partner cocked her hip. "You betcha.

Summer Sunshine is the perfect cover name for a girl from Florida who's a speech and language therapist in Orlando. No one would ever be suspicious of someone with a name as sweet as that. Plus, I call you Sunshine all the time, so I won't accidentally blow our cover. It's the perfect backstory to help us establish rapport with our subjects next door so we can ferret out what they know about Tara. We have to find her before the Kellys do, because if you're right and she wasn't involved, they'll likely kill her. She won't be able to be a material witness against the Kellys if she's dead."

There were plenty of other reasons they didn't want Tara O'Connor to end up dead. Lily's gaze tracked to the two little girls making sandcastles on the beach. No child should go through that.

"Sitting here and doing remote surveillance until Tara O'Connor maybe shows up isn't going to break this case open. Didn't we both go to the FBI undercover school to enhance our careers?"

Her partner's last question was a little on the cheeky side, but it was undeniably true. Separately, they had both enrolled in the specialized school, which made them eligible for cases where going undercover was deemed necessary to gather more evidence. No one could deny the advantage it provided. When the undercover agent managed to create trust and camaraderie, intimacy even, persons of interest got more comfortable and shared things related to their case.

Having an innocuous given name for this undercover assignment couldn't be more important. No one in their right mind would suspect Summer Sunshine of being an FBI agent, even Robbie O'Connor, who'd been a cop long enough to be suspicious to his core. Plus, she'd known people who went by some version of that name. Granted, it was only in hippie and New Age circles. Maybe that was why it bothered her, given her background.

"Fine, I'm Summer Sunshine." She fought a frown.

"It totally suits since you're so sweet... Now, based on my assessment of our neighbors, I've ruled out Tim O'Connor for an approach—too nice and steady, based on his social media, which would need a longer approach. That leaves the other two. You have a better shot cozying up to Lieutenant O'Connor with your bleeding heart background while I'm more Billie O'Connor's type. Again, his social media tells the story. He seems like an *easy come, easy go* kind of guy who likes a voluptuous gal like me. They'll be putty in our hands." Sheila had the audacity to make kissing noises.

Lily grabbed her coconut water and drank deeply to disguise the nerves that started jumping when she thought about kissing Robbie O'Connor. So not professional and something that might not even happen. Kissing while undercover was something she'd successfully avoided so far. "Not if one of them realizes you've taken your cover name from two very famous movies. What if someone puts two and two together?"

Sheila gave her a gentle punch in the arm. "Oh, please. No one's going to hear Clarice Malone, snap their fingers, and say, hey, you combined two characters from *Silence of the Lambs* and *The Untouchables*. Not even Jodie Foster or Sean Connery, God bless his soul, would pick up on that."

"Just don't do your Sean Connery impression. It's not the greatest, but everyone in the FBI who hears it knows who you're doing."

"You're just getting the usual undercover heebie jeebies!" Sheila half hugged her. "Come on. We should be enjoying this! It's not every day we do undercover at the beach. Hell, I'd be enjoying myself more if I looked that good in a bikini."

Lily suddenly wanted to wrap her blue and white-flowered sarong around herself like a towel. "It's just a swimsuit, Sheila." They'd had a little undercover vacation shopping spree the previous evening after their operation had been approved.

"Not on you, Sunshine," Sheila continued. "God, I envy you. When I wear two scraps of cloth over my unmentionables, I feel like one of those blow-up dolls men buy for—"

"You look great in a bikini, which is why you've been undercover as a stripper," Lily reminded her. "I'd have trouble with that role without a rack."

"I'd kill for your cup size," Sheila said with passion, coming to stand next to her, drinking her Starbucks, dressed in yoga pants, looking like the casual city slicker from Washington, DC who was down for a much-needed vacation with her single friend. "Heck, I'd kill for your height too. If I'd wanted to be in the Bureau before 1975, it wouldn't have even been possible. You had to be at least five foot seven."

"Sheila, back then your bigger problem would have been that the FBI didn't allow women until 1972." Her partner had a good self-esteem, but she was teased mercilessly for being five-four and "rounding out a uniform," as more than one jerk had said out loud. Not that Lily hadn't had things said about her, but her height of five-ten was deemed more acceptable in an organization of mostly tall men.

"One of the first female agents had the last name of Malone," Sheila said, "so maybe I'm honoring her."

Lily had to think back to her coursework to remember the woman's full name. "Susan Roley Malone. Nice ploy, but I still think you were going for the Sean Connery feel."

Her partner gave her a saucy wink. "But you'll be wondering, which is why I'm such a good undercover agent. I get into your head."

That made her start laughing.

"All right. I think it's time for your approach, Miss Sunshine. You finally look less stressed from all the hoops we had to jump through to get here."

"Nah, this one was easy."

Normally a field office liked to be in charge of what was going on in its territory, but given that the Kelly investigation was part of a big investigation out of Boston, their office was running it. And with money from their own budget, which the local office in Charlotte loved. Buck hadn't had to do much convincing to let them run the undercover op independently given the Charlotte office was stretched to the limit with a manhunt for the kidnapper of a six-year-old boy.

Lily prayed they would find the boy soon, because the more time passed, the worse it would be. She'd be working on high-risk cases like that if she got her promotion, and nothing motivated her more than looking for a lost child.

She surveyed the two sweet little girls she was here to protect while conducting the case. Screaming aside, both children seemed fine. Reagan was trying to console Cassidy, who was wailing against Robbie's shoulder now, pointing at the ocean.

"You look like the kind of sweet little neighbor who would offer assistance to a screaming kid." Sheila slurped the last of her Starbucks. "No one would know in that getup that you'd been 'sworn' in as an officer of the peace today."

"Stupid to be on an investigation and not be able to exercise our police powers on something other than a straight federal crime due to being in a different state than our HQ," Lily bandied back. "Let's hope we don't have to bust anyone. We just need Tara to meet them here or have them tell us where she is." Assuming they knew and had a way to communicate. They would be looking for a phone. Likely a burner.

"Or for the Kellys to find them." Sheila opened the glass patio door. "Not that we want that, but it would help our case. We could bust them for more than money laundering and destruction of property."

She cracked her neck, hating that the worse this situation

got, the better her career prospects would be if she resolved it. "It's a long way from Boston for the Kellys. All right, I'm going in. Wish me luck."

"Say hi to that cat for me." Sheila smacked her butt playfully—so not regulation. "That tracking device on its collar saved us."

They'd peeled off from following the O'Connors when they'd gotten onto the main road taking them into the Outer Banks. At night, there weren't many cars on the local roads, and Lily hadn't wanted them to get suspicious. If they'd slowed down, they might have seen the Massachusetts plates on their vehicle, and Robbie was a cop—trained to notice such things. Besides, they'd needed to find a place to stay for the night and kickstart the paperwork needed to run an operation in another state. Two days later, she and Sheila had acquired a green Ford Taurus with Carolina plates they'd rented locally along with their strategically located rental house. With their cover stories in place, she didn't see any reason the O'Connors would suspect anything.

"You'd better get going on that yoga of yours," she told her partner. "We want to make sure Billie notices you right away. In case you're wrong about their types."

"I'm not." Sheila grabbed her new sea foam blue mat and rolled it out as they slid the patio door open and walked across its length, one bigger than Lily's current apartment. "I think I'll bend over so he can see my ass. People are wrong about the way to a man's heart is through his stomach. For some men it's all about the ass."

She didn't dignify that with a response as she flipped her sunglasses down and trotted through the sand to the beach. God, she couldn't fault the view. They could only speculate about why the O'Connors were in this house on the Outer Banks, but Lily was betting Tara had arranged it. From the side windows of their rental, she could see into their house, and it looked very cozy for a bunch of bachelors. Theirs was similar—a bright home full of windows and decorated with beach themes and sayings. It was shades better than the flea-infested motel she'd stayed in two months ago the last time she went undercover, and truthfully, she loved the light and the space.

Billie O'Connor caught sight of her first. She knew he was thirty-seven—one year younger than Sheila—the second of the O'Connor kids, owned two mechanic shops in Southie, and had never been married. His driving record was somehow free of speeding tickets even though he owned a number of classic hotrods.

He grinned with male appreciation the second he sighted her. He nudged Tim, who'd just turned thirty, was the seventh kid of the eight, and had surprised her by being a nurse in a retirement home. That explained the more quiet and sensitive demeanor they'd seen on his social media compared to his other brothers. Robbie was still soothing Cassidy, bouncing in place in black swim trunks that showcased a very fit physique. Many cops his age didn't keep in shape, but it seemed he did, and honestly, it was hard not to admire his body.

"Hey, neighbor!" Billie called, bringing her attention back to him. "I saw that we had someone move in this morning, and I must have the luck of the Irish, since you look like an angel sent from heaven."

Oh, he laid it on thick. Tim rolled his eyes while Robbie's gaze locked with hers. She felt a blip in her stomach as their eyes met. His were a deep, piercing blue. Attraction? Okay. She could work with that. "Not an angel. I have to say that's the best sandcastle I've ever seen in real life. Did you make this?"

She directed her smile toward Reagan, who was quietly watching the scene in a mermaid-colored swimsuit that shimmered in the sunlight. "Yes," she answered shyly, tucking her chin to her shoulder, "but I had lots of help."

Cassidy's crying shuddered to a halt as the little girl swung her head toward her sister's voice. Lily regarded the curly-haired cherub with the wet streaks on her cheeks. Despite looking so unhappy, she looked adorable in her pink swimsuit with purple flowers. "Oh, sweetie, you look like you've cried yourself out. What's the matter?"

The little girl started whimpering immediately, turning into Robbie's shoulder. His large hands cupped her protectively. "She might need another nap."

"She just had a nap," Reagan said, digging in the sand with a red plastic shovel. "And she never cries like that unless something is wrong."

Robbie's face darkened as he patted Cassidy's back. "Got any ideas for cheering her up, Reagan?"

She shook her head. "I gave her my Barbie to play with and that didn't help."

"Maybe it's her tummy." Lily ventured closer, aware of Robbie's eyes following her every move. "I'm a speech and language therapist, so I work with children a lot. What did she eat today?"

"Our favorite," Reagan offered, jumping up and coming over, clearly past her initial shyness. "Chicken nuggets. And Cassidy ate like twenty of them."

Robbie cleared his throat as his mouth tipped up rather adorably. "She's exaggerating."

She gave an answering smile, sensing he didn't want her to think badly of him. He jostled the little girl as they watched each other. Suddenly the hot moist air seemed to steal her breath. Tough and tender—a killer combination.

"Yeah, but she stuffed them in her mouth so fast Tim had to tell her to slow down or she'd puke," Reagan said in a rush.

"Maybe it's just a tummy ache, then," Lily said, sharing a

conspiratorial smile with Reagan. "When one of my students has one, there's this point I massage. Would it be all right if I showed you?"

Robbie's brow furrowed. "Ah..."

Trust was hard for him, and she imagined his protectiveness was off the charts given the current situation. "I promise it will help her."

"You want to feel better," Reagan said, gently touching her sister's little foot. "Don't you, Cassidy? Sometimes my mom massages her tummy."

"Well, I'm only going to massage the fleshy area between her thumb and forefinger." She cast another glance at Robbie, knowing he was sizing her up. "But only if you feel comfortable."

She was aware of Billie and Tim watching the scene from their place in the sand. Obviously, Robbie was the lead decision-maker here. "If you think it will help," he said after another long look, one that made her heart race faster. Because when he looked at a person, he *really* looked, and she hadn't been prepared for the intensity.

Stepping closer to take Cassidy's hand put her near enough to feel the heat radiating from his body. She could smell the sand, the surf, and something that was all man on him. God, it was potent, so potent her belly tightened. Her gaze took in his rippled muscles before she drew herself back. "Here, sweetie. Let's see if this will help."

As she massaged the soft impression slowly, Cassidy studied her with big blue eyes, clearly mesmerized. Lily was aware of Robbie's regard as well, and she hoped he couldn't see her pulse beating in her neck. Cassidy lowered her head slowly to Robbie's chest, and Lily had to fight off another wave of attraction as his muscles flexed from reflexively tightening his grip on her.

"She seems a little calmer," Robbie said quietly.

"Yeah, she is." Reagan looked at Lily with a pinch of awe in her eyes. "That's amazing. I'll have to remember how to do that when she has another tummy ache. She gets them a lot."

Robbie seemed alarmed by this news as he shot Reagan a concerned look before glancing back up at Lily. "Thank you."

"You're welcome." Her pulse was pounding in her ears, and she had to fight the urge to take a step back from him to give herself room to breathe.

"Well, we don't want to keep you from your swim." He cleared his throat again. "It's good to meet you. Ah..."

She found her cheeks warming, imagining what he would think of her undercover name. "Don't laugh, but my name is Summer. It's a joke for all seasons, especially with the last name Sunshine. I blame my New Age parents."

"Summer Sunshine," Billie drawled out in his rough Boston accent as he jumped to his feet. "I couldn't think of a better name. I'm Billie. That's Tim, our baby brother, and this here is Reagan. The baby you just soothed is Cassidy. We're the uncles of these two beautiful little girls. And their dad is my brother, Robbie. He's divorced, and this is his time with the kids."

Lily couldn't help but notice Robbie's tight smile at the blatant lie.

"We're here to help," Billie continued, clearly selling it. "He's also deeply in need of a vacation, as you can tell. I hope we see you and your friend around."

She made sure to smile brightly and enjoyed watching Robbie's eyes darken. "Hard not to run into each other, being next door. Well, I hope Cassidy feels better."

A sound like mottled gunfire sounded from Cassidy's diaper. Tim grinned. Billie winced. Robbie's brows flew to his hairline.

"Well, I said she *would* feel better..." Lily managed, biting her lip to keep from laughing.

"Acupressure for the win," Tim said, tipping up Cassidy's little face. "All you had was a bad case of gas. No more crying now. Right, baby girl?"

"Man, Cassidy, you had a lot of magic inside you, didn't you?" Reagan asked, patting her tummy soothingly.

Cassidy gave a wide grin at last, drool spilling from her mouth and onto her swimsuit.

An awkward silence descended as the air swam with the smell of rotten eggs. Reagan started gagging and holding her nose, making Cassidy laugh. Billie and Robbie shifted on their bare, sand-covered feet. Embarrassment was so not in their alpha vocabulary, and honestly, Lily could never have imagined a first meeting quite like this one.

Robbie winced after sending her a chagrined smile. "Ah... we've got a diaper to change from the smell of it. Again, thanks for your help. I'm sure we'll be seeing each other."

"Yes, let us know if you need anything," Billie said, his deep voice playful. "Sugar, milk, eggs. Adult conversation. We'll need it after another diaper changing."

That made Summer's mouth twitch. "I'm sure you'll be all right. You guys look pretty tough."

"Some days it's a mirage," Robbie joked half-heartedly as he held Cassidy away from his chest.

"You guys are being such babies," Reagan said with a snort. "It's just a diaper."

Robbie looked to be biting the inside of his cheek when he turned back to her. "Any chance you're a miracle worker with changing diapers too?"

She gave it a momentary thought before dismissing it. She didn't want to look *that* maternal. Somehow, she didn't think it was the right note to set with him. "I'm sure you'll do just fine. If you need a break afterward, you know where to find me and my friend. Good luck."

She made a strategic retreat, waving as she started walking

down the beach in the other direction. Stopping to pick up a seashell, she watched as Robbie strode to the house, the little girl babbling now as she twirled the ends of his hair, wet from his earlier dip in the ocean with her.

From his rigid gait, he clearly wasn't thrilled to be on diaper duty. All of a sudden, she found herself wondering why he and his ex-wife hadn't had any kids. Of course there were a million reasons people didn't have children, whether they couldn't or didn't want to, but he was part of a big family. Had that cured him of wanting any of his own? God, she really shouldn't be thinking about this stuff...

"So we're babies, huh?" Billie plucked Reagan onto his shoulders, making her cry out in delight and clutch his bald head. "Did your mom pack a gas mask? Because your sister might look all sweet, but she stinks as bad as a Southie garbage truck."

Reagan held on laughing as Billie started jogging toward the house, catching up to his big brother. Tim followed more slowly, picking up seashells in a way that suggested he was the romantic of the bunch.

Lying back in the sun, Lily wished her mind was on how good the warm sunlight felt on her skin. But all she could think about was how downright adorable Lieutenant O'Connor was when he was joking and looking repulsed at the thought of changing a dirty diaper. She could never have learned that from studying his file. Now she had a fuller picture. He was courageous, honorable, handsome, and funny. And smart. She couldn't forget smart.

Summer also couldn't let herself get too attracted to him.

She was, after all, here on a job.

CHAPTER FIVE

Parents needed mobile hazmat teams on call twenty-four seven.

How had no one suggested this?

As Robbie peeled back the diaper he was helping Tim change, he nearly let out a cry at the contents. No chemical spill could be as bad as this mess. Carefully, he drew the diaper out and folded it, trying not to gag. Cassidy kicked her little legs, babbling, as she lay on the living room floor on the changing pad Tim had snuck under her, clearly unaware they were saving her from the battery acid she'd emitted.

Talk about bad luck. He shouldn't be still thinking about the gorgeous blonde they'd just met on the beach, one both mega-hot and sweet. Was the universe laughing at him? Was this its follow-up joke after he'd thought closing a case on a bad guy was better than sex? It had to deliver a girl he would totally go for normally at a time when it was impossible.

"Ugh!" Reagan's face scrunched up. "That's the most magic you've ever had, Cassidy. Too bad you don't make glitter instead of poop."

Cassidy giggled in response. How could she be so happy when she stunk so bad?

Billie nudged him hard in the ribs. "I'm going to have nightmares. You owe me, brother. Like *a case of Irish whiskey* owe me."

"Look." Robbie gave him a shove back as he secured the radioactive package. "It's not my fault she had a hurricane in there."

"'Cane," Cassidy said, clapping as she lay on her back.

Tim lifted her up. "Someone grab me our new baby garbage pail. I'm going to need a lot of wipes."

Robbie felt the urge to hurl, but he grabbed the can after depositing the diaper. Cassidy tried to roll onto her side to see what was going on. "Grab her," Tim cried as Billie lurched forward on the floor to gently hold her in place. "She's a shifty one. Who knew anyone who looked so sweet could do a poopsie like this?"

A poopsie? He and Billie traded a look. Tim was showing them why he'd been voted Nurse of the Month six times at the retirement home, a record their father had told them all about. Suddenly, all he could think about was how his dad was faring in Ireland. Probably worried sick. Kathleen, too.

He wondered if the Kellys had visited O'Connor's Pub or any of his other brothers. They'd probably gone by Billie's two mechanic shops, but the guys who worked there knew how to wield a wrench or a crowbar. Some of Billie's guys had even done time, although not for anything that would make Robbie worry about having them around his family.

The biggest concern he had right now was about Tim's girlfriend. If the Kellys sent someone to check out the retirement home, they might find out he was dating another nurse. They could question her. Maybe even grab her.

When he'd shared his concerns with Tim, his brother had told him not to worry. The relationship wasn't public, given they worked together, and it had only started three months ago, so there was no reason for the Kellys to find out. Besides, he hadn't told Helen about Tara or the kids—he'd just said he had to leave town to help his brother with an urgent family matter and couldn't be in touch while he was gone.

God, it was too bad he and Mickey had agreed that his partner would have no contact with any of the O'Connors while he was gone, but it had seemed wise since Mickey was working with Internal Affairs. He had to be extra careful with everything at stake.

"Earth to Robbie," Tim called after sanitizing his hands. "I'm ready for the fresh diaper."

"Here." He snagged one from the bedazzled diaper bag, which was now thankfully free of mob money, and thrust it out. "And don't make this worse by quoting Shakespeare."

"Yeah," Billie added in solidarity. "Don't do it, Timmy."

Since they'd been stupid and given Tim ammunition with the whole Shakespeare crap, their baby brother had been a quoting fountain, knowing it was driving them nutters. Worse, the girls loved it when Tim poured on a British accent and belted out those "funny words" as Reagan called them.

"Too bad. I had the perfect one from *Hamlet*," Tim said, deftly affixing the diaper and lifting Cassidy up for a kiss on the cheek.

"I want to hear it!" Reagan cried, jumping up and down.

"Please!" Cassidy added, throwing out her chubby little arms.

"My offense is rank, it smells to heaven."

His lyrical booming British voice was completely different from his usual rough Southie accent. It was incredible. Suddenly, Robbie wished he could take a video and share it with the rest of the family. Even if it was ridiculous, it would be a good laugh. God, he even missed sending around his stupid criminal videos. His mood crashed.

He was used to action. To doing what he wanted, when he wanted. Now he was in Kiddieville, changing diapers, dressing Barbies, and preparing chicken nuggets. His bravest act was chasing a toddler down so she didn't drown in the ocean. Jesus, this trip was already killing him. And the cat still hated him...

He spied the family room, sensing it was around.

"Hey!" Billie gave him another nudge to the ribs. "What about our beautiful neighbors? Especially that angel, Summer—"

"We're here to look after the girls." Even Tim turned from making baby faces at Cassidy at the sound of his gruff voice. "I was just thinking it was fate's big joke on me to meet a woman I'd like to ask out while we're here, but let's stay focused."

"You'd like to ask her *out*?" Billie glanced at Tim, and then both of them stared at their older brother. Even Reagan was studying him, which made Cassidy turn her big blue eyes toward him too.

"My oldest brother who has been off women—"

"We have a job to do, Billie, one I take very seriously." Maybe he would need to remind himself every time he saw Summer, but there wasn't another option. "I expect you to do the same, and not go off like you're on the prowl on a Friday night in Southie."

"What's on the prowl?" he heard Reagan ask.

That made him wince. He turned, feeling like he'd failed at being a good role model. God, he'd done his best with that responsibility as the oldest of eight kids. He'd savored never having to do it again.

"What's with the whole magic in the pants thing?" Billie

bandied back at Reagan as Robbie took the opportunity to wander off toward the patio window.

Mr. Deflection was in the house. Robbie wondered if that was how his brother handled women when they said they loved him. Not that his brother led anyone on. He was always completely straightforward. But that didn't mean people didn't fall for each other, even if it was one-sided. Billie said people suddenly up and "got ideas."

That was something Robbie understood firsthand. He'd tried to be straightforward with the women he'd dated after his divorce, but he quickly fell into a pattern with everyone he dated. In the beginning, she'd say she understood his need to keep things casual, but a few months in, she'd get all clingy and gushy about how great he was and how she'd fallen for him.

The hurt, the drama, and the complications had led him to stop trying, resigning himself to getting laid less, sure. Pouring himself into work and being with family helped. But he still felt a hole in his life—not that he'd ever admit it out loud.

He carried another hole around inside him, from when his mother had died. He figured he could learn to carry this one too, after a near lifetime spent carrying the other.

He'd loved his ex-wife, but he was a cop, through and through, and after five years of marriage, she'd started to pressure him to quit and find another profession. She'd used ruthless words, whispered after hot sex.

If you love me...

If you believe in us...

God, she'd tried to manipulate him and guilt him at every turn until he'd finally concluded she wouldn't stop. Southie girls were like that. In the end, they were both miserable. Unfulfilled. He'd packed up what he'd wanted from their apartment and left, leaving her a brief note on the kitchen counter after telling her they should get a divorce. *I'm sorry. I can't change.*

If you asked him today, he'd still say no one should have to change who they were to have someone love them or stay with them. Love was a choice. First, last, and always. His ex had gone back on her choice to love a cop. He loved his job and he was good at it.

"Hey, Robbie!" Tim called, coming over and putting his hand on his shoulder. "Reagan said Tara didn't want the girls to feel bad when they fart, so she told them it means they have a lot of magic inside them. I can't wait to use that at Serenity Gardens. Come on. We're going to fly that kite Billie bought."

"Yeah, come on!" Reagan said, running over and taking Tim's hand. "Cassidy wants to fly a kite too."

"She does?" Tim danced over to the little girl on the floor and scooped her up. "Then fly it we shall. High into the heavens, where all the magic in the universe lies."

Robbie regarded Billie as they left the room to find the kite. "Magic, huh?" he said distractedly. "Our baby brother is beyond addled. He's—"

"Just because I appreciate a beautiful woman doesn't mean I'm not taking this situation seriously." His brother lifted his massive chin. "Same goes for you."

His exhale was charged with frustration. "I'm sorry I implied that. I'm... Hell, I'm not used to playing on the beach and changing diapers. I'm used to—"

"I know what you're used to." Billie planted his feet. "Which is why it's so colossal that you actually admitted to wanting to go out with that sweet woman next door."

He was so not having this conversation. "Don't turn into Tim and make me talk about my feelings."

Billie's mouth tipped to the right, and a rusty laugh snuck

out. "Fine. How about we throw the football around outside and act like real men? Not diaper-changing pansies."

Now they were talking. "Tackle or touch?"

Billie cracked his neck. "What do you think? And hey... maybe our next-door neighbors will enjoy a game of shirtless football. It's the least we can do for Summer for helping soothe Cassidy."

Robbie's pulse sped up. He'd noticed Summer sneaking a glance at his bare chest earlier. "You've got a one-track mind."

"Which I thank God for as a meat-eating, women-loving man." He slung his arm around Robbie. "You might try easing up on yourself. Flirting with the girl next door could release some of your tension. Are you always like this at work?"

He thought of his partner giving him a gift certificate for a massage last Christmas. *Mostly* as a joke. Of course, he hadn't used it. He'd given it to Tara instead. God, Tara. Where was she today? What was she doing? "I'm worse," he finally answered. "I'm every criminal's worst nightmare."

Billie erupted with laughter, dragging him down the stairs. Miss Purrfect hissed as they appeared, jumping off her sunny perch on the couch with a menacing meow before tugging at her collar again.

"Evidently, she doesn't like the new collar," he noted to Billie. "Maybe it's all the rhinestones."

"Yeah, Tim caught that, but Reagan said Tara told her to never remove it, or she'd get lost. Besides, it's not like I want to get close to that cat."

"Me either." He watched as Miss Purrfect gave them another glare, put her tail in the air, and grandly swept past them to the kitchen.

"Talk about the cold shoulder," Billie joked, clutching his heart playfully. "Maybe I've lost my sex appeal."

"I can't stand to look at you."

Robbie grabbed the football Billie had bought and followed his brother out onto the beach. Tim and the girls were already up a ways flying the kite. Summer and her friend were sitting on their towels, talking, clearly checking them out.

Her obvious regard gave him permission to admire her. Summer made quite the picture with the ocean breeze ruffling those long blond locks. Sunlight kissed her tall, slender frame and all the places that brought men to their knees. Her slow smile seemed in response to his appearance, and God help him, he felt the urge to smile back.

Billie ran over to them, grinning that "sex appeal" smile he was famous for. Summer—he still couldn't believe her parents had chosen that name—smiled as his brother started talking, but her friend leaned forward in her black bikini and swept her hair over her shoulder, clearly interested. She was so Billie's type, sexy with a voluptuous body to match, and Billie puffed up like a rooster when she laid her slender hand on his forearm. Idiot.

Robbie sent the football flying, knowing it would annoy his brother. Billie's head jerked to the side moments before the perfect spiral nailed him in the shoulder, and he caught it one-handed. Sending back a raised brow, he refocused on the ladies and said something to make them laugh.

Only Summer snuck a peek Robbie's way...

Their eyes locked, and his heart picked up speed. So, he appreciated a beautiful woman. He was still a man. Didn't mean he was going to do anything about it. But God, he was tempted, seeing her lying on her side, her bare legs a feast for his senses. She was gorgeous and nice. What stranger would help a screaming child and then handle an explosive diaper with humor? This was not a Friday night pickup kind of girl. This was a woman who was comfortable with herself, clearly good with kids, outgoing—

She wasn't smiling now. What was she thinking as she

looked so seriously at him? That he needed a good woman to soften him? Make him happy? Right. Until she decided to start changing him and the life and career he'd made, one he was proud of, one he'd hoped his woman would be proud of.

He let his gaze sweep over the nice line of her trim shoulders and back. Her blond hair was windblown and a little frizzy. Oddly, it made her look sexier. She had a trim waist to go along with those endless legs. When she'd come to stand beside him earlier, he'd noted she was tall, coming to his shoulder in bare feet. Five-ten, he'd bet.

Her eyes had been as green as a shamrock and warm with compassion. He could feel himself wanting to look more, and that was a problem. At one time, he might have decided to pursue a vacation fling, but he was older and wiser, and he had a serious job to do, protecting Tara's girls.

But damn, she made it hard for him to concentrate, which Billie proved easily by sneakily throwing a pass back to him when he was admiring Summer.

The football nailed him in the face.

CHAPTER SIX

ROBBIE O'CONNOR DIDN'T LOOK LIKE HE WAS GOING TO give in to his attraction and cozy up to her.

Sure, she'd known he was going to be a hard nut to crack, but she'd thought she'd laid a brick in the foundation of rapport between them when she'd helped Cassidy. But while he'd looked his fill and earned a bruised cheek for his trouble, he hadn't come over with his brother to strike up a conversation.

He'd simply walked away with the football to where his other brother, Tim, was flying the kite with the two ecstatic girls jumping up like colorful little pogo sticks at the edge of the glittering aquamarine water.

"Don't mind my brother," Billie said, catching her glance, his shadow looming large as he stood beside Sheila. "Robbie's a great guy. He just has a lot on his plate. But tell me more about you ladies. How long are you here?"

Sheila tipped her oval face up and gave him a beaming smile that showed off the pink lip gloss she'd carefully applied. Billie leaned in closer as she delivered an account of their cover story. Two childhood best friends. Yada yada.

Billie said he thought it was great how tight they were. That good friends—like family—were what mattered most in life. Yeah, he was selling them a story too in his own way.

Lily let her friend do her thing, her attention drawn to the others as Reagan and Cassidy screeched in delight. A smile snuck across her face. Robbie had boosted Reagan on his shoulders and was running as she flew the billowing orange and turquoise kite. Tim scooped Cassidy up and jogged behind them, the little girl waving madly in encouragement. The football lay forgotten on the beach, the tide flirting with it on each rush toward the sandy shore.

Lily rather liked the fact that Robbie wasn't going to let himself be distracted by single women on a beach holiday when he had a bigger goal—protecting those sweet girls.

Ironically, he seemed to be exactly the sort of guy she really wanted to date. Because the FBI preferred for their agents to have had previous work experience before joining the Bureau, she'd chosen to be a kindergarten teacher in the Bay Area, knowing she wanted to ultimately work on cases involving children. During that time, she'd been in a two-year relationship with a tech engineer. He'd known she was planning to apply to the FBI once she'd reached the "magic" entry age—thirty years old—but when the time came, he'd told her he liked things as they were and wasn't interested in being involved with someone who worked in a high-stakes profession that involved plenty of moving around the country as part of climbing up the career ladder.

Even though she'd loved him, she'd wanted to be in the FBI since she'd been a young woman. She was not going to give up her plans, especially not for someone who didn't truly understand how important they were to her.

It turned out he wasn't the only one who felt that way about dating an FBI agent. While she was never without invitations to go out, most guys didn't call her back for another date once they learned what she did for a living.

Sheila liked to say it was akin to wearing flea repellant instead of perfume.

As she watched Billie crouch down onto his haunches next to Sheila, flirting like it was his job, she wondered what the Vin Diesel doppelganger would think if he ever learned the truth. Would Sheila still be making him grin, or would he feel threatened? Hard call. As a successful mechanic, he likely hung around men all day—much like Robbie. Men who worked in alpha male hives were often threatened by strong women.

The FBI was the perfect example. She'd been asked out by other officers, but most of them were arrogant and used to getting any woman they wanted because they were FBI officers. Fit. Hot. Cocky.

Some women really got off on that, and while Lily saw the appeal, she'd made it a policy to never date a fellow officer. There was enough sexual harassment regardless, and opening that door to being seen as "easy" or "available" was a good way to cause even more trouble, not to mention professional suicide. She was known for being an effective officer but reserved, despite her Sunshine nickname. That was fine by her.

Women at the FBI needed to work harder to prove themselves, much like women in many professions. While her superior female officers said the FBI had gotten better, it was still an old boys' network. She navigated that as best she could by busting her butt and keeping up with her cases. Collaring the bad guys and bringing in money were two things that got you promoted and left alone.

This current case with the Kellys involved both, and they were still waiting to hear whether Internal Affairs had reported the mob money from Tara's nail salons to the Organized Crime task force that involved Boston police, the FBI, the DEA, and other law enforcement agencies. Sheila had bet her a case of coconut water it wouldn't be reported. Lily had countered with Lindt chocolates, arguing that if it wasn't, it might be because IA wanted to run a contained operation. Too many cooks in the kitchen and all...

"You know, Summer was just saying how gorgeous it is here too!" Sheila swatted Lily playfully, drawing her back into the conversation. "This is our first time in the Outer Banks, and there's so much to explore. We read about this great bar and grill that has live music a couple of nights a week. What's the name again, Sunshine?"

She wanted to grit her teeth as Sheila's hazel eyes danced with glee. "Umm...something with brewers in it. I'll have to check." Being too prepared was a no-no on cover ops.

"I can ask our landlady for suggestions." Billie rubbed the back of his clean-shaven head, which she hoped he'd smeared with sunscreen. "Maybe you two would like to go out for a drink after our girls hit the hay? The last couple of nights they pretty much fell flat on their faces after dinner. My mom would say too much fresh air and sun."

"I understand the feeling." Sheila gave her signature murmur, arching her neck, eyes closed, and rubbing her fingers through her thick black hair. It worked like a charm on every man. "I'm still exhausted after finishing up a huge audit with one of my clients. I was practically whimpering by the end."

Lily almost hoped Billie would ask her more about her work because Sheila could back it up. Interested in working on major fraud and corruption cases someday, her partner had gotten an accounting degree and practiced as a certified accountant until she'd applied for the FBI at thirty.

"Sounds like you haven't had much fun lately," Billie commented, shifting on his haunches as his hand came closer to her towel, clearly uninterested in shop talk. "We should do something about that."

"Yes, we should." Sheila opened her eyes and gave him another beaming smile. "You should see if one of your brothers wants to come along. That way someone could still stay with those cute little girls. Or... Me and Summer could swing by with the drinks. I make a very authentic margarita."

Lily knew this line. "Trust me, it's not to be missed."

Someone shouted up the beach, and they all turned. Robbie was flicking his hand in their direction, as if beckoning his brother to join the family. Billie rolled his eyes before saying, "I'd better get back to family time. Let's figure something out, though. Be fun to have a drink."

"You know where we are," Sheila murmured, turning on her side to show off her luscious curves as Billie rose to his feet.

He pursed his lips, clearly admiring, and then gave another winning smile. "I sure do. See you, ladies."

As he ran off, Sheila lay on her back and sighed. "He's going to be easy, just like I thought. Robbie, however, seems determined to fight his attraction for you, which has me wanting to throw you at him."

"Sheila, I doubt you could throw me," she said dryly.

"If Billie gets us into their house, we'll see if they have a phone we can ask for a wiretap on. Maybe Tara's in touch with them, checking up on her girls."

"Robbie would know it's a risk."

Sheila took a drink from her water bottle. "True, but we'll still tap something if we can. Oh, and I'd like to extract the cat tracker—unless you think we should leave it in case they run on us like Tara did."

They didn't have an official search warrant for the house, but they could look around. If they spotted something, they could ask for one. "Let's keep the tracker," Lily commented, watching as Billie scooped Reagan off his brother's shoulders and took off farther up the beach, the kite continuing to streak through the clear blue cloudless sky.

Sheila sat up. "You know, Billie *is* kinda hot and he does seem good with kids. Let's hope his flirting will lead him to unburdening himself on little ol' me."

Lily studied the group as Tim chucked Cassidy under the cheeks, making her squeal and flail her little arms. Robbie stood staring out at the ocean. In profile, he was compelling. Hard angular jaw. A solitary demeanor. Yet connected when needed—like when Cassidy reached for him. He took her easily from Tim and propped her on his hip, saying something to Tim that made him throw back his head with laughter.

"I don't think either of Robbie's brothers up and took vacation from their full-time jobs without being told why." She pulled her knees to her chest, analyzing. "They're tight. Did you notice how Billie said nothing about them and kept the questions about you?"

"Yeah, but players are good like that." Sheila opened the sunscreen and squeezed some onto her arms. "The less details, the less to remember with multiple women."

"That's true, but I don't think he's going to reveal anything that might hurt his cousin or those little girls." Lily took the sunscreen and applied some to her shoulders, grimacing at the greasy feel. "They were raised in Southie. People get cut or killed for talking out of turn."

"Meaning they have trust issues." Sheila lay back and rolled her shoulders. "We really are kindred spirits. I know you won't want to make a run at Reagan to see what she knows."

Her stomach knotted with tension. "I know it's part of the job, and as a kid who helped an undercover FBI agent unknowingly, I understand the merits. But I'd prefer to go for adult source info if possible."

Sheila patted her hand. "You're all tense now, and I'm sorry. I know it bothers you. It's not my favorite way to get information either, but if we need to go there—"

"Then we will." She pressed her hand to her locked diaphragm. "When we've exhausted other options."

"Meaning we need to figure out how to get Robbie talking to you, since he has the most info. Clearly, you've turned on his reptilian brain."

"Sheila, that's so gross."

"That football nailing his face almost had me guffawing."

"It was a big compliment, wasn't it?" she said, her lips twitching at the memory.

"One of my best moments was when a man ran into a lamppost as I was walking out of Quincy Market," her partner added, readjusting her thick black sunglasses. "Between your looks and your Miss Confessor profile, you're a shoo-in to get some useful information."

She sure hoped so. She had to trust in her skills. Adults had told her their secrets since she was a child, sensing both compassion and a safe space. She had more confidential informants than anyone else in her division because of it. In truth, knowing things no child should have known at her age had helped her. The undercover female FBI agent who had infiltrated the cult her mother had joined had done the rest. Brie Thierry was the FBI agent who had inspired her to join the Bureau. She was the FBI officer that Lily Meadows wanted to be.

"Why don't you run into the ocean and then pretend you have a cramp?" Sheila suggested, reaching into her beach bag for a bag of pistachios. "Robbie just handed Cassidy back to Tim. We know his protective instincts are high. He'd surge into the surf and save you, and then you'd be all wet and slick in his arms as he carried you safely back to shore. Then he'd lay you down and hover over you in all his masculine glory and likely put his hands on your poor little calf. Batting your eyelashes could seal the deal."

She suddenly felt sick. God, the job sometimes was too much. She spotted the football they'd been throwing roll into the ocean with the surging tide and float off. "How about I just go get their ball?"

Sheila snorted with laughter. "Make sure to use both your hands, Summer. It looks awfully big."

Chuckling to herself, she jogged up the shoreline and darted into the surf as the ball floated past. Untangling the seaweed clutching the pigskin, she felt the sand give under her bare feet as the tide went out again. As a child, she'd always feared this moment. Maybe it was because she'd already understood how dangerous life could be when the ground under you started to shift and change. There was nothing to hold on to. She'd learned to navigate that feeling well, and she was smiling as she left the waters.

She had this.

Robbie was watching her when she turned with the football in hand. She looked back at him, knowing Sheila was right. This was another opportunity, an opening. She could jog over to him, giving him a good view of her bikini-clad body. But he'd proved he wasn't a man who could be so easily swayed by a flash of ass. She'd read his file over a dozen times, looking for insights into his personality, the drivers anyone undercover looked for to tip things in their favor. He was divorced, she knew, and unlike many cops, he hadn't remarried right away. In fact, he hadn't remarried at all in the past five years. That suggested he'd gotten a tough lesson about law enforcement—that it often didn't mesh with family life. Still, family was clearly critical to who he was.

He wouldn't be looking for an easy score. He'd be looking

for an equal, someone who could challenge him. She drew back her arm and let the ball fly. In her previous career as a teacher, she'd played with plenty of balls during recess. She was a good athlete—hadn't she set a record for running up Radar Hill at Quantico during her FBI training? As an FBI officer, she'd been part of team-building exercises involving flag football and softball. She threw a damn good spiral.

His look of shock as he caught the ball against his chest pleased her. Even at thirty yards away, she noted the way his brow lifted, amused. She let her smile coast over her face, and this time, it wasn't her fake cover smile.

Then she turned around to walk back to Sheila, and if she let her butt sway more than it needed to, well, that wasn't part of her cover story either.

She had just found her strategy with which to hook Robbie O'Connor.

CHAPTER SEVEN

A QUIET HOUSE HAD NEVER SOUNDED SO GOOD.

Robbie cocked his ear, savoring the peace. At least there was one upside to getting up early. First thing every morning, he went online to his account on the encrypted messaging service Internal Affairs had set up for him and his partner to use. There was still no message from his partner. He knew it was only going on five days since he'd arrived at the gym to pick up the girls, but he was restless.

Robbie tried to tell himself that was a good thing as he closed his IA-issued laptop. But no break in the case meant they weren't any closer to getting Tara cleared and her and the kids reunited and safely home. Surely the Kellys weren't laying low. It wasn't their MO. When you fucked with a Kelly, someone got hurt. Bad hurt.

Pushing those dark thoughts away, he pulled on his running shoes and tiptoed over to the next room to check on Reagan and Cassidy. Cracking the door, he noted they were still asleep in their beds, Miss Purrfect spooning the baby in the playpen. The cat lifted its head and bared its teeth as if he were an intruder. He made a face back. He didn't even want to know how the cat had gotten into the playpen. Likely used its demon-like claws to climb the netting. He let himself out before the cat could give one of its nasty hisses or growls and tiptoed down the stairs.

All that mattered was the kids were asleep as dawn's fingers spread across the sky, after yesterday's exhausting, patience-testing day filled with *what can we play next?* and *how many more days until we see Mom again?*

Truth be told, he could suck it up and play more girly games—anything from fixing Barbie's tangled hair to using shot glasses as baby teacups for a tea party, with the stuffed bear and rabbit sitting at the table with their beady little staring eyes. Yes, he could take even that freak show.

But he couldn't take the Mom question.

Because he didn't *fecking* know when they'd see Tara again, other than at the end of the two weeks. Tim, true to his usual positivity, had told him to be grateful they hadn't asked anything about their dad yet. After that honest-to-goodness slap in the face, he'd stewed about what to say if the topic came up. Tara had done a good job before she'd left, but he might need to tell them not to go off with the father if he *were* to show up—not that Robbie expected that. Scotty was on the run from the Kellys. He was probably in a *no questions asked* motel swigging his favorite beer, hoping to, at best, keep his fingers and toes.

The uncertainty of the whole situation was driving him nuts.

And so was all of Billie's harping about having a drink with their next-door neighbors. For two days, his brother hadn't stopped talking about Clarice's famous margaritas, or how it would do them good to get out of the house for an adult evening after being in Kiddieville all day. Of course, Billie had already secured Tim for babysitting. Bully for him.

"Morning," Tim called as Robbie entered the rosy-lit

kitchen. His little brother was bright-eyed and bushy-tailed like usual at the early hour, since his shift at the retirement home started at five a.m. "I've already had a walk on the beach. It's going to be a beautiful day."

Robbie grunted in response. Every morning his eyes tracked to the stupid saying in a matted heart frame behind the cozy white plank table: *This Kitchen Is Seasoned with Love.* Every morning it made him want to puke. He thought about what kind of saying they could frame at the precinct. *This Breakroom Is Splattered with Blood.* Now that would be funny!

"You sound like your normal cheery self," Tim said, pointing to the fresh coffee in the corner of the massive black granite countertop. "Grab a cup before I tell you what I found this morning."

Every cell went on alert. "What did you see? Sketchy guys on the beach? Someone weird drive by? Tell me."

Tim put his hand over his mouth to cover his smile. "Nothing dangerous. You might get a little freaked out though. Ah...Miss Purrfect decided to use your shorts in some kitty defecation ritual."

"What?"

"Check out her litterbox. I'm not sure how she stole your shorts, but I don't think you're going to want them back now."

"That damn cat was sleeping with Cassidy when I checked." He strode into the laundry room and stopped short, horrified by the sight of his black shorts, scratched up and covered in cat shit. "Dammit! That fu—"

"Language," Tim called, coming to stand beside him. "Look, it's not uncommon for cats to get like this when their normal routine is upset. Plus, you tossed Miss Purrfect off the couch last night when we started watching *The Little Mermaid*."

God, like he needed to be reminded of that sing-along

nightmare. "Because that feline is an animal, not a person." He ground his teeth. "Tim, I've been more than patient with the girls..."

His brother's mouth twitched. "I knew you were reaching deep yesterday when Cassidy insisted you put a bow in your hair. For the fourth time."

"Well, Billie can't seem to get it right, so I did what I had to do." They both snorted at that. "But, Tim, I can't take a bad-tempered cat. After this, I want to throw it outside and be done with it."

Tim put an easy hand on his shoulder, giving him those understanding *I'm a good listener* eyes that probably rocked his girlfriend's world. "I know you do. Billie would agree. He and Miss Purrfect had a standoff in the bathroom at lunch when the cat wandered in while he was taking a piss. He didn't like that the cat was standing there watching, and when he tried to slam the door in the cat's face, it sprayed him. He didn't say anything, but he bitched to me about it stinking to high heaven."

"That's why you sprayed Febreze upstairs." Robbie turned around and marched to the stairs. "Okay, that's it. We will not be terrorized by some—"

"Those girls love that cat, Robbie," Tim said softly behind him. "It's all they have of home right now besides each other."

He halted, fists clenched at his sides. Guilt broke through the concrete around his heart. "It needs to learn a lesson in manners."

"My girlfriend has a cat, so trust me when I say you can't win a power game with a cat."

Robbie throttled back his anger. "Fine. When you're right, you're right, but something's gotta change. For Billie too."

"Don't I know it. Why do you think I put her in with Cassidy last night?"

"And yet it managed to steal my shorts and shit on them while I was asleep." He shot his brother a look. "Wait. Is a kid sleeping with a cat even sanitary? It's not on Tara's list. You read it, right?"

"We'll take Cassidy into the ocean today if she's covered in cat hair, don't worry, and of course I read Tara's instructions." He detoured to the kitchen, so Robbie followed. "Billie, not so much. Have your coffee. You'll feel more human."

How could he feel human when that cat had somehow gotten the slip on him and snuck into his room and stolen his underwear?

"No, I'm going for a run." He ran his frustrated hand through his hair. "Billie had me this close to agreeing to go out with those women next door to let off some steam last night after hearing you guys singing along to every freaking song in that really disturbed movie."

"*The Little Mermaid* is a classic, and honestly, it's better that they're singing than crying. Don't you think?"

Who said his baby brother didn't know when to go for the jugular?

"You win that point. Tim, I don't know how people do this. From the moment they wake up, it's nonstop. Where is Cassidy running off to? Is she sticking something in her mouth? Is she trying to drown in the ocean? What accessory does Reagan want to put on her Barbie? What do they want to eat? What do they want to play? I swear, I'm starting to agree with Billie. If I was in a relationship, I'd make an appointment for a vasectomy."

Tim was trying not to laugh. "Easier ways to prevent kids than having someone go in with scissors and stop your swimmers. But your call. I personally like being around the girls. They're like my seniors in some ways. Erratic, yet very dear.

Innocent, yet so wise. Demanding, yet easy as all get-out. Yesterday afternoon, Reagan and Cassidy were happy to have their feet in the air on the beach and laugh for ten minutes. Tell me that isn't special."

He leveled his brother a hard look, very much feeling like the old grouch he was so often accused of being. "I'm glad you think so, Tim. Personally I can't believe we ever did that as kids. It's a complete waste of time. Putting your legs in the air and laughing for no reason. What's the point?"

"Go run!" Tim walked to the door and opened it. "You obviously need it. I'll have pancakes and sausage waiting for you when you get back."

Tim had been doing most of the cooking, being that he was the best cook of the bunch.

Robbie sighed. "Sorry I'm bitching. Thanks for cooking. I'll...buy some hot dogs and burgers. We can grill tonight."

"Sounds good. Watch out for jellyfish on the beach. Those onshore winds last night brought a bunch up with the tide. And I know how much you hate them."

He didn't just hate them. He loathed them. Why had God created something that could practically reduce a man to tears with one sting? Bees had nothing on jellyfish. "Yes, Mama. I'll keep my eyes peeled. Oh, and Tim. Did you quote Shakespeare as you watched the sun rise this morning?" he asked, feeling the satisfying need to poke at his brother.

Tim flipped him the bird after looking around to make sure the girls weren't there to witness it. "Yes, and I looked up some insults the girls wouldn't understand. Don't let this one hit you on the way out. *I scorn you, scurvy companion.*"

Now *that* was what he was talking about. Brotherly baiting. A little roughhousing to start the day. Better than coffee. "Don't you get scurvy from a lack of Vitamin C?" He lunged for his baby brother. "What am I, a pirate?"

Tim evaded him with the grace of a much-plagued

younger brother and grabbed a chair for protection. *"Out, damned spot."*

"I swear to God, Timmy, I'm going to put you and that cat in a body bag if you keep this Shakespeare thing up."

"Nothing will stop me." He raised his fist like a plagued hero making a vow in some off-Broadway drama. "I've finally found something that gets under your skin and Billie's. I will not surrender. I won't."

Robbie pretended he couldn't open the door fast enough as Tim began spouting more Shakespeare gibberish. Honestly, he was feeling better already. His tennis shoes sunk into the sand as he made a beeline toward the beach. The lure of the scene had him breathing easier. The frothy tide was breaking as it reached the gorgeous stretch of golden sand. The sky was mottled with red, orange, and bright blue, all competing for real estate in the open expanse.

The beach was empty of inhabitants, another bonus. Being a city dweller, he craved being alone, and running in the national parks or fishing outside of Boston were his escapes from the madness. He was going to enjoy this run and force his brain to stop bitching. Because even he was getting tired of himself and his damn thoughts.

Maybe that's what that Shakespeare guy had meant with the *out, damned spot* comment. He chuckled to himself and started running, enjoying the way the sand challenged his legs at first. Keeping to the wet sand, he let it rip, doing what his weird Shakespeare-quoting brother had suggested—bypassing the legions of dead or dying jellyfish on the beach.

He ran until he was at his peak cardio level, something a quick pulse check told him. Maintaining his pace, he let his gaze crest across the beach and out toward the ocean, the earthy scents of salt and ocean coming in with each inhale. Used to the rocky shores and cold waters in the Boston area, he thought the Outer Banks was a lot like a steam room, the water so perfect it was almost too warm to swim in.

He'd always preferred the cold water, often winning the longest time in the Atlantic when he and his brothers went to the beach up their way. His mind flashed to his family. He wondered for what had to be the millionth time how they all were, but most especially if any of the Kellys had paid a visit to Danny at the pub. He'd been tempted to call on the burner even though he knew better, and that had made him finally realize why stupid criminals always got caught calling friends and family. They couldn't resist. But he would. He had to. For Tara's sake as much as everyone in their rental house. With his mind on Tara, he pushed his pace faster. He wasn't a religious man anymore, but he wasn't too proud to call in some prayers. *Please let her be safe and back with her babies soon.*

The seagulls cried and squawked around him, some fishing for breakfast while others chased a puffin who'd hauled out a decent-sized trout. He and his brothers should charter a boat and take the girls fishing. Usually, when they came to the beach, they went out on the water to fish or shoot the breeze and drink beer, but it hadn't dawned on him to do that here.

Would the girls be okay on the water? Or would they be happy for about ten minutes and then get bored? Was there whale watching this far south? But would *he* be bored with a bunch of other tourists waiting for some big tubby water mammal to spew water through its spout?

God, he missed work. Give him a breaking and entering or a carjacking, and he'd be happy as a clam. He didn't like domestics. Never had. Any man—or woman—beating on someone they were supposed to love was the scum of the earth in his opinion, and he had zero respect for them and their problems. Nothing justified that kind of behavior. Some murders he had an easier time understanding. Like the mob. You screw them, they cut you. Any idiot knew that.

Again, why in the world had Scotty played with the Kellys? If they caught him and killed him, Robbie wouldn't be sad. The girls would be better off without a man who'd knowingly put his family in that kind of jeopardy.

He felt a presence at his back moments before something flashed by him. "Hey!" he shouted, unnerved that he hadn't heard the person coming up on him, and so closely for that matter.

A woman with a blond ponytail bobbing and long, slender legs he would recognize in a police lineup. Hadn't he been staring at them every time she and her friend appeared on the beach for suntanning or reading? *Well, hello, Summer Sunshine.* She was wearing a blue tank and matching short shorts as she looked over her shoulder and grinned at him.

Surprise rolled over him at her speed—the same way it had when she'd thrown that perfect spiral his way. She didn't slow down, but that coy smile she was giving him over her shoulder suggested she was pleased with herself for catching him off guard. Then she was facing front again, her strides eating up the beach. He punched up his speed, but even a seasoned runner like him couldn't keep up. She left him in her dust, and he was more than a little embarrassed by that.

How in the hell did a speech therapist run like that? She must have run track in high school, maybe college even. He watched as she continued a brisk pace up the stretch of beach that rolled out to the left. When she turned around, running back his way, he felt his muscles burn as he extended his pace. Part of him knew he was trying to impress her.

He watched her smile at him like the cat who'd gotten the cream—damn, he could never use that phrase again after Miss Purrfect's assault on his shorts.

Summer was as pretty as a picture, all slender and sweet as

she ran his way. Until she passed him again in a blur. A blur! Man, she was fast!

He thought about turning around and following her, but when he looked over his shoulder, she hadn't slowed. If she had, she would have been signaling she was interested, right? God, he was clearly out of practice with women, but something told him she was amused by him. She might even be having fun with him. First the football, and now outrunning him...

She was a mystery. A challenge.

Surely, she had to know he was fighting his attraction for her. They stared at each other every time they were on the beach together. So far, she hadn't pushed it. Clearly she'd decided to show off today.

"Okay, that's kind of hot," he acknowledged to himself.

She was stretching when he turned around to come back. He could see her in the distance on the beach, doing that whole lunging warrior thing and other seamless moves that suggested she was not only fast but flexible. Again, really hot. He thought about Billie's near pleas about going out for a drink and music with adult conversation. Last night, he'd nearly succumbed to temptation when Tim and the girls had started singing along with that Jamaican-talking animated crab.

Would it be such a bad idea? he'd thought.

Then he'd dismissed it, the same way he'd fought the urge to pick up the burner phone and check in with Danny. Call him cautious, but he didn't want to leave Tim alone with the girls while he and Billie went off on dates. If something bad happened, Timmy couldn't stop it. He couldn't live with himself if his brother and the girls were hurt because he'd let his guard down.

Robbie had to assume they were in danger—every day.

Staying home—where he'd beefed up security—was the

best plan. The saying among cops who lived to old ages was simple and often repeated to stupid cadets like he'd been, full of bravery, bravado, and balls: stick to the plan; going off half-cocked will get you killed.

He had a plan, a damn good one, even if it wasn't his usual.

So as he returned to the house, all he did was flash Summer a friendly smile before heading toward the patio door. But as he got closer to their rental, he decided he could have a little fun of his own if she were still watching. She was. Hot damn.

He slowly tugged off his shirt.

CHAPTER EIGHT

Her strategy had paid off.

Granted, it had taken her two days to find the right opportunity, but Robbie had flirted back but good. He'd stolen her breath when he'd stripped off his sweaty shirt, revealing the kind of muscular, masculine back guaranteed to make women drool. Of course, it wasn't professional to check out a target like that, but she was only human.

Lily practically skipped back to the house at her success. The moment she entered, she caught Sheila fanning herself as she fussed with the flowers they'd bought at the store and stuck in a round white vase. Little domestic covers like that could help an op seem legit. Buck always said it was the details that counted, and as Lily looked around their rental, she decided it was starting to pay off.

"Robbie O'Connor certainly takes care of the body God gave him," Sheila declared with a breathy sigh as she righted a red gerbera daisy. "I'm only sorry you didn't get a chance to see his chest. It was *hold the phone* gorgeous!"

Lily could imagine. If it was anything like his back...but

she refrained from saying so aloud. "I told you he wanted a challenge."

Sheila's soft drink hissed as she opened it, and she took a healthy sip before smacking her lips. "I assume you have another challenge planned for Lieutenant Hottie O'Connor? Wanna bet how long it takes before we have a dinner or drinks with him and his brother? Poor Billie has wanted it so bad the last couple of days even I felt sorry for the guy. But he gets props for not pulling the trigger without his brother's consent."

"Billie loves those girls and his family." She grabbed a coconut water from the fridge and then a beach towel she'd set out earlier on the white barstool, rubbing it over her sweat-slicked skin. The humidity was suffocating outside, and it was barely eight o'clock. "But I think I got us some new momentum. I'm going to do a little surfing with the surfboard I rented so I can intrigue Robbie a little more. How could I pass up the best surfing on the Atlantic Coast? Later, how do you feel about some bikini volleyball? Do you think you can maneuver the O'Connor boys into a game?"

Honey." Sheila mimed striking the ball as she shot her a dry glance. "Putty in my hands—only I'd better wear my sports bra. The girls would fall right out of my bikini when I serve. While some would love the view, there are children around."

Lily saluted her as she left for the shower. "I give it two days before Robbie breaks and agrees to a date. Which will put Billie out of his misery."

"One!" Sheila shouted back.

Grinning, Lily headed upstairs. Sheila really was an optimist sometimes. Nothing would please her more than for her partner to be right. She was itching for movement on this case.

When she exited the house again after a light breakfast, carrying her new yellow surfboard, the men were playing with the girls on the beach. Reagan was shoring up a new sandcastle with Tim while Cassidy attempted to shovel their construction material into her matching red plastic bucket with Robbie as her assistant. Billie was making some kind of moat with his pointer finger. If she was a normal person not on an under-cover case, she would have thought they all looked completely adorable together. Three large men and two little girls. Quaint.

"Put a sway into those little hips of yours, Sunshine." Sheila sauntered beside her, decked out in a white sports bra with matching bikini bottoms, white sunglasses, and white flip-flops. She looked hot. Like straight out of a music video hot.

"I'll do my best," she answered, throwing a little motion into her gait. But she knew she didn't have the curves or hip rotation Sheila did.

One pair of eyes found them immediately. Billie waved, which prompted Reagan and Cassidy to pause their playing and do the same. She and Sheila both returned the greeting, but Lily kept her pace casual as she left Sheila to spread her towel and catch some sun.

Carrying her board toward the water, she could feel Robbie's eyes on her. She didn't know why, but she knew it was him. His gaze seemed to sear her skin. No question about it, he knew how to watch and assess discreetly—but thoroughly—like any seasoned law enforcement officer. She wondered if he'd worked undercover before. They would have that in common.

Stop it, Lily. Eyes on the prize.

"Hey, Summer!" She turned as Billie called her name, sprung up like a giant, and jogged over. "Wow! You surf?"

"Yeah." She kept walking as he trekked alongside her, waving at Sheila playfully with his power-watt *you know you want this* smile. "Since I was a kid. I can't wait to get out on the water."

"Cool!" His fingers skimmed the board with obvious appreciation. "I've only boogie boarded and even then, they don't make too many boards big enough for me. Hey! Watch out for jellyfish. There seems to be a ton today."

"Thanks!" she responded, heading into the water, not wanting to get stopped for more conversation.

She had a focus, and that was intriguing Robbie O'Connor more. She waded out into the ocean, enjoying the feeling of the warm water moving against her skin. Growing up beside the Pacific, she'd had to balance her love of the water with its coldness, ensuring her core temperature stayed strong. Here, she was already misting with sweat.

The ocean was one of the few places she felt safe, free, and in control, perhaps because she had no one to rely on but herself. No one interfering with her. That had been a heady feeling for a young girl who'd often felt trapped.

Breathing deeply, she tuned in to her surroundings, letting the waves rock over her. Sure enough, she spotted a pale brown undulating jellyfish. She wasn't thrilled about the bell-shaped stingers, but the ocean always carried some risks. Undertow had been her greatest in the Pacific, but she'd managed. She'd manage today too.

She slid onto her board and started paddling out, eyeing the crest of approaching waves. God, they were beautiful with their turquoise and darker blues mixing with the white where the waves broke. She chose her wave, preparing herself to rise up onto her board and ride it out. Right before it reached her, she pushed up gently onto her board, setting her feet and balancing her weight. The thrill of it had her heart dancing in her chest.

God, she loved that moment. The wind rushed over her face, and she felt the water hold the board as she moved in harmony with the subtle movement under her feet. She'd tried to teach her ex-boyfriend to surf, but he'd fought the water. One had to move with the water to balance on top of it and let it carry you.

Much like she'd learned about life.

When the wave brought her in and receded, she heard enthusiastic clapping from little people. She'd wondered if the girls would be curious. Not all children liked the water. Sure, Cassidy seemed to try and run into it every chance she had, but so far, none of the O'Connor brothers had let Reagan and Cassidy into the water much past the tide coming in.

They were smart about disguising their protectiveness by putting the girls on their shoulders and wading into the water, but she'd noted it. The girls had floaties for safety, but the brothers didn't let them get in the ocean alone for one minute. She wondered if they would have been as vigilant if the girls were older. When she'd been young, no one had worried about her being in the water, and frankly, she'd been glad. There had been enough stifling in other quarters.

When Lily slipped back into the water, she heard a male whistle of appreciation and Sheila's hoot. Sure enough, like he had for the last couple of days, Billie was sitting next to her partner on the beach as Sheila slowly applied sunscreen to her arms. He hadn't reached for the bottle to help yet, but Lily wouldn't be surprised if Sheila let him help her with her back today.

What a girl had to do on a case...

"That was so cool!"

She glanced to the right. Reagan was running over, Robbie jogging behind her. Tim rushed after Cassidy, who was flailing her red sand shovel in the air with glee. Waving again at the girls, she turned and swam out, smiling. The girls were going to make this easy. So far, they'd kept their distance, something she imagined was due to Robbie. But today she was going to change that. She might even give Reagan a little surf lesson if the O'Connors approved. She was a certified swimming teacher, after all, something she'd enjoyed doing when she'd run children's programs during summer vacations. Plus, the extra money had been nice.

Riding the board a few more times, she started putting on a show, punching up her hops onto the board as she rode a wave in. The girls were now cheering her every move, jumping up and down, the sandcastle long forgotten. Tim was grinning in that easy way of his.

Robbie was trying not to look intrigued as well as downright concerned. His arms were crossed over his shirtless chest. She should have known his protectiveness would come out with her on the water. Clearly, he didn't like it. Attitude radiated from every hard, masculine line of his gorgeous body. Like he was pissed off she had forced him to pay her attention, worry about her even.

God, she loved her job sometimes.

She upped the wattage of her smiles and waves to the girls as she danced with her board and the ocean. On her final run, she did a backflip off the board before heading into shallow water, a trick she'd mastered when she was about Reagan's age. Not from her mother, of course. A kind surfer had taken her under his wing when she'd showed an interest in surfing. He'd given her one of his old boards, and to her back then, he'd given her the sweetest gift of all: freedom.

When she surfaced, more cheering sounded. Feeling that rush of excitement in her veins she always got from watersports, she grabbed her surfboard and swam to shore. She noted the large jellyfish before it collided with her right leg, and she darted out of its path. When she looked up, Robbie had waded into the water with a massive frown.

"Do you have a cramp?" he called.

She shook her head. "Jellyfish."

His jaw popping reached her ears. "Did you get stung?"

The edge of his voice was razor-sharp with concern. "No. I'm good."

Had he planned on saving her?

When she reached the shallows, she kept her gaze on the water for any other stinging inhabitants. She sidestepped a trio of smaller jellyfish and broke from the water, the sand pulling under her feet. Robbie had a protective arm around Reagan, who had a tense, worried look on her little face.

"You okay?" he asked as she approached. His gaze ran over her, as if to ensure she hadn't been stung. She kinda liked that. After the kind of abuse she'd been around as a child, she was a sucker for a guy who so obviously cared about other people's well-being.

You are undercover, Lily.

"I'm great! The water feels terrific and being back on a board was heaven."

He finally lifted his hand from Reagan, who rushed up to her with wide and excited eyes. "I'm glad you're okay because that was so cool! You were like a ballet dancer on the water."

"Thank you," she said humbly, slicking the water from her ponytail. "I've been a water sprite since I was younger than you. There's nothing better."

"You looked like you were one with the ocean," Tim commented as he walked over with a gurgling, drooling Cassidy. "Having tried surfing once, I know you made it seem easier than it really is."

Cassidy thrust out her shovel, like she was inviting her to join their party. "Are you a water baby?" she asked with a grin.

"Cassidy likes to play in the water, but there's a lot of jellyfish around," her sister supplied. "Can I see your board?"

Robbie continued watching quietly as she smiled and looked over. "If your dad says it's okay."

For a moment, she saw the truth ripple across Reagan's face, and then Robbie was putting his hand gently on the little girl's shoulder. "It's very nice of you to offer," she said in a small voice.

"Sure thing. If you want, your dad or one of your uncles can help you paddle on it. Or I could."

She turned around and beamed a smile at Robbie. "Can I?"

"Me too!" Cassidy cried out, waving her shovel wildly.

Tim glanced at his older brother, and there was enough silent communication in the look to speak volumes.

"Reagan, I'm a little worried about the jellyfish," he told her, kneeling down in front of her. "It would really be bad if you got stung. Trust me. I know. It feels terrible. Like *I'd have to buy you a new Barbie* terrible. Let's see if the water is clearer tomorrow, and then we'll reassess. Did you see how Miss Sunshine had to swim really fast to get out of the way of one? She's a professional, and it almost got her. Okay?"

Reagan looked down, fingering Summer's board. "You promise about tomorrow?"

Lily noted the way he tipped her face up and nodded very seriously. "You have my word. But with the ocean—or any water—safety is our number one concern."

He sounded so much like a by-the-books law enforcement officer, her mouth twitched. His brow suddenly rose, and his blue eyes blazed with challenge.

"That's what Mom would say," Reagan said with a heart-felt sigh before turning back to Lily. "Would tomorrow be okay for you, Miss Sunshine?"

"Please call me Summer." She laid the board on the wet sand. "Tomorrow would be great. But how about you start your first lesson on land? Try standing on the board and holding your arms out. See if you can balance. If it's okay with your dad, of course."

Robbie's jaw tightened. "It's fine."

Calling him dad clearly struck a nerve. She would have to remember that. She only smiled at him innocently, knowing it would drive him a little crazy. Her smile seemed to make him frown sometimes, and she suspected it was because it had a powerful effect on him, one he really wanted to resist. *Well, too bad, Lieutenant O'Connor*.

Reagan cast a glance between them before stepping on and bobbling a little as the board gave. Her eyes flew to Lily's. "It *is* hard!"

"Told ya, Miss Pixie." Tim set Cassidy down and took the little cherub's hand as he helped her onto the board as well. "All right, sweetheart, keep hold of my hand. Let's see what you've got."

Cassidy jumped up and down, waving her shovel in the air, making Reagan wobble again. Before Lily could steady the little girl, Robbie was next to her in a flash. His capable hands closed gently around her shoulders.

"Bend your knees a little more, Reagan. There you go. Feel your feet."

He was a good coach, she realized. Patient. Competent.

Stop it, Lily Meadows. Next, you'll be seeing him in knight's armor.

"Cassidy is trying to topple me," she cried out with a laugh as Cassidy gave another series of delighted jumps, squealing nonstop.

Billie and Sheila walked toward them, close enough to touch each other. Progress. Lily studied Robbie surreptitiously. He was paying attention to Reagan, but she knew he was watching her too.

God, he was good at it. In fact, he made that kind of regard totally hot.

"Summer!" Sheila's hips were all an easy sway, filled with

feminine allure. "Billie and I were just saying you're like a gazelle or something. Girl, you were amazing!"

Her friend put her arm around her waist, and Lily did the same. Two friends having a moment on vacation.

"I know I was impressed." Billie nudged the back of Robbie's knee with his sand-covered foot, earning him a glare while Tim fought a smile. "You outran my brother this morning, I heard."

Robbie looked to be biting the inside of his cheek. "She clearly had someplace to be. I'm on vacation."

"Well, there's always tomorrow to see if you can match my stride." She gave a challenging smile, her insides zinging at the possibility. "Reagan, feel free to play with the board as long as you'd like. You can bring it over when you're done. Clarice? Are you ready for a little volleyball?"

Sheila swatted her butt. "Girl, you're insatiable. Why don't you grab a drink, and then yes, we can play some volleyball. I know how much you love it. It's been a while for me, so be gentle. Okay?"

Oh, the double entendre. Billie fell for it like the player he was. "If she isn't, you can count on me, Clarice."

Her partner batted her long black eyelashes at him, giving a low feminine murmur Sheila swore shot straight to a man's crotch. Robbie clearly didn't like the interaction by the pointed glance he sent his brother. She tried to keep her mouth from grinning. He certainly wasn't going to be happy about her partner maneuvering them into playing some volleyball.

"Give me a sec, Clarice," she said with extra cheer in her voice. "I'll be right back with the ball."

"Thanks for letting me play with your board, Miss Sunshine," Reagan called as she walked off.

"Yeah, Miss Sunshine," Cassidy echoed.

She waved without looking over her shoulder, knowing

Robbie was watching her all the way. A little sway of her butt, and she wanted to break into a full-on celebratory dance by the time she hit the kitchen and chugged her coconut water. When she returned with the volleyball that came with the rental, as did the already set up net, Sheila was beaming that conspiratorial smile of hers. She could almost hear her partner saying *see, putty in my hands*. The O'Connors were all standing behind their rental house now, as the volleyball net was positioned off the main terrace.

"We have some fellow volleyball enthusiasts, Summer." She caught the ball when Lily threw it her way. "How do you feel about having Billie and Robbie play against us?"

She shifted her weight to her right side, knowing Robbie would want to give her sun-kissed body a slow, full-on perusal. But he kept his gaze focused on her face as his jaw tightened, as if resisting his impulses cost him.

Their eyes locked. Her mouth went dry at the heat hovering in his clearwater blue eyes. Man, he was intense—and really hot, standing there with sweat glistening on his hard, muscular chest. Sheila was right. The view from the front was as good as the back.

She let her mouth tip up, wondering how Sheila had gotten Robbie to agree to play. Then again, her partner had a way of convincing men to do things without them realizing they'd been influenced, a trait she swore she'd gotten from her mother, who'd used it as a prosecutor before ascending to the bench as a federal judge.

"I'd love some healthy competition," she responded, opening her hands for Sheila to throw back the ball. "Reagan, do you want to keep score for us?"

The little girl jumped in place and turned to Robbie. "Can I? Please?"

"Sure." He broke his regard from her and turned to Reagan, smoothing her hair down. "You can count that high, right? Because we O'Connors have been known to score a lot of points. Right, Billie?"

"You bet, bro!" He went over and high-fived his brother, putting his arm companionably around his shoulders. "And if the women need a big shoulder to cry on afterward, I've got one right here for them."

Robbie pointed to his shoulder as well, as if to suggest he would lend his gorgeous musculature to Lily. Swagger? Oh, this was going to be fun! If she hadn't been holding the ball, she would have rubbed her hands together in sheer delight. They had no idea who they were dealing with, and now they'd paved the way for neither Sheila nor her to go easy on them. When she glanced over to Sheila, her friend nodded slyly.

They were going to beat the O'Connor boys senseless.

CHAPTER NINE

ROBBIE'S COMPETITIVENESS HAD GOTTEN THE BEST OF HIM.

"You ready, bro?" Billie asked, holding out his hand for a fist bump when he finished using his foot to sketch out the game's boundaries in the sand, something that had amused the opposing team. But if they were going to play, they were going to play by the rules.

"I was born ready." He rolled his shoulders before lowering his voice. "You're the one who needs to get his head off someone's curves and focus on the game. We have a rep to uphold."

"I'm flipping you the bird in my head, so I won't set a bad example to the kiddies," Billie said in an equally low voice, kicking some sand at him as he walked to the net.

Robbie cracked his neck and jogged in place to charge himself up as Summer and Clarice pivoted at the hips and stretched. He couldn't help but take in Summer's long, slender legs. Since the first moment he'd seen them, he couldn't take his eyes off them. To look at her, one wouldn't imagine she was so athletic. Hers was an understated grace and power. Then she gave him that cocky grin of hers as she palmed the volleyball, her eyes nearly dancing in anticipation. She was enjoying the game they were playing as much as he was. And one thing was for sure...

She was going to make him sweat to earn every point. Frankly, he was juiced.

"Shall we toss a coin or something to see who goes first?" Summer offered, practically smirking. "Since you insisted on sketching out a legal court."

"Maybe we should give them the ball first because they're such big, lumbering men," Clarice shot back, anchoring her hands on her hips with a grand laugh.

"Lumbering, my ass," he muttered under his breath.

Billie made a show of pounding his chest. "Big is right, sweetheart."

"Bigger *is* usually better." Clarice gave a heartfelt sigh before shaking her finger at him. "But not in this case, honey. We are so going to own you. You'll be begging for us to get to twenty-one points fast to stop the pain. Do they make Band-Aids in your size?"

"Whatever you want to tell yourself, honey." Billie dug his feet in the sand, finding his stance. "Losers buy dinner."

Robbie felt the pull. He'd told Tim he was going to cook, but if they won like he planned, he'd have a night off of kitchen duty. Plus, there was no way they were going to lose. Nothing against Sheila, but she had a serious height challenge being so petite. They were going to own her at the net. "Second!"

"Deal!" Summer shouted back, dancing in place. "But you're going to be the ones buying."

He saluted her across the net. "Why don't you go first? Since you're so going down."

"Girls, just so you know, bragging about beating someone else is not considered very nice," he heard Tim say from the sidelines where he was standing with Reagan and

Cassidy, who both had sticks in their hands to keep score with.

He wanted to wince as he glanced over. He really should dial back his boasting. Maybe he'd finally found the outlet for his recent frustration. Because he hadn't felt this good in a really long time, and he was going to savor every freaking minute.

She tossed the ball in the air, clearly playing with him, her smile as bright as the season she'd been named for.

He planted his feet, preparing for her serve. God, he should be old enough to know better, but he'd always loved a challenge. His mother had told stories about how he used to throw his rattle ahead of him when he was first crawling, only to then crawl toward it, triumphant when he reached his prize. "Even then, you loved to push yourself, Robbie," she'd say. When he'd gone to school, she'd been smart enough to realize it also worked with schoolwork. She wouldn't just ask how well he'd done on a test. She'd inquire about anyone who'd done better.

Few kids had beaten him—in the classroom or in athletics. Pickup sports were common in his neighborhood back then. Someone was always playing baseball, football, or soccer after school. He'd join in with glee, scoring again and again.

When he'd gone through police training, he'd loved all of the tests—on the gun range, with physical fitness, and in the classroom. He'd graduated at the top of his class again, to the surprise of none of the O'Connors, and had gone on to excel in the department. His close rate was high, so he'd been promoted quickly. After he stopped being so cocky, of course. Even though he was turning forty this year, he'd resisted a desk job, keeping his physical fitness standards high. Sure, he wasn't a cadet at the police academy, but he wasn't a midlife windbag who ate too many donuts and couldn't run down a suspect.

"Anytime you're ready, Sunshine!" he called out.

She grinned, looking every bit a hot babe on the beach in that bikini. "I was giving you guys a minute to get ready. You might want to take some deep breaths and do some more stretching. I'm trained in CPR, but studies show it's easier on old guys when they take the right precautions."

Billie hooted, slapping his knee. "You just worry about you, Sunshine. Right, bro?"

"Right." Robbie lowered into a deeper stance, knowing she was going to pack a wallop with her serve. He'd noticed the slender ropes of muscles there, because his eyes couldn't seem to keep away from taking in every wicked inch of her gorgeous body.

She had shown him up, running him down the beach, and he damn well knew she was more graceful on a surfboard. But volleyball... Not only was he tall, but he had bigger muscles, a clear edge in hitting the ball back. He'd played his fair share on the beach, and he'd demonstrated every time what a debilitating serve and killer spike he had. Forget about his net play. He could outjump most guys.

When Summer had taken off with that cute little swaying butt to grab a drink, he'd let Billie think he needed to twist his arm to get him to play with the women. It never worked to look too eager. But he'd *wanted* to show Summer he could hang with her. Desperately so.

He didn't care to analyze his reasons. Obviously, he couldn't get involved with her. But he could spend time with her like this. He was just a guy playing a healthy game of volleyball with a hot woman who could more than handle herself.

Despite his attempts to prepare, her serve caught him right in the center of the chest, hard enough to sting like a jellyfish and leave a mark. He fought a curse.

"Ace!" Clarice shouted, hooting and turning in a celebratory circle.

"One point to the ladies," Tim called as Cassidy cheered before being hushed by Reagan, who drew a one in the sand with a stick, which Cassidy tried to mimic.

He closed his mouth as Billie glanced at him and gave him a *WTF* look. Picking up the ball on the ground, he tossed it to Clarice, who had a shit-eating grin on her face. Her flirtatious demeanor clearly hid a competitive streak. Gritting his teeth, Robbie watched Summer's hips sway as she walked over to her friend and high-fived her. With the ball back in her hands, she returned to her serving position.

"Ready, boys?" Clarice singsonged, shaking out her thick black hair, probably to distract Billie. Not a difficult task, truthfully.

Robbie wanted to make a rude gesture at his brother, but the girls were watching from the sidelines. Nodding instead, he dug his feet into the sand and focused on his opponent. Her second serve had the same bullet-like quality as her first, but he was ready this time. He set his weight and returned it. It sailed over the net toward Summer, who jumped up and spiked it directly at Billie's body like a missile.

His brother caught it against his chest before it dropped to the ground. "Lady, you just made a serious mistake."

Summer's response was infectious laughter. "Oh, did that hurt, big guy?"

"We have a first aid kit if you need a bandage," Clarice practically trilled.

"I'm fine!" Billie grumbled, no semblance of his usual *charm the ladies* grin visible. "You take care of you, honey."

"That's two points to the ladies," Tim shouted with way too much pleasure. "Make another mark, Reagan."

"The ladies are really good, aren't they?" she asked Tim in a hushed voice that reached Robbie's ears.

Glancing over, he noted Tim's goofy smile. Cassidy had abandoned the stick and was digging with her shovel in the sand while Reagan's face was strained with worry. Was she concerned about them losing? Well, not on his watch.

On Summer's next hammering blow over the net, Robbie caught the ball and gave it air, setting Billie up to lob it over the net. With his height, he got it behind Clarice, but Summer skidded through the sand, landing on her stomach as she returned the ball to play with an impressive dig. Clarice caught the low hit, knocking it back into the air. Summer jumped to her feet and rushed toward the net, knocking it to Billie's right. Robbie lunged for it, but the ball landed on the ground in front of his face. All he got was a mouthful of sand.

"Three!" Tim shouted.

Robbie spit sand out of his mouth as he pushed himself up. Billie glanced at him with a grimace. Jesus, who were these women?

"You okay?" Cassidy asked him, swiveling on her little diaper-puffed swimsuit butt as she tried to stand up in the sand.

He didn't want to risk her running into the field of play and potentially getting hit with the ball, so he strode over and scooped her up. "Yes, I'm fine, sweetheart. I happen to like having a sand beard."

He rubbed her soft cheeks gently with the remaining sand, making her squeal to high heaven, playfully pushing him away. Satisfied, he plunked her down in the sand and handed her back her shovel. "Can you make me a really nice sandcastle?"

"Yep!" She scooped up sand with force, spraying him.

He spit out more sand, feeling Reagan's hand on his arm. Turning, he rubbed more sand off him. "You want to feel beach Santa's beard too?"

She shook her head, dancing away. "Are you mad that you're losing?"

He wondered if there was a right answer, but he figured the truth was always best. "Yes. We shouldn't have bragged. Now Billie and I need to do something about it."

"It's okay if you lose." She lifted a shoulder. "Mom always says what matters most is doing your best."

"Our mother used to say that too." Even at a young age, he'd known it was bullshit.

Tim was chewing on his lip like he was fighting laughter. "I'm sure my brothers will do their best. Maybe they're just outmatched today."

"If the kids weren't around..." he muttered as he walked closer to Tim, bumping him on purpose. "All right, let's play. Sorry for the delay."

"That's okay." Summer waved brightly. "It's important to take care of our little fans on the sidelines."

"Hi, Miss Summer!" Cassidy called. "I'm making a sandcastle."

"So I see." She tossed the ball back and forth in her hands. "Should I serve again to your dad and uncle?"

Robbie's stomach dropped. He'd told the kids not to use their names, but Cassidy was little...

"Yes!" Reagan yelled, coming over next to Cassidy. "But be nice to them, okay?"

"Yeah!" Cassidy repeated. "Nice is best."

Robbie didn't think that was on the agenda after the way he and Billie had shot their mouths off. Robbie cracked his neck and mouthed *"No mercy"* to Summer. She sputtered out a laugh and then gave a leaping jump and hammered another killer serve his way. He had to step back to set the ball and return it, but he managed it. Clarice was ready for it and lobbed it into the air for Summer to drill over the net. Billie was ready this time, jumping at the right moment and blocking the shot. The ball hit at Clarice's feet.

Robbie hooted before he caught himself. His little cheering section clapped and squealed. Billie gave a few *whoof whoof whoofs* before rushing and chest bumping him.

"That's what I'm talking about," his brother spat out. "Now you serve and make them wish they'd never tangled with the O'Connor brothers."

He caught the ball when Clarice threw it his way. Positioning himself at the back of their makeshift court, he stared at Summer. She was wiggling those slender hips of hers, her gaze focused on him. A satisfied smile shone on her face, and his breath caught for a moment. God, she was so beautiful. Her oval face was flushed from the heat. The blond hair she'd twisted into a ponytail to stay out of her way glinted like gold in the sun.

"Anytime you're ready," she called merrily.

He felt an answering smile spread across his lips. *You bet I'm ready.* Time for them to take over this game. Which way was she going to move? If he could fake her out, he had a chance at an ace. God knew they needed a point. He let his eyes and body drift to the left, as if he were planning on sending the ball in that direction. Then he threw it in the air and drove his palm into it, shooting it across the net, angled the other way.

Her body turned sideways in a flash, and before Billie could jump, she sailed the ball over his head. Robbie lunged for it, but he caught it too low. Grumbling, wiping off more sand, he watched it roll across the ground.

Billie winced as he picked up the ball and tossed it to Clarice, who'd just finished cooing and high-fiving Summer. "Sorry, bro. She's wicked fast."

"Be faster," Robbie spat back. "Also, how tall are you? Can't you use that to your advantage?"

"Don't get surly." Billie put his hands on his hips, his face darkening. "We talked about that, remember?"

He bit the inside of his cheek to keep from delivering a salty response. Little ears were the worst. He was going to explode if he didn't start swearing again. How did people release all this pent-up frustration on the inside if they didn't drop an f-bomb or two? "I'm as happy as a lark," he quipped to his brother. "Ask Shakespeare."

Billie threw his head back and laughed. "Hey, Tim! Did you hear that? Robbie's comparing himself to a lark. Where's that from in Shakespeare?"

"I can't give a direct quote, but I do remember a passage or two about the sweet song larks give in the morning." Tim pointed to Robbie. "Girls, do you want to hear what a lark sounds like? Go ahead, Robbie."

Timmy was going to die after the girls went to bed. "I flunked the class on bird sounds. Let's play!"

"Too bad, I really wanted to hear your lark impression." Summer took her ponytail down and shook her hair out, her captivating smile making his chest tight. "In fact, we could stop playing if you want to give us a show. Did I hear you talking about Shakespeare? I love Shakespeare!"

God, what was it about chicks and Shakespeare? "You can talk to Tim after the game. He's the wannabe playwright. Come on, Clarice. Let's see what you've got."

She gave her hips a wiggle. "I can't wait to show you, boys. Especially that big hunky bald guy across the net. You ready, honey?"

"I'm always ready." Billie pounded his chest. "Let's see what you've got, little mama."

Robbie grimaced. Were they supposed to talk like that around the girls? Tara's lengthy list of dos and don'ts had only included not swearing. Figuring it was better to err on the safe side, he said, "Hey! Watch the language."

Billie looked over his shoulder. "What did I say?"

Before Robbie could respond, Clarice jumped up and pounded the ball over the net, catching Billie in the chest.

"You weren't looking!" She rushed over. "Are you all right?"

His accusatory frown in Robbie's direction was answer enough, but it fell from his face as Clarice gently ran her hands over the spot where she'd nailed him with the ball. "That's much better. You have a woman's touch."

"Oh, for the love of...Pete!" Robbie mumbled. "Let's play!"

"Maybe we should call it," Summer offered, walking to the net. "You don't seem to be having much fun."

Fun? Getting creamed by two gorgeous women in beach volleyball was supposed to be fun? They'd clearly never been to Southie. He and Billie would never live past the disgrace if his other brothers ever found out about it. They would have to hang Tim upside down from his fingernails or something and get him to promise to never share the details of this horrendous butt kicking.

"No way," he called back. "We agreed to play, so we play."

What Clarice's serve didn't take care of, Summer's net play did. While she wasn't as tall as either Billie or him, she was plenty tall enough and the most wicked fast female he'd ever met. And strong. Laser strong.

He caught a few more balls to the chest, and while they didn't sting as badly as other injuries he'd sustained—like taking a bullet with a bulletproof vest—it still competed with a jellyfish.

By the rally for the winning point, he was sucking in air and downright pissed off. At himself. Summer was serving, of course. He dug his feet into the sand, determined the game wouldn't end on an ace.

She jumped and slapped her palm to the ball. It sailed over the net, wobbling erratically. It fell well short of her other serves, so he and Billie weren't prepared. They both lunged for it, colliding with each other as the ball bounced off the ground.

"Winner!" Tim shouted as Clarice let out a cheer. "Now that was some final serve. What *was* that?"

Robbie looked up as Summer walked over to the net and ducked under. "A float serve. I thought it might catch you by surprise."

"Well, it sure did." Robbie shook his head ruefully, pushing past his own anger and frustration over losing.

His mother had been wise here. *Be a good loser. Just make sure you don't do it too often, okay?*

God, he wondered what she was thinking about them from her perch in heaven—out here talking big while being run ragged by two little girls who wore more than their fair share of glitter. She would probably laugh herself blue. He was smiling as he came forward. "Good game, Summer. Clarice. Looks like we owe you two dinner."

He'd been raised to be a good sport, so he stuck his hand out for extra measure. Summer glanced down before extending her hand to him. His was sweat-slicked while hers was positively cool in comparison. His palm sparked at the electricity of her soft touch, and he was pleased to feel her fingers contract around his. Their eyes locked, and he watched her pupils dilate, the gold around the iris surrounded by green.

Holding her hand and her gaze a moment more, he felt his heart pumping faster in his chest. Awareness of her gold-kissed skin in nothing but a blue bikini filled his awareness. He wanted to touch. He knew he couldn't. "You played some game."

"When I have to, I play to win," she answered, no smile on her face now.

That sounded practically cryptic, but before he could

search her features, a small hand touched his hip. "Okay?" Cassidy asked, patting him with her shovel. "You did great!"

What kind of bullshit was Tara feeding these kids? He picked her up and gave her a kiss on the cheek. "No, sweetheart. Billie and me stunk to high heaven. Like one of your hurricane diapers. But we don't need to dwell on that."

"Hurricane diapers?" Summer asked.

Now she had a smile on her face, one he shared. "Inside joke."

Then he not only heard Cassidy give a trio of farts but felt them against his arm. He winced. "Is that the power of suggestion or something?"

"Magic!" Cassidy declared, dropping her shovel and clapping her hands.

Summer bravely fought laughter. Instead, she nodded with a serious expression. "That's incredible, Cassidy! Can you do magic anytime?"

Her little head nodded, and Robbie shot Summer a hard look. Was she purposely encouraging more of Cassidy's so-called magic? Her whole acupressure thing had already delivered one diaper disaster. She'd better not be trying to bring on another, because changing a stinky diaper after getting their butts kicked would only make him more surly.

"Hey, Robbie!" Billie jogged over with Clarice. "Since we owe the ladies dinner, do you want to take them out or invite them to the BBQ you were planning tonight?"

Right. He'd justified that wager and gotten burned. Now he was cooking dinner *and* visiting temptation alley, all in one night. Part of him grew excited, realizing he'd have an excuse for spending time with her, time he'd been refusing himself. Surely one night would be all right...

"A BBQ here would be better. The girls will probably be tired after all this excitement." Plus, he wasn't sure he wanted to go out to a local restaurant. Going out publicly would be a risk.

"I'm not tired," Cassidy mumbled, putting her sweaty head against his shoulder.

He smoothed his hand down her pink swimsuit, brushing off sand. "Sure, you aren't."

"Can we bring anything tonight?" Summer asked, her green eyes suddenly soft and slumberous.

Then he realized she was looking at him like that because of how he was holding Cassidy. He cringed inside. Women had some weird thing for men who treated kids good. Must be some kind of evolutionary impulse. He wanted to tell her not to get too gushy. Cassidy wasn't his kid. But he couldn't, and the thought of perpetuating the lie—especially to a woman he was attracted to—made him tight on the inside. Lying about who he was was worse than bragging, and look how that had turned out.

"You can bring your famous margaritas," Billie said, looping an arm around Clarice. "If the offer still stands. I'll need something to wash out all this sand in my mouth from your killer plays. Right, Robbie?"

He didn't deign to reply. He glanced over to see where Reagan was. Tim was standing by her as she kicked the sand. For a minute he didn't know what she was doing. Then it hit him. She was brushing away the scoreboard, clearly upset. Crap. "Hey, Reagan!"

A soft hand touched his arm, arresting his breath. "Let me talk to her," he heard Summer say.

He met her gaze and nodded. Her mouth tipped up at the sides before she strode off. When she knelt in the sand before Reagan, the little girl ducked her head to her chin. She was upset for them, and the knowledge made his heart shift in his chest in a weird way. Funny how she was as protective of them as they were of her in some ways. Well, she was an O'Connor, he supposed. They took care of their own.

Tim wandered away a few steps as Summer spoke to Reagan. Robbie couldn't hear what she was saying, but he watched as Reagan nodded a few times before tipping her head up and giving Summer her full attention. A few moments later, Summer ran a light hand down Reagan's arm. They shared a smile before the little girl shot past her, running his way. When she reached him, she banded her arms around him, making Cassidy giggle.

"I think you're a winner," Reagan told him. "You're absolutely the best!"

She might as well have knocked him in the head with that one. Is that what Summer had told her to say? And why did it affect him so? He needed someone to smack him upside the head.

But Reagan didn't let go, so he put a hand to the back of her neck, not knowing what to do in the face of this fierce affection. Suddenly he was rocked by another memory of his mother—of coming home and finding her upset about something. He'd run to her and told her how wonderful she was too—and she'd kissed the top of his head and told him what a sweet boy he was.

Even knowing he had an audience, he leaned down with Cassidy in his arms and laid a kiss on Reagan's wind-tangled hair. Her arms squeezed tighter around him, and another pang went through his chest. When he straightened, Summer had that gushy look on her face again. His heart must be feeling all the gushy girly stuff around him because it went sideways again in his chest.

Then another barrage of bullet-like sounds came from Cassidy's diaper. Reagan jumped back and started laughing. The stench of rotten eggs rose up, and he held Cassidy out with a grimace. She laughed, dangling her feet in the air. "'Cane," she announced, clapping her hands again.

The absurdity of his life crashed over him like a giant wave. His shoulders started to shake from laughter, and he looked over to see Summer holding a hand to her face, doing the same.

In a different situation, a different life, he'd have gone over to her and asked her out. Just. Like. That.

But he had kids to keep safe and a diaper to change.

CHAPTER TEN

THEY HAD THEIR IN.

Sheila hadn't stopped humming a spicy salsa beat since they'd beaten the O'Connor brothers hands down. Besting cocky FBI guys in sports usually had Lily singing herself, but this win had affected her differently. It was the grim expressions on Robbie's and Reagan's faces, she decided. They'd taken the loss to heart in different ways. She hadn't expected that.

"Quit your brooding," Sheila said, adding ice to the blender. "We have a lot to celebrate. Your strategy worked. God, sometimes guys are so predictable."

The appliance being switched on stopped Lily's reply. She searched the cabinet for something to bring the little girls' drink in, her hands still smelling strongly of the fresh limes she'd helped squeeze for the margaritas.

The blazing sound died. "We kicked butt and have progressed to a closer inspection of our subjects. Maybe we'll even find a phone. Sunshine, do I need to give you a pep talk before we go over?"

"I know the whole *avoid making out with your person of interest* rule." Despite how much she might want to caress and explore that firm, sexy mouth of Robbie O'Connor's.

"His kiddie protector side is getting under your skin." Sheila spooned a taste of the margaritas and smacked her lips. "De-li-cious. I wish I could drink more of these babies tonight but duty first."

Indeed. She needed to tattoo it on her hand right now to keep focused. Because the way Robbie looked at her was stealing her breath and making her mind go blank. "At least you don't think Robbie's dirty anymore."

"I *mostly* think that, but I've seen plenty of low-life criminals who are good with kids." Her partner cut her a knowing look. "So have you."

She'd done plenty of work on the trauma of her childhood, so the reference didn't ping her the way it used to. Sighting a container for the girls' drink, she snatched it out of the cabinet. "Aha! This is going to have to work."

"A cocktail shaker?" Sheila dumped the frozen margaritas into a large glass pitcher. "What are you giving those girls to drink again?"

"Coconut water shaken with ice will make them feel special." She knew from all her work with kids how important that sentiment was. "Besides, it's good for them. Cassidy's tummy has to be really upset, judging by the way she...expresses so much magic."

Sheila chortled, practically falling back against the counter. "I wanted to yell *Duck, we're under attack*, but I didn't want to blow our cover. I've got to admit, it's a brilliant way to talk about farting. My brother could fart on command as a kid. His big moment to this day was when he farted to 'The Star-Spangled Banner' at a baseball game with his friends. They were seven. I've never seen boys laugh that hard."

Having been a teacher, Summer had experienced her

share of such antics. "I had one kindergarten boy who would fart every time he said thank you. His older brother, clearly a bad influence, told him it made his point stronger. I had to convince him otherwise. The girls in the class couldn't steer clear of him enough."

"I don't blame them." Sheila dumped the salt and extra limes in their beach bag with some plastic glasses as Lily made up her own concoction and closed the top of the shaker. "You should put on some of that berry lip gloss. Just because you can't kiss Robbie O'Connor doesn't mean you don't want him checking out your lips along with the rest of you."

She reached for her purse with an eye roll and smoothed the raspberry color over her lips. "You're the one who's going to have trouble keeping Billie's mouth and hands away."

She made a shooing motion. "I've got a plan. Plus, I have you to start yawning and falling asleep if needed so we can bounce. As your best friend, I can say you've had too many margaritas—being the lightweight you are—and that I have to take you home. Works every time."

They had used that strategy with success before. "Good to know the playbook."

Sheila opened the door, balancing the margaritas in the blender on her hip. "You look nice, by the way. If I were a guy, I'd have trouble keeping my eyes off you. I can't pull off those beach dresses. My curves always stick out in them."

"You're being too hard on yourself as usual." She grabbed a towel for the shaker and locked the door behind them. "You look great, and the expression on Billie's face the moment he sees you will only confirm it."

Sure enough, when they went next door, Billie was the first to reach them, taking the beach bag and the pitcher from Sheila with a delighted once-over glance at the short sleeveless red dress that hugged her body.

"You look totally scrumptious," he said, leaning down and kissing Sheila's cheek before turning to Lily. "Both of you. Make yourselves at home."

Sheila wiggled her fingers at Lily to precede her inside. Good idea. That way she could be alone with Billie. Letting herself in after a soft knock, she welcomed the air conditioner on her bare skin. The humidity was suffocating outside even as the sun descended in the sky, its glow less intense.

She scanned the house, with its homey décor and inspirational signs on the walls, ones Lily couldn't imagine impressed the O'Connor boys. Definitely a Tara pick, then. That was a good thing. If she'd secured the house, that meant she knew where Robbie was with the girls. Having confirmation on that point would be good news for them. Buck certainly would like some hard evidence that Tara might show up here. She did a quick perusal but didn't spy a phone lying around. Damn.

Cassidy's giggles erupted with Reagan's laughter in another part of the house, making her smile as she walked into the kitchen. Robbie swung around from the back counter immediately, dropping the raw hamburger patty he'd been putting on a plate with a thunk. Every muscle was poised for action, and she winced.

"Billie let me in," she said quietly. "Sorry I scared you."

"Few people come up on me unawares," was all he said.

Then he cleared his throat. His blue eyes narrowed with heat as he swept his gaze over her white, nearly transparent sleeveless dress. While it was full-length, it floated like clouds. Lily had loved it on sight on their shopping spree. She'd freeze to death most of the year in such a dress in Boston, but it was perfect for the moist heat of the Outer Banks. She'd thought Robbie would find it more captivating than a short sundress, and as he continued staring, she struggled with the feeling of being pleased he liked it. Like he might be speechless because of it.

Her heart rate was spiking, which was so not how she was supposed to be feeling undercover.

Another beat passed between them, attraction flaring, her heart knocking against her ribs. She saw him swallow thickly, and she fought the urge to shift on her feet. Usually she was not off-balance, but she was floundering here.

"I thought our company was here!" Tim said as he walked in, carrying Cassidy. Reagan jogged after him, still giggling. "Welcome to the nuthouse. Make yourself at home."

She let out a shallow breath, telling herself to relax. "Thanks. We appreciate the invite."

Tim bit his lip to keep from smiling as he set Cassidy down on the counter. "You two more than earned it."

"That's all...in the past." Best not to poke at Robbie's smarting male pride. "Hey, girls, I have a little surprise for you. Clarice might have brought margaritas for the adults, but I brought something special for you two."

"You did?" Reagan asked, running over to her side.

"I wanna see too," Cassidy said, starting to crawl across the kitchen island.

Robbie was next to her in a flash, catching her deftly. "None of that. We don't want you falling off, do we?"

He kissed her wild, curly head, and she gave him a drooling smile before laying her cheek against his chest. Without the blazing sexual energy from earlier, she could take in what he was wearing. His navy T-shirt was nicely worn, making her think one of his brothers must have packed him a bag before they'd left. She *had* seen three duffel bags in the back of their Suburban parked out front. They'd already run the plates, and the vehicle belonged to a Garret Kilkenny, an eighty-year-old man who lived in Southie. No relation. They still didn't know how the O'Connors knew Kilkenny or how they'd ended up with his vehicle, but they imagined it was likely related to Billie's mechanic shop.

So far, the O'Connors had done things smart. For their sakes, and the kids', she hoped that continued. As she looked down at Reagan's delicate china-doll face, she thought of the danger they could be in with the Kellys. She knew it wasn't below them to threaten a child to get what they wanted. Well, that sure as hell was not going to happen on her watch. She reached out and ran her hand down Reagan's ponytail, secured by a silver glittery bow, and they shared a smile.

"I love your dress," she said, touching the fabric. "You look like a princess."

"Thank you." She gestured to the little girl's purple cotton dress that said *Future President* on it in silver glitter. "I like a woman who has high aspirations."

"Mom always says we can be anything we want," she said shyly. "Even president of your own company. Like she is." Then she cast a look at Robbie, as if wondering if she'd said too much.

"Your mom is a boss, and we all know it," Robbie said, sending her an assuring smile. "Who else would come up with calling gas magic?"

Reagan's mouth twitched as Cassidy lurched off Robbie's chest and shot her hand in the air. "I do magic!"

"You sure do!" Robbie held her out. "Too much for me."

That had the little girl laughing as he brought her close and kissed her on the top of the head again. Lily felt a strange pull to keep watching him with Cassidy. God, they looked so sweet together, and right before her eyes, Robbie seemed to become taller and more handsome than ever. Like he was suddenly the most handsome man she'd ever seen.

Shit.

She had to force herself to turn back to Reagan. "Do you have any special glasses we could use?" She shook the shaker, making the ice clank against the metal. "Why don't we serve it up? You can try it and see what you think."

"Let's do it outside," Robbie suggested, setting Cassidy on his hip. "That way we don't have to worry about the Drool Baby spilling anything since she won't be using her sippy cup."

God, Lily had a very hard time not smiling just then. Hardened police officer Robbie O'Connor was talking about spills and sippy cups?

"Good idea, bro." Tim grabbed a bottle of insect spray from the counter. "How is your fellow victor this eve, Summer? Still wearing a crown of laurels after laying my brothers so low?"

Lily wasn't sure how to respond, but she couldn't keep her lips from twitching. Tim clearly wanted to poke at his brothers.

"Ignore Shakespeare over there, Summer." Robbie jerked his chin toward his younger brother. "Someone dropped him on the head or something, and the madness is finally coming out."

"Though this be madness, yet there is method in't." Tim lifted Cassidy from his brother's arms and set her on the counter. "Close your eyes, sweetheart. We don't want you getting all bit up outside."

He shielded her eyes, then turned to Reagan who did the same so she could get sprayed. Finished, he turned swiftly and sprayed Robbie before his brother could stop him.

"Hey!" Robbie shot out. "I'm going to toss you into the ocean for the jellyfish to eat for dinner if you don't cut that out."

The younger man danced out of reach. "Girls, let us pour you this drink the lovely Summer made for you this eve. Hark! I wonder what it might be."

Robbie's mouth was a flat line. Obviously, he hated the

Shakespeare stuff, and Tim knew it. Which was why Tim was doing it, his dramatic theater accent only making it more amusing. The girls started giggling, and Lily couldn't help but join in. "You obviously have a gift for making people laugh."

"There's just something about iambic pentameter and a dramatic British accent," Tim said to her. "I use it at the retirement home with my patients all the time and it makes them laugh. Seems it works on pretty little princesses too."

"That's me!" Cassidy yelled, wobbling on the counter, prompting Robbie to grab her and set her on stable ground. "I'm a princess!"

"Me too!" Reagan cried out. "So is Summer!"

She inclined her head at being included, and they shared a smile.

Tim thrust his hands on his hips as he looked down at the girls. "Then where is thy crown?"

"We don't have crowns here." Reagan made a face. "They're at home."

"What injustice is this?" Tim thrust his hand into the air and headed to the cabinet under the sink, pulling out aluminum foil. "We must remedy this travesty immediately. Come!"

Reagan ran after him with Cassidy trotting along behind them as fast as her glittering pink sandals could carry her. Adorable!

"He found out the Shakespeare thing drives me and Billie nuts," Robbie explained with an aggrieved sigh.

She strove for a straight face but mostly failed. "I kinda got that."

"Sure, you're laughing now. Just wait. It gets old. Like *mold on Chinese takeout* old. Never, ever show a weakness to a sibling. I must be having a slow week since I allowed it." He paused, looking at her, then added, "I was out of line when I shot my mouth off about how we were going to best you and

Clarice today. Beating me and Billie senseless today was just deserts."

She couldn't contain her surprise. "Is that an apology?"

"Yes." He lifted a shoulder, his awkwardness obvious. "Can you tell your friend? She seems to be tied up with my brother."

She nodded, glancing out the window with the view of the patio to see what Sheila and Billie were doing. Sure enough, they huddled together at the patio table, knees touching. He was already sipping a taste of the margaritas from a spoon they'd brought over, her partner batting her eyelashes at him. Sheila had him well occupied.

"Let's forget all about that." She picked up part of her dress and waved it. "That's a white flag reference in case it's not obvious."

His mouth tipped up to the right in a deliciously sexy smirk. He practically smoldered male sexuality now that he'd dropped some of his guard. She was going to have to fan herself when he wasn't looking to keep from inhaling all of his potent pheromones.

"It wasn't." His eyes slid down her in a longer appraising fashion this time. "Reagan was right. That is a nice dress."

She curtsied, thinking about Shakespeare. God, she couldn't pass up the opportunity to tease him a little. "Thank you, kind sir."

He shot her a narrow-eyed look before giving a reluctant laugh. "Don't you start or that white flag won't last. Besides, why does that Shakespeare stuff appeal to women anyway? I'd think you would hate it. Didn't most of the gushy stories end with the lovers dying or something? That's hardly what I'd call romantic."

Okay, her mouth was twitching now. Flirting with him was as easy as gliding over the ocean's waves. "What about eternal love between two people? Love strong enough to die over?"

"Maybe it's the cop in me, but there's nothing romantic about two people dying." He sighed heavily, his mouth working. "Excuse me. I shouldn't have mentioned my work. I'm on...vacation. It's better if I don't...for the girls."

Nice cover, she admired, but his anger at the slip was obvious. "No worries. I totally understand not wanting to talk about work on vacation. But I'll only say I really admire what you do. We all need to know there's someone out there doing a job that keeps us all safe at night."

She meant it, but he only looked uncomfortable before saying, "So what *did* you bring the girls to drink?"

The towel had absorbed the shaker's condensation when she picked it up. "Grab a glass and see. Then we'll put it in the fridge because the ice is melting."

"Evidently, crowns trump girly drinks." He grabbed a juice glass and thrust it out. "Fine, I'll try it. Consider me that poison taster guy."

She shook the shaker and poured him a finger. "Poison taster? Someone has imagination."

He eyed the drink suspiciously. "This had better not be a Cosmo."

"I work with kids." She started chuckling. "Would I give a child an alcoholic beverage?"

Another nonanswer. He lifted the glass and sniffed, his face scrunching up before he took a dainty sip. "Coconut? What is this stuff?"

"That's coconut water with ice cubes. It's very hydrating and good for you, especially upset tummies." She poked him in his hard abs when he made another face.

"Last I looked, coconuts were white on the inside." He set the glass aside with a frown. "You have access to some pink coconuts or something?"

Oh, Robbie O'Connor, I really like you.

"How did you know? They're back at my house with my crown."

He studied her, his gaze roving over her features. She felt like he was assessing her, practically asking for permission to see her soul. She almost gave it to him. On some level, she knew he would take care of what he learned. From the very beginning, when he'd first shown up at the gym to pick up the girls, she'd thought he was a man to trust. No wonder Tara had given her two little girls to him when she was in trouble.

"Look!" Cassidy ran back into the kitchen, her little feet stomping from her speed. "I've got a crown."

Robbie grabbed her before she ran into his leg. Scooping her up, he held her out and examined her. Tim's impromptu crown was more like a simple diadem, but from Cassidy's beaming grin, the little girl thought she'd won the ultimate prize.

"See!" She touched it lightly, grinning as drool came out of her mouth. "I'm pretty."

"You are." Robbie used the edge of his T-shirt to wipe her mouth. "Princess Drool Baby. Go! Find your kingdom."

Okay, that had Lily practically melting against the counter.

He set Cassidy down gently, and she touched her crown with careful little fingers. "Gonna show Miss Rosie."

They watched as she toddled out again. "Who's Miss Rosie?" she asked.

"That's what she's named her teddy bear." He walked to the doorway as if to check her progress. "Tim! Cassidy is coming your way."

"I hear you, fine sir!" his brother shouted back. "Miss Pixie and I are still working on her crown."

"Oh, for the love of God..." Robbie gave a short smile. "I know we owe you dinner, but if it's too much of a zoo over here, I can drop it by when it's cooked. We're not having

133

anything fancy. Only hamburgers and hot dogs with bag salad and some veggie sticks for the kids. Okay, and some chips. Because you have to have something to crunch on."

He scratched his ear then, suddenly looking like a fish out of water. Usually he seemed so capable, but taking care of two little girls wasn't his usual, as she knew. Clearly not when it involved having a woman he found attractive over for dinner.

"Burgers and dogs are one of my faves," she answered truthfully. "I might drink coconut water, but I love the classics."

"Great." He nodded crisply, picking up the shaker and putting it in the fridge. "Consider yourself forewarned, though. I know you brought adult drinks, so do you want a margarita? Ah...if they aren't melted already. Billie and your friend seem to be enjoying them on the patio." Another glare. "He'd better have turned on the BBQ like I asked."

She turned and looked over. Sheila was laughing at something as Billie gestured with his hands. A margarita with a salt-lined rim was in her hand. "I'm good for now," she answered, not wanting to interrupt them.

Obviously, Robbie was annoyed with his brother by the way he huffed as he looked out the patio window. "Tim suggested we buy some wine as well. We have red or white. Or beer. We weren't sure what you liked."

It was kinda sweet that they'd gone on a special trip for wine. "I'm not much of a drinker, honestly. Lightweight here. But I'll have a glass of white if it's no trouble."

"It's not." He started opening the drawers, clearly looking for a wine opener. "I'm missing my little helper. I usually tell Reagan to look through the cabinets like a treasure hunt since we don't know where anything is."

"Rental house problems," she joked. "I'm doing the same at our place."

He made a satisfied sound finally and held up the

corkscrew. "Whew! I didn't check to make sure we had one before we went to the liquor store."

"It wouldn't have been a thing," she told him, watching him meticulously open the wine. "And if you break the cork, I won't care."

He pulled the cork out perfectly after biting his lip in a very sexy way that made her zoom in on that area more than she should. "You're awfully easy to please."

"Was that a compliment or an accusation?" She crossed her arms as he glanced over sharply. "I figure there are plenty of bigger items to get worked up about. Personally, I try and have few of those on my list."

She'd made that decision when she was a senior about to graduate from high school, and it had helped change her life. Before, she'd fallen into anger and worry easily—depression too. Growing up in a foster home had been stressful and often lonely. But when she'd finally been able to strike out on her own, she'd wrapped herself in the freedom like it was a warm blanket.

She was finally calling the shots of her life, and she was going to make them count. No secrets or abuse in her personal life. From anyone. Working through her triggers and hurts had helped. She had put the past behind her, and by God, she was proud to have the nickname Sunshine at the Bureau most days.

"Only an observation," he mused, grabbing a wineglass and pouring her half a glass before handing it to her. "So how are you liking the Outer Banks?"

They weren't tourists, so she went with some of her personal impressions. "The beach is great, and our house is open and comfortable. That's all I really need. I'm only missing a hammock. I love curling up in one with a good book as the hammock sways in the ocean breeze."

"Read anything good lately?" he asked, selecting a beer from the fridge and using the countertop edge to pop the top.

"A really great romance fantasy by Kathia called *The Lies of Gods*." She took a sip of her wine, wondering if he was going to relax. "It's a little King Arthur and *Game of Thrones* with a happy ending."

"No wonder you like Shakespeare." His mouth turned up in amusement. "Hang on a sec. It's too quiet. I want to make sure Tim has the girls and Cassidy's not off doing God knows what with Miss Purrfect."

She choked on her wine. Surely that wasn't the cat they'd put the tracker on... "Who?"

"The cat. It's my current nemesis. Be right back."

He jogged out of the room, leaving his beer on the counter. She took a moment to take a cleansing breath. God, he was a good caretaker of the girls and a good listener. Connected. Intense. Tantalizing.

Get your head in the game, Lily. She forced her mind back to the kitchen, looking for a phone, but there was nothing. Not that she was terribly surprised. Obviously, no one was posting on social media right now. Billie usually posted updates about cars he was working on—a business and personal hobby he was clearly successful at—while Tim liked to share nature scenes from his favorite parks but little else, suggesting he might be into photography.

Robbie wasn't present on social media in his name, which wasn't unusual in law enforcement. Neither was she. Social media was a new challenge for undercover work so she had a few accounts she could use, depending on the situation. Her name wasn't mentioned, of course. Accounts with names like Lady of the Night or lover387 kept her somewhat protected, although it was also possible to change the name on a Facebook account once every thirty days.

Neither Robbie nor Billie seemed like the type to ask to

be "friends" on social media, and she was honestly glad. When had people stopped wanting to pick up the phone and call? But she and Sheila were prepared all the same. While she didn't think Robbie was going to check them out online —why would he suspect anything?—it paid to be ready for every eventuality, and they were. She'd bet he was as well.

So where was he keeping a phone?

"I found our little princess," Robbie said, walking back into the kitchen with Cassidy in his arms. She was holding the cutest gingham-clad bear with a matching bow between her ears. Tim and Reagan followed, strutting in impromptu capes made out of beach towels. Both wore aluminum foil crowns with the same detailed whimsy displayed in the sand-castle on the beach.

"What ho!" Tim called out.

"Language," Robbie corrected with an edge in his voice.

"It's a greeting," Tim explained, throwing his towel covered in tropical fish over his shoulder. "Not the word you're thinking of."

Oh my God! Robbie had thought Tim had meant *ho,* as in a promiscuous woman? Lily bit her lip to stop her laughter.

Robbie let out a frustrated sound. "Better not be, man. There are women present."

"Not only women—I see a fair maiden without a crown in this room," Tim bellowed, making Reagan sputter with laughter. "Princess Sunshine. Would thou wish for a crown? Being in disguise does not suit thee. You are the sun itself in that gown."

"The sun is yellow," Robbie ground out. "Her dress is white."

"The moon then!" Tim said without missing a beat as Lily chuckled at their exchange.

Oh, this was fun! "I would love a crown, kind sir."

Robbie sidled up closer to her, Cassidy thrusting out her

bear for Lily to see. "Egging him on will only extend the show," he said for only her ears.

She set her wineglass down so she could shake hands with the bear. "I know, and I find myself much entertained. Cassidy, is this the incredible Miss Rosie I've heard about?"

The little girl grinned and nodded. "Mine."

"Why, she's absolutely beautiful," Lily declared, punching up her own theatrics. "The perfect companion for a princess like you. But you seem to be missing your magic wand?"

Her eyes went huge in her little face, and Reagan stopped playing with her crown, clearly fascinated with this development. "Magic wand?"

Lily spied the utensils crock by the stove. She pranced over to them, making her dress billow around her, and plucked up the crock. Carrying it over to her new friends, she handed a plastic spatula to Cassidy first, still cradled in Robbie's arms. The little girl squealed and thrust it in the air, nearly knocking him in the eye. Oops.

Turning, she presented the crock to Reagan. "You should pick your own wand like a proper princess."

The young girl shyly pointed to the knife sharpener. "I want that one."

Robbie looked a little worried, but before he could say anything, Lily said, "Interesting choice, Princess, and one filled with great magic, I'm sure. So you'd best be careful with it."

"I will," Reagan answered with awe.

"I've got magic," Cassidy said, scrunching up her little face and tensing her arms like she was trying to...

Robbie glared at Lily. "If she lets out some magic now and I have to change a diaper, your white flag is going into the BBQ to feed the fire."

Spinning around, knowing he was joking, she bowed at

the waist to Tim, offering him the utensils. "And you, kind sir?"

He selected a whisk and spun it in his hand. "Thank you. You are a kind and beautiful maiden."

She curtsied again before turning back to Robbie. "Would you want to be selecting your wand, Sir Robbie?"

A wicked look entered his eyes before he replied, "I already have one, Princess Sunshine."

Tim snickered while Lily's mouth moved in amusement. "Ah, to be a man. Always with a wand."

His smile was downright flirty, so she turned away for a distraction. "Now, Princess Cassidy, what wish will you make with your wand?"

The little girl's face immediately lit up. "Mommy coming!" she cried out.

It felt like a crystal vase had shattered on the floor. Robbie and Tim both went stiff. Reagan's face crumbled, and then the little girl was running out of the room, her impromptu cape falling in her haste.

Lily gestured with the utensils. "I'm so sorry. I..."

"It's okay," Robbie assured her with a tight jaw. "She's just missing her mother. I'll go after her. Tim, can you take Cassidy?"

His brother grabbed the baby easily. Her lip was curling up, and she pointed in the direction where Robbie left to go after Reagan. "She's sad."

Tim kissed her cheek. "Yeah, a little. But you... Let me see that wand of yours."

Cassidy thrust it out at him, which he evaded easily.

"Is there anything I can do?" Lily asked.

"Nah." Tim took the crock from her and set it on the counter. "It's nothing to be concerned about. Robbie's got her."

Sure enough, Robbie came back in with Reagan a few

moments later. The young girl's eyes were still wet, but she gave Cassidy a brave smile when her sister called her name and thrust her wand out. Tim put the little girl on the floor, and she immediately toddled over to Reagan and put her arms around her, patting her on the back with little hands. Their sweet hug was heartfelt and endearing, the comfort in the embrace making Lily's heart turn over.

"They really are the sweetest kids," Tim said, coming up to stand beside her. "The wand idea was a great one, Summer. Thanks. I'm going to get a lot of mileage out of that if it rains tomorrow and we're stuck inside. I might even see if my seniors enjoy it."

He was trying to comfort her in his own way, and that was also sweet. She kissed his cheek softly. "Thank you, Tim. That made me feel a little better."

"Good." Tim was about to put a hand on her shoulder in camaraderie, but he stopped, and she was surprised to see Robbie was cutting him a hard look. "Aha. The green-eyed monster doth appear. I'll just go and check on my other brother. Girls, come on, let's show our other fair companions this eve our crowns and wands."

Breaking apart, Cassidy rushed over to grab Miss Rosie while Reagan shot Lily a sad smile before following them out onto the patio. Billie didn't seem to notice them until Tim dropped Cassidy gently in his lap, breaking the intense conversation he and Sheila were having over their nearly drunk margaritas.

"You have nothing to feel bad about," Robbie said, pulling her gaze back to him. "It was an innocent comment. I wouldn't have guessed Reagan would react like that. She's been happy to be on this adventure since it started, but she's clearly missing her mom more than she's let on. That's all to say that Tim doesn't need to be comforting you. I've got a perfectly good shoulder here."

So he *was* jealous? Interesting. "I hate knowing I did or said something to make a child cry. I didn't know my question would lead to her mom. Is she going to be coming here—like Cassidy hoped?"

Finally, she could ask a question that related directly to their case, although she hated to admit she was tempted to make use of his shoulder. For completely different reasons...

His gaze shuttered. "Like I said, you didn't do anything wrong, so let's drop the whole thing. Don't make me grab Tim again so he can spout off some more Shakespeare crap to get you to smile."

She wasn't pleased by his evasion, but she couldn't push on whether Tara was coming to join them. "Your brother is a very nice man."

"Everyone says he's the nicest of the O'Connor boys for sure. But no one's perfect, as the Shakespeare thing proves."

Did he think she was suddenly into Tim? "When I say he's nice, it's a compliment. I imagine he'd be fun to hang out with."

He crossed his arms, his muscles flexing with tension. "He's seeing someone."

She closed her mouth, trying not to laugh. "I'm not interested in Tim, Robbie. You don't need to wave me off. There aren't many truly nice men in the world, and he's one of them. I bet he'd make a good friend. That's all I meant. I'm sorry if that ticked you off."

Picking up her wine, she heard him exhale like an angry beast. "I must be losing my—I'm glad you clarified that, because I was getting pissed thinking you'd started liking my baby brother."

His mouth moved like he was clearly fighting with himself and that green-eyed monster inside. My, how that gave her a warm little buzz.

"Over me," he added in a husky voice, giving her a slow once-over.

She felt the punch of his honesty. Her pulse turned thready in response to the shot of hot awareness between them. "We're on the same page," she rasped out, letting her gaze drift and linger over his strong, hard jaw down to his wide, broad chest.

Checking him out is part of my cover. There's no reason not to make it look believable.

God, she was lying to herself. Her personal feelings had woven their way into this assignment since the first day she'd seen him.

He was staring at her when she looked up, his blue eyes smoldering. "I hate to say this, but we aren't on the same page. I'm on vacation with two young girls who are in my care. I'm not here for any complications. I mean this as a compliment, to use your phrase, but you, Summer, are one giant complication."

Her chest grew tight and she fought for breath. This was her response to him as a woman—nothing undercover about it. "I didn't come here looking for anything either. You surprised me."

That was honest at least.

He crossed the kitchen until he was standing inches away from her. "I'm old enough to know better. So even though I want to kiss you right now, I'm not going to. We have an audience for one, and second, I have a feeling I'm not going to want to stop."

That arrested all the oxygen in her lungs. His hungry gaze ran over her face again. His hands fisted at his sides, as if he was fighting the pull to touch her. She could feel the heat from his skin and wished she could lift her hand and touch him. But she couldn't cross that line either. "Then we're agreed. This would be stupid."

"The stupidest." His voice dipped to a sexy whisper, and from the way his eyes hovered on her mouth, she knew he was imagining all of the stupid things he wanted to do to her. She could suddenly see him lifting her onto the kitchen counter and stepping between her legs, all hard man and muscle.

She took a step back. "I should go and...see how..." She stopped herself from saying Sheila's name. Wanting to slap herself for her near mistake, she walked swiftly to the patio door and let herself out.

The warm humid air only made her more aware of her hot cheeks. God, she was flushed. Sheila looked up immediately from canoodling with Billie, who was holding Cassidy on his lap.

Her friend's smiling face changed to a look of concern, making Billie glance over his shoulder. "Everything okay in there? My brother didn't growl at you, did he? I told him to be nice tonight."

She had to think about how to respond so she wouldn't cause a problem. "Of course not. I just wanted to come out and try one of Clarice's famous margaritas."

"Well, they're mostly melted." Sheila stood and walked over to her, taking her by the elbow. "Oops."

"That's okay," she made herself say. "Better for me since I'm a lightweight."

Sheila jiggled her arm as if to bring her back to herself. "Come on, Sunshine, we'll grab you some more ice from our place."

"We have some inside, ladies." Billie stood and put Cassidy over his shoulders, making her squeal and hang on to his bald head. "I'll go with you. In case someone *is* still huffing and puffing."

Robbie had his head buried in the fridge when they came back in. He swung around with the hamburger platter in his hands. "Billie, grab the dogs and the buns. You're just in time to help me BBQ."

He walked past Lily swiftly, every muscle locked. His T-shirt and shorts might as well be made of armor. Her partner had warned her that first day about thinking of him as a knight. But there was one thing she hadn't realized.

Knights could repel people with their armor too.

CHAPTER ELEVEN

THE CAT HAD IT IN FOR HIM.

Robbie scooped up the T-shirt Miss Purrfect had managed to steal for her litter box and balled it up, wincing at the putrid smell emerging from whatever that hideous furball had done. To one of his favorite running shirts!

Wasn't he nice to the girls? Didn't he bend over backward to play whatever they wanted? Answer their every crazy little question? Didn't he check his computer every morning at the crack of dawn, praying for an update from his partner? When he'd come down to the kitchen this morning, he'd found yet another empty space in his account where a message would be...and then the ruined shirt.

The "bad guy" currently plaguing his life was a furball. If it were up to Robbie, he'd cuff that cat and put it in jail. Twenty years to life would be good for it.

"I see your battle with Miss Purrfect continues," Tim commented as he strolled into the kitchen in an old Pats T-shirt and boxers.

Robbie stormed into the adjoining laundry room and threw the shirt in the makeshift diaper pail before returning, setting his weight as he regarded his brother. "What is that cat's beef with me anyway? It doesn't mess with anything you or Billie own."

Tim turned and started making coffee, the dark aroma a godsend. "Maybe you should talk more sweetly to it like I suggested. Billie changed tacks."

Be nice to a furball?

"When hell freezes over," he spat, grabbing two mugs.

"Language," Tim called out, setting the coffee to brew.

"The girls aren't up, and I'm going to explode if I don't—"

"Take care of your raging attraction to our neighbor?" Tim supplied, leveling him with a knowing look. "You always do this to yourself. Fight against what you know is true and then get all grouchy because of it, affecting everyone around you. You were rude last night, and you know it."

"I was rude so I wouldn't do anything stupid."

He'd purposely avoided being near or alone with Summer for the rest of the night, a task which had proven both difficult and frustrating. Wasn't it just his luck that he'd met a really hot woman who also seemed to be a decent human being, and he couldn't do anything about it?

"Why would it be stupid?" Tim pulled out the sugar bowl and grabbed two spoons. "Look, I know I agreed that we should stay focused on our reason for being here and not spend time flirting with women. But I mostly said that for Billie, of course. You compartmentalize things all the time. Why can't you have an innocent romance with Summer on vacation? The girls will be all right. We've got them squared away."

He straightened, fisting his hands. "Because this isn't a real vacation. I can't leave the girls and go on a date. Or sleep over anywhere but here. Especially since it will give Billie the green light he's looking for. And trust me, bro, he sees green already."

Tim's mouth curled, a rare sight. "You don't want to leave me alone with the girls. Dammit, you don't think I'm tough enough to look out for them."

Shit. He ran a hand through his hair. "I brought you both along for numbers as much as your caretaking side, because I didn't think *I* could handle the girls alone or stand up to what might come after us."

"I buy the caretaking part, sure." Tim stepped closer, anger in his expression. "But the rest is crap. You brought me along because you didn't want me in Boston in case the Kellys decided to pay me a call."

Terrific. Now the nicest O'Connor was picking a fight with him. "Tim, I brought you because my emotional intelligence when it comes to love and nurturing is zilch. That's your specialty, and you're damn good at it. My contribution is protecting the kids. I'm not the guy who knows what to do when they go to pieces missing their mom."

"Bullshit." Tim poked him in the chest, and his use of a cuss word wasn't lost on Robbie. "You helped me and Kathleen when Mom died. I don't know what I would have done without you. Pop was silently falling to pieces and working all the time like a tough O'Connor is supposed to do. You—"

Robbie's eyes were burning suddenly at the shine in his brother's eyes.

"Oh, never mind. I know you don't want to hear it."

"No, say what you were going to say."

Tim's mouth worked before he said, "You've let yourself get hard, but that doesn't mean you've lost those things. They're still in there. Just like they were when I needed you. You did fine comforting Reagan last night after Cassidy's innocent outburst about their mom."

Had he? Finding that young girl with her hands pressed to her face, crying, had grabbed him by the throat. He hadn't known what to do, so he'd just said her name softly. Thank

God she'd launched herself at him. He'd held her until she'd finally let go and told him she was okay. "Look, I didn't do anything. She bawled. I patted her back like a moron who had no clue what to say."

Tim gave a long-suffering sigh before turning away to pour two coffees. "There's *nothing* to say sometimes, especially when you can't change anything. Like Mom dying."

His insides roared with grief. "I don't want to talk about that."

"Fine! So let me use another example. When I'm with a patient who's just had horrible health news or a bad family visit, I sit there with them. I show them I care by being there. That's what matters in the end. Oh, why am I even talking? You won't give yourself a break. Drink your coffee, and then go for a run. You need to blow some of this off before the girls wake up."

He glanced outside. Summer was probably already running or soon would be. He didn't want to chance meeting her on the beach. When she and Clarice had left last night, the final look she'd given him had said it all. The usual sparkle in her green eyes was as absent as her bright smile. He'd hurt her, and he knew it. And dammit, he felt like shit about that too. Even though they'd been in agreement about not doing anything about their mutual attraction.

"If you don't go, you're a coward," Tim said, picking up his coffee. "And you know it. That's not who you are. You should apologize. She's a sweet woman, and she doesn't deserve your shit."

With that final smack to the face, his *nice* brother left the room. Robbie picked up his coffee and burned his mouth taking a sip. He let out a trail of swear words since no one was around, fighting the urge to kick the kitchen cabinets with his bare feet. He was boiling on the inside, and he knew it. Running was the only outlet for him at the moment.

He headed upstairs for some socks and shoes, not seeing Tim anywhere. The girls were sleeping when he checked on them again, but he spotted Miss Purrfect splayed out on his unmade bed the moment he entered his room. She rolled over, pawing at her collar, and gave an audible hiss.

"Hey!" He lurched at the cat, who screeched and took off for the hallway. "It's not my fault we're here, dammit. It's Tara's."

He froze. That wasn't fair either. Yanking out some socks from his duffel, he pressed his free hand to the headache starting at his nape.

Tara. Where was she? How was she? Jesus, being in the Outer Banks was like being in an alternate universe. The Kellys were out there, looking for Scotty and Tara—and potentially him and the girls—and their money. So far, nothing had changed. They were coming up on a week.

Something needed to break and break soon—or he would.

No, he needed to suck it up. Why was he letting a random attraction to a virtual stranger get to him? He yanked on his shoes and socks, tying his shoelaces tightly. He knew the answer. Because he was horny, that was why.

No—it was more than that. Summer was freaking gorgeous, from her long legs to her blond hair and green eyes, but that wasn't the only reason he felt drawn to her. She was also graceful and kind, grounded. That smile of hers could make him forget what he was about to say. And the way she looked at him, like she knew him on the inside and liked him, understood him even, had been burrowing under his skin, causing all sorts of discomfort.

Tim was right. She didn't deserve his bad attitude. He needed to apologize.

Leaving the house, he headed next door, not wanting to risk that she'd zoom past him on the beach, leaving him to chase after her—*if* he could catch up. God, how freaking embarrassing if she left him panting in her dust again. He wanted to apologize, not be humiliated.

Clarice was visible in the kitchen window as he stepped onto their patio. The way her black brows rose with disdain was enough to confirm he was on their shit list. Knocking lightly, he straightened his shoulders, ready to take his medicine.

She cracked the door with plenty of attitude. "Looking for your jerk uniform?"

"Actually, I realized I was still wearing it." He blew out a breath. "I was coming to apologize."

She touched her ear with a long red fingernail. "I'm sorry. What did you say?"

He was supposed to apologize to her? Wasn't Summer the one who deserved an apology from him?

Well, he had ruined things with her and Billie last night, he realized. His brother had given him a pissed-off shove after the two women had left shortly after picking at their food. Only the kids' presence had prevented a further blowup.

"I'm sorry for my behavior last night. I *was* a jerk with a capital *J*. It won't happen again."

"Forgiven." She motioned him toward the kitchen. "Come inside and wait for Summer. Since you owe her an apology too. You know... Some people actually embrace having an attraction to someone. You might try it."

He could see why Billie liked her. She had a frank, straightforward attitude to go along with the curves his brother liked. "My life is complicated right now. I didn't come here looking for anything."

"Well, it's like pigeon shit in the park. No one wants it, but it doesn't mean you don't embrace the good luck it brings."

He'd lived in Boston long enough to have heard that one

from Italian Americans. "We Irish Americans don't believe getting crapped on is good luck."

She walked over to the coffee pot and poured him a cup. "No, but you believe in leprechauns and pots of gold under rainbows, so you shouldn't really judge, should you?"

He took the coffee and drank it slowly, his eyes widening at how strong it was. "Somehow I don't think you really believe in tall tales."

Leaning her elbows on the counter, she gave a short smile. "You're right. I'm an accountant. I like numbers and data. They're straight up and straightforward like me. Do you like the coffee?"

He imagined Summer had shared his profession with her, so he decided he could be straightforward too. "The guys in my precinct make coffee like this. Practically pops your eyeballs out of the socket."

"It's my recipe for getting through tax season. But I can't seem to give it up. Summer can't stand it. You've seen her girly water."

"Reagan and Cassidy loved it." He felt like crap again when he thought of how sad the girls had been to see the two women leave so early last night. "Maybe I should come back."

"Not on your life." Clarice playfully picked up a paring knife and held it out. "I know plenty of men like you. The impulse to apologize is rare. The actual apology is even rarer."

"This is the second time I've apologized in less than twenty-four hours," he pointed out, frowning.

"So I heard." She put the knife down. "But here's what I know about men. By the time you walk back to your house, you'll think you did plenty, saying what you did to me, her friend. No, you're going to stand here and drink coffee until she returns. Then I'll leave you two star-crossed lovebirds alone and you can apologize to her sweet little face."

His mouth tightened. "Star-crossed lovers? Have you been reading that Shakespeare garbage too?"

"Your brother, Tim, is adorable!" She gave him a sly grin. "It's too bad I saw Billie first, because your baby brother is a real romantic. I'll bet he knows how to treat a woman right."

Had she and Summer analyzed him and his brothers? He didn't want to know. "Tim has a girlfriend."

"That's no shock." She gestured to him. "You clearly don't. In fact, you act like you wiped your whole dating and romance program from your motherboard. Is the girls' mother that bad?"

Terrific. They were wondering about his and his brothers' personal crap. It was just like women to dig in deep. "You've seen the girls. They're wonderful. And that's all I'm saying on that subject."

"Fine. If you'd like, we can stop trying to have an adult conversation, and you can simply grunt like an animal. Might save you a lot of trouble."

He couldn't help but puff out a laugh. "Right. And maybe I should stop walking upright too and just hunch over and drag my knuckles on the ground. Stop confusing people."

Her cackle carried across the room. "Now that's a fabulous idea. Give that ape a wide berth, it'll say. He's not fit for human company. Robbie, you should start practicing today."

Her wicked humor had him cracking a reluctant smile. Yeah, he could see why Billie liked her. Okay, she was a little weird, but balls-out honest. Billie didn't take to women who played games. "As long as my new act entertains Reagan and Cassidy, I'll do it. We're reaching that part of the vacation where the glow of the adventure is fading. They're getting restless."

"Then we should do something fun!" Clarice said enthusiastically, wiggling her hips. "I remember being bored on vacation as a kid. The only antidote is something exhilarating.

How about an amusement park? I think I read in a brochure there's one in Nags Head."

He still wasn't sure about going out in public. "Cassidy is still a little young for that, but thanks."

A knock sounded before a door slicked open in another part of the house. "Hey!" Summer called. "It's me."

"Great!" Clarice shouted back. "We have company."

He set his coffee aside. "You two knock before you enter the house?"

Clarice picked up the knife. "You're damn right we do. We're women alone in a house. Beats going around with a weapon. We also lock the doors. There are weirdos in vacation spots too, you know."

"I've busted a few," he commented, watching for Summer. "Thanks for the coffee."

"You're welcome." Clarice made a show of putting the knife away. "You might start that practicing—and grunting—just in case the apology doesn't work."

He hadn't allowed himself to imagine the possibility that it might not. Shit. "Point taken. But I might try flowers first. Hunching like that would give me a bad back."

"Whatever, O'Connor," she called, sailing out of the room.

Muffled conversation sounded from the direction she'd gone. Moments later, Summer walked into the kitchen wearing a sleeveless light green dress that stopped mid-thigh. Her long legs made his mouth water before he lifted his gaze to her face. The green of the dress punched up the green in her eyes, and she had her golden locks pulled back in a ponytail that enhanced the delicate curves of her oval face.

She was so damn beautiful she was making his heart knock against his ribs. His hands were starting to sweat, and he thought about what Clarice had said about apologizing. It *was* harder doing it with Summer. He realized why. Because it mattered more, and he wanted her to think well of him. Tim was right. He was fighting with himself, and he was losing.

"I was a prize jerk last night." He met her surprised look straight on. "I came to say I'm sorry. Again. That's not usual for me. I'd like to say it won't happen again, but I don't make promises I can't keep. I'm not in the habit of being a jerk per se, but I'm frustrated and a bit restless and...hell, I'm completely out of patience. I want you. I don't want to. That's it. Do you want me to leave?"

Her mouth tugged toward a smile before it smoothed out. "I know you don't want this, but I didn't expect to be ignored. It surprised me how much that hurt. We barely know each other."

Her honesty as much as the soft rasp of her voice grabbed him by the throat. He crossed to her, his hand lifting to caress her cheek. "I'm sorry I hurt you. God, I really am. Maybe that's why we should just call this and go about our vacations. Separately."

But even as he said it, his fingers slid along her jaw and neck, the softness of her skin this side of heaven. She squeezed her eyes shut, her breath shaky as she leaned closer. Into his touch. "This isn't what I expected either, you know. Especially you having the power to hurt me. I don't give that to anyone anymore."

"I hate that I hurt you, Summer." He pulled her against him, wrapping his arms around her, desperate to undo what he'd done. "I'm all out of making sense right now. Tell me to stop. Tell me to leave."

Her hands gripped his sides. "I should. But I can't. God... I just can't."

His mouth swooped down, meeting her raised lips. Then she was gripping the back of his head and kissing him. Their mouths clashed. Their teeth grazed sensitive, urgent flesh. When she tore her mouth away, he caught the gleam of heat in her bright green eyes. Then she rested her face against his chest, sinking into him.

Like that kiss had liquified her knees.

Yeah, that's exactly how he felt too. Except it had melted something inside him, the fire hot enough to ravage walls he hadn't known he'd erected. He cradled her tenderly, his mind totally blown. The smell of something floral and beach and woman reached his nose, and he felt the urge to tip her face up and take her mouth again.

Touching her had been a mistake. It had opened a whole other world of attraction, passion, and shit—tenderness—and it was a door he desperately wanted to walk through. One he needed to close just as much.

"The timing couldn't be more wrong here," he told her, caressing her back slowly. "My life is complicated—"

"I know," she interrupted sharply, looking up. "I don't care."

The words made his balls draw up. "This can't go anywhere," he said gravely.

She inhaled shakily and nodded. "Yet here we are. We're just going to have to find a way to enjoy it now. Knowing there's nothing after we leave here. You have your life, and I have mine."

"I'm here for the girls." His voice held conviction, thank God. He hoped she could understand without knowing all the details. "They're my first and last priority. They have to be."

"That's the way it should be," she said, running her soft fingers over the rough stubble of his jaw, which he hadn't bothered to shave yet. "I won't get in the way of that. You have my promise."

She was more understanding than most women he knew. God, he hated lying to her, but that was the way it had to be. Nothing could make him tell her the truth. There was too much at stake. And what would it matter anyway? This attraction needed to have a short shelf life.

"The girls are little, and you saw how much they miss their mother." He ran a thumb down the middle of her nape, making her shiver, which made him want to find other places that would cause that reaction. "I need to be close to home. In case they need anything. After they go to bed, of course."

Pulling back, she took a breath, her face suddenly tense. "That's a little fast for me. Why don't we have a drink tonight and a walk on the beach? I need you to understand. I don't do one-night stands, and flings aren't my usual."

There was a whisper of something in her tone, something heavy with the past. He wondered what it was, but given his own dissembling, he wasn't going to press. "All right. We go as fast as you want. Always. You have my word on that."

"Good." She laid her hands on his chest, and he covered them with his own, his heartbeat rising again to her touch. "You know...I had no idea what was in store for me when I came here."

If she only knew. He let his fingers play with the ends of her hair. "Me either. I was just supposed to get out of town with two little girls and my brothers along for company."

Her mouth tipped up to the right, sexy and adorable all in one. "Clarice might want some time with Billie as well, you know. But he should ask her if he'd like to."

He glanced off toward the door Clarice had left through, wondering if she was somewhere in earshot. God, he hoped not. "Billie's pretty pissed I ran you guys off. I was lucky he couldn't give me the business in front of the girls."

She brightened. "I have something for them."

"You didn't need to do that, Summer," he said, even though something weird fluttered in his chest at her thoughtfulness.

She left the room briefly before returning, walking back

in with a shopping bag from a store he and his brothers had also visited for supplies. She thrust it out and then smoothed her ponytail after he took the bag. "I didn't wrap them, but..."

He looked inside, his Adam's apple shifting in his throat. "You bought them wands."

"Every princess should have one," she told him, that sparkle back in her green eyes, he was relieved to see. "Also, there's one in there for Tim. It was the most masculine one I could find, but in some circles, I imagine it wouldn't pass muster."

Digging deeper in the bag, he spotted the only non-pink one. She was right. The baby blue wasn't exactly a guy's color. "He'll love it. They all will. Thank you. I don't know what to say. Especially when you were out buying these after I was such a jerk to you last night."

"Well, they weren't, and I wanted to do this."

She laid her hands over his rough ones, making him achingly aware of how different they were—she was soft and he was hard, and he wanted to explore every... "Again, it's really nice."

God, he sounded lame.

"I thought it might help them wish for whatever was in their hearts right now," she continued, pressing her hand to the center of her chest, where her heart had raced for him. "It's tough when little girls have worries. Having something to hope for, to wish for—well, that's everything. Even if it's make-believe."

Again, the past seemed to cast gray shadows on her face. "It's not one of the inspirational sayings hanging in our house next door," he said lightly, trying to pull her out, "but I imagine there's one about that phrase. *Make. Believe.* In a girly font, of course."

"The word *Receive* would probably go after *Believe.*" She

broke off a laugh. "You going to make a crack about me saying something like that?"

"Never." He tipped her chin up, seeing the promise of something happy and hot in her eyes. "We should decide on a time tonight before I give in to the urge to kiss you again."

She let out a shaky breath. "Clarice is probably still listening in the other room."

"At least she's put away her paring knife." He cupped her shoulders when she gave him a puzzled expression. "How does nine o'clock work for tonight? For just you and me? No eavesdroppers or angry brothers—or pissed-off cats. Don't ask."

She caressed his chest, making him aware of the power her fingertips had to make him burn. "Okay. Were you planning on running this morning?"

"I was." He wouldn't tell her he'd feared he wouldn't be able to catch her to apologize.

"Want a running partner?" she asked shyly. "Seems a waste to wait until tonight...I just need to change."

He skewered her with a look. "You planning on running a seven-minute mile? Because while I hate admitting this out loud, lest you think I'm a wuss, that's too fast for me."

"I think I can handle your leisurely pace for a day." Her mouth twitched sexily, making him want to run his finger across those amused lips. "But tomorrow all bets are off."

Who knew what tomorrow would bring? Tonight they would have a casual drink and a romantic walk along the beach. He could already feel himself holding her slender hand as the washes crashed in the distance. His thoughts would be on her and her only. Being alone was going to change things between them. There was no getting around it. He'd have to face that. But not now.

"I'm forewarned." He gave her soft cheek a final caress

before stepping back. "I'll just drop these wands off next door and meet you outside. Unless you want to give them——"

"No, please don't wait! Waking up to a present is one of the best things in the world."

He wanted to make a note of that. For her. But giving her presents would sure as hell make whatever they were doing more than just a vacation thing. "I'll see you shortly. And thanks again. For everything."

She gave that bright smile of hers, and he turned to leave, nearly walking into the counter. Clumsy he wasn't. Idiot he'd just added to the list. But at least his temporary jerk badge had been removed.

When he let himself into the house, Billie was sitting having coffee with Tim. His brother immediately stood, his big jaw already out of joint. "You and me need to get something straight."

"Clarice is waiting for you to ask her out," he simply replied, walking over to Tim. "These are presents from Summer for you and the girls. I'm going on a run."

He headed back to the door, relieved not to hear Billie's heavy footsteps following him.

"Oh, and by the way, Tim," he said, turning around to face them, "I'm going to have a drink with Summer after the girls go to sleep around nine—with a walk on the beach afterward." He put his hand on the doorframe. "I'd appreciate it if you'd keep an ear out for the girls."

Billie's shock turned to a sly smile. "About damn time."

"Of course, kind sir," his brother replied in that irritating Shakespearean accent. "It would be my honor to serve you so humbly, especially as you are in the pursuit of love."

Robbie narrowed his eyes. "Let's be clear. I'm doing this against my better judgment, but I'm going to control my own stupidity. If I turn into an idiot, I want one of you to hit me.

As hard as you deem necessary. Because I won't let Tara or those girls down. I couldn't live with myself. Got it?"

They both nodded crisply.

"Good. I'm glad that's clear. Because dammit, Tim, this ain't no Shakespeare romance. I won't let it end tragically."

He slammed the door on the way out.

CHAPTER TWELVE

THEY HAD A PROBLEM.

Or at least Lily did. She was falling for a person of interest while being undercover. The line between Summer Sunshine's feelings and Lily Meadows' was blurring. Usually on undercover assignments, she could justify the masquerade. Pretending to be someone else so they could put bad guys away was her job, a job she was proud of, a job she was honor bound to execute.

But suddenly, when she spoke to Robbie, all she could think about was how she was lying to him about who she was and why she was really here. He was going to hate her when he found out, and that was a new worry wrapping itself around her ankles.

The likelihood of him discovering she was FBI was high. The case was going to be solved. She was going to solve it, get her promotion—do her job. That might benefit Robbie and his family, but she couldn't imagine he would be thrilled with her subterfuge.

God, what a mess.

"I think you can expense those wands to the FBI, right?"

Sheila studied her as she downed half a bottle of coconut water to coat her dry throat. "Since they were your idea to get back in with the O'Connors after last night. But it seems like we've progressed to a whole new level. And men complain about women changing their minds."

"Sheila, I'm—"

"I know what you are." Her partner strode forward and put her hands on Lily's shoulders, her gaze direct. "I've developed feelings before while undercover. It happens. Which is why the trainers address it in undercover school and sometimes you have to talk to someone in the shrink shop after an assignment. But I trust you, Lily. You should trust yourself too."

She nodded, aware of Sheila's intentional use of her first name. Her partner was trying to remind her she was Lily Meadows, an FBI agent, who worked undercover. Right. She wanted to tap her own skull to drill that truth back into it. "I do trust myself, Sheila, but God, why do I have to feel this way *now*? Why can't I just meet a normal guy during my off-hours and date?"

Sheila laughed harshly in the sunny kitchen. "One, because we work like dogs. Two, because most guys' balls shrivel the instant they hear we're FBI. And three, because you don't want a normal guy. You had one. It didn't work out for you."

She chugged more coconut water as her heart silently agreed by giving a hard thump in her chest. "I know you're right, but I want to..."

"Roar?" Sheila grabbed the coconut water from her hand. "Go ahead. Then head upstairs and change. You have a running date with your person of interest."

"Maybe I should cancel it?"

"Is that seriously a question?" She chewed her lip before

heading to the fridge. "I'm getting you more pink water. Obviously, you're dehydrated."

She gave into an understated roar. "No, what I need is to get my head on straight." One smell of Robbie, and both Summer and Lily were going to start going gooey-eyed again. Especially if he ran without a shirt on. My God, his chest made her fingers itch to trace all those hard muscles. This lunacy was the kind that killed promotions. She needed to keep her focus on the prize—not his gorgeous chest and ocean blue eyes. God, she was rhyming now. Maybe that Shakespeare stuff was catching.

Sheila slapped another coconut water into her hand and propelled her to the doorway. "You aren't going to blow an operation because you've found a hot yet grouchy knight in shining armor who protects little kids—especially since this is the job that's going to give you the promotion you want. I don't care how sweet under that hard exterior Robbie O'Connor is. Now, I believe there's a gorgeous, tall, bald hunk of a man coming to our back door who also zings my girly parts. Both Sheila's and Clarice's."

She craned her neck to their terrace and spotted Billie sauntering toward the patio door. "What are you going to do?"

"Same as you!" Sheila slapped her butt. "Do the job. Now, move it, *chica*!"

Her partner only used Spanish when she was emphasizing a point. "Fine, I'm going. Unless you need a chaperone. I delivered my *this is too fast for me, and I don't do this kind of thing usually* speech to Robbie. What's your plan?"

Waving at Billie, who was now standing in clear view, she lowered her voice and said, "I'll tell him I've got my period and it's a bloody massacre. And then I'll tear up and say the timing is terr-i-ble because I'm really falling for him. Guys like him run like the wind from shit like that."

She coughed out an unexpected laugh. "Why didn't I think of that?"

"Honey, I aced my undercover test on how to get out of difficult situations," she whisper spoke. "Okay, now I'm opening the door to my gentleman caller. You go out the front when you leave."

Gentleman caller? Tim O'Connor's Shakespeare jokes *were* certainly catching on if Sheila was using them. She jogged up the stairs and headed to her bedroom at the end of the hall, chugging more coconut water. The extra walk reminded her that Sheila always insisted on being in the first bedroom off the stairs because she was a lighter sleeper and a better shot in case someone breached the house.

Right. Focus on FBI stuff. Like shootings and bad guys—the reason we're here.

Finishing off her water, she took pleasure in crunching the bottle with her hand, the physical action keeping her focused. The shooting aspect of the job had been tough for her in the beginning, mostly because she didn't want to use violence to handle anything. Fortunately, her mentor and friend had told her it was her desire *not* to use violence that would make her a better agent. All she needed to remember was to follow procedure, keep her wits about her, and rely on her team. If she did that, she'd rarely have to pull her weapon, let alone use it.

So far, Brie Thierry had been proven right. Lily hoped it would stay that way. Especially since she'd be working on cases involving children. She'd been lucky that the cult her mother had joined hadn't used guns. Not that there hadn't been violence, but it had been the quieter kind, the kind that came behind closed doors and after dark. She'd been lucky to be too young for it. Some of her friends hadn't been so lucky, though. Ironically, given the excuse Sheila planned on making to Billy, it had been Lily's lack of period that had saved her.

The crunched bottle rested in her hands. She looked down, realizing that was how she could have ended up. Broken. Crushed. Brie had given her a shot with a good foster home and mental help. The rest had been on Lily.

She wasn't going to mess up how far she'd come. Shaking off the memories, she walked into her bedroom and intentionally put the crunched bottle in the garbage can. It had served its purpose.

Crossing to the stack of undercover clothes she'd arranged in the top drawer of her dresser, she pulled on a green tank top that covered her middle along with a white tennis skirt. No need to amp up the mind-blowing sexual energy between them with a more revealing outfit. She wasn't a masochist. Telling herself she was going to walk the narrow line she was on the best she could, she reached for her socks and running shoes.

Her phone buzzed on the bedside stand where she had it charging, and she walked over to it. She hoped Buck wasn't going to pull them. Usually they were the ones who contacted him with updates. She took a breath and picked up her phone, heading into the bathroom. Their communications were always secure, but since Billie was in the house, she closed the door to make sure the sound wouldn't travel.

"Agent Meadows," she answered even though she knew it was Buck. One did not pick up and say, "Hi, Buck," to one's supervisor.

"The Kellys appear to be trying to flush Tara O'Connor out of hiding," Buck informed her without greeting. "Obviously they know she's removed the money because a mysterious fire started in her primary location around seven o'clock this morning when the chairs were packed to the gills with women looking to be pampered before they headed to work."

"Oh no," she breathed out.

"Exactly," he agreed in a clipped tone. "There was a shit

show stampede of screaming barefooted women with those girly rubber thingamabobs between their toes, according to the officer I sent to have eyes for us. But it was also on the morning news, which gives me indigestion as I finish my onion bagel. There are reports featuring victims complaining about their manicures being ruined. Can you believe that? I didn't even know nail salons opened that early or career women cared about shit like that."

No, Buck wouldn't understand the desire to look one's professional best when it involved beauty products. He'd been known to tell new female officers, fresh out of Quantico, if he thought they were wearing "too much makeup," saying it was the FBI and not a clown house.

"I don't know what the world is coming to, sir," she answered deadpan.

"According to early police reports I'm getting from a confidential source, Tara's second-in-command at the nail salon was freaked out, but she maintained that her boss is on a much-needed vacation after ending her marriage and will be back soon. I'll tell you, those Southie women don't scare too hard. This fire screams of arson, and I'm guessing Tara's people would suspect it."

"It's hard to know what she told her staff, sir," Lily reasoned. "I doubt she would mention the money laundering."

He grunted. "You might be right. If Tara O'Connor can give both you and Sheila the slip, she's one smart cookie. Either way—the Kellys are likely to hit back harder if Tara doesn't appear soon after this initial scare. I don't want to think where they go from arson. What do you think the odds are of her coming back to Boston like the Kellys want?"

Lily ran it over in her mind. "I've read everything I can about Tara and now that I've gotten to know her children a little, I'd say she has very protective instincts and is loyal to the people in her circle. She'll be sick to her stomach about the fire, especially since she knows her husband was the reason for it. She's going to want to prevent further damage. My bet is she knows there's only one person she can fully trust."

"Robbie O'Connor," her boss surmised. "Any word on them making contact or meeting up?"

There was no way Robbie knew about this yet. If he had, he wouldn't have come over to discuss his attraction to her this morning. His jaw would have been granite, and he would have been wanting to kick something before hovering close to those two sweet girls.

"Like I said in my report last night, sir, the youngest daughter mentioned wanting her mother to come, but I don't have anything more right now. We haven't seen a phone, but we've only been in two rooms in the house. I've made some further headway with Lieutenant O'Connor since my report, though, and hope to have better access. We have a drink and a walk planned for this evening. Alone. And today I'm teaching the girls to surf—or something of the sort. Our face-time with our subjects is growing stronger by the day. Perhaps he'll learn of the fire and confide in me."

Or would he simply cancel their outing? She had to make sure that didn't happen.

"Too bad you haven't found a phone. Nothing has popped on our end from his work phone. I tend to agree with you that he likely turned it in to Internal Affairs at the toy store meet. We also have nothing from his brothers' phones."

"Robbie would have advised them all to dump them since they're traceable," Lily broke in.

"We need something more, Lily."

Pressing them was his job, so she strove not to be irritated and say, *Of course, we know we need a phone, sir.* "We'll expand our efforts today, sir."

"Good. If you can discover a phone, find out the number. I'll initiate a warrant for a wiretap. If he has a phone, one would imagine Tara would call him now. We want to have the wiretap in place so we don't miss any evidence."

Lily walked to the window where she could see into the house next door—and their subjects. Tim was chasing Cassidy around as she shrieked, clutching Miss Rosie. The little girl was still in her pajamas and had wild bedhead. Reagan, she noted, was lying on the floor reading a book with Miss Purrfect cuddled up to her. None of them suspected they were under surveillance or that their family cat still boasted an FBI tracker on its bedazzled collar. More guilt pricked at her skin.

"Tara will weigh the risks of contact given her children are here, sir, but the arson changes things." How could it not?

"She trusts Lieutenant O'Connor big-time," he said flatly. "Otherwise, she wouldn't have given him both her kids and the money."

"Agreed." She froze when Tim caught her looking as he tossed Cassidy in the air, forcing her to give a cheery wave while her stomach gave a troubled flip-flop. "Sheila and I will make a concerted press on the phone issue. So far, none of the brothers have used one in our presence. I have an idea on how we can push it."

Photos of the girls learning to surf for their mother. They would see how Robbie handled that innocent request.

"Good. We need a break, Lily. I hate telling my boss how you and Sheila are off in the Outer Banks in a vacation beach rental sipping Sheila's famous margaritas and getting tans."

She winced. They were going to get ragged about their tans when they returned to the office. Great. "Sir, I need to go. Lieutenant O'Connor is waiting for me to run with him."

He sputtered out a rare laugh. "Are you running your usual

Olympian speed that hurts a man's pride or doing a sweet undercover run that makes O'Connor feel like he's a god?"

Her reputation for speed was well known, and she'd dealt with hurt pride and pissed-off alphas in the Bureau because of it. "I deemed Lieutenant O'Connor would like a challenge. I left him in my dust the first day."

"I'd almost pay to see that," Buck said with another strangled laugh. "All right, it sounds like your cover is progressing. Keep pulling. We're going to untangle this case and put the Kellys down. This fire could be just the thing to push things over the edge."

She pressed a hand to her now upset tummy. A fire during a busy business time was bad enough. Beyond the actual damage it would cause, the fear and intimidation would leave a scar. Next time, it might turn more personal. Would the Kellys go after one of Tara's employees? Maybe one of Robbie's other brothers? She'd pulled all of their driver's licenses. Every last one of them was over six feet, looked Southie tough, and hadn't smiled for his photo. She had to believe Robbie trusted his brothers to take care of themselves.

She gripped the towel on the towel rack, biting her lip. She wished she could ask Robbie if he knew about the fire and what his fellow cops were planning to do about it. His partner had to already know what was going on, right? So did Internal Affairs. Surely the Southie police would do more drive-bys at Tara's other nail salons and hopefully some of her employees' homes. The FBI couldn't help without blowing their cover.

"Summer!"

Sheila's shout brought her out of her reverie. "Coming!"

She tucked her phone out of sight since it was charged and tugged on her running shoes. Jogging down the stairs, she found Robbie in the kitchen alongside Billie. They were talking to Sheila, who stood at the stove.

Robbie's demeanor was the same as earlier, so he hadn't heard the news yet. He was wearing a T-shirt, evidently not planning on running bare chested. They were in sync on the no-inflaming moves memo. When she entered the kitchen, he immediately broke off what he was saying, his mouth tipping up to the right. Her insides fluttered over her queasy stomach.

Get back into your cover, Lily.

Shaking her hair back, she said, "Sorry for making you wait. I was tugging my shoes on when a friend called on her way to work. I was telling her how great the Outer Banks is. She's so jealous."

"Was it Amy?" Sheila asked, serving up scrambled eggs for two. "She texted me last night asking for photos. I fell asleep before I could text her back."

"Yeah, it was Amy." She sent her partner a wink—their agreed upon sign to tell her something important *had* happened to delay her upstairs.

Sheila winked back to confirm she understood, her flirtatious smile remaining in place as she pushed a spatula at the eggs, Billie hovering close. "I'll text her after I have breakfast with this hunk."

Billie grinned when she reached over and gave his giant bicep a squeeze. "She's a doll for feeding me."

Robbie gave a dramatic eye roll. "Ready?"

She crossed to where he was standing, smiling. "Are you?"

His answer was a grin filled with challenge and heat. Her heart started tapping to its new Robbie cadence in her chest.

Remember why you're here.

"Hey! Did you remember that you promised Reagan that I can show her how to surf today?" she asked.

His mouth worked like he was amused, and God, the way

it highlighted the hardness of his jaw had her falling way too easily back into character. She could lap him up. Summer Sunshine could, that is.

"I did." He inclined his chin to his brother. "Eat fast. Tim is alone with the Drool Baby and Miss Pixie. You know how Cassidy is in the morning."

"Wild as a banshee." Billie pointed to the door. "Run fast."

Robbie's jaw tightened as an uneasy silence descended in the kitchen. God, when two alpha males locked horns...

"Oh, don't worry, Mom," Billie practically huffed after a beat. "I'll be back to babysit in no time. Maybe I can even convince our sweet little neighbor to join me."

"We can dish up our eggs and head over there straight-away," Sheila told him, patting his hand with an overbright smile.

Lily could see that Robbie was considering saying something, but she decided to head off an eruption between the brothers. They wanted things to stay harmonious. That kind of vibe led to double dates and frivolities. To saying more than was prudent. "Come on. The faster we run, the faster we get back. Unless you're not up for the challenge."

That statement had his fiery blue eyes meeting hers. "Oh, I'm up for it. Let's go."

She wiggled her fingers at Sheila, who wiggled hers back— God, she hated pretending to be a witless woman. Crossing the terrace, they walked in silence to the beach. She stretched her arms overhead on the way, gazing at Robbie surreptitiously. He was looking back at the house, his jaw tight.

"I'd understand if you don't want to leave Tim alone," she told him, bending at the waist to stretch her hamstrings.

He cracked his neck, a sound rife with tension, and started to stretch his own limbs. She had to look away as his muscles rippled from the motion, making her head turn fuzzy with instantaneous lust. So not part of her undercover packet.

"No, it should be fine." Another crack sounded in his back as he gave a side stretch. "My mother used to say that if someone wasn't screaming, there probably wasn't blood on the floor. I don't hear any screaming."

A puff of laughter erupted from her. "Your mother sounds like she had her hands full." Lily fisted her hands behind her back and arched her chest, telling herself to walk the line. Like the professional she was. Summer Sunshine didn't know that he'd lost his mother when he was fifteen.

Then she caught Robbie's eyes lingering on her and felt another bolt of white-hot heat explode in her midsection. Oh shit. "No one could say my mother had it easy with eight kids, seven of us boys. After spending time with the girls, I don't know how she did it. They never stop. Even when they're sleeping, they make me think about them. Reagan mumbles and tosses and turns while Cassidy is splayed out, making baby snores. I have renewed respect for mothers—"

He broke off, his face scrunching with distaste. She wondered if he'd felt he was sharing too much.

She started jogging, Robbie matching her speed. "And their mother?"

His mouth tightened. "I've always had respect for her. Never as much as I do now though. All right, let's go."

With that, he punched up his speed, stopping all conversation. She easily matched him, feeling the tug between guilt and a genuine desire to know more about him. Instead, she fell into her body and focused on her pace along with the nature around them. The seagulls were out screaming as they hunted in the ocean and soaring overhead. A few early swimmers were in the water, some with children, but the beach was mostly theirs, and theirs alone.

Robbie said nothing more, clearly focusing his strength on keeping up with her. She wasn't breathing hard, but he was.

Since it was near impossible to have a conversation this way, and she had questions, she cut back her speed.

His head whipped toward her, and his glare had her heart skipping a beat. "Don't you dare go easy on me."

There was a warning there, so she heeded it. He didn't slow, so she increased her pace again. Sweat broke out across his arms and face. The hot humid air enveloped her like a steam room, but the ocean breeze and the sound of the waves made her happy as her body did its thing. She rarely got out to enjoy the beach in the Boston area, this being her first summer there. People raved about Cape Anne and Cape Cod, but she'd only gotten away once, only to be pulled back into the office over the weekend because their case had gotten hot. Running like this had always helped her feel like she could do anything.

"You have the nerve to smile like an angel while I'm puffing like a freight train?" He grunted, every muscle locked in his personal battle with himself.

Grumpy looked hot on him. Then again, she'd be hard-pressed to think of anything that didn't look hot on him.

"*You* were the one who wanted to keep running at this pace. I was all for throttling back so we could have a pleasant conversation."

"Running isn't for chitchat." He swiped an arm across the sweat on his forehead. "It's to test yourself. To push yourself. To go past your limits. But dammit, Summer, you push me hard."

She didn't know what to say and looked off into the waves crashing on the beach beside them. His hand grazed her arm. She glanced over, uncomfortable moments with other men rising up in her mind. Her ability to outrun them had changed the way they'd interacted with her. Surely...

"I like it." His sexy grin made her practically giddy. "Push me some more."

Her internal temperature skyrocketed with those words, and the images that swam up in her mind weren't fit for her undercover report. Ones that involved two sweat-slicked bodies falling to the sand. Locked around each other. Mouth to mouth. Skin to skin.

Sexy visions dancing in her head, she did as he'd demanded, pumping her arms more quickly as she increased her pace. The sand under her gave a little more with her speed. He was breathing hard, every muscle working, as he matched her. They raced up the sweep of the beach that fanned out to the left, and then he was throttling back.

"Okay, I'm going to have a heart attack if I keep that pace up," he said in a raspy breath. "I'm almost forty, you know. Jesus!"

She bit her lip, trying not to laugh. "That old, huh? Well, I'm glad you told me, Grandpa. Like I said yesterday, I'm trained in CPR. But you should probably run with a phone on you if you're worried about collapsing. Or maybe you forgot your medical call alert bracelet back home?"

He had this sexy way of bunching his mouth when he didn't want to be amused. She wanted to trace every inch of those chiseled lips. And then jump in his lap as she kissed that look off him.

Lily Meadows, remember your promotion.

"Why do you think I brought my home nurse along?" he bandied back after sucking in more oxygen.

Her laugh was as easy as the tide. God, he was so fun to be with. Why couldn't she have met him in a normal setting? Would he have still been interested if he'd met her as Lily Meadows, FBI agent? Once he found out the truth, would he be able to see past the subterfuge and understand?

He's lying about who he is too, she reminded herself, a thought that made her immediately feel better. They were both lying to each other as part of their respective jobs, so she could stop feeling guilty.

Why hadn't this realization dawned on her earlier?

"What in the world are you laughing about?" he practically spat as he bent over at the waist, still breathing harshly.

"You!"

She studied him as his brow quirked in response, feeling a pull, same as always. He was the most compelling man she'd ever met. *Could* they start over as just themselves once this case was behind them? Because Lily Meadows knew the direction her heart was heading, and she very much wanted to keep whatever this thing was going...

"Given your medical status and all that huffing," she said, now grinning from ear to ear, "we should stop and take your pulse."

Her body felt rejuvenated from the run and the realization, and she was feeling lighter than air as she reached for his wrist. He slanted her an amused look but let her take his pulse.

"You're within normal levels, albeit at the high end of the range." She let go of his wrist and patted his sweat-slicked, hard chest. "You aren't in danger of keeling over, Grandpa."

He stepped closer, pressing his fingers to the pulse at her neck. "We should probably check you too. You're way too precious to me at the moment. I'd hate to have something happen on my watch."

Her heart did a jumping jack in her chest, and an ache of longing started in her belly before fanning out across her skin as he touched her. His fingers were rough-tipped and blistering hot, but it was the arousal in his liquid blue eyes that had her fighting a sensual moan. She wanted to close her eyes and lean into him, savoring the sensation of his sweat-slicked body against her own as the ocean thundered around them. But that would be too fast, especially given the night ahead.

So she locked her muscles and fought the inner tension rippling through her, urging her to take things further.

His fingers trailed down her neck, causing a streak of fire before falling away. "Your pulse kicked up for a moment there. I wonder why."

She pushed at his chest before starting to jog again. "You know why," she called flirtatiously over her shoulder.

He let her run ahead of him as she punched her speed. They'd both fought the pull of the moment back there. Tonight might be another matter.

She bit her lip to shift her focus back onto the case. Robbie hadn't responded to her comment about the phone, but she could press the issue later while teaching Reagan to surf.

Somewhere in that house, there had to be a phone. He had to be communicating with either his partner, Internal Affairs, or both. Maybe even Tara. Surely, very shortly, he would know about the arson at Tara's salon. How would Robbie react to the news? Their attraction only added a new urgency to the case.

The sooner they closed the case, the sooner they could stop lying to each other and find out what was really between them—assuming he could get past how they'd met.

CHAPTER THIRTEEN

S<small>UNSHINE, SAND, AND SEX.</small>

Robbie wished he could have the girl and all the rest, but he knew better. So he took care of business as he showered, gritting his teeth. He laid his forehead against the tiles and let the cold water pour over him.

Summer had him so hot he was burning. He must have bad luck or something, because how could he meet a woman like her now? When he was pretending to be a single dad with two girls? Maybe he needed to ask Kathleen to send him a four-leaf clover from Ireland because, Jesus, the timing and situation couldn't be worse. The longer he spent time with Summer, the more he felt like a louse for lying to her.

Part of him knew it shouldn't matter. He was doing what he had to in order to protect the girls. Besides, he and Summer were just two ships passing in the night. Feeling guilty was a wasted emotion when they would never see each other again after this trip. He just needed to force the other crap out of his mind and enjoy her as much as he could safely allow.

Safely allow. What a joke. He was a raging inferno of lust mixed with a rare desire to get to know her better. Idiot was too soft a word for him. He needed to remind his brothers he might need them to knock him out soon.

Spying his erection, which was growing even though he'd taken care of business only moments earlier, he wanted to kick something. He gave an audible growl instead.

An answering hiss sounded behind him. He swung around and slipped on the wet tiles, landing hard on his ass. "Ouch!"

Miss Purrfect fell into a crouch and bared her sharp little white teeth, giving another angry hiss. The water from the showerhead rained down on him as they continued their standoff, Wet Naked Bruised Alpha against Bitchy Clever Cat.

"Okay, that's it!" He shoved off the floor, wincing at the pain from his fall, and grabbed the shower wand, turning and spraying it in her direction. The cat shrieked and darted out of the bathroom.

"Chicken!" he shouted. "Freaking furball. I'm showering in here."

He lowered the wand to his side, stretching to ease the sharp pain in his ass. Cursing again, he eyed the dripping mess of the bathroom. God, he hoped he'd gotten that cat wet, but now he was going to have to clean this crap up. And he had a grapefruit-sized bruise swelling on his butt. Terrific.

He spied the cracked door. How in the hell had the cat gotten in here? He knew he'd closed it behind him, not wanting any little children—Cassidy mainly—to come wandering in and find him naked. Jesus, he wasn't a prude, but that wasn't something he wanted either one of them to endure. He secured the shower wand back in its holder after turning off the faucet and grabbed a couple extra towels to mop up the floor. Muttering cuss words under his breath felt good, and when he finished his cleaning, he heaved the towels in the corner as hard as he could.

Erection now gone, he pulled open the door to his bedroom, determination in his every step. He was done with this. The cat. This stupid *not a vacation* vacation. Lying to Summer. All of it.

A light rap of knuckles sounded on the door. "What are you barking at in there?" Tim asked loudly.

"Yeah!" Cassidy repeated. "Barking."

Groaning at being asked to explain himself, he tugged on some shorts and crossed to open the bedroom door. As he let his brother and Cassidy in, he tensed. "That cat is still in my room. Otherwise, this door would be open too."

"I don't know what you're talking about," Tim said, clearing his throat. "Robbie, you don't look well."

What the hell did he care how he looked? He scanned the room. "It has to still be in here. You'd better come out, you damn furball."

"Language," Tim cautioned, pointing to the little cherub in his arms who was grinning at him.

"I'm past that." He grabbed a pillow, and that was when he saw the vomit on the other side. "Miss Purrfect puked on my bed! Oh, you are so going to get it."

"You're in big trouble," Cassidy cried out—at him or the cat, he wasn't sure.

"Robbie—"

He started beating his mattress with the pillow. "Come out you little—"

"Hey!" Tim practically shouted as a streak of white fur raced out of the room with an angry meow.

"You chicken," Robbie cried, taking off after the cat.

Tim stepped in front of him before he could leave the room. "Stop this! You know when you asked us to hit you when you started acting like an idiot? We're there. Except the cherub is watching so I can't clock you. Get ahold of yourself."

He ground his teeth. "Cover Cassidy's ears."

Tim shook his head and stood his ground. "No. If you give in to old tendencies now, it's going to resurrect old patterns. You're an adult. Use your nice words."

If a child hadn't been present, he would have picked his baby brother up and hauled him into the shower and hosed him down. But Cassidy was still smiling and drooling, her light brown curls sticking up all over her head, clearly amused by the situation.

Was Miss Purrfect like this at home?

"Look, that cat not only vomited beside my pillow, but it hissed at me in the shower!" He forced a tight smile at Cassidy as she babbled. "That feline is totally out of control. Is she like this at your house, Cassidy?"

She laughed and nodded. "Yep, with Daddy."

Okay, that made him feel like total shit. He spun away. Now he was in the same category as a suspected money launderer and home-wrecker. Terrific.

"Out of the mouths of babes." Tim was clearly trying hard not to grin, and it made Robbie's teeth hurt. "I'm telling you, Robbie. Feed her or cuddle her. That's the only way you're going to bond with Miss Purrfect and get over this battle. Because look at you. Beating a mattress with a pillow like a— Don't make me say it. Right, Cassidy?"

His brother nuzzled Cassidy's neck, making her shriek with laughter as she cried, "Miss Purrfect loves cuddles. Like me."

He was not cuddling some stupid cat. But he could fight the urge to glare at his brother. Cassidy might get scared.

"Do you need a hug?" Tim's mouth tilted into a grin.

"You're lucky you have a human shield." He went over to his bed and started ripping off the bedsheets, his nose scrunching at the smell. "Great! Now I'm going to have to wash these."

"Housework is never done." Tim gave Cassidy a smacking kiss on the side of her neck. "You finish up and then join us on the beach. Your lady friend is all freshly showered and ready to give her next surfing lesson. Billie is already out there with Reagan, talking to Summer and Clarice. Oh, and by the way, Miss Purrfect *can* open doors."

"Sh—" He was proud he'd broken off mid-curse before Tim could open his mouth. "Tara would have a smart cat."

"Miss Purrfect is so smart," Cassidy said, sending him a shy smile. "Like me."

"I've yet to meet a dumb feline." Tim glanced at his shorts. "We're changing into our swimsuits, aren't we, Cassidy? You might do the same, Robbie."

"I haven't checked out the jellyfish situation yet."

Tim made Cassidy into a human airplane and headed toward the door while she made the corresponding buzzing sounds. "You're not the only one with eyes. Besides, the water looks better today. Didn't you notice on your run, or were you looking at other things?"

He glowered at his brother.

"Plus, we'll be in there with them," Tim continued with a laugh. "Robbie, nothing is going to happen to the girls. You might take a minute and calm yourself down."

He took a deep breath. "Fine. I'll see you shortly. But that cat had better not mess with me, or I'm telling you, I'm locking it outside."

"Don't do that," Cassidy burbled out. "Miss Purrfect sleeps with me."

Tim planted a kiss on her cheek as his eyes blazed with disapproval in Robbie's direction. "He's just kidding, sweetheart. Now, let's go change into a swimsuit and find your princess wand. Maybe you can make fish appear in the water."

"I want a whale!" Cassidy cried out.

"Whatever you want, cutie pie," Tim said, patting her back. "You might want to grab your wand too, brother."

He flipped him the bird since Cassidy wasn't looking. "Already done."

"Jeez, and that didn't help?" Tim winced before tipping up the little girl's chin. "Cassidy, we're doomed. Doomed! The frustrated Prince Robbie has no place to quench the fire in his hot sword."

Robbie went over and closed the door with an audible click, proud of himself for not slamming it. God, when had his baby brother become a nutso Shakespeare act? His brothers were going to pants it out of him if he kept this up after they returned to Boston.

After they returned to Boston...

God, what were they doing? Holed up in Familyville with two girls, hoping to evade the bad guys who were over twelve hours away in Boston. He was going crazy at the lack of movement. They had over a week before Tara had agreed to call it. Nothing had happened yet to break open the case.

Give him a chance to break the case open. He could knock some heads together. Interrogate some bad guys. He wanted to...

Fisting his hands, he tapped his bare foot on the plush carpet. This waiting game was killing him, all right. God, he'd have given his right arm to be going through the door of a violent drug dealer's hideout.

Or better, on a real date with Summer.

He rubbed the back of his neck. Tonight was as close as they were going to get to that, and the prospect already had him losing his mind. How was he going to stop himself from doing something stupid?

Then it hit him. He could time their date. Yeah, that was right. Thirty minutes for a cocktail and then another thirty walking along the beach. He couldn't do something stupid in under an hour, right? Then he'd bid her good night and head inside.

To his freshly laundered sheets.

He hung his head. God, who was he kidding. He didn't want to roll around in his sheets alone. He wanted Summer to be there with him.

"Not happening, man," he told himself.

Grabbing his swim trunks, he changed and headed to the kitchen to grab a snack before joining the others outside. The air was still like breathing through a wet blanket and the sun was raining down in hot waves as he trudged through the sand to the happy party. Reagan was already standing on the surfboard, trying to stop it from rocking on the ground. Her little sister was running back and forth across it, Tim bent at the waist to make sure she didn't trip. Billie stood cozily beside Clarice, his hand tucked casually around her waist.

And Summer...

She was wearing another eye-popping bikini, this one in a sexpot red that highlighted every sweet little part of the body he wanted to put his hands on.

She looked up and smiled as he reached them, putting her hand on Reagan's shoulder to steady her. His earlier anger started to drain away, and in the moment, he knew he was in real trouble.

His father had always said his mother had possessed the power to calm him down when he was at his most pissed off. *Son, when any of you find a woman like that, you'll know she's a keeper.*

He took a half step back, reeling from the shock. Summer's gaze narrowed in response.

"Look at me!" Reagan cried out, her extended arms teetering slightly. "I'm balancing."

"She's a fast learner," Summer said after a long moment, finally looking away from him and gently positioning the girl's shoulders. "Remember, Reagan. Keep yourself angled straight on the board. Your feet are going to want to move. It's the set of your shoulders that is your helper. Now bend your knees and tighten your belly. I'm going to rock the board a little."

Summer continued her instructions as his mind buzzed like an old emergency broadcast system, emitting one solid ear-grating note. A warning of potential tragedy. He was falling head over heels for a woman under false pretenses. And there was no way he could tell her the truth...

Once Tara's situation was resolved, they'd be out of here so fast it would make his head spin.

Would he tell Summer the truth once everything was resolved? The only good reason for doing that was if he thought they had a future together. That would mean long-distance dating—assuming she didn't punch him when she found out he'd been lying to her the whole time. Even if it was for a good reason. You never could guess with women.

Hadn't his sister, a cynical girl from Southie, all but kicked out her now-husband for not being totally truthful to her before they got engaged? And they'd been together for a while, doing the whole dating lovey-dovey thing. He and Summer—

"Hey, bro!" Billie called, his brow furrowed. "Why don't you take Drool Baby from Tiny Tim here and see if you two can make a whale appear?"

"I have my wand," Cassidy cried out, running over to her red bucket tucked in the sand beside a half-made sandcastle the tide hadn't completely destroyed.

He met his baby brother's concerned gaze. Tim crossed his arms and stared at him, his usual jovial smile absent now. God, was his mood that much of a vibe killer? If so, why were they giving him baby duty? Wouldn't a beer be better? Kids usually ran away from moods like this, didn't they?

A soft thunk landed against his leg. He looked down.

Cassidy was beaming at him, drooling with her angelic smile. She thrust out her wand and then pointed to the ocean. "Whale! Now!"

Then she started running into the surf, shrieking in delight as the water rushed over her bare feet. He had no choice but to sprint after her, scooping her up and heading into the ocean. When he was waist high, she slapped the water with her wand and then started laughing when it sprayed them both in the face. He gritted his teeth, keeping an eye out for jellyfish.

He stewed. She played. From the cheers on the beach, the surfing lesson was going great. He did his best not to watch Summer and her sweet and sexy form. But her laughter stopped his dark thoughts in their tracks. Then he would gaze at her and be unable to think of anything else, his heart beating heavily in his chest.

Cassidy hugged him a few times, taking him down an even deeper emotional rabbit hole. There was a weird sweetness in his life right now, one he'd never experienced before, and it was making him go out of his ever-loving mind.

Tim and Billie finally accompanied Reagan and Summer into the ocean with the surfboard, and Robbie watched as the water lapped at Summer's skin. He wanted to be that water.

Billie hoisted Reagan onto the board, and he and Tim held her arms while she practiced balancing more, with Summer caging her waist to make sure she didn't slip. Clarice was on the beach, he noted, taking photos with her phone.

His blood chilled.

Cassidy caught him in the neck with her wand, making him wince. What was he going to do about those photos? Surely, she wouldn't post them on social media. Especially without asking permission.

Dammit! He'd hoped there wouldn't be anything awkward like this. Certainly, he could say he believed in privacy for the girls. He wasn't on social media as a cop, but his brothers? How was he supposed to explain Tim's and Billie's reticence? They had social media accounts.

Shit.

"Where's my whale?" Cassidy asked, laying her head against his chest.

He didn't want to tell her that you couldn't summon a whale with a magic wand. Hardened cynic though he was, he knew that was akin to telling a kid Santa Claus and the Easter Bunny were the biggest parental lies in kid history.

He wasn't even a father and here he was beginning the journey of lying to a kid. Hell, and he was already lying to the woman he was attracted to.

This was the worst pseudo vacation ever.

"The whale's sleeping." He started walking toward the beach. "Maybe he'll come around later. After you have lunch and take a nap. Okay?"

He kissed her cheek for extra measure, feeling like super slime for lying.

"I'm taking Cassidy in," he called to others. "Reagan, you're doing great!"

He knew his enthusiasm wasn't up to his normal, but she was impervious, thank God, as she balanced on the rocking board while three protectors helped her find her feet.

Clarice was waiting for him when he strode out of the water. "I have some great photos of Reagan surfing. Do you want me to send them to you? Maybe their mom would like to see them?"

"Mommy!" Cassidy cried out, waving her wand.

He halted, trying to find his polite smile, the one he used when he had to deal with customer service people or assholes from the FBI who wanted to horn in on his cases. "Thanks. You can send them to my phone, but call me a concerned kind of guy. I'd prefer none of them be posted on social media. In case you were posting about your vacation. I'm a cop, and I'm a little nervous about stuff like that."

Her big brown eyes widened. "I would never put photos of someone else's kids on social media. Especially without asking."

He punched up his smile and patted her arm companionably. "Thanks," he said with an earnestness he didn't have to fake. "Some people don't understand. Even my bros laugh it off, so I'd appreciate you not sending them any photos. It'll save me from having to knock their heads together later if they ignore me and screw up." Okay, that was a total lie too.

"Of course!" She blew out a huge breath, practically grimacing. "Trust me, I get why you'd be protective about that. There are a lot of sickos online. I have creeps messaging me all the time. Oh, never mind. Anyway, if you'll tell me your number, I'll text you right now."

He nodded with another lying smile taxing his mouth. Crisis averted. "Great." Reciting his number to her, he patted her again on the shoulder. "Thanks, Clarice. That was very thoughtful of you. I'm sure their mother would love to see them." That much was true at least...when she finally came out of hiding.

Walking off, he tucked Cassidy up higher on his chest so she could see her sister over his shoulder. God, he deserved a medal for lying under fire, and damn if he wasn't proud of himself.

He'd had her send the photos to his real phone, which was tucked securely in a Faraday bag with Internal Affairs to make sure no one could track them.

CHAPTER FOURTEEN

CHOOSING A DRESS FOR AN UNDERCOVER DATE HAD NEVER been so difficult.

Not that Sheila had seemed to have any issues preparing for her date with Billie. She'd already finished getting dressed. Lily wanted to kick herself as she held up the strapless yellow cotton dress, still worrying over her choice as she regarded herself in the mirror.

"Too much of a *don't touch me* vibe," Sheila commented from her spot on the bed. "After Lieutenant O'Connor routed me soundly today with the photos, we need a dress that will have him either swallowing his tongue—"

"If he does that, he can't give us any info," Lily pointed out, tossing the dress aside onto a spare corner chair.

"Fine." Sheila walked over to her large closet filled with her limited selection of eight summer dresses, all of which had been under ten dollars at the local discount store. "This one. He'll be hot for you, but it'll also show off your sweet, nurturing side."

She'd liked the celery-green shimmery dress the moment she'd spotted it on the end-of-summer sale rack. It hugged her average bodice with its scoop neckline before flaring out flirtingly and stopping just above her knees. Likely no one had gone for it because it wasn't exactly a casual *hang on the beach* dress. The dress was a mix of cotton, spandex, and something else that made it a dress-up or dress-down kind of outfit, depending on the right shoes, hair, and makeup.

"We're walking on the beach, so I'll have to carry the sandals I was thinking of," she commented, crossing to her bathroom to change into it.

"You're wearing those fuck-me pumps, right?" Sheila asked, following her.

Lily slanted her a look. "Hey, I'm changing in here."

"Call me a voyeur." She laughed, fluffing her already blown-out sexy wavy beach hair. "Plus, I have the same parts. Nothing to see here. I'm just glad we don't have to figure out how to carry a gun in these dresses. I don't think Thunderwear would get the job done."

Lily snorted as she pulled on her dress. "I was glad Buck didn't ask me directly if I'd packed mine. On the last undercover op, he told me to keep it in the car since it's not exactly something you can buy at the local clothing store."

"It reminds me of Mormon underwear," Sheila commented. "Don't ask."

Shoulders shaking from silent laughter, Lily pulled a few locks of hair off her face and secured them with a tiny clip. "Good?"

Sheila studied her like she was crashing for a final exam at Quantico. "Yeah. He'll want your hair blowing in the ocean breeze. You aren't going to want it getting stuck in your lip gloss. Because it is so a *come hither, big boy* lipstick kind of night."

"Oh, Sheila, where do you come up with things like that?" she asked, reaching for her mascara.

"Rap mostly. It's the most honest assessment of the male

mind in my opinion. The entire lexicon is like the FBI manual set to music. But really, it doesn't matter if the guy is from the hood or waltzing down Wall Street in a twenty-thousand-dollar suit."

This she had to hear. "How so?" she asked as she curled the brown-coated wand over her lashes.

"One, a man gets money however he can. Two, he'll shoot something if it comes at him or have someone else do it. We're talking murder one and two. Three, if he can fuck it, he will. Every single time. Sometimes he pays. Prostitution, anyone? And don't get me started on the whole, if he can smoke it part..."

Lily clapped. "You should give a special training."

"I'll email a proposal to Buck." Sheila stuck her face next to Lily's in the mirror and smoothed the smudge of mascara in her right corner. "Did I mention it used to drive my mother nuts when I listened to rap? She'd stop in my doorway and say, 'I put men like that in prison every day, Sheila Rae, and they aren't good role models for you to be listening to.'"

"To which you'd reply?" Lily asked, applying her favorite raspberry lip gloss, trying not to think about Robbie kissing it off later. Her nerves were already jumping.

"'Yes, Mother.' I had no voice back then."

Since that was hard to imagine, she patted her partner on the back. "I've met your mother, so I get it. She's formidable."

"Wouldn't be a federal judge if she wasn't." Sheila winked at herself in the mirror. "I sometimes wonder how she would feel if she saw me like this, dolled up like a hottie on an undercover assignment."

They both regarded themselves in the mirror. Looking at them tonight, no one would think they were FBI agents. They both looked their scripted part: two best friends getting ready to go on dates with men they'd met on a beach vacation. "I'd bet she would know it was necessary."

Sheila rubbed the corners of her eyes. "She gets my case files from someone in DC. That I know. And she tells me every Christmas how proud she is of me and all the bad guys I've put away, the justice I've dispensed. But I think she'd lose her shit if she knew about this underbelly of justice. Then again, this is the woman whose sole maternal advice was: if you take the *F* out of life in every situation, you'll remember there's always a lie. Justice balances the lies."

Justice?

"Is that what tonight is about?" Lily asked, turning from the vulnerability in her eyes reflected back at her in the mirror.

Sheila lightly grabbed her shoulders. "Yes! The same way it is when we're sitting in the car for hours surveilling someone, or when I have to give a lap dance to someone on a yacht or at a strip club. The O'Connor boys are good men, but they have information on the likely whereabouts of a very important person of interest. The one who landed in your lap, Sunshine, when your CI told you about the Kellys laundering money through Tara's nail salons."

She nodded. "Thanks for the reminder. I needed it. Sheila, I hate to ask this..."

Her partner rested her hip against the sink. "You wonder if I've ever enjoyed kissing someone undercover when it couldn't be avoided."

"Yes," she said quietly, hoping her blush covered up the sudden heat crawling on her cheeks. "I've evaded it so far."

"Tangled limbs did the job, huh?" Sheila got a rare soft motherly look on her face. "Sure, I have. There was one guy we'd turned as a witness who was going back into a major drug operation with me so we could take down his boss. He was the kind of ripped, charming bad boy I've always found attractive. He wasn't a killer, so he had that going for him."

"Always a plus," she said dryly.

"Word. He was in the sales side with other countries. Spoke four languages. Smart. Posing as his girlfriend not only involved a lot of public PDA but sleeping in the same bed on his boss' yacht for three days and pretending we were having sex at night. Because the boss was paranoid, the room was bugged and videoed, and if we hadn't fooled around—"

"Your cover would have been blown," Lily finished, crossing her arms from the tension she imagined Sheila must have felt in that situation.

"That made it part of the job. So we fooled around, and it got very intense. No full-on penetration but lots of mutual stuff happened. I told myself, how could it not? He was very skilled, and we had chemistry. But when we finished the op, I felt guilty. So every time I did, I looked at the photo of the drug lord I'd helped bring down. Then the guilt would go away. Because if I hadn't gotten onto that yacht and done what I did, I wouldn't have secured the hard evidence we needed to bring him down. It ain't pretty, but it's the job."

Lily tipped her head back and studied the ceiling. "I want to have sex with Robbie."

"I know." Her partner lightly punched her in the arm. "And I want to have sex with Billie."

"But you've got the whole bloody massacre going on," Lily said, gesturing to the loose-fitting purple dress Sheila had chosen.

"Sunshine, don't look so forlorn. Maybe you and Robbie will have sex in the future once the truth is out. I know the status of your love life back in Boston—not that mine is any better. You two certainly seem to fit."

Wincing, she turned away to run a brush through the ends of her hair. "Maybe don't say that now. I'm trying to keep focused on the case."

"Good." Sheila strode to the door, pointing to her wrist-watch. "Because it's showtime."

Lily took one last look at herself and followed her partner down to the kitchen. The men were a minute early with Billie leading the way, decked out in a tight-fitting black T-shirt with freshly washed jeans free of travel wrinkles. His cheeks looked recently kissed by a razor, and when Lily let them in, she scented citrus aftershave when he kissed her sweetly on the cheek, a little surprising, and told her she looked gorgeous. Then he was striding purposefully toward her partner, who gave some kind of shriek. Lily noted Billie had dipped her and was kissing her neck playfully.

When she turned back, Robbie stood silently before her, hands fisted at his sides. She jerked a moment, seeing him in the same white button-down shirt and slacks he'd been wearing when they'd first spotted him at the Beacon Hill gym. Then she reasoned it was probably the nicest clothing he had with him and found her ability to smile at him. He'd wanted to look nice for her.

His mouth took some persuading too, his smile slow to reach his ocean blue eyes. "My brother's right. You do look gorgeous, but I hope you're okay with me not dipping you like that moron."

She suddenly felt unsure of herself and finally remembered to let him inside. "No dipping needed. I wouldn't want you to drop me."

He stopped close to her, inches away, his heat and musky male scent making her head swim. "I would never drop you, Summer."

The truth was in his gaze, throwing her insides into turmoil. Her heart started its telltale rat-a-tat-tat in her chest. A fuzzy sensation filled her head. And goodness, her skin tingled with an electricity it had never experienced before. But it was the warmth spreading through her, giving her a kind of floating feeling, that had her the most worried.

Feeling like this about a guy was a rarity for her. Being

with a good guy like Robbie would be a gift. She knew it down to her toes. *Oh, please, Robbie, let's not screw this up because I think you're feeling the same way even though we're both lying to each other.*

"Do you want a drink?" she asked, stepping back to give herself space to breathe. "Sheila didn't make margaritas, but I noticed the beer you drank last night and made sure we had it stocked."

"That was nice of you." He cupped her arm as she started for the fridge, a gesture so shocking she jerked a moment before laughing at herself. "What are you drinking?" he asked.

Lily glanced over at Sheila and Billie. The other O'Connor brother had Sheila nicely caged between his body and the end of the kitchen island, where he was whispering something in her ear that had her partner's shoulders shaking with laughter. "I could do white wine. Clarice?"

Her partner tipped her head back from Billie. "It seems we're taking a short drive."

Lily pursed her lips. That wasn't something Billie had mentioned when he'd asked for a date, but then again, he'd said he was going to surprise her. But she knew Sheila could handle it.

"I thought you two might enjoy a drink alone since Robbie wants to stay close to home," Billie told her with a wink. "We won't be long."

"Take as long as you'd like," Lily said with a smile as they left holding hands and grinning at each other.

"No, he won't," Robbie said when they were alone. "We had an agreement about keeping you guys out too late. You both had a huge day helping Reagan learn how to surf and playing with the girls."

So he was setting boundaries. Of course he was. He was a man who didn't allow himself much freedom.

Feeling on firmer ground, she opened the fridge for

Robbie's beer and the wine bottle. "That's understanding of you." She handed him the beer and went to the cabinet for a wineglass.

The sound of him popping the beer reached her as she poured herself some wine. Extending her glass, she said, "I usually work with kids, so a little teaching doesn't faze me. Reagan and Cassidy must have been tired though. And then there's you...the self-proclaimed grandpa who complained to me about our pace this morning."

Any struggle he'd been having with himself disappeared, and he flashed her that hot, challenging grin she couldn't get enough of. "Grandpa's got plenty of energy in him, don't you worry. Especially when he's watching you in that dress. What is that color?"

She laid her elbows on the counter after strategically positioning herself across from him at the kitchen island. "Celery."

"They named a color after that pathetic vegetable?" His brow knit in bafflement before he gave a snarky laugh. "I hate that stuff. It's always on some sad veggie plate at a holiday party next to those bone-dry carrots no one wants to eat. Ranch dip can't even make it edible. But I'm off my point. I've never seen a woman wear celery, but it's never looked more captivating. You really are a beautiful woman, Summer."

That darn heat was spreading over her cheeks again, making her feel like a young woman with her first crush. "Thank you. I see you cleaned up."

"I didn't think shorts and a T-shirt would do for a night with you." He tipped his beer back, studying her while he was drinking. "And my tux was at the cleaners."

"Funny." She took a sip of wine, feeling her body loosen. She was relaxing around him, and it felt good. Even though she was undercover, she felt like she could be herself. God, this was the weirdest op ever.

"So...we're having a drink as we planned. Do you want to sit outside? It's still muggy but the sunsets here are pretty spectacular. We might catch the big orange ball before it gets swallowed in the ocean. That's how Reagan describes it, at least."

She came around the island slowly, unable to look away from his blue eyes. "They're really sweet girls," she said with an easy smile. "Getting to know them and the rest of your family has been a lovely surprise." That was true, at least.

"You mean that." He set his beer down when she reached him and traced her jaw lightly, making her knees give for a moment—a first. "Don't think I didn't realize you were choosing to put a barrier between us before. But we both know why, don't we?"

Her breathing turned shaky as his finger trailed slowly down her neck, a weapon of fire. God, she wanted to be covered in it, every single pore of her skin.

"Because both of us are trying to fight this," he said almost harshly as he gently traced the neckline of her bodice, making her nipples hard. "I told you this morning that I didn't expect this. But Summer...meeting you has been one of the best parts of the trip."

"You mean that," she echoed in shock, making him chuckle in a *low-octave, make her girly parts sizzle* way.

"You can take it to the bank." He made a crossing motion over his heart, and she felt the absence of his touch way too much. "I'd planned to fight it by allotting us thirty minutes for a drink and then another thirty for our walk."

She bit her lip to hold back her very pleased smile. "I got a sense you were trying to manage our time together. It's kinda hot."

His chuckle was rusty and out of practice. "This is the first sign of sick humor I've seen in you. I kinda like it. Summer, I don't want to have a beer. All I want is to kiss you senseless. Maybe run my hands over you and try and push out of my mind the fact that your dress color was inspired by someone's love for celery."

Laughing now as well, she didn't move as he slid closer, brushing the fronts of their bodies together, making her laughter stop. Their eyes met again, his burning with amused heat, a look she wanted to get lost in. Instead, she pointed to the clock on the wall. "But we're barely ten minutes into your first time allotment. Doesn't that seem reckless?"

He gave a rough sigh. "I'm not a reckless man. Everything I do is about cleaning up after other people's recklessness. But you make me want to get a little reckless even though I know it will only lead to stupidity."

She angled back to study his face. "What kind of stupidity?"

"Forgetting this can't go anywhere."

For a moment, she wondered why he'd concluded that. Because he thought she lived in Florida? Because everyone thought vacation romances didn't last? Or because he was closed off after his divorce? God, she was starting to have as many questions about their personal interactions as she did the job.

He reached for his beer. "You said this was fast for you. I'm suddenly talking like someone put a quarter in me. Maybe we should take our drinks outside."

"Do you want me to bring the kitchen timer with us?" she joked, hoping to bring back some levity to both her thoughts and their time together.

"Only if you long for speed dating," he quipped, opening the patio door.

She grabbed her wine and stepped outside, Robbie following closely behind, the heat and promise of him singeing her. "Well, while I haven't attended an event, it does hold a certain logic. Asking questions of each other for five minutes beyond the initial *do I find you attractive?* assessment is very efficient."

He pulled her patio chair out before she could reach for it and waited for her to be seated. "Okay, I'm shocked. I'd pegged you for a romantic."

"And yet you didn't bring me flowers or chocolates," she said with a sigh, pressing her hand to her forehead dramatically. "If Tim were here, he'd have a good Shakespeare quote. I've got nothing."

"Not a fan?" He slid into his chair. "That's a point in your favor. You had me fooled with all the wand and crown stuff."

"Are we keeping score?" She sipped her wine. "Does running time count as a point?"

He shifted in his seat. "Grandpa is going to be crying uncle way too early tomorrow. I'm a little embarrassed to tell you why."

She kicked back in her chair, crossing her ankles. "I love that we've agreed it's a morning thing, my kicking your ass."

He grunted. "I prefer to think of it as you being a serious drill sergeant helping me up my game."

"So what's your excuse?"

"I fell in the shower and bruised my ass. My glutes are killing me."

Leaning closer, she narrowed her eyes. "You fell?"

"Are you inching closer so you can try and see my bruise? I can stand up if you want to give it a thorough examination."

The idea of seeing his naked butt had her breath arresting in her chest. She could kiss it and make it better. Instead, she pulled a Sheila and fluffed her hair. "I'm not in any hurry."

"Liar."

She jolted.

He immediately took her hand. "Whoa! You should see the look on your face. I was just kidding. Clearly, I went too far."

No, he'd only reminded her they were both lying to each other. "Fine. I do want to see your butt, but not when it's five different shades of eggplant and celery."

His look was endearing, almost boyish. "I'm never going to hear the end of that. I should just have said you looked pretty. When a guy gets into colors, he's in trouble. You'd think I would know that from having two artists in the family who are women."

She knew about his sister, Kathleen, the metal artist living in Ireland. Of course, she couldn't let on that she knew. "Who? If family questions aren't too personal."

"I've just talked about my bruised ass," he said with a lopsided grin she'd never seen on him before. "Plus, you've met two of my brothers. I have four others. But the women are my sisters. One by blood, Kathleen, the youngest of the lot, who's loved making things out of metal since we took her to a junkyard as a kid. The other one is her best friend and kinda adopted sister. She works in stained glass. They both live in Ireland now and are rising artists. We couldn't be prouder of them."

The love he had for his family had already been evident from his willingness to take off and protect two little girls. But the sheer joy in his words as much as his lighthearted expression opened a door to a greater understanding of him. Sure, he was sweet with the girls. But they were kids. These women... He adored them. "No wonder you're so good with the girls. Clearly you started early, with your sister and her friend."

"I was eleven when Kathleen was born." He lifted a shoulder. "Ellie came way later, but they make it easy, being all independent and full of sass. That's how women in our family are. What about you? Is family talk too personal?"

Her mouth turned dry. "No, only tragic. We're better off

talking about your bruised butt. Do you want to tell me how you fell in the shower?"

His perusal of her was intense, as if he was trying to unlock her secrets. In that moment she could see how he would be a good listener with a victim but also a patient interrogator. "I'm not sure I like the sound of tragic. Maybe it's the cop in me, but it pushes my buttons. Hell...it's more than that. I want to know more about you. Are you sure you don't want to talk about it?"

She lifted her wine to her mouth to cover her surprise, drinking slowly to give herself a moment. Usually anyone who heard her typical deflection was happy to change the subject. Usually she kept that part of her life sealed.

Her mentor had told her she'd seen victims join law enforcement with good intentions only for their pasts to haunt them. Brie hadn't wanted that for her, and neither had Lily, so she had accepted every referral Brie had made for her. She'd pored over her past in therapy as a teenager and later as a young woman, making sure there were no more tentacles waiting to take her down. It had been hard work, and she was damn proud of it. It had paid off. "It's really dark and not something I share often. My ex got all fidgety and didn't talk to me for two days after I told him." But the pull to share something real with him was so strong because there had been so many lies.

He set his beer on the table and leaned back. "I'm not your ex, and I don't spook easily."

No, he would set his shoulders and face whatever came— like he was doing with Tara's girls. "I didn't expect to veer into a personal direction tonight."

His smile was rueful. "Neither did I, but here we are. Honestly, I'm kinda glad. My personal confession of the night —I'm tired of the shallowness of dating. Have been for a while. Maybe I am turning into a grandpa, or Tim is right about me turning hard after my divorce. But this conversation feels more meaningful than any of the dumb first-date conversations I've had about my hobbies since I know I can't say I love the intricacies of pulling fingerprints, matching DNA, and putting away bad guys."

She couldn't help but spurt out a laugh. At some point in the future, she hoped they could talk about that because she rather liked the smell of gunpowder after firing her weapon. "All right, here goes. I was raised in a foster home after I turned twelve, taken away from my mother by a court order. Part of a larger case..."

Stop talking like an FBI agent, Lily.

Inhaling deeply, she set her wine aside. "My mother was into the *free love, smoke anything* movement that runs in some New Age circles. She ran away from home as a teenager, hooked up with some other street kids, and ended up at a community farm and ashram. Think hippies back in the sixties. She didn't know who my dad was since everyone slept with everyone as part of some universal bullshit about love and nonattachment."

His mouth tightened a fraction, and she had to give him credit for keeping his gaze open.

"We raised our own food. Made our own clothes. Self-sustainable living. As a kid, it wasn't bad. I went to a local school, but no one thought I was weird for living in a community like that. It was California. To this day, I can still make better yogurt than anything you can buy in the grocery store."

"What changed?" he asked, crossing his arms now, looking imposing.

An image of her mother surfaced from that time, her long hennaed hair pulled back with that vacant look in her green eyes. "My mother got a little bored. Her drug intake wasn't doing the job anymore, I think, so she started looking for something else. She and a few other friends heard about this incredible guru who had started an open community everyone in their New Age circles was raving about. She joined his cult when I was ten."

His mouth hardened, but he didn't move. His eyes remained soft on her, waiting for her to continue.

"The drugs were more hallucinogenic. We didn't just meditate as a community. We listened to this guru go on and on about... It doesn't matter. Spiritual stuff that impresses people seeking those kinds of things. I didn't like him from the first."

She could still see his wavy blond hair and piercing blue eyes, his arms muscular from yoga and surfing. Shivering, she cleared her throat and folded her hands together tightly.

"He...had this way of putting his hand on you—like he was blessing you with his presence. It made always me want to shift away. Anyway, long story short. Everyone treated him like a god. It was considered an honor to have sex with him. But he also believed it was his duty as a spiritual god on earth to initiate girls into womanhood, so when they had their first period, they were sent to him."

Robbie's blue eyes turned into glacier ice. "That moth-erfucker."

"Yeah." She cleared her throat, remembering her older friends coming back in shock, sometimes with their shirts inside out or their skirts on backward. "He was smart and told them never to talk about what happened. That it was their divine part to keep what had happened between them a secret. The parents knew, sanctioned it even, so they helped keep what he was doing secret. They didn't see it as wrong."

"I've arrested people like that, and I still can't fathom allowing that kind of abuse," he said tightly. "Keep going."

Taking a breath, she continued. "Anyway, he made the mistake of buying and selling some pretty serious drugs and doing some human trafficking on the side, not to mention tax evasion. His community was raided by law enforcement officials. It happened two months before my first period."

This time he shook his head. "Jesus, I don't imagine it's easy to see that as luck, but in my neighborhood, we'd say someone was looking out for you."

Her mouth was dry, but she nodded. She didn't mention how Brie had pulled her aside at one point and told her not to tell anyone if she got her period. "I *was* lucky, but other girls weren't. I had to get over my guilt about that—along with a whole lot of anger that my mother couldn't wait for me to get my period so I could be 'blessed' by the guru. She was so high and crazy by then, she made it easy for the court to place me with another family. They were nice people, but I didn't really feel like I fit in. Anyway, that's the story."

"You're talking about that cult in Marin, right? About twenty some years ago?"

"North of Petaluma, yes." Her mouth parted as shock hit her. "Not too many people put that together. Although it did make national news."

"I was planning on going into the police academy, so I started paying attention to those kinds of stories." He extended his hand, which she took, liking the way his fingers curled around hers. "The cop in me has a million questions. But the man before you wants to say you're a remarkable woman. No wonder you went into a profession where you could help kids."

More shock. Her ex hadn't understood. Of course, Robbie didn't know what her real profession was. "You got that, huh? Well, enough story time. Do you want to take that walk on the beach?"

He didn't let go of her hand as he stood. "Sure. How do you feel when you talk about it now?"

Her smile was easier as she rose from her chair. "Free, honestly. It was another life, one that planted the seeds for who I ended up becoming. My good friend and mentor always told me that you have to take the good from everything you face—even if you have to squeeze hard to find a single drop. That's what I did."

He brought her close against his body and cupped her face with his free hand, his touch soft. "Yeah, you sure did. And I admire the hell out of you for it."

His eyes shone with tenderness and something she didn't want to name. But the intimacy between them was undeniable. They had grown closer from her sharing. Fallen even harder for each other. Neither of them could deny it. She was pretty sure neither of them wanted to. "Don't kiss me now. I'd rather we wait until there's a little more romance. If that's okay."

The smile that broke over that sexy mouth of his had her muscles going lax and heat spreading through her belly. "I'll rein myself in, but I think you know how badly I want to kiss you. Your story only made me want it more. Before you were just a girl I really liked that I met on vacation. Now, you're someone I'm... Maybe we should start walking."

Neither of them moved.

Was her breathing harsh to his ears suddenly? It was to hers, and all because he didn't dare finish what he was saying. She hadn't imagined it.

"Summer Sunshine," he mused, tracing her cheek. "Now I understand your name."

She wanted to lower her head and bang it against his chest. Just when they were growing closer, she'd been reminded of the reality of their situation. Of the fact that he didn't know her name, and she wasn't supposed to know he wasn't the girls' father.

Finally, she shook herself and tugged on his hand, starting toward the beach. "I'll race you to the water," she said, already unstrapping her heels one-handed before they reached the sand.

His hand only tightened more firmly around hers. "No way. Grandpa here just wants to take a stroll with the most amazing and beautiful woman in the world."

Her heart rolled over in her chest as she let her shoes fall. "Robbie... You're not so bad yourself. Since we're talking personal, can I ask why you became a cop?" Because she knew so many details about him, but not the why underneath, and that was what made him who he was, the man she wanted to know everything about.

He leaned to the side and toed off his shoes, dispensing with his socks before pulling her forward with him. "Sure. I think you know we're from Boston, but do you know about the neighborhood Southie?"

God, here she went. "Like from *The Departed*? Clarice loves that movie, but it's a little violent for my taste."

His sigh was long-suffering. "Yeah. That one. Don't get Billie going about how that movie kicks *Good Will Hunting*'s butt. The stale narrative about Southie is that it's rough, crime-ridden, and run by the mob. Mostly true. There is also a strong sense of community and people who live by a code. My parents were like that. Well, my dad still is. My mother passed."

"I'm sorry," she said, even though she'd already known.

"Anyway, I worked as a stock boy for a grocery store in the neighborhood. I'd known Mr. Kincaid since I was a kid. My mom shopped there, and when she wasn't looking, he'd sneak me a lollipop or a piece of bubble gum. He was always smiling. Loved kids. It was one of the happiest days of my life when he asked if I'd help him at his store. I was twelve. And yes, I know I was too young according to child labor laws, but it wasn't like that."

She wondered if he'd bust the man now for that kind of an

infraction, but she remained mute on that subject. "He sounds nice."

The roar of the surf filled the silence. He looked off toward the ocean, the silver and blue twilight highlighting his chiseled features. "Yeah. The best. His family and my family went to the same church, school, baseball field. You name it. His wife got cancer, and the treatments were expensive since insurance never covers it all. He fell behind in his protection money, and that's when my life changed for the second time."

Lily could guess what was coming next, so she stopped on the beach and faced him, pressing a hand to his chest. His smile lit up his face, and she went all soft inside when he covered her hand and stepped closer, making them a unit.

"I was in the store when two tough guys from a local mob family showed up, demanded he pay his tab, and then proceeded to break things in his store. I tried to stop them, and one of them grabbed me. Started tapping me on the cheeks and telling me I'd better learn to keep out of other people's business. I can't tell you how angry that made me. Being humiliated in front of a man who was a hero to me. Mr. Kincaid told them to take whatever they wanted, he'd get the money, but they had to let me go."

Lily found she was holding her breath because she knew something bad was coming.

"The lead guy—because there's always someone in charge —tapped Mr. Kincaid on the chin with his powerful fist and said that wasn't good enough. Then he turned to me and said I was going to be his lesson about being late with their money. He signaled to his buddy, and before I could blink, he jerked up my arm and broke it."

She touched his face. "Oh my God! No."

He kissed her palm. "You're sweet. And yes, that sucked. Mr. Kincaid went to pieces, and trust me, reducing a man like him to tears was a feat. My arm hurt, so I had an excuse. But he just held me in his lap and rocked me after they left, saying over and over again how sorry he was."

Unable to help herself, she wrapped her arms around him, the scene vivid in her mind. "Those bastards!"

He nuzzled her neck. "Such language. But I like it. Honestly, while it was awful, my mind was totally clear. Like crystal clear. I kept telling Mr. Kincaid that he had nothing to apologize for. Those mob guys did, and they deserved to be punished. That was the day I decided I was going to grow up and stop guys like that from hurting young kids like me and old men like Mr. Kincaid."

She leaned back and ran her hands down his arm. "Which side was it?"

"My right, which really pissed me off. I was the pitcher for our baseball team."

Kissing the upper bicep, where she imagined that kind of forcible contact would break a bone, she laid her head against it. "Seems like we both saw a pretty nasty side of humanity when we were about the same age. I was twelve too when..."

She trailed off. That was when she'd decided to become like Brie—an FBI agent. Of course, back then she hadn't known she'd need to have another career before applying, but she hadn't minded being a teacher because she'd known it was leading to her ultimate goal.

As she looked at Robbie's face, she desperately wanted to tell him her whole story. Would she ever be able to do that? Did she need to plant the seeds now? Before he found out the truth of who she was?

"You understand me better than any woman I've ever met, Summer Sunshine."

That did it. She cupped his strong jaw and met his gaze. "I know we've just met, but I have to be honest. You understand me better than any man I've met too. I told you this is rare for me. I wish I could explain how much. Do you...ever wonder if this thing between us could continue?"

His eyes narrowed. "I've wished I could have met you under normal circumstances. That sounds weird. Let me clarify. Like out on the town in Boston or at a friend's BBQ."

"I've thought about that too," she said softly. "I know it seems impossible. We've just met and have different lives. But I just want you to know I wish there wasn't an end to us knowing each other. And that's where I'll stop."

She lowered her hands from his jaw, telling herself to regain her balance. Give them both a little space after the intensity of their sharing. When she started to step away, he tugged her back to him.

"Oh, no, you don't." His hands framed her face. "Don't pull away from me. This entire evening has been a deep dive into knowing each other, and I don't want that to change. Summer, I wish we could keep seeing each other too. I just have no idea how that could happen, so right now, I'm telling myself to soak up every single moment I can with the most beautiful and special woman in the world."

"Oh, Robbie," she said, closing the distance between them and stepping into the warmth of his body. "I wish everything weren't so complicated."

"Hey! Don't get all sad on me. You asked for romance earlier before I kissed you. Right now, I wish I had a red rose or something to tuck behind your ear."

God, who knew he could be this sweet? "Maybe you could find me a seashell?"

He levered back and slanted her a look. "Tomorrow, when it's light out, I will take Cassidy and Reagan on a seashell hunting excursion for the best seashell on this beach. But I'm afraid it's getting dark, and all I can think about now is that I won't be able to see the jellyfish washed up on the beach."

She twined her arms around his waist. "Maybe you wanting to protect me is romantic enough."

"You should aim higher," he said, enclosing her in his embrace. "You deserve more. Summer, you deserve everything."

The blues of his eyes were darker now, in the scant light, but the desire was as clear as the rising moon. "All I want right now is for you to kiss me."

"Then we'd better make it count," he whispered before laying his lips over hers.

The frisson of heat as their mouths met rocked her back. His hands kept her in place as they learned each other's textures, sipping softly as their heartbeats started to race. Her eyelids drifted shut on a breathy sigh when he kissed the corner of her mouth. Wanting more of him, she threaded her fingers into his thick black hair and pressed him closer to her heat, closer to where she needed him. His breathing fractured, increasing the pressure of their mouths until she opened hers and let him in.

His tongue swept inside, sending a jolt through her, making her tighten her arms around him with an agonized moan. He answered with a guttural sound as she traced his tongue, dancing with him. The tide surged around her feet, but he was there to steady her against him. His mouth. His body. His hands. They all kept her grounded as his mouth did wicked things to her and made her want more.

She slid her hands around to his front, wanting to feel the power of his pounding heart against her palms. He wrapped his hands around her hips and pulled her tightly to him. His erection was obvious, and feeling it against her had her moaning again. "Oh, God, Robbie," she said, wrenching her mouth away.

His mouth followed. "Not yet," he whispered harshly as she heard a car door slam in the distance. "God, not yet."

The kiss took on more urgent demands, and his hands slid down to her bottom, grinding her against him. She felt a rush of heat in her middle so strong she threw her head back, crying out softly.

"Yes, that's right. Moan for me. Tell me what you need."

She needed *him*. Her body knew it, and she feared her heart did too. "We're getting out of control here."

"I know." He pressed his forehead to hers. "I know, and I still can't seem to stop touching you."

Inciting words, ones she couldn't ignore. She tugged his head down for a kiss. This time she took the lead, sweeping her tongue inside and making him groan.

A porch light went on, pulling her awareness toward it. Heated voices sounded. She slid her mouth to his jaw, kissing it softly, her eyes going toward the disturbance. She spotted Tim standing in the light with another petite woman, his hand on her arm—

Tara O'Connor.

"Oh, my..." Her training kicked in. She took in the understated nature of the woman's clothing, so different from her usual *see me* outfits shot with bling, but she knew that profile like the back of her hand. "You have a visitor."

Robbie's head swung toward the house. "Jesus Christ!" His hands slid slowly from her, and she had a moment to take in his poleaxed expression before his face transformed into one filled with unadulterated emotion.

Then he was running toward the woman. Tim's hand dropped from her, and Tara started running too. They met halfway to the house, wrapping their arms around each other. For a moment, she was arrested by the sight. God, they really loved each other. She'd never had anyone love her that fiercely. What would it be like?

Catching herself, she dug her nails into her palms so she could focus. Lily started walking, her heart battling with the lingering desire from their kiss. She needed to flip her internal switch so she could feel the excitement that their case had just broken wide open.

When she reached them, Robbie had his hands on Tara's haggard face, one devoid of practically any makeup. She'd transformed herself by going plain with a nearly frumpy outfit of neutral shirt and shorts with ugly white tennis shoes. What a change. Lily was impressed.

"Are you okay?" Robbie finally managed with a hoarse voice. "Jesus, Tara, do you have any idea how much you scared me?" Then he was pulling her to him in another fierce hug.

Tim walked over to Lily, valiantly trying to smile. "So this must seem weird, but we heard the girls' mom was almost in an accident earlier, and it totally freaked us out. My brothers didn't mention it because they wanted their time with you and Clarice to go well. I mean, Robbie and Tara might not be right for each other romantically, but they still share a family. You know?"

Lily nearly blinked multiple times in shock. Who would have thought Shakespeare would be so good at lying on his feet? "I'm glad she's okay. Was the near accident on the way here?"

"No, it was on her way home from work before she headed out." He heaved out a breath. "Long story. Her work stuff changed, so she decided to pop down. She really missed the girls. And despite them getting divorced, she and Robbie have a strong bond. But it doesn't mean anything."

"Good to know." How sweet of Tim to try and manage her relationship with Robbie. But he couldn't realize why she was so impacted by the sight of their affection. As she watched Robbie and Tara hold on to each other, she felt swept away by the love they had for each other. Tara had run scared after the fire in the nail salon and come straight to the one man she knew she could count on.

Heck, that was more than love. That was loyalty.

"You wouldn't happen to know if Clarice is back with your brother, would you?" she asked, wishing her partner were here for backup.

Did she reveal herself as an FBI agent right now or wait until Sheila was with her?

Later, she decided. She didn't want Tara to run. The woman's face had looked haggard before she'd hugged Robbie with all her strength. She would likely be more cooperative if she talked with her cousin, saw her girls, and got some sleep. Neither Robbie nor Billie was going to slip away without saying goodbye to them. After tonight, Lily was sure of that. She and Robbie had crossed into new territory. When she revealed herself as an agent, it was going to be a total shock to Robbie too. The whole situation had to be handled delicately.

"Ahem," Tim said, clearing his throat loudly.

Robbie's head turned, finally noticing his brother. Tara pulled back, and with the porch light, Lily watched the woman's eyes narrow in suspicion. Of course they did. This woman had been terrorized. Lily would be suspicious too in her place.

"Tara," Tim began, clearing his throat again. "This is our neighbor, Summer. She and her best friend are here on vacation too. Billie is off with Clarice tonight. They've been terrific with the girls. Wait until you see the magic wands Summer brought over."

Robbie seemed to shake himself, looking down at Tara before glancing over at Lily. She could almost hear him say *oh, shit* in his mind.

"Hi, Tara," she said, forcing a smile at her person of interest. "I've heard so much about you."

I can't wait to interview you and nail the Kellys.

"Hi, Summer." The woman's forced smile fell quickly from

her face. "I didn't realize Robbie and Billie had met anyone on their vacation."

Robbie scrubbed his face. "Everything since the day we left Boston has been one surprise after the other."

Tara only raised her perfectly waxed eyebrows at him, crossing her arms. Even though she was five-four and tiny in comparison to her older cousin, Lily could see her backbone. Tara wasn't going to make things easy for them.

A patio door slicked open somewhere, and moments later Billie and Sheila appeared. "Hey, we heard— Oh, Jesus!"

Billie lurched forward, scooping his cousin up and twirling her around. "You had us crazy out of our minds, girl."

Sheila had a smug look on her face, and Lily met her gaze. She shook her head subtly. Her partner knew the code. She was telling Sheila to hold back, that they wouldn't introduce themselves as FBI right out of the gate. Her partner only batted her eyelashes in response. Lily winced. She knew what that meant too. *Fine, but I'm still going to press for information.*

"Hey, big boy!" Sheila called, cocking her hip. "Do you want to tell me who you have all scooped up and cozy like? Because I might be getting jealous."

Billie set Tara down, his mouth falling open, clearly speechless. Tara cocked her own hip in response and glared at Sheila. "I'm his brother's ex-wife, that's what," the woman answered, an edge in her voice. "Which means I'm family."

Sheila's mouth pursed like she was a little put off by that answer. "Interesting... I thought Robbie here had the girls for a couple of weeks while you were working."

Lily fought a wince. Sheila adored pressing their subjects with questions when everyone was off-balance. She insisted it was the best way to shake information loose.

"There was a change in plans," the woman responded, a bit haughtily. "I'm going inside. Should I wake the girls now or should we catch up first? You know how Cassidy and Reagan get when they see their mommy."

Tara might as well have lifted her leg and given a little tinkle by how proprietary she sounded. Lily bit her lip, waiting to see how Robbie was going to handle things.

He pinched the bridge of his nose before looking up. "I hate to call it a night, but we should probably hear about Tara's change of plans. Seeing as how it affects the girls. Right, Billie?"

His brother nodded solemnly before walking over to Sheila, closing his hands on her arms, and bending to meet her gaze. "Sorry to cut our night short, sweetheart. Catch you in the morning?"

She ran her finger slowly down his chest. "Not if I catch you first, handsome."

As Billie leaned down and kissed her partner sweetly on the mouth, Lily looked over at Robbie. His inner conflict was evident from his locked jaw and creased brow. He strode forward, touching her arm softly. "This wasn't how I wanted our night to end, but this concerns the girls."

She could tell he was hoping she'd understand—like they'd discussed. As she traced his jaw, she hoped *he* would understand when he found out the truth.

Because this was her last call as Summer Sunshine.

"I totally understand." She kissed his cheek as her heart wrenched. "We'll talk tomorrow."

Nodding, he strode over to Tara, putting a protective arm around her and leading her inside. Billie lifted his hand before following. Tim did the same after giving them a rueful smile.

Sheila cozied up next to her as the porch light went dark. "Well, it seems our little friend was flushed out after all."

"Yes," she replied, chewing her lip. "We're not going to be able to go with a normal approach here."

"No, things have gotten pretty personal, and that's when

people's backs get up." Sheila glanced over. "How was your date?"

She winced. "Wonderful. Emotional. Complicating."

Her partner uttered a reluctant laugh before saying, "Mine too. I hate to say this, but Robbie is the key here. We have to persuade him of our next steps."

"I know." She rubbed her arms against the sudden chill in the air, dread already rising inside her. "God, it's gotten cold."

"Feel your promotion in the air," Sheila told her, bumping her with a hip. "Tara and her girls are going to be able to go home because of us. We're going to bring those bad guys down for good. That will warm you up. Come on. We need to strategize and then call Buck."

Lily let herself take one last look at where Robbie had disappeared.

Right now, she felt like their budding relationship was as wild and unpredictable as one of the waves crashing to shore. Well, she had mastered the way to stand tall and work with the elements she was given. They cared about each other, and she hoped they both could ride that wave once he got over the shock of learning who she really was. But she couldn't just leave that to fate.

She needed a plan to get Robbie to trust her and cooperate with them to bring the Kellys down, and it had to be flawless.

He'd become too important to her—his family as well, Tara included—for her to lose him.

She was not going to let anyone down, least of all herself.

CHAPTER FIFTEEN

THE MOMENT THEY WERE INSIDE THE FAMILY ROOM, Robbie pulled Tara to him again, Billie and Tim be damned.

"What happened?" Because he knew she was running scared from the way she'd started trembling the moment he wrapped his arms around her.

"The Kellys set a fire at my main nail salon this morning." His arms tightened around her when her voice hitched, helping him suppress the rage rising inside of him. "The chairs were full. My clients had to run barefooted into the street. My ladies held up, but they looked terrified. I didn't know what to do."

He rocked her as Billie and Tim patted her back tenderly, their faces tense with the same combination of anger and worry battling inside him. "You did good to come here. They meant to scare you, Tara. All the way back to Boston."

"I know!" She pressed her face into his chest before raising her troubled, mascara-smudged eyes to his. "And I knew it would be the stupidest move ever to go back. But I can't leave my nail girls hanging like that. Or my clients. Robbie, I drove here the whole day from Cincinnati—"

"Why Cincinnati?" Billie broke in before Robbie could ask.

"Because it was over twelve hours away from Boston, like the Outer Banks, and I thought it would work in my favor that it's not a common tourism destination. I figured it was smart to be about twelve hours from everything—including my girls. God, it was a long drive today, but I knew I finally had to meet up with you. Robbie, promise me you can look after the girls and me. Otherwise, I'll..."

"Hey!" Billie said, punching her lightly. "Don't you see three O'Connors here? Tara, we've got you and the girls. But Jesus, you scared us!"

Robbie finally pulled back to study her. She looked scared too. Her usually perfect makeup was understated, and her hair was pulled back into a serviceable ponytail. She had on a plain brown T-shirt and tan shorts along with pitifully ugly old ladies' white sneakers. Was this Tara's version of undercover?

"You did a really good job with everything," he said in a soothing tone. "I mean, look at you. Nothing to make you stand out or draw attention to yourself. Exactly what you should do on the run."

"I know!" She rubbed her nose, which was dripping. "Look, I hated scaring you, but I had to make a decision, and separating—"

"It's fine," Robbie said. "We work from now. Okay, let's sit down and talk this out. I should probably check my computer—"

"Your computer!" Tara practically shouted. "But you can't—"

"It's encrypted and untraceable," he assured her, taking her shoulders and looking into her wild eyes. "Now, take a few deep breaths."

Tim handed her a tissue as she did her best to suck in air.

He could see her pulse beating fiercely in her neck, a combo of shock and stress. He hated seeing normal victim behavior in her—his family. Billie started to open his mouth, but Robbie shot him a look. He glared at him but stayed quiet.

His mind started to play out various scenarios. If the Kellys were willing to start a fire, it meant they didn't think their money was on the premises. "When did the fire happen?"

She sniffed and blew her nose. "After eight sometime. I saw the reports on the morning news online. I watch it every day and pore through *The Boston Globe* for info. But there wasn't anything until today."

"I'll need to watch that footage and check my messages." He kissed the top of her head. "I checked my computer before the fire, so I didn't know about it. I need to find out who's running point—"

"Not to butt into police work," Tim said, wrapping an arm around Tara. "But have you eaten anything today, sweetheart?"

She shook her head. "No, I just...went to pieces and then sat down and thought things through. When I decided the best option was coming here, I packed and jumped in the car."

"Let me fix you something," Tim said, glancing Robbie's way to make sure he wasn't stepping on toes.

"That's a good idea." He let out the breath he'd been holding as well, but it didn't diminish the weight pressing suddenly on his shoulders. She was here, she was scared, and the Kellys had just taken another shot at her.

"Then we should talk about when you want to see the girls," Tim continued calmly. "Because they've missed you despite all the fun we've been having. The kids are doing great, Tara."

"I'm so glad!" She put her face in her hands. "You have no idea how scared I was for them."

"All right now," Tim said, continuing to earn Robbie's respect with his measured, thoughtful approach. "We've got you."

Robbie spotted the feline before it started to weave figure eights around Tara's feet. She bent down with a cry and scooped up the cat. "Oh, Miss Purrfect!"

As she snuggled the cat, he caught the unblinking stare it gave him. He gestured to Tara, wishing he could say: *Look, fleabag. I'm taking care of your mistress. So cut the attitude.*

"An omelet okay, Tara?" Tim asked.

"I don't think I can eat anything, but I'll try." She buried her face in the white fur again and then put the cat back on the floor.

Robbie stepped back when the cat settled at her feet like a little feline sentinel. *Like* you *could shoot bad guys.* God, he was being bitchy, he realized. Was it because his body was still processing all the lust stirred up by his date? He thought about the abrupt end of his evening with Summer. Up until Tara had arrived, he'd been having one of the best nights of his life. Now it would all have to come to an end.

Probably.

They'd talked about continuing to see each other, but for the foreseeable future, his entire focus had to be on Tara and the girls, especially when things with the Kellys were escalating. He needed to talk to his partner. Stat.

"Tara, sweetheart, why don't you go into the kitchen with Tim?" Robbie suggested, trying to send her a smile. "I bet you didn't drink much today either."

She stroked her throat. "I am thirsty, now that you mention it."

Robbie kissed her temple and urged her in Tim's direction. "Totally normal. Go follow Tim. We'll be there in a sec, sweetheart."

Billie nudged him in the side after she had gone, Miss Purrfect giving him a final once-over before following. "I can see the smoke already," his brother said quietly. "I'm glad you're already working things out. But what can I do? I can't make a fucking omelet, and right now, I'm feeling a little out of sorts about Clarice and really pissed at these Kelly assholes. Robbie, I want to break them into little pieces."

Robbie took another deep breath, falling into that quiet place he went to after being called to a crime scene. "You can help me to check to make sure there's no one watching the house."

"You think someone could have followed her?" Billie asked sharply.

"I don't think so, or they would have picked her up already," he answered. "But I want to be sure. I'm going to check the back. Can you take the front? Pick a good place in the window with the best view of the street and give it about two minutes. Usually that's long enough to spot someone shifting position if they're surveilling from a car."

Surveilling from a beach would be different, and as he let himself out of the house, he positioned himself against the end of the house at the patio's edge. He kept his eyes scanning right to left on the beachfront, but nothing was visible other than the inky black sky and the white of the breaking tide. He noted the lights were still on next door and wondered if Summer and Clarice were still keyed up after the abrupt end of their night. He hated the thought, but there was nothing for it.

Satisfied they were still safe from the Kellys' guys, he went back inside and locked the door behind him, pulling the curtains. Tara was picking at the omelet Tim had made for her, a half-drunk glass of water beside her. She looked ready to fall headfirst into the plate. Miss Purrfect was on her lap, purring softly. Tim's quick glance over had a flash of worry before he bravely smiled. Robbie made the corners of his mouth lift in response.

Billie inclined his chin when he joined them in the kitchen a moment later, and Robbie heard the message loud and clear. They were good. "Tara, I'm going upstairs to check the messages on my computer, okay? I'll be right back."

She glanced up, her dark brown eyes unnaturally wet with tears. "I can't tell you how much I appreciate this. All of you guys upending your lives to protect me and the girls. I'll make it up to you, I swear."

His throat thickened. "You don't owe anybody anything. We're family. This is what we do."

Her eyes gleamed again, slaying him. Billie's jaw audibly popped.

"Personally, I think Billie could use a serious pedicure on those giant feet of his," Tim said, pinching his nose for effect. "God knows we'd appreciate some treatment to cure his stinky feet. Tara, girl, help us out."

She gave a weak smile. "Pedicures on the house for life."

Billie's mouth lifted to the left as he gave a feral attempt at a smile. "Baby bro, I think you're talking about Robbie's feet. They smell worse than bad ass."

Everyone chuckled rather pathetically, but it was a start. He shot Tim an approving look, to which his brother nodded. As he surveyed their group, he reflected that he'd brought the perfect people along with him, not just for the girls but for Tara. Maybe even himself. "I'll be right back."

He was quiet on the stairs as he took them two at a time. When he logged into his account on the encrypted messaging services, he had a flurry of messages. From both his partner and Roland in Internal Affairs, the only two people with access to the message board besides himself.

There was an initial report on the fire at the nail salon, followed by a later one describing the initial fire inspector's conclusion that it had been arson. No special signature. No fingerprints. Roland noted there had been no chatter about an arson on the streets either before or afterward from any of their CIs. Then again, the Kellys ran a tight organization.

His partner reported that there still was no trace of Tara's ex or his new side piece from the nail salon despite the time he'd put in off-hours checking highway and other police cameras around the city. But now they had a crime that the Southie PD could legitimately go after.

Except there were rumblings by the officer in charge about Tara being on vacation and not being accessible by phone. Him too, for that matter. Johnny O'Malley had strolled into Mickey's office before his shift had ended to inquire whether Robbie might be at the same vacation spot with his cousin, something Mickey had been able to truthfully deny.

Everyone in the department was stirred up now, thinking Robbie's family issue, leading to his very rare vacation, had something to do with his cousin. With the arson involved, no one in the department would be thinking their sudden vacations were solely about her marriage ending. His boss was going to want to talk to him, and so would the rest of his police brothers. Usually they looked out for each other, but he'd gone off alone. There were questions flying. Especially ones surrounding whether the Kellys had dirty cops on the payroll, which was why Robbie had gone AWOL to protect family.

Mickey and Roland's final message to him was pretty much the same. Has Tara contacted you yet? And what do you want to do now?

Robbie sat against the headboard and tipped his head back. *What was the best move?* He could bring Tara back to

Boston alone and leave Billie and Tim here to watch over the girls. But his protective side started to itch when he considered it. Sure, Billie could handle himself, but he didn't want to leave him in charge like that. He wasn't trained, for one.

He needed another professional, but that was going to be tricky. He'd slipped out of Boston before anyone had time to watch him, but the situation had changed. He couldn't just ask Mickey to come down. Someone would be tracking his every movement, especially now.

"I told Tara to look in on the girls tonight so she could assure herself they were okay, but to let them get some rest and see them in the morning."

Robbie looked over. Tim had cracked his bedroom door open. He waved him inside. His brother entered and shut the door quietly behind him, his face fully grave, showing his every emotion.

"I'm bunking on the couch so Tara can get some sleep," his baby brother continued, looking at him, unblinking. "From the look of you, I imagine you're feeling the weight of Sisyphus on your shoulders."

"He's the guy who carried the rock, right?" he asked dryly. "Sounds about right."

Tim walked over and sat on the edge of the bed. "I figure the O'Connors are like tandem runners, handing off the rock to one another when it gets too heavy. Why don't you give it over to Billie and let your mind settle for a while? He's drinking coffee in the kitchen now and playing solitaire. Like he's preparing to keep watch all night."

That knotted up his throat hard. "Shit."

"I won't call you on the language." Tim waggled his brows with effort. "Tara's in the house now."

"Yeah, she is." *Thank God.* "We're in a whole new ballpark, Tim."

"I know." His brother folded his hands. "Billie told me the house is still safe—"

"Which is why I don't think he needs to stay up on guard duty."

"He needs something to do, Robbie." Tim clenched his hands. "This is his way of handling his anger and his worry. And his lust. Hope it's okay to call that out."

"Yeah, there's a lot of that going around," he mumbled, the feeling of Summer's soft blond hair suddenly on his fingertips.

"I take it your date went as good as Billie's?" Tim asked, his lean face knitted with concern.

"Might have been the best ever," he admitted to his baby brother with a hefty sigh. "But Tara arriving—"

"Shifts everything." Tim studied him. "I did my best to explain to Summer why you were worried about Tara. I made up a whole story—"

"You did?" Robbie sunk back and regarded his brother. "You lied for me?"

"For us," his brother corrected. "And to preserve a relationship I think is coming to mean quite a bit to you. In a very short stretch, I might add. Not that time is the best barometer. We're Irish. We know when we know."

God, he didn't need to be reminded of his Irish genes, so he said nothing in response. "Thank you, Tim. For thinking fast on your feet."

"That's what people who can quote Shakespeare do," he quipped, making Robbie reluctantly smile. "Why don't you get some rest too? You'll know what the best course is when you know it."

Robbie closed the laptop on his lap and set it aside. "That's not what Mickey or Roland Thomas are saying exactly."

"Are they instructing you to come back to Boston?" he asked, his blue eyes pinched with concern.

"No, but the officer in charge of the arson at Tara's salon knows my absence is linked to hers. He visited Mickey today."

"So what? That doesn't mean you need to make a move. Besides, while I hate saying this out loud—and I never would in front of Tara—isn't the arson a blessing in disguise? Before, it looked like she could be part of a money laundering scheme. But doesn't she look more innocent now that the Kellys are going after her?"

He lifted his shoulder. "It doesn't exactly clear her. Someone could say they were sending her a message about taking their money."

"But why would she take a stand against the Kellys if she was working with them and benefitting?" Tim shot back. "I would think a junior prosecutor could make that kind of argument easily."

"I'm impressed. All those *Law and Order* reruns are paying off for you."

Tim shot him an uncharacteristic bird. "Is there anything else I can do? I know I'm not sentinel material, but I'll hear something on the couch. I'll have the baseball bat with me."

His brother suddenly looked vulnerable and fierce all at once. Robbie scooted over until he could put a hand on his shoulder, suddenly feeling very much like an older brother. "Honestly, Tim, right now I'm thinking my smartest decision was bringing you. Not discounting what Billie brings to the table, but Danny, Riley, Caden, and Brennan would have brought the same things. *You* took care of Tara tonight. You helped her settle down. You fed her, and you probably even changed the sheets on your bed so she'd have fresh ones. Then you helped her see her babies in the best way possible given her current state."

Tim's blue eyes swam with emotion. "That's the nicest thing you've ever said to me. It means a lot."

Robbie's chest tightened. "I know you don't think I have as much respect for you as our other brothers, but why don't we stop that shit right now? Because it's not true. You bring something really special to the table, and I respect that. Tim, I admire you."

When Tim hugged him, he hugged him back, feeling that bond of blood and brotherhood with him in a way he never had before this trip. "Now, get out of here and let me rest this frenetic brain of mine because I do need to figure out our next steps. And soon."

Tim was smiling when he pushed back and stood. "I have one more thing to say since you're looking at me like I'm a cute little puppy."

Robbie groaned. "I kick puppies, Tim. Kidding. God, you'd better not be about to lay a Shakespeare quote on me."

Grimacing, he pointed to his lips. "I'll hold it in, but I'm going to step on a ledge."

"Don't fall," Robbie warned, bracing himself.

"I think you can take it." His brother stepped exaggeratedly toward the door, however, making Robbie's mouth twitch. "I've seen you with plenty of girls since you went out on your first date with Katie O'Sullivan. And I stood by your side on your wedding day."

Robbie knew where this was going. "Run, brother."

He shook his head, setting his weight. "I've never seen you look at a woman like you do Summer."

"Tim—"

"I want you to be happy, dammit. I heard you laughing with her last night—in this house. Do you have any idea how rare that sound is? You stopped laughing like that after Mom died."

His heart tore in two. "Jesus, Tim. Just stop!"

"I won't. You admire me, remember, so I'm saying what I see. And I see *that*. What if coming here wasn't just about you seeing me differently but yourself? What if meeting Summer turned out to be fate's gift to you for being the kind of man you are? Because you aren't just tough and hard, you're loyal and caring and as straight as an arrow."

He wanted to put his hands over his ears. "You might as well run off to Ireland, talking like that."

"If I could tell Kathleen about all of this," he said, lifting his chin, "she'd be on the next plane over to see for herself, and then she'd knock you in the back of the head about passing up a woman like this. Since I can't call her, I'm doing the knocking my way. So, knock knock."

"My life isn't a damn—"

"I'm not letting you finish that sentence." He held his hand out like he had the power to stop his older brother from speaking, when they both knew he didn't. "I'll get out of your hair now and say, I love you. You're my brother. I've looked up to you my whole life. I admire the hell out of you. And whatever you're planning, I'm with you. All the way."

He nodded, swallowing a whole lot of love for his baby brother. "I know you are. Good night, Tim."

"Night, Robbie."

He let himself fall back onto the bed, staring up at the ceiling. Images of a stricken Tara filled his mind. On the tail end of his cousin was Summer, standing in front of him on the beach in the soft light of the moon. He could still feel her hands cupping his jaw, hear her softly confess she wished they didn't have to end. Tim was right, God help him.

He closed his eyes, searching for answers. He didn't have just one plan to figure out, he realized. His second was what he was really going to do about Summer.

Because, in the quiet of the night, he could finally admit to himself that he didn't want to let her go.

CHAPTER SIXTEEN

THEIR PLAN WAS BRILLIANT, AND HER PROMOTION WOULD be a sure thing.

Robbie, though? She had no idea what would happen.

She could only hope that the man she'd come to know and care about would at least meet her halfway. After he blew his top, which she feared would be his initial reaction. She'd continue hoping that coming clean to Robbie would mean they could go on a real date as themselves when all this was over. Because if she didn't lead with hope, she felt like she might lose her balance and make a mistake, and that was something she could not do.

Lily finished another bottle of coconut water and then checked the clock, eager to kick things off. This time she was the one who patted Sheila's butt. "Showtime."

"God, I can't believe you talked me into this. The sun is hardly up, and we barely got a catnap." Her partner's glare didn't have its usual punch given the dark circles under her eyes from a long night.

When they'd checked in with Buck last night, he'd wanted them to immediately bring Tara into the North Carolina FBI office before transporting her and her girls back to Boston in protective custody. Basically, pissing on Robbie and the Southie PD and pulling rank with the racketeering case they'd been working on to nail the Kellys. Not to mention frightening some very little girls.

Hairs rising on her skin because of how badly she knew that was going to go over—with both Tara and Robbie—Lily had told Buck they were going to go over everything they had so far and call him back with a detailed plan. Her brainstorming session with Sheila had been rocky at first, because her partner was reluctant to worry about egos and stepped-on toes. Sheila loved pissing contests, something she swore she got from her mother.

But she'd agreed about not wanting to traumatize the little girls they'd both grown fond of. In the end, Sheila had called her "my queen" and sent a fatigued bow her way.

Lily had gotten totally choked up, but of course Sheila had quickly followed it up by saying it was her eighth cup of coffee that had enticed her to agree to Lily's unconventional plan. Her partner had collapsed on the couch while Lily had called Buck back and laid out her strategy.

He'd argued nearly every point with her, which was what made him a good agent and boss, making her defend each part of her scheme. He'd finally caved at four fifteen, telling Lily that she'd better be right, or he was going to transfer her to Anchorage and tell the officer in charge to put her on moose poaching cases. Did people poach moose? She'd shivered but hung up victorious.

With two hours of sleep, she was wired from an entire six-pack of coconut water. But ready...

"You were the one who initially thought of this idea, remember?" Lily said slyly, not wishing to start an early row. They had one hell of a day in front of them.

"But I wanted *you* to pretend to get stung by a jellyfish to hook Robbie." Sheila thrust out her yoga-legging-clad leg. "I hate acting like a damsel in distress."

"It won't work with me, Sheila," Lily shot back. "I've shown my prowess evading jellyfish. Plus, we need to get our ace in the hole alone. What better way than to create a scenario where he's in his element?"

"Fine!" She fluffed her sagging curls and yanked open the patio door. "But I swear. If I pretend to be stung and no one sees me, you'd better not laugh. Or video me flailing around in the sand, moaning from a pretend sting."

She knew not to waver. "Trust me. Just remember to cry out loudly. Do you need to practice?"

"Girl, if I holler now, it will blow your whole plan." She sailed out the door and into dawn's morning light. "Close it behind me and stay out of sight. I need to look like I'm craving alone time."

Lily bit the inside of her lip as she secured the door and then took a hidden position where she could see her partner. Sheila was shuffling her feet, as if she'd tossed and turned over an aborted night with Billie. Truthfully, Lily was glad they'd had no time to think about the men.

Okay, not much time, she admitted. She'd only admit to having one or two thoughts, hoping and praying Robbie wouldn't just understand, but would be in awe of the way she'd chosen to handle things.

Sheila's low scream on the beach had Lily's heart rate kicking up. Her partner clutched her right foot and then hopped around before collapsing in the sand. Writhing in pain, she started rocking and moaning, turning her foot so she could see the bottom.

A man ran out onto the beach—all alone, like she'd hoped, given her knowledge of his early morning schedule. She clenched her hands as Sheila turned her pitiful face up to him, pointing toward her foot, which she'd wisely pointed down to cover its lack of a real sting.

Lily's eyes shot to her hairline as the man scooped her friend up and started walking briskly toward the house. She ducked around the side walls until she was out of sight in the entryway. The patio door slid open.

"Summer! Hey! I need you. Your friend is hurt."

She made a show of running loudly in place, like she was coming from upstairs. Bursting into the kitchen, she found their hero lowering Sheila into a kitchen chair, his face calm, his hands professional as she reached for her foot.

"Tim," Lily called softly.

He turned his head. "I need some tweezers and some boiling water."

God, he was really so adorable. Dark hair had fallen onto his forehead. She crossed until she was standing in front of him. "Tim, Clarice is fine. I need to tell you something, and I didn't want you to get mad in front of your brothers. It's really important, or we wouldn't have done this."

Glancing sharply at Sheila, he frowned darkly as she showed him her perfectly fine foot.

He stepped back, his brow creasing. "Joking about a serious injury is low, but I believe you had a good reason, so I'll let my anger go."

"Thank you." She grabbed her purse from the counter, where she'd strategically placed it, and discreetly pulled out her badge and ID, palming it. "Tim, we're here to help you guys. I want you to remember that when I show you this. And I want you to promise you'll hear me out before you leave."

His blue eyes narrowed to slits. "Summer, I don't like the sound of this."

"Tim, we're FBI agents here to help Tara and the girls," she told him slowly, holding up her credentials.

His face paled, and he took a step backward, as if totally off-balance.

"Look, I know it's a shock, but we knew about Tara's ex-husband laundering money for the Kellys, and we've been working on bringing them down." She kept his shocked gaze as she lowered her badge face up on the counter. "We were going to help her the day she went to the gym because we knew the Kellys had threatened her, but she snuck out a side entrance. Smart, right? Then your brother showed up, and we decided to follow him because we knew your cousin would meet back up with her girls. Tim, it's obvious how much she loves her family. Just like you guys love them."

He was watching her steadily, his palms flattened on his thighs. His training as a nurse was solid. He knew how to stay calm in a crisis. "Why are you talking to me and not Robbie? You know he's a cop."

She nodded, again slowly. "Yes, and he's a good one. He's proven it over and over again. But Tim, you've seen how personal it's gotten between us. Being undercover can be complicated, and while it's unprofessional for me to tell you this, I've developed feelings for your brother."

"So have I, if we're confessing," Sheila interrupted, pulling their attention toward her. "Billie. Not Robbie."

"I don't want to hurt Robbie, but he's going to be shocked to learn I'm FBI, don't you think?" she continued, blowing out an aggrieved breath. "You have shown time and time again how levelheaded you are. You don't fly off the handle. You listen and you understand—"

"You want me to keep Robbie from blowing his top," Tim drew out, pursing his lips. "That's not going to be easy. You're right. He's going to be upset you lied to him."

She made a face. "That's what I thought at first, and it is true. But you know what? He was technically lying to me about being a single dad, so I'm thinking we're even."

Tim laughed low in his throat. "Good luck getting Robbie to see it like that."

Sheila shot her a look, clearly ready to take over. Lily shook her head subtly. "I want him to see it like that, Tim, for personal and professional reasons. Because I have a plan that will help keep Tara and the girls safe and allow us to take down the Kellys for good. Will you help us?"

He studied her before saying, "I'll do my best to encourage Robbie to listen to you and not storm off. Because that's your biggest problem up front. He likes you, Summer. Ah... What is your real name?"

"Lily Meadows," she told him, giving a short smile. "Not too much better than Summer Sunshine, right?"

"I call her Sunshine as a nickname because she really is so sweet," her partner broke in, standing at last and thrusting out her hand. "Tim, I'm Sheila Morales."

He shook her hand with strength before turning and doing the same with Lily. She rather liked that. "Also, we're based out of Boston."

"You are?" His eyes widened before a smile appeared on his face. "Is there some rule about cops and FBI officers not being allowed to date?"

She and Sheila shook their heads simultaneously. "Not a one," Lily answered. "But helping Tara and the girls is the priority."

"You sound like Robbie." He suddenly started to laugh, pressing a hand to his forehead. "Oh my God. This is perfect. Like Shakespearean perfect. The two love interests next door aren't who they say they are. Only...everyone is lying to each other as they develop feelings for each other. I wish I were a playwright. This would make a great story."

Sheila punched him lightly in the shoulder. "Hey! Every work of Shakespeare I had to read in school ended in tragedy. We don't like tragedy, do we, Lily?"

She crossed her arms. "No, we most surely do not. So are you in?"

He nodded swiftly. "How do you want to tell my brother?"

"I thought you might go over there and tell him I have something urgent to tell him. Billie can look after Tara and the girls. We've checked the area. No one followed her."

"We checked too, but Billie stayed up all night until I sent him to bed at dawn—"

"Oh, that big galoot." Sheila put a hand to her heart. "How mad is he going to be, do you think?"

Tim shrugged. "I have no idea really. I say we start with Robbie. He can talk Billie down if necessary."

"Good." She and her partner shared a look. "Let's summon the beast."

CHAPTER SEVENTEEN

ROBBIE WAS SCRAPING HIS RAZOR DOWN HIS CHEEK WHEN someone knocked on his bedroom door. He rinsed his face and left the bathroom to open it. Tim was standing on the other side, looking a little pale.

"Did you get any sleep on the couch Miss Purrfect has covered in cat hair?"

His brother shook his head. "Billie slapping cards on the table in the kitchen playing solitaire was the bigger culprit for my lack of Zs. Besides the obvious elephant in the house. Got a sec? I need some help. Clarice got stung by a jellyfish—"

"When?" he asked, going on alert. "Is Summer all right?"

"She hadn't gone out onto the beach yet. Anyway, Clarice also took a hard fall hopping around, and while I got her into the house and tended to the sting, I'd like to carry her upstairs so she can rest. I thought she'd be more comfortable if we lifted her together. Billie finally crashed when I woke up, or I'd..."

"Sure thing." Clapping his brother on the back, he followed him quietly down the stairs. "Is Tara up?"

"She hasn't come down yet," he said quietly. "And the girls are still out."

"Well, it's barely six." He hoped his cousin had gotten more rest than he had because they had a lot to talk about.

He had an initial plan, but he wasn't sure how she was going to react to being in touch with the Southie PD, especially when they had reason to suspect the Kellys had someone on the payroll. Robbie wanted to bring the officer leading the arson case into the larger Internal Affairs investigation. He didn't see any other way. He could not handle the Kellys alone. He and Tara had to work with the police, and if Internal Affairs had to run the case, then so be it. The biggest issue he was having was where to keep the girls until the situation was resolved.

He didn't think it was wise for everyone to stay together. They needed protective custody, but he wasn't sending them off with strangers. His brothers couldn't keep taking time off. God, he could finally fully understand the agonizing choice Tara had made to leave them with him in the first place.

"Lot on your mind today, huh?" Tim asked as they left the house. "Well, it's a new day. Thanks for coming over with me."

"You know it." Besides, he would have a chance to see Summer and tell her he wanted to stay in touch but didn't know how long it was going to be before he could call her again. He couldn't keep his focus with her around, and his every waking hour had to be dedicated to solving this case so Tara and the girls could go home.

When they reached the women's patio, Robbie spotted Summer resting her elbows on the kitchen island, wearing a white yoga outfit, her face tense and pale. Clarice was sitting on a barstool, also in yoga attire, also looking tense. Tim knocked on the patio door, and when Summer rose and waved them in, he slicked open the door.

"I hear someone got stung by a jellyfish, Clarice." Robbie winced. "Having experienced a sting before, I sympathize. Let's get you upstairs. Then I need to talk to Summer."

"Actually, I need to talk to you too," Summer said, coming around the island with a smile on her face.

Except that smile was a little tight, and suddenly his stomach was tensing in response. "Ah...if you're a little upset about how things ended—"

"Not at all." She came and stood in front of him, and he caught her shallow intake of breath. "Actually, Robbie, I have a question for you."

He glanced over at Tim and Clarice, wondering whether they should find a private place to talk. But her green eyes were locked on him, and she didn't seem bothered by the audience. "Shoot."

Clarice puffed out a laugh; Summer slid her a look before returning her focus to him. "First question. Do you trust me?"

Shock landed first, and then he was narrowing his eyes. "Yes, mostly. We haven't known each other long..."

"No, I suppose not." She laid her hand on his forearm, igniting a fire on the bare skin below his T-shirt. "Well, I'm telling you that you can trust me all the way, and I'm asking you to believe that."

His brows slammed together. "Okay, this is getting a little weird. What's going on here?"

"She's not planning on tying you up and hauling you off to Vegas to get hitched, so don't worry," Clarice answered with an evil grin.

"Haha." Oddly, his stomach didn't flip-flop at the thought of her dressed up in a casual white dress as they stood before a preacher in Sin City. "Very funny, Clarice. You know, you certainly aren't acting like someone who got stung by a jellyfish." He eyed the group staring at him, knowing when he was being cornered. "So what's all this trust talk about?"

Summer reached into her purse and pulled out something that looked like a black wallet before flipping it open. The words *FBI* screamed at him. The gold badge and identification photo slapped him in the face. "No, you can't be…"

"I am," she said softly, guilt lighting her face as she set her ID down on the counter. "Lily Meadows out of the Boston office. This is Sheila Morales, my partner. And we're here to help you with Tara's problems."

He watched her lips say the words, and all he could think over the rage boiling in his blood was that he'd kissed those lips and told her he didn't want their time together to end. That he'd fallen for her. "Well, fuck you! You've been undercover this whole time? How dare you not tell me. We are so done here."

Turning on his heel to leave, he was shocked to see Tim standing in front of his exit, arms clenched across his chest. "I know you're mad, Robbie. I was a little too. But they're here to help, and honestly, bro, don't you feel better knowing you had two law enforcement officers looking out for the girls all the time along with us?"

He got in his brother's face. "No, I fucking don't, Tim. Get out of my way."

"No," he answered sternly, even as his Adam's apple shifted in his throat. "You need to listen to them. Come on, Robbie. Lily didn't like lying to you any more than you did her. You both have feelings for each other. Now, set it aside and open your ears."

He could not believe his baby brother was challenging him. "You don't tell me what to do. Move, Tim, or I *will* move you."

"Robbie, please don't walk out," Summer—Lily—pleaded. "I went against my boss for a plan that doesn't involve bringing Tara in officially."

Spinning around, he realized his heart was pounding

against his ribs. "You are not fucking bringing her into the FBI. Over my dead body."

Clarice—God, what was her real name?—gave a giant sigh. "The Kellys would love it if we were all dead, don't you think? That's why we're here, isn't it? Now take a moment and work it out. You're a good police officer. You know what's at stake here."

He glared at her before Summer—dammit, Lily—stepped into his vision. "We both know how things work when this much mob money is involved, Robbie," she said calmly. "Stop and think for a minute over this shock. It's why you gave Roland Thomas in Internal Affairs the cash in the toy store parking lot outside Boston after you picked up the girls from the Beacon Hill gym."

Boils might as well have covered his skin for how enraged he was. "You've been watching me this whole time? How long have you been on this case? When—"

"My CI told me Janice Brewster was bragging about the Kellys paying for her new fur coat."

"Jesus Christ," he said, running his hand over his neck.

"Janice said her boyfriend, Scotty Flanagan, was on their payroll and going places in the organization. Two days later, Tara found out her ex was cheating. At the time, we weren't sure whether she was involved in the money laundering. Then we watched her haul a rather heavy bag out of the nail salon. You know what's next. We started to surveil and caught the Kellys slashing her tires—"

"You didn't protect her!" He cursed, clenching his fists as he stared her down. "Her kids were in that house."

"We were prepared to step in if it got uglier," Lily told him, her brow knitting. "Take a minute and let that sink in. The cops have the same MO."

He spun away, his jaw popping. The cop in him was warring with the cousin, the one who hated knowing Tara had been so terrified out of her skin she'd run and sent her girls away. To him.

His ears buzzed. His heart knocked in his chest. He clenched his eyes shut, his emotions flying out of control like unruly fireworks.

"Robbie," she said again in a calm voice, one he could hear entreaty him. "No one hauls mobsters in for a first misdemeanor destruction of property. That's all we had then. No evidence. No witnesses. We were building our case. Like any good law enforcement official. We were tailing her when she went to Costco and had a buying spree. She looked like she was fleeing—"

"She was!" he finally exploded, spinning back around. "She was running scared. Like she is now. All you've done here is sit on us and twiddle your thumbs."

He knew it was below the belt, but he couldn't stop himself. Seeing her flinch made his gut twitch.

"Sorry to say this, Robbie, but isn't that what you've been doing here too?" Clarice asked with an edge.

He had to rein in the urge to lash back. "Why aren't you out looking for Scotty—"

"We are, trust me," Lily continued in that same calm voice, although her face was several shades paler. "He hasn't surfaced. Neither has Janice. If they do, we'll bring them in immediately. But I knew Tara wouldn't leave her girls alone forever, so here Sheila and I sat. But we weren't twiddling our thumbs, and you know it. Just like you weren't."

He heard the steel in her voice and reluctantly nodded. "I have a plan—"

"Mine is better," she said, her eyes flashing with that familiar challenge.

The punch to his gut was heavy-hitter quality. Now it all made sense. The initial foray to become friendly and then create rapport. He knew how the job was done, and God, they had done a good one. "I can't risk her or the girls with you after all of this. I don't trust you, which brings us back to your original question, doesn't it?"

Hurt flashed in her green eyes, but her face remained stiff and wooden—so unlike the woman he'd come to care for.

"Robbie, you can't do everything yourself," Tim said quietly. "Tara said the Kellys have people on their payroll in your precinct."

He was breathing hard as he turned to look at his brother. "You don't know what the Feds are going to do with Tara. I do."

"Robbie, didn't you hear what Lily said?" Tim gestured in her direction. "She argued with her boss for a different way. At least hear her out. They care about Reagan and Cassidy and us. It's not going to be like your other dealings with the Feds."

"I could quote case after case of them grinding people down for a collar." He made a rude sweep of his hand. "This — This is all an illusion. A mirage. That's what undercover is. A bunch of lies wrapped up in pretty packages. Fed style. I won't put my family in their hands, Tim. You don't know how badly things could end up. It gives me fucking nightmares to think about it. If I didn't believe it would screw with your head, I'd have my partner back in Southie send me a few photos of some crime scenes where the Kellys did their worst to a woman or a kid. Do you hear me? I can't risk it!"

His brother studied him before giving an explosive breath. Then he walked over to Clarice—Sheila—and whispered in her ear. The woman blurted out a shocked laugh before rising. He watched in shock as they left the room together. "Tim, you come back here! We're leaving. I swear to God, I'll go get Billie. If we have to hog-tie you—"

"Violence is not needed here," Lily said in a raspy voice in the now empty kitchen. "Cooperation is. Look, I know some of the cases you're talking about. I even probably know those FBI officers, and while I work with them, that's not how I do things. People matter to me."

His throat suddenly felt raw.

"The story I told you about the cult my mother put us in is true." She took a deep breath, her green eyes bright with emotion. "I know what it feels like to be scared and vulnerable—like Tara and her girls. What I didn't mention is that an undercover female agent brought it all down and saved me. She inspired me to join the FBI. So I'm not just a hotshot Fed going after a collar. Everything I do on a case is about protecting people and putting the monsters away."

He had to look away from the pain in her gaze.

"I have a plan that will keep Tara and the girls safe. The Kellys will be caught and go away for a long time for a whole host of offenses—"

"Summer—Lily—stop." He exhaled harshly. "I believe you care. But I can't just go with feelings. How long have you been assigned to Boston?"

Her brows tensed. "Six months, but I'm—"

"My guys were born and raised in Southie," he said in as even a tone as he could muster, "and they know what they're dealing with. It's our community. Forgive me for saying this, but you're a rookie in our backyard."

"I'm sorry you think so little of me." She crossed her arms in a protective gesture. "I didn't want to go here, but you don't seem to be willing to give me the same respect I'm giving you. Robbie, Sheila and I are such good agents that you didn't see us once on your tail the whole way here. And you didn't suspect us on this fake vacation."

He felt the slap of that on his face. "You're right. Clearly, you and your partner took a few liberties with your undercover assignment. Because you used your feminine wiles to hook me and my brother—"

"I did not!" She fumed, fisting her hands at her sides. "I beat you at every sport we played. I purposely did not use the damsel card, not only because I knew it wouldn't work, but because I wanted you to see me as an equal. Clearly, you're too much of an ignoramus to do that."

"Your partner already thinks I drag my knuckles on the ground," he shot back.

"Well, Lieutenant, if the shoe fits." She sucked in a breath. "We're getting totally off track. I didn't want to get personal."

"Well, it is personal, dammit." Calling it out there had something breaking free inside of him. He grabbed her to him, feeling her heart pounding in her chest. "You made me like you. Want you. Care about you. I'd decided to try and see you after this! How the fuck do you think I feel knowing this was just a job to you? And you say it's not personal. Sweetheart, you've made me as raw as they come."

Her face flinched. "It wasn't just a job to me. I fell for you too! Do you think I liked lying to you? But you were lying to me too. Why can't we just call it even?"

"Because your lies were bigger than mine." He cupped her face, his fingers wanting to feel the burn from her touch. "And you kissed me!"

"You kissed me too!" She shoved him, but he didn't move. "Lying about being a single dad isn't a big deal? Oh, this is rich. You think you're on some high horse. Well, buddy, you aren't. But all this arguing isn't going to get us anywhere. Because Tara is still in trouble, and I still have a case to close."

He dropped her arms and took a step back. "You should have told me who you were before now."

"I couldn't, and you know it," she argued, looking over as Tim and Sheila walked back in.

He turned to his brother. "Tim, I don't know what is

wrong with you, but we're going. Now. Don't make me cold-cock you."

His brother walked up to him while Sheila came and stood beside Lily, huddling in closer until all four of them were standing close. "What? Do you expect us to put our hands into the pile and say Go Team?" he scoffed.

"Not exactly." His brother whipped the arm he had resting behind him and grabbed Robbie's wrist. His reflexes dulled by shock, Robbie felt something cold and metal touch his skin before he heard a click, and then Sheila was grabbing Lily's wrist. Another click sounded. He looked down in shock.

They were handcuffed together.

"What the fuck is this?" he shouted.

Lily rattled the cuffs, their arms grazing each other. "Sheila, stop this! What in the hell are you thinking? I am not going to be handcuffed to this blockhead."

"Blockhead?" Robbie eyed Tim and Sheila as they backed away toward the patio door. "Tim, you are a dead man."

"After our talk about your unique feelings for Lily, I'm risking it." His brother gave him a lopsided smile. "Destiny brought you here—"

"Tara brought me here!" He started to move toward his brother, but when he jerked on the cuffs, Lily cried out in pain. "Sorry. I'm not usually the one in the cuffs."

"On that we agree," she said dryly. "Tim. Sheila. I know you two think you mean well, but you're only making things worse."

"Listen to your partner." Robbie turned to Lily's partner, desperation rising in his veins. "Come on, Sheila. Give us the key. You can't cuff a police officer."

"I didn't technically, and honestly, I've cuffed law enforcement officers in my private life before. More than once," she said with a smirk, opening the patio door. "Your brother keeps surprising us. He had the idea and executed it brilliantly."

Tim had the audacity to take her hand and grandly kiss it. "Thank you, kind lady."

Robbie glared at him. "You've totally lost it, Tim."

Sheila clucked with her tongue. "No, he hasn't. We both agree you two are perfect for each other. That's why you're making a mountain out of a mole hill."

"This is such bullshit," Robbie ground out.

"You're both competitive, highly intelligent, protective, and nice," Sheila continued despite his outburst. "Okay, that's mostly Lily. You're in the same profession mostly, which means you get the job. And you live in the same city. Neither of you has dated much lately, wanting something more, and *voila,* here you are—practically a love match after a week."

"This is so not happening," Lily moaned.

Robbie thought about lunging for his brother, but from the set of his jaw, it was clear he intended to see this through. "I'm blaming your Shakespeare crap for this, Tim. You have one last chance to uncuff us."

Tim lifted his chin. "I know what I'm doing. Besides, after thinking about it last night, I've concluded you and Lily have a shot at a very un-Shakespeare romance."

"What the hell does that even mean?" he spat, feeling Lily straighten next to him.

"Yeah, I'm eager to hear this theory as well," Lily replied, standing way too close to him for comfort.

"You said his works end in tragedy." Tim's blue eyes were warm but unrelenting. "While that disregards the fact that half his plays are comedies, all his tragedies do end badly, and man, you have been living in one. Deceit. High drama. Intrigue. Good versus evil. But we don't want your story to end predictably. I think you and Lily have a shot at a real happily ever after."

He heard Lily's sharp intake of breath beside him and ground his teeth. "That's the biggest bunch of bullshit I've ever heard. Tim, we need to get Tara out of here—"

"That's where you're wrong, O'Connor." Sheila put her hands on her hips and practically breathed fire back at him. "Lily's plan is flawless. Hear her out. Now, Tim and I are going next door."

"Sheila, you're my partner!" Lily said in a raised voice. "This is so not okay."

"You're both going to pay for this!" Robbie shouted. "I don't like being handcuffed."

"Who does?" Sheila quipped, giving Tim a gentle shove out the door. "And keep your voices down. You don't want to wake Reagan and Cassidy or upset Tara. We'll come back in a while and see what progress you've made. Work it out! And don't leave the house. It would suck to have someone call the police after seeing two people handcuffed together fighting on the beach."

With that, the patio door slicked shut.

His gaze swung to Lily. "So this is how the FBI does the job, huh? Nice."

"It was your brother who must have instigated this." She bit her lip, breathing harshly. "You are the most close-minded, obnoxious man I've ever met."

Then she planted her hot mouth on his, rocking him back.

CHAPTER EIGHTEEN

Robbie's heat scalded Lily as he met her mouth and pulled her body to him one-handed, kissing her feverishly.

Progress!

Because if he thought she was done with him, he was crazy. The way they'd scraped each other to the bone with their earlier jabs only showed how deeply they cared for each other. She opened her mouth, giving in to the torrent of desire rolling between them. The kiss went wild, tongues tangling, breaths shattering.

He suddenly wrenched his mouth back, staring stupefied at her, his fingers caressing her thigh where their handcuffed hands rested. *"What are you doing?"*

"Showing you I have feelings for you too." She thumped his chest to get his attention. "That this is real!"

His mouth worked like he was about to shoot back a comeback, but she was so done with his bullshit. She pinged his ribs again with an angry flick of her finger and watched in delight as his blue eyes fired even hotter.

"Your baby brother is the only O'Connor male I've met with any sense. So...you wanted to keep things going too, huh? Well, now you know we can. And I happen to be done listening to you bitch and moan about me being a Fed and duping you while being undercover, especially since you lied through your pretty teeth too. You're as guilty as I am, bucko."

"I am not interested in rehashing this shit." He picked her up with one arm and started hauling her over to the kitchen counter. "We need to find something to pick the lock."

If he did that—and she doubted he could—he would be gone. No way she was letting that happen, personally or professionally. She climbed onto his body and clamped her legs around his waist. The hard evidence of his desire was as clear as day.

"Aha!" she cried out, delighting in the knowledge he wanted her. Badly.

"Stop that! If you knew how much control I'm having to—"

"I'm not letting go." She arranged their cuffed hands between their stomachs and then slid the other hand around his nape, locking gazes. "Robbie O'Connor, so help me. You're going to listen to me and you're going to listen good. Until last night, we were totally into each other. The truth doesn't change that. In fact, it makes it more feasible for us to have a future."

"There is no us," he ground out like the total blockhead he was. "You can't start a relationship on a lie. Now unwrap those sexy legs—"

She only squeezed them tighter. "Everything I told you— everything that mattered—was true. You were the same with me."

He was silent.

"See! We were both real with each other."

His pulse drummed in the side of his neck as he stared at

her. "I opened up to you because I thought you were some sweet therapist who worked with kids—"

"I'm still a professional who's worked with kids." She planted another kiss on his mouth, making him groan, before pulling back. "Before the FBI, I was a primary school teacher. I worked with at-risk kids. I have a strong desire to empower young people, but I also have a crazy desire to protect them and make very bad people pay if they hurt them. We have that in common."

"Summer—Lily—stop this." He rested his forehead against hers, rubbing them together longingly as if she were torturing him. "It's not going to work."

The hopelessness in his voice had her heart tearing. "We don't know unless we try, and I happen to want to. Now that everything is out in the open, we can. We finish this case. Together. And then we—"

"How am I supposed to trust you after this?" he asked harshly, levering back.

"Do you lie outside the job?" she asked baldly.

"No. But that doesn't—"

"Neither do I." She cupped his jaw, her fingers massaging away the tension there. "Come on. Give us a chance. Hear me out. It upset me to keep lying to you, and I was scared about you finding out I was FBI. Because I've fallen for you, dammit."

A muscle leapt in his cheek. "I'd fallen for you too. That's what makes this so hard."

She could feel him softening, hear the anger he'd been using to cover up his raw emotion. "Robbie, thinking about not seeing you again is ripping my heart open."

His face tensed. "Don't say that."

Yeah, under all that tough guy routine, he was still human. "It's true," she pressed, wrapping her arm around him. "You think this is easy for me? Exposing myself and how I feel to you when you're acting like a hotheaded idiot?"

He spurted out a reluctant laugh. "You sounded like my mother earlier when you were all like 'Robbie O'Connor, so help me. You're going to listen to me and you're going to listen good.' It's what stopped me from taking you here and now, something I'd never want to do in anger."

"Me either," she said, running her hand up his back soothingly, "so thanks for reining yourself back."

Rolling his eyes, he said, "I have some self-control despite feeling like an emotional yo-yo since I walked through your patio door this morning. And if I believed in woo-woo stuff, I would swear my mother was speaking through you from heaven, trying to get through my thick skull. You're not the first to complain about my hard head."

He seemed calmer, his muscles loosening from their locked position. She felt safe enough to nestle into him, laying her head on his shoulder. His hand came under her butt to support her better against him, a good sign, she thought. His pulse wasn't pounding against her now, the anger draining out of him. But his arousal was still there, hot and persistent, and that made her smile weakly against his shirt since she knew he hadn't let his desire get out of control.

Him dialing it back was only another indication of how deeply he cared for her, and knowing that made her feel raw and happy and a whole host of other crazy things that all led to one conclusion: she felt good with him, really good, more cared for than she ever had. She was almost scared to say anything, not wanting to shatter this moment. They still had a ways to go. So she went with it, embracing him warmly and letting her guard down all the way.

"I didn't have a chance, did I?" he whispered, tucking his face against the curve of her neck. "I knew it on the beach the other day. I was all keyed up, and then I saw you, and all the stress and strain seemed to just disappear. My dad likes to say that's the kind of woman you scoop up and never let go of."

She found her voice, raising her head and tracing his jaw. "Well, you have me scooped. Maybe you shouldn't let go."

He pulled her tighter against him. "I don't want to. If we do this, everything changes."

Clenching her legs around his waist, she gave a soft smile. "We both knew that last night."

His breath was a harsh rasp. "Yes, we did, because I don't just up and tell people the reason I became a cop."

"Me either," she whispered, her throat catching.

"I can't believe I'm about to do this."

His mouth tightened, and she braced herself for what he was about to say next. "What now?"

His sexy smile started slowly before spreading across his face, lighting up the last shadows in her heart. "I'm about to tell you that you can share your plan with me later. Assuming we don't have somewhere to be right now."

"Really?" Relief and a shaft of happiness shot through her. "You'll listen? But why later?"

"Answer the question."

His gruff command made her pulse skip. "No, I don't have anything scheduled immediately. I was waiting for your compliance before I initiated the next steps."

"That's good." His finger traced one slow line down her neck, making her burn. "That's really good because right now, I want to make love to you. How do you feel about that?"

She softened the opening of her legs, brushing his hardness. He sucked in his breath in response. "I'm going to agree we can take some time for each other. Because, Robbie, I really want your hands on me."

He lowered his head after giving another heart-turning

smile, taking her mouth in a slow, seeking kiss. There was no rush anymore, no impatience. Only the first foray...his lips telling hers this moment was the first in a long sensual adventure. Thank God. Her mouth opened when his tongue quested, and they danced, their breaths matching.

"This one-handed crap is going to drive me nuts," he whispered in a masculine rumble against her neck as his lips cruised down. "You don't happen to know where the second set of keys is?"

"No, and I doubt Sheila would have left them here." She bit the line of his rugged jaw. "She's thorough."

He jangled the cuffs resting between their bodies. "So I see. I still can't believe Tim came up with this idea. He's... never been like this before."

"You mean he's always been your good baby brother," she finished, nipping his earlobe. "These kinds of situations have a way of showing us what's inside us. I happen to adore him."

"You would, given your propensity for wands and tinfoil crowns." He tipped her neck to the side as his mouth slid down the line of it, making her fight a low moan. "Enough talk of my brother. Any thoughts on how we're going to do this, handcuffed together? Because I cannot contemplate the ragging we'd get if we go over now and ask to be uncuffed, only to come back here for some personal time."

"Sheila would have us for lunch."

"So would my brothers, and then there's Tara." His face shadowed. "I'm going to tell myself she'll have some time with the girls while we're over here, so I won't feel guilty."

"I prefer a guilt-free zone too." She laughed to cover up her own nerves, tickling the back of his neck with her fingertips. "You might start for the stairs. My bedroom is the last at the end of the hall. I figure we're both smart people. We'll manage with the cuffs."

He hoisted her more securely and started walking. "I want

to do more than manage. I want to make you call out my name."

"Oh, goodie," she breathed out, holding on and enjoying the rub of his generous length as he ascended the stairs.

"Hell, I want to destroy every ounce of control inside you." He met her gaze, his ocean blue eyes pure challenge now. "How about that?"

She laughed low in her throat. "Are we going to have a little competition here too? Think you can keep up, Grandpa?"

He gave a wolfish smile. "Wanna bet who cries out first?"

"Maybe not our first time, huh?" She nudged her lower body against his hardness. "Crying out is part of the fun, and I expect to be crying out often from the way you make me feel inside."

"How do I make you feel?" he asked, stopping at the doorway to her bedroom.

She tightened her hips around him, the motion making him groan audibly. "Hot. Happy. Needy. I know it's going to be good with you."

His mouth swooped in for another soul-claiming kiss, heating up the rising fire in her belly. "Yeah, no doubt about that. Summer—Lily—"

She tensed at the use of both names, watching the struggle on his face. Holding her breath, she waited for him to come to terms with whatever he was about to say.

"I don't do this lightly," he finally managed in a low voice. "Making love to you means I've decided that I want you in my life. That I'm prepared to trust you."

A hard ball of emotion stuck in her throat. So here they were, both on the precipice of committing to things that weren't easy for either of them. "I'm glad you told me. It's the same for me."

"Good," he rasped out, resting her against the doorjamb.

"Now, maybe we can figure out how we're going to manage getting you out of your clothes because I don't think I can wait another minute to touch you."

She unwrapped her legs slowly, and with his help, she lowered herself to the floor. Looking down at where they were cuffed, she studied their situation. "Well, how do you feel about your shirt?"

"Why?" he asked, cupping her hip with a large, hot hand.

"I always carry a pair of seamstress scissors with me on the job. They're invaluable and a seemingly innocent weapon if needed."

His mouth kicked up to the right. "I like a box cutter myself, but your approach is more understated. You know...it's going to take a little bit to get used to you being FBI. As I said, I haven't had great experiences—"

"I get that. If we're being honest, not all my interactions with the police have been terrific. But I'm hoping we can have a clean slate with each other."

He nodded. "Done, seeing as how we both catch bad guys and probably drink the same bad coffee."

She sighed in relief, appreciating him trying to make a joke. "Are you willing to talk it out later? Our jobs."

"Yeah." He gave a haphazard chuckle. "You know, I've talked more in the last few days than I have in the last three years. I'm looking for a little more balance in my life. I miss the action."

"Well, come this way," she said, leading him to her bedside drawer, pulling it open for the scissors. And condoms, she realized. Right.

She held up a foil packet, and he nodded, taking it from her and putting it beside the pillow.

"You're a Glock girl," he said, pointing to the gun in the drawer. "That explains everything."

She shot him a look. "What is *your* preferred weapon? Besides the obvious..."

He gestured to his erection before lifting his shoulder. "We have three department-issued Glock choices, but personally I like a Benelli M3."

"Twelve gauge," she said, grabbing her scissors and closing the drawer. "Predictable. Now, tug your shirt down at the hem and be still. It's not easy to do this one-handed."

She opened the scissors and started cutting upward. She caught sight of ripped abs and then hard pecs as she cut the front open. My goodness, this was now all hers.

He jangled where they were cuffed. "We still have the sleeves—"

"I know." She slid the remnants of his shirt to the left where they weren't cuffed. "Just shrug out of it, and then I'll cut the shoulder off the other arm."

Oh, my, my. Her insides tightened as his bare chest appeared. Biting her lip, she had to look away to concentrate on her task. With one last snip, his shirt fell to the floor like discarded rags. He was taking the scissors from her hand before she could look up.

"Let's see if I can cut you out of this yoga top," he said, his brows clenching together. "Don't distract me."

She pursed her lip to keep from laughing. Not distract him? They were about to have sex handcuffed together. "I didn't imagine our first time would involve cutting each other out of our clothing. Kinky."

"Behave, because I don't want my hand to slip when I start seeing all that soft, gorgeous skin of yours." He gave a strong, powerful exhale. "Maybe a story will distract me. You should know I wasn't lying. I really do hate being handcuffed. When I was a hotshot rookie, I solved the case of a ranking officer. I thought he'd thank me. He handcuffed me to his cousin's garbage truck for about four blocks. I had no choice but to ride along as he cruised beside me, explaining to me respect for rank and police hierarchy."

She didn't dare laugh. "Law enforcement 'teasing' was a bit of a shock to me when I landed at Quantico. Teachers aren't so brutal."

"I imagine," he agreed, cutting in one clean, focused line. "You're the girl next door. Not your typical hard jaw, tight-assed Fed."

She didn't bite the hook since most police officers felt that way about the FBI. "When I arrived for training, they thought I was there to fix the Xerox machine," she told him, remembering how mortified she'd been after she realized the mix-up. "They laughed at me and shared a look that screamed *she won't last*."

"I bet you ran them into the ground like you did me, right?" he asked, snipping the straps to her yoga top.

"You bet I did. Set a Quantico record, even."

He smoothed the material against her skin, making no move to remove it from her as he opened the drawer and set the scissors inside before closing it firmly.

"Good girl," he said, tipping up her chin. "I'm sorry I insulted you earlier. I was totally out of line."

She met his gaze. "I appreciate you saying that. So are we through with all that now?"

He slid his free hand around her waist and pulled her close to him, his hard chest teasing the edges of her yoga top open where he'd cut it. "Yes. Maybe this is a good time to start over. Hi, I'm Robbie O'Connor."

"Lily Meadows." A whisper of a smile flirted with her lips. "Nice to meet you."

"Yeah, it really is," he said in a dark, low rumble. "Meeting you was exactly what I needed, despite everything else going on. And just to be clear...I don't want you to go easy on me. About anything. Running me down on the beach—"

"Or making you flop face down after we have sex?" she asked, playfully waggling her brows.

He lowered his head slowly, his hand already tugging away her mangled yoga top and throwing it aside, bringing them skin-to-delicious-skin at last. "Let's see if I can surprise you."

With that, she rose up to meet his descending mouth and gave a purrlike sound as he sucked on her bottom lip. Tangling her fingers in his thick black hair, she pressed their mouths more firmly together, punching up the smoldering heat between them. A needy feeling rose within her, and turning, she pressed him back on the bed, straddling his lap, maintaining their connection. He groaned, opening his mouth, inviting her tongue to dance with his own. God, yes, was all she thought.

His hand ran up and down the length of her back, igniting fires along her sensitized skin. She was fighting for air as she continued to kiss him, unwilling to give up that hot, all-consuming connection. Feeling her heart pounding in her chest, she changed the angle of their kiss, taking it deeper. He gripped her hip in response, rocking into her. Their anguished moans rolled out. That was the only sign she needed to push off his lap, press him down on the bed, and tug on his pants.

"Now who's in a hurry?" he asked, baring his teeth as he helped her with his zipper.

"You know I excel at speed," she shot back with a playful smirk. "Besides, why wait for what I want?"

He lifted his hips to help her, given they were both effectively one-handed. She slid his pants down, and before she could blink, she was flat on her back beside him. He rose up off the bed, stripped the rest of his clothes off, and then tugged her leg so her hips ended up at the edge of the bed.

"I can handle your impatience," he said, falling to his knees and arranging their cuffed hands beside her knee, tickling the underside of it. "But you're going to have to let me play a little."

His free hand slid up the inside of her thigh, shattering her already rapid breathing. "I'm totally fine with that. Play away."

"Oh, I plan to, don't worry." He tugged down her yoga pants, and she lifted her hips to aid him, wanting to feel his heat, his mouth, his body on her.

"Promises, promises," she breathed as he slicked the pants off her ankles, leaving her completely bare before him.

His hot gaze slowly traveled the length of her body, that telltale pulse of desire beating fiercely in his neck. "God, you are so ridiculously beautiful. Later...I don't know when...I'm going to want you to put one of your bikinis on and sit on my lap." He fitted his shoulders between her legs, spreading her wide. "But until then, let me show you what I can do without my hands."

She was already arching up as his mouth touched her core, making her cry out harshly. Electric shock waves shot through her pelvis. Her eyelids drifted shut as he used his mouth and tongue to bring her to the brink. She was panting hard as the first wave hit, the force bending her back onto the bed. "Yes, oh, yes, oh yes!"

"I should have known you'd be loud—even though you look so sweet."

Her breath was heaving after her orgasm, so she had to suck in more air before she could answer him. "Are you complaining?" She cracked her eyes open. "Because I'd think you'd be pleased I was so vocal about your performance, Grandpa."

"No way you cried out like that for a senior citizen," he said with a hearty laugh, playfully kissing his way up her belly, before turning his attention to her breasts, putting his mouth on first one and then the other.

She arched into him. "Yeah, you're right about that. Oh, Robbie—"

"Talk to me," he urged, his voice low and harsh and filled with heat as he made her moan again. He used his mouth with the same kind of focused intensity he did everything, until she was pulling his head to her breast, urging him to use more tongue and teeth. He did, and they both groaned audibly, fingers tensing on each other's skin.

"I need—"

"So do I."

His response was harsh and urgent, and she gripped his shoulder, pulling him up. Their eyes locked, his gaze wild and determined. She touched his jaw. "Are you finished playing?"

"Never," he ground out before laying his forehead against hers and rubbing it deliciously. "You make me want everything—all at once. God, Lily. I never saw this coming, but I am so glad you're here."

"Me too," she whispered, feeling tenderness as well as desire as he angled back to gaze at her face.

His erection nudged her core, and they both froze for a moment, anguished groans pouring from their chests. "That felt like an electric shock all the way to my—"

"Yeah," she said. "Condom. Now."

"Bossy." His head whipped up, the tense angles of his face clenched with need as he gave a tight smile. "I like it. We'll do slow later."

"I'm going to want to lap you up," she panted as she watched him tear open the packet with his teeth.

"Later." He looked down at her under him before studying the condom. "Jesus, we're going to have to work together to get this on me."

"I excel at cross-departmental cooperation," she told him, levering herself up so she could help him fit the condom over his very sizeable length. "God, you are so pretty."

He shot her a wicked look. "You're going to have to do better than that, sweet girl, but right now, I don't care what you call it. God, I'm about ready to explode. Lie back and hold still."

She choked out a laugh. "Oh, you are so hot when you're dispensing orders. What else do you want me to do, Captain?"

"It's Lieutenant, and I want you to shut up, so I don't buck into you like a bronco right out of the gate." He eased into her, making her cry out. "Please don't tighten up around me yet."

"Oh, I got a please," she said hotly, bringing her hips up as he shifted deeper. "God, yes, that makes everything better."

He thrust into her core and then froze, groaning loudly. Lifting his head, he sought her gaze, his heart in his eyes. "Lily."

The use of her real name was important. Epic. She felt her throat catch right before he started thrusting, first deep and searching before their mingled cries sent the pace faster, urgency driving them on. He brought their cuffed hands to the side of her head, tangling his fingertips with hers as the wave built. Levering her hips to meet him, she pushed him on, feeling the hot rush start in her belly.

Their gazes locked as it swept over them, and she watched as blind shock crested over his face. Then he froze and threw his head back, crying out loudly. Pulsing, heart beating wildly in her chest, she wrapped her free arm around him as he levered onto her, holding up his full weight by an elbow. His lips cruised into her neck, his hot breath panting madly against her skin.

"God," he rasped out. "God, Lily."

She turned her head, needing to see him. His eyes were clenched together, desire still raging through him, making the line of his jaw and brows tense with passion. She felt the pulse, the way their hearts pounded in unison, and knew she'd just experienced a connection greater than anything she'd ever had before. "Robbie," she whispered.

His eyes opened immediately, a bright blue filled with tenderness and something she wasn't ready to name yet, not until he did. Then he smiled, a smile so warm her heart somersaulted in her chest. They gazed at each other, neither moving as they breathed shallowly, and Lily welcomed the moment of stillness, knowing it was precious. Her heart settled down inside her chest, filled with a new warmth and contentment.

"Well, Lily," he said unevenly, his exhale harsh and charged from their mutual lack of oxygen. "I don't think you can call me grandpa now."

Sliding her hand into his hair, she tugged him closer so she could lay a kiss on his gorgeous mouth. He slid them both onto their sides, kissing her softly until she pressed back, a totally happy smile stretching across her face. "No, probably not. I'm actually pretty relieved."

His reluctant laugh brought a black lock of hair onto his forehead, making him look boyish. "Me too. Now...as we lie here together, it's getting harder and harder for me to ignore that the handcuffs are as sweaty as the rest of me and that we still need to get them off."

She worried her lip, already wincing with embarrassment at how much ragging Sheila was going to give her when she caught sight of her after this. "We're also going to have to get dressed again. Somehow. Before I beg Sheila for the key."

He cursed. "Right. I didn't think that one through. I probably should have left my shirt on."

"No way." She ran a slow finger down the center of his chest. "I wanted all of you. I've had fantasies about this chest."

He closed his eyes, a satisfied smile coasting over his face.

"Good to know. We probably need to start thinking practically. In a minute or so. Before we face the music together."

Liking that he was as reluctant to rejoin the real world as she was, she cuddled into him as best she could, arranging their handcuffed hands on his hard stomach. "Despite how much I wish it were otherwise, we should. How about we hop in the shower, wash each other's backs, figure out our wardrobe, and then find our jailers?"

"Because you have your brilliant plan to unveil," he said, kissing her sweetly on the mouth. "I'm all ears now, in case you didn't know."

She traced his face, savoring this final moment with him before they had to return to the job. "Good. Because it's a bit unconventional."

CHAPTER NINETEEN

Robbie ran his hands through his wet hair, his mouth falling open.

"That's your plan?" He studied Lily as she sat across from him on the couch, legs crossed, while Sheila beamed with pride. Tim didn't move a muscle on the couch next to him, but he glanced surreptitiously at his brother and watched a canny grin break out over his face. His brother was having way too much fun. He'd chuckled heartily when he and Sheila had finally returned with the key, ten minutes after Robbie and Lily had showered and found something to cover her, and learned he needed to grab his brother a new shirt.

"It's perfect." Tim leaned forward to fist-bump first Lily and then Sheila.

"Right?" her partner bandied back. "Buck, our boss, wanted to go by the regular playbook, like Robbie feared, but Lily was like no way. We can't use Tara like that. No sending her undercover with a wire. No putting her in the crosshairs of the Kellys where actual harm could come to her. She has two little girls we need to protect, she said. And you know

263

they'll be safe with your brothers and an agent in the FBI safe house. Now, before you get your shorts in a wad, Robbie, I'm going to be playing Tara after—"

"After you release social media footage of her playing around with her new boy toy." He coughed on the word, earning him a backslap from Tim. "Which you plan to use the real Tara for."

"Not only macking on him, but living it up large," Lily added, her hands clenched in her lap as though she was nervous.

He turned to look at his baby brother, trying to keep an open mind, especially as Lily was sitting still as a rail, her green eyes practically imploring him to see things her way. Upstairs, they'd been so in sync, and he missed that. Now he was struggling to understand.

"How is it you see the brilliance of this, and I don't?" he asked his brother. "Tim, you've lived in Southie your whole life. Why in the world do you think the Kellys are going to send some of their guys down to the Outer Banks because they think Tara is in a hot new relationship? I don't get the whole boy toy, living it up part."

Lily opened her mouth, but Tim held up a hand. "Let me. We know the Kellys want her, but what Lily is suggesting is downright Shakespearean. *Hamlet. MacBeth*—"

"Here we go again," he ground out, tempted to put his hands over his ears.

"They're going to think it's a trap if we just put Tara out as bait." Tim tapped the side of his nose. "But this way, we're going to make it look like you have the girls while Tara is off doing what women do best in this instance—or so it's broadly thought."

"Keep going," Robbie practically pleaded, shooting Lily a tight smile.

"Tara is going to look like she's taking her revenge—on both the Kellys and Scotty. First, she's going to have a new plaything—total vacation rebound. Second, she's going to look like she's spending the Kellys' money like there's no tomorrow."

"That's what worries me," he said, pressing a hand to his belly.

"A total fuck you to both the Kellys and her ex will drive them both nuts," Sheila informed him with a delighted wiggle on the couch. "We're talking serious revenge."

"Plus, Tara is going to look like she's gone wild," Tim put in. "Crazy. She'll look uncontrollable. Even by you, the serious, don't mess with me—"

"I get the picture." What he was getting was a migraine. "So I'm supposed to tell my boss and the officer working the nail salon arson case that I took Tara's girls so she could get away for a while and party? Jesus, I'm going to look like an idiot."

"Exactly!" Sheila exclaimed. "We don't want to feed anyone's suspicions that you're using Tara as bait, seeing as you're a cop. It's better for them to think she's being reckless. And trust me, men don't have a hard time believing that about women."

"You'll tell them you told her to get out of town and lay low," Lily broke in, smoothing her palms on her thighs, which he had to force himself not to stare at. "But she's not thinking logically. Just like a woman. She's angry."

"Pissed!" Tim cheerfully added, crossing his ankles. "And you know what they say about women and revenge?"

He'd been a cop for years and heard plenty of confessions, but he looked at his brother blankly. "No, Tim, what?"

His grin was downright devilish. "Hide your credit cards. And you know what they say about men?"

"I'm a guy, Tim, so you don't need to spell it out."

"Oh, but it's so much fun to dissolve into stereotypes," Sheila bandied back. "No guys like to be a cuckold. Tim, I used that term for you."

"You're a lady and a scholar," he said, blowing her a kiss, making Robbie groan.

"A woman isn't supposed to spend a man's money like it's nothing," Sheila followed up. "Especially when it's not hers and she doesn't have his permission."

"I love it!"

Robbie's head whipped toward the kitchen doorway as Tara breezed into the room, wearing jeans and a beige T-shirt she'd jauntily tied at the waist. "Where the hell did you come from?" he asked.

Tim slowly raised his hand. "I snuck her into the kitchen with Sheila's blessing to expedite things. I figured our cousin could come to her own conclusions."

"Tim told me your new squeeze is FBI." Tara gave him a playful wink, her usual sass back in her smile. "And he convinced me not to look a gift horse in the mouth. We have the Feds on our side. That puts the Kellys in boiling hot water, not just warm Southie water. It also protects us from the Kelly snitches on the force."

"Precisely!" Sheila snapped her fingers. "There's a long list of crimes we plan to tie them to."

Tara rubbed her hands together delightedly. "Music to my ears. I'm so ready for this to be over. Besides, all Reagan and Cassidy could talk about was their sweet friends next door, who taught them to surf and bought them princess wands. And clearly you like her, cuz. How could I not listen to her plan? Besides, I like that I'll look like one of those idiots in your stupid criminal videos. Except the joke will be on them for believing it."

"Stupid criminal videos?" Sheila gasped. "I love watching those. I send them to Lily all the time."

Lily met his gaze. "Now you can send yours to me too," she said, a soft smile taking sail across her face.

"After this nightmare is over." He put his head in his hands after Tara cast another knowing look at him and then Lily. "So you're totally on board with this? Tara, I was planning on taking you back to Boston and having you talk to my guys on the force informally—"

"What does that accomplish?" Tara blew a curl out of her eye. "Nothing. Just more talk-talk-talk. Plus, I believe the Kellys when they say they have a mole in your department, maybe more than one. I'm assuming you haven't smoked them out yet."

He breathed fire before shaking his head. "No, we haven't."

"I don't know the full scope of Lily's plan—nice to meet you with your real name, by the way—but I imagine she's got a plan for catching the mole or moles too."

"I do." Lily nodded with killer confidence. "We just need you to lay a few false breadcrumbs—with Internal Affairs' full knowledge, of course."

He tipped his head toward the ceiling. "God, I knew this was coming. I'm going to be persona non grata."

"No, you aren't." Lily leaned forward, a determined fist resting on her knee. "Robbie, you're going to put the Kellys down so they don't come back and hurt your family. I'm including you in our case. I told Buck I needed you to pull it off. We share the collar."

"And that's really big of her considering how much this case matters for the promotion she's going after," Sheila added, making a big boom noise afterward. "We're talking a chance to join the Child Exploitation and Human Trafficking

Task Force, in Boston, something she's worked toward her whole life."

He swallowed thickly, knowing the seeds of her motivation. "I'm humbled, and I'm on board. If I get a little grouchy, it's only because I hate deceiving cops."

"At least you aren't a mole selling people out to the Kellys." Tara crossed and cozied up next to him, punching his arm lightly. "Look, I want this done. I don't care if I have to play kissy-face with the ugliest undercover FBI agent in history to accomplish that. I want to be free of this problem and back in Southie with my girls. *Safe*."

There was a silent plea in her eyes, one that spoke of the fear and vulnerability she was pushing back to stay strong. "We're going to take every precaution," he promised her.

"Of course," Lily said with assuring hands. "I'll show you all the details. We'll execute our plan flawlessly."

"Down to me dressing up like your cousin here," Sheila said, closing in on Tara and studying her like a hawk. "I'll need to study your mannerisms. All the way down to how you like to do your makeup and nails. Oh, and by the way, you won't have to suck face with an ugly FBI officer. The agent Lily has in mind has set records for blowing panties off."

"Sheila Morales!" Lily cried out. "That is totally unprofessional."

Robbie cleared his throat while Tim sputtered with laughter beside him.

Her partner only sashayed her hips. "Come on, Lily. You set running records at Quantico. Tyler Darren has set records for having women practically fling their panties at him. Everyone knows it. That's why he's the most wanted undercover agent out there. That guy has played everything from a male stripper to a pretty boy Ivy League Wall Street type."

Tara made a girlish sound that had Robbie wanting to

bash his head in. "Got a picture?" she asked in a sultry voice he was sure would scramble his brain.

"You bet." Sheila pulled her phone out of her yoga top, making Robbie cringe, as Tara got up to take a look.

Tara whistled. "Okay, you weren't overselling. Nothing is photoshopped?"

"No, ma'am. That's all Tyler. Sometimes I wonder how he gets his reports in and finds the time to stay that ripped. Because there's ripped—"

"And then there's ripped." Tara made another one of those sounds Robbie wished he could unhear. "Scotty is going to lose his shit when he sees me sipping a Mai Tai off this honey's washboard abs."

"Tara, for the love of—"

Tim elbowed him. "She's getting into character. Let her be."

Sheila glared at him as well. "What he said. Tara, Tyler and I have done dozens assignments together, and I can promise you...you're about to have some serious fun, girl."

Fun? Were they insane?

"Sheila is trying to assure Tara—"

"I know," he told Lily, holding up his hand. "It's just a little jarring."

She crossed and sat down next to him on the couch, more serious than he'd ever seen her. "I say this with the greatest care and respect for you. You're going to have to forget you're related to Tara and just be a cop right now. I need Lieutenant Robbie O'Connor by my side, not Robbie, the concerned cousin."

He bit the inside of his jaw, glad for the reminder. "You have him. Once I get rid of Billie and Shakespeare here. Ah... by the way, Tim. What exactly did you tell Billie about why you've been over here? I can't imagine he was thrilled to be babysitting the girls alone."

Tim turned sheepish. "About that...I kinda told him Sheila was preparing a big surprise for him with our help, so he needed to stay out of the way."

"Well, it's kinda true," Sheila said with a wince.

"And he bought that?"

"Dude likes Clarice." Tim lifted a shoulder. "He bought it hook, line, and sinker."

Robbie pinched the bridge of his nose, wondering how Billie was going to take the news. He hoped he'd simply laugh it off with his *easy come, easy go* grin. Because they had enough balls in the air. "Your lying is starting to worry me, Tim."

"Except the story *is* true," Tim followed up with glee dancing in his eyes. "And handcuffing you and Lily together so you'd listen to her wasn't lying exactly—"

"*What?*" Tara interrupted. "You two were handcuffed?"

Robbie squirmed, and Lily gave a humorless laugh. "Tim has become very theatrical all of a sudden."

"Tim's plan helped these two lovebirds come together for real," Sheila said, making loud kissing noises.

"Tim came up with the idea?" Tara lifted a hand for Tim to high-five, which he did, rising and putting his arm around their cousin. "Way to go. Respect, man."

He broke free to give one of his new regal bows, to which she responded with a curtsy. They'd created a monster.

"Tim has grown quite a bit on this trip," Robbie said diplomatically. "We might keep the handcuff thing in this room."

"No way, cousin!" Tara gave a bawdy laugh. "This story is going to be told again and again at O'Connor's Pub."

"Don't forget about BBQs and family reunions," Tim said, giving Tara another high five.

Lily was looking down in her lap, a slight flush on her cheeks. "Do you see what you've gotten yourself into?" he asked. "Think you can take it?"

She lifted her head, her green eyes filled with that all too sexy challenge he loved. "You bet I can, Grandpa. Can you take this plan I've cooked up?"

He laid his hand close to her leg. "You're right. It's brilliant. But I'll need you to add something to your equipment list."

She gave a beaming smile, looking very much like the girl next door. "Anything."

"Antacids."

They shared a smile. "And here I thought you wanted a Benelli M3."

"That too."

Sheila gave a pretend swoon. "Oh, gun talk. That's so sexy."

It really was, he thought, as he stared at Lily and realized this could be the rest of his life if he wanted it. And he did. God help him, he really did. "Glad that's settled."

"I have a request for that equipment list too," Tara said, garnering their attention. "I need a new wardrobe and a shirt that says Running Wild in rhinestones."

Lily's mouth twitched. "I'll see what we can do, but I don't think you're going to complain about the wardrobe I have in mind. Or the accessories. We're talking luxury brands with loud screaming labels. And wait until you see the car I have in mind that we confiscated from a drug dealer. Tara, you're going to look like you've spent at least three hundred thousand dollars with your new boy toy on vacation."

"Wow, you guys really mean living large." She fluffed her unusually flat hair. "Oh, this is going to be fun."

Lily rested back against the couch next to him, which felt not only right, but perfect. This wasn't a woman who'd want him to have a different job. This was a woman he could talk cases over with—and she, in turn, could talk her cases through with him. Their passion for each other was as great as their passion for justice. God, he was getting cheesy. He put his arm casually over the back of the sofa, toying with the ends of her hair where no one could see. But deep down it all came down to one truth: she was his perfect partner.

"I think we've laid out the initial steps for everyone," Lily said, very much in charge, a position that looked good on her. "Now, let's go and catch some bad guys."

CHAPTER TWENTY

T IM AND TARA RETURNED TO THE HOUSE TO PLAY WITH the girls so Sheila could tell Billie about his so-called "surprise."

Lily's nerves were strung tight. Not only for Sheila but for Billie. Robbie insisted on staying in case his brother acted like a jerk. Sheila had only nodded with a fixed smile. Lily knew that smile. It was part of her poker face.

She dragged Robbie into the living room to give her partner and Billie a little privacy in the kitchen, which Sheila had decided was the best place to reveal her cover, joking about the kitchen island being a good barrier.

Billie rapped lightly on the patio door before slicking it open after being welcomed inside. "You part of this surprise too?" he asked, stopping short, seeing them.

Lily cleared her throat. "Sort of. My friend will tell you. She's in the kitchen."

"Great!" He craned his neck, heading that way. "Come out, come out, wherever you are."

Robbie gave a low groan as Lily clenched her teeth.

"Hi, Billie," she heard her partner say.

"There you are! I hear you have a surprise for me. Where is it?"

"It's not a physical present," Sheila responded, irony in her voice. "In fact, you aren't going to believe it when you hear it."

Lily heard her partner's voice drop then, the kind of low mumble she gave when she was giving a field status. Professional. To the point.

"FBI?" After a moment, Billie's deep belly laugh filled the house. "Summer too?"

Her partner must have nodded, because his laughter became louder. "Oh my God! You're kidding! I didn't know Feds could look like you two. Robbie must have lost his shit. Hey, bro? You need a diaper change in there?"

Lily looked over at Robbie, who silently shook his head as if to say he didn't know how things were going to go down yet. But teasing was good, right?

"And you and—what are your names again?"

"Sheila Morales and Lily Meadows," her partner answered factually.

"Right. Sheila. Good to meet the real you. So you followed us all the way from Boston, huh? And have been watching the whole time? God, I wish I'd known that last night when I played solitaire and kept an eye out. I've never been more worried in my life."

Honest, Lily thought. No thread of anger in his voice. That was good too.

"You've got a gun, right?" he asked.

"Upstairs."

"Can I see it? Chicks with guns are so hot. What about handcuffs? You can cuff me anytime."

Sexist and yet playful, which was so very Billie. Robbie pinched the bridge of his nose. "I think it's going pretty well, don't you?" she whispered.

Robbie gave a strained thumbs-up.

"I hope you aren't upset—" Sheila began.

"Upset?" Billie's laughter boomed out again. "Are you kidding? My guys are going to love this story. Meeting you has been one of the best parts of this fake vacation. I'm thrilled you went for me while undercover. I take it as a compliment. I know Robbie was the perfect mark being the cop, but you could have always gone after Tim. You chose me."

Lily could almost see him puffing out his chest.

"I seemed more your type from your social media account," Sheila said with a relieved laugh.

"That you are, sweetheart." Another sexy chuckle. "So, you're going to protect Tara and take down the Kellys. You might be my new hero. To think, I'll be able to say I briefly went out with the hot Fed who put those guys in the slammer. Can I have a selfie with you? I'm so putting the photo up in my garage."

"Maybe not that part since I work undercover," Sheila sputtered, clearly amused.

Robbie's mouth parted, and Lily pressed her lips together to keep from laughing. So they'd been worried for nothing. Billie saw the whole thing as a lark. True to form. She knew her partner liked him, but his response didn't cut off the possibility of a future connection, did it?

Sheila entered the family room with a bemused look on her face. "I'm about to be immortalized in a mechanic shop. Lucky me. I'll just grab my phone."

Lily gave her partner a finger gun along with her own bemused look. "Aren't we all glad that's behind us?"

"So glad," Robbie ground out.

Billie strolled in, his hands tucked in his jeans. "You stayed because you thought I was going to go ape shit. Brother, you've got me all wrong. This is the best thing that's ever happened to me. A hot chick in the FBI choosing me for her undercover side piece. Man, it's like ascending a new level or something."

"Glad you think so," Robbie said, studying his brother.

"I know I am." Lily stood up and thrust out her hand. "I'm Lily Meadows. Good to meet you, Billie."

He took it gently, caressing her hand. "Do all the chicks in the FBI look like you and Sheila? Because maybe I need to apply."

"Billie."

"That's a compliment, bro." Billie put his arm around her shoulders. "I hope you know my brother totally is into you."

"That rumor has been confirmed," she answered, her lips twitching since he didn't know about the handcuffs yet. "I happen to be really into him too."

"Excellent." He turned as Sheila came in, holding up her phone. "There's the hottest chick in the FBI. Come on, sweetheart. Let's take that selfie. Afterward, I want to get a photo with all four of us. The two gorgeous Feds who hoodwinked the O'Connor boys. God, this is awesome."

Lily breathed a sigh of relief. Now they could start the operation.

Billie sported his usual *easy come, easy go* smile from then on, helping Tim with the girls after Tara told Reagan that the women she'd known as Summer and Clarice were undercover guardian angels, watching over them while she was gone. Lily had thought it was a sweet way to explain things, and while she could see the questions in Reagan's eyes, the little girl had hugged her warmly and given her an enthusiastic thank you. Then she'd given both Lily and Sheila tinfoil guardian angel badges she'd made with Tim, something that had warmed their hearts.

After a full day of working toward their joint goal—something that felt right and invigorating—they all played with the kids and had a BBQ to celebrate the new direction of events.

She and Robbie even found some moments to sneak away and explore their burgeoning passion for each other. Then they went through the same thing the next day.

Everything was going according to plan.

Until Tyler showed up.

Because when alpha males occupy the same playground...

When he got out of the car, Sheila stepped out onto the patio to greet him, and Billie's face tightened as he watched the FBI agent pick her up off the ground in a big hug, making her partner laugh wildly. Billie, Robbie, Lily, and Tim were all out on the beach with the kids—one last beach hangout before the kids left—and Billie took one menacing step toward the house before Robbie stopped him with a hand on his arm.

"I've changed my mind," Billie said tersely as he shook Robbie off and continued toward the house. "I'm not leaving."

She and Robbie shared a shocked look as they followed him, shooting Tim and Reagan an assuring smile as they paused in their sandcastle making.

Robbie snagged his brother's arm, halting him while he was still on the beach. Billie's easy grin was gone, replaced by a *ready to brawl* set of his jaw and big body. Lily approached cautiously. Did Billie have deeper feelings for Sheila than he'd let on since learning the truth? Sheila had been realistic about Billie's lighthearted reaction, saying he went through women like Lily went through coconut water. Tim had later commented that this O'Connor brother didn't do the green-eyed monster.

She laid a gentle hand on Robbie's arm as she heard Billie's teeth grind together. Sheila punched Tyler playfully in the arm after he set her down, falling into their comfortable rhythm, but Lily wanted to wince as she imagined the scene through Billie's eyes. The noon sun was practically glowing on the six-foot-five blond agent. Sheila had joked Tyler's good looks made her believe in God last night as they'd all had their final dinner together after the kids went to bed. Billie had laughed along with everyone else—before Tim had started all of his Shakespeare nonsense again about Tyler being a rose...

"You know, Billie—I've lost count of the number of cases Agent Darren and Sheila have worked on together," Lily said, doing her best to be diplomatic and save Robbie from having to step in.

She and Robbie were still finding their groove—as lovers and as professionals—but so far, they seemed to have the whole complementary leadership thing down pat. He could be the bad cop, and she excelled at making things work as the good one, so to speak.

Buck had told her he liked Robbie after their first joint operational call, and Buck didn't even like Santa Claus or the Easter Bunny, saying the holiday sham led to increased crime.

"Their rapport is part of what makes them so successful," she continued, trying to assure him.

"They certainly have some rapport," Billie commented darkly.

She immediately shelved the idea of suggesting he take a gander at the sports car Tyler had driven down for their photo and video op—an orange McLaren. Somehow, she thought that would only make things worse. "You don't need to meet him. In fact, why don't you give us a moment to talk to Tyler alone, Billie?"

"There's no need for that," Robbie said, facing his brother. "Right, Billie? In fact, it's downright rude of you to pull this attitude. You assured everyone you were good with this situation."

"That was before I saw this joker!" He gestured rudely in

Tyler's direction. "You can't trust a man that pretty. He looks like he went to Harvard—"

"He did," Lily murmured, not surprised someone from Southie would feel angst toward someone in that part of Boston.

"And I'll bet you a beer at Danny's he was in one of those fancy fraternities—"

"Billie, there's a lot more to Tyler than meets the eye," she interjected, because Tyler *had* been in one of the most exclusive fraternities on campus. "I wouldn't choose another agent for this job. I promise you."

Robbie got in his brother's face. "Don't you dare fuck this up by being jealous over a woman you assured me and everyone else was just a fun time," he said between clenched teeth. "And don't insult Lily. Ever."

God, he really was her knight in shining armor.

Billie held up his hands immediately. "Look, I meant no insult. Okay? But Robbie, tell me you trust that guy. Because that jackass looks more like a pretty boy who's more inclined to lap dance someone than to read them their rights."

"You're making no sense, Billie." Robbie punched the air. "Is he a stripper or a Harvard asshole?"

Lily cleared her throat loudly as Sheila and Tyler both looked over. "Brothers! They're going to miss each other so much. Hey, Tyler! I'll be with you in a just a sec. Good to see you, man."

Robbie poked his brother in the chest as she forced a smile at their audience. "Billie," he said in a hard undertone, "so help me... If Lily says he's a hardened FBI agent, you believe her. I do."

She couldn't help but get a happy little glow from the way he was backing her. Since he'd set aside his own reservations, he'd been with her every step of the way, smoothing anything needed—including Reagan's fears about leaving without him, which she voiced at bedtime last night. That had torn him up, but it had also made him more focused. *The Kellys have to go down because I can't take seeing tears in that little girl's eyes ever again,* he'd told her, and she'd fallen even more in love with him.

"I'm only being protective because that joker is going to put his hands on...Tara," Billie spat out badly.

Even Lily knew he'd meant to say Sheila. Tension raced up her spine as Robbie stepped even closer to his brother. "That's not what this is about, and you know it. You and me are going to have a problem if you do or say anything to make either Sheila or Tara uncomfortable. Now, smile, dipshit. They're coming this way."

Billie elbowed Robbie back, breaking his professional smile for a moment.

"He's going to behave now, Lily," Robbie assured her tightly. "Or I'm covering him in jellyfish."

Lily laughed weakly as Tyler and Sheila reached them. Her partner was practically sashaying over, and she sent her a warning look as she said, "Tyler Darren. Meet Lieutenant Robbie O'Connor and his brother, Billie."

"I've heard a lot about you guys." Tyler extended his hand to Robbie first. "Nice to meet you, although I know we all wish it wasn't necessary."

Lily watched as Robbie clasped his hand. When he needed to, Tyler had a granite handshake, and clearly, he knew it was necessary with the O'Connors. He met Robbie's eyes head-on, showing him the steel behind his good looks. Should she have mentioned to Billie that Tyler was a Rhodes Scholar? She'd shown Robbie his agent file to assure him of both his competency as well as his track record with the Bureau.

"It's good to meet you, Agent Darren," Robbie said in his

flat, professional voice. "Lily and Sheila sing your praises, and they're no pushovers."

"That's one of the reasons why I like working with them," Tyler said, showing his perfect white teeth.

"Oh, stop!" Sheila said, hitting him again playfully.

Lily wanted to strangle her partner. Sheila damn well knew that Billie was acting weird...and also why.

Lily watched as Billie proved her partner right by aggressively extending his hand to Tyler.

The agent shook his hand, gripping it tightly, giving Billie the same unflinching look.

Billie didn't let go right away but leaned in and said in a menacingly soft voice, "Yeah, a pleasure, but if you get my cousin or any of these other beautiful people killed, we're going to have a problem, you and me. And no freaking tongue when you're playing boyfriend. With either of them. Got it?"

Lily's eyes widened as Sheila puffed out a laugh. "Well, that ruins my day."

Tyler shot her partner a look. "I'll bet..."

Robbie politely laughed before glaring at Billie. "My brother is a protective kind of guy."

"We have that in common, then," Tyler said, suddenly looking dead serious despite his casual white T-shirt, worn jeans with a rip in the knees, and black flip-flops. "Trust me. They're in good hands."

"The best." Sheila grinned as she grabbed one of Tyler's. "I mean, jeez, look at the size of these. I'm surprised you can find a gun that works, Tyler."

"Cut it out, Sheila," Tyler said, saving Lily the task of threatening to kill her partner. "I'm trying to assure Mr. O'Connor here. I know it can't be easy leaving here today, but I promise you that Lily's plan is one of the smartest operations I've been involved in. From the moment I heard she'd smoked my training officer at Quantico in a run up Radar Hill, I knew she was someone to watch."

"Thanks, Tyler," she said, ducking her chin a little. "Tara is inside putting her little girl down for a nap."

"Not anymore," Robbie said as she stepped out onto the patio.

"Is that my new friend?" she called breezily.

Lily braced herself for the next possible drama, wishing Tim wasn't still trying to keep Reagan occupied with building a sandcastle. The little girl had to be watching everything, especially since her mother had told her how they were kind of putting on a play to explain her new clothes and why she was staying behind for a day. Just this morning Reagan had made a point of telling her mother how pretty she looked in her new sleeveless black Dolce & Gabbana dress. *"I'm back to myself, Miss Pixie,"* her mother had said with a wink.

And Tara did ooze confidence as she sauntered over in her new undercover dress, wearing the killer designer gold heels they'd had expressed from Manhattan with the rest of her spending spree items. How did she walk on the beach with those?

"I heard your car drive up and told Miss Purrfect to keep Cassidy company until she fell asleep. Hi, I'm Tara."

"Agent Tyler Darren," he said, extending his hand, professional to the bone. "I appreciate you trusting me to take care of you and do my part while we're executing Agent Meadows' plan."

Tara shook his hand with both of hers, a fixed smile on her face, but Lily caught how her shoulders seemed to drop their tension. "You have no idea how much your help means."

"Lily and Sheila know this," Tyler said in that relatable way of his, "but I became an FBI agent because someone hurt a woman I cared about. Lily specializes in cases involving kids. I specialize in cases with women in trouble and in dangerous situations."

Wetness shone in Tara's eyes momentarily. "Well, that's me! Agent Darren, you are heaven-sent—like our guardian angels Lily and Sheila here."

"I'm only doing my job, ma'am," he said, continuing to let her shake his hand.

Billie rolled his eyes, making Sheila putter out a laugh, but Robbie sent Lily a half smile. She could all but hear him thinking, *Okay, I like this guy*.

Billie didn't seem so convinced. He was staring at Tyler like he was a cockroach he'd like to crush with his boot.

"Tara, why don't you and Agent Darren go inside and sit down with Sheila and talk through the itinerary today?" She patted her cell in her cotton drawstring pants. "I need to see how close Agent Petris is to arriving."

"It would be a pleasure."

"Hang on," Tyler said, reaching into his pocket. "Lily asked me to pick this up for you, Robbie."

When Robbie noticed the bottle of antacids he'd requested, he sent her an amused look. "I was kidding. Mostly."

"Details," she only responded as he pocketed them in his shorts.

"Lily doesn't forget anything, does she?" Tara linked arms with Tyler as the trio walked off. "So tell me a little more how you see things working between us."

Lily glanced over at Billie as she pulled out her phone. His face looked set in stone now, and she wondered whether there was anything to do. If he wanted to see Sheila again, he could ask her, right? Interfering didn't seem like a good way to kick off her new relationship with the O'Connor clan. Also, just because Billie looked jealous didn't mean he wanted to date her partner. Everyone knew his reputation.

"Agent Petris is going to be here in thirty minutes," she said after reading his text.

"I'll tell Tim and Reagan they need to get changed and ready for our road trip," Billie practically growled, shoving his hands in his pockets and striding off.

"Ignore him." Robbie jerked his head in his brother's direction. "He'll get his head on straight. I know he's not happy we're splitting up."

She laid her hand on his arm. "Neither are you. You look like you tossed and turned all night after you left me." They'd agreed it was better for him to continue sleeping in the O'Connor house, which meant no sleepovers.

He shrugged. "I missed you. We haven't woken up together yet."

She leaned a little closer to him, aware they were in a public space. "You have a standing invite to sleep over at my apartment back in Boston."

His eyes narrowed. "I'm in love with you, and I don't even know where you live."

She'd suspected how he felt about her, but hearing the words made her heart zing. "I'm in love with you too, but I know where *you* live," she joked.

"I'm glad we're in agreement on how we feel, but I still don't—"

Oh, he was so serious suddenly. "So, we have a lot of details to share. Like the fact that I live alone and don't have pets. Near Harvard. Kidding!"

He didn't laugh.

"Come on. That was funny."

"Robbie!" Reagan cried.

They turned to see the little girl running toward them, covered in sand, her ruffled purple swimsuit still wet in spots from her surfing attempt earlier with her uncles' help.

"Billie says we need to get ready to go." She arrived with

repressed tears in her eyes. "But I really don't want to leave Mommy and you here. Why can't you come with us?"

Lily's heart broke for the little girl. Since Tara had arrived, Reagan had been practically glued to her side, while Cassidy had preferred to be held more. Even Miss Purrfect hadn't been far away, either weaving figure eights around Tara's legs or resting beside her feet. She glanced over at Robbie, whose face seemed to get harder before he crouched down to his little cousin's level.

Cupping her slender arms gently, he said, "Because I have to stay here and help your mom fix some of the things your daddy did with our little play. Remember how she told you that last night?"

She nodded fiercely, biting her lip. Lily admired Tara for being as honest as she could with the two girls about why things were the way they were. She knew some parents just wanted to gloss over things and tell their kids everything was fine, but they always sensed it when something was wrong. She'd felt that way at Reagan's age.

She hoped Reagan and Cassidy would only remember this short trip as a blip on the screen away from their mother, not knowing until they were much older, perhaps, how dangerous things had been. Of course, losing their father was likely to be a continued reality, and Lily hoped she could find some way to help soften that now that she was in Robbie's life.

"Your mom will be back with you tomorrow night, okay?" He tipped her chin up. "Billie and Tim will make sure you and Cassidy have a ball until then, along with Lily's work friend, who's going to be with you guys."

"It won't be the same without you," Reagan whispered softly, and Lily laid her hand on Robbie's shoulder. If she had a ball of emotion lodged in her throat now, she couldn't imagine what he must feel.

This little girl was losing her protector, the one who'd

been there from the beginning of this misadventure. Separating from him would be like ripping off a Band-Aid. But Robbie had been resolute in his desire to stay in the Outer Banks and be on-site when the Kellys sent their men for Tara. She'd given him the option, even though she'd already known what his choice would be.

"I'll be with you soon enough." A smile flickered on his face. "But I need to stay here with Lily and Sheila until you guys can go back to Boston. It'll only be for a little while longer."

Reagan lowered her head again, studying her sandy feet.

Tim arrived with Billie, holding the red bucket and shovel. They shared the same grim expression as Robbie, but then Tim shook himself and stuck the bucket on his head.

"What ho!" he cried in his fake British accent, spitting sand out of his mouth as the dregs rained down on his face. "What doth thou think of my new hat? Does it suit me? Or is it missing a feather?"

Reagan slowly raised her head, but her young face was pale and strained. "You don't have to cheer me up, Tim. Mom says it's okay for me to be sad sometimes."

The men all seemed to jerk as if they'd been electrocuted by her honesty. Time for Lily to step in. She lowered herself to a knee. "She's right, and I'd be sad and a little scared if I were in your shoes—even though you aren't wearing any."

That had her mouth tipping up. "I know what you mean. Mom says you have to walk in someone's shoes sometimes to understand them."

"I agree." She touched Reagan's heart. "Since you love princesses, I'll bet you remember the other thing they have inside them besides beauty and magic."

Curiosity smoothed out the tension in her O'Connor blue eyes. "Maybe."

Lily smiled, aware of Robbie's gaze on her. "Some call it

courage. Others bravery. But it's a strong trait all people with O'Connor blood seem to possess from what I can see. It means you do what you have to when things aren't perfect and you don't like them."

"Like my mommy and Robbie are doing," Reagan said hesitantly. "And Billie."

The tall man straightened at the mention of his name, but she answered before he could respond. "Yes, but actually, I was thinking about you. Because you don't want to leave today, but you know it's what your mommy and Robbie want you to do. So you're going to do it. And you're going to help Cassidy have a good time so she won't be too upset."

"We don't want her to cry." Reagan took a few steps closer until she was standing inches away from Lily. "Do you want to stay here?"

"I do actually." She tucked Reagan's thin hair behind her ear. "Because I love my job, but mostly because it's going to help us make sure you and your family can go home to Boston."

And never have to worry about the Kellys again.

"I'm glad you're with Robbie, then." She brightened at last. "That means I'm going to see you in Boston. Since you really live there."

"It does." She smiled at Robbie when he turned his head, his gaze warm with that new tenderness she couldn't get enough of. "Maybe we can have a princess wand shopping date sometime soon."

Reagan nodded. "I think Tim should come along. He's really good at accessorizing. I told Mommy as she tucked me in bed last night, and she couldn't stop laughing. I didn't see why."

"It's the Shakespeare thing," Robbie said, playfully shoving his baby brother. "Tim seems to have discovered his inner goofball on this trip."

Tim gave a lopsided smile. "The enlightened appreciate my special gift. Before we go, we need to do one more thing. Reagan, will you kneel, please?"

"What the—"

Lily silenced Robbie by touching his arm, and they watched as Reagan gave Tim a puzzled look before lowering to the sand. He stood above her, grinning as he touched her little shoulders with the red shovel. "For your courage and bravery on this trip, I hereby reward you with a new title. Arise, Princess Pixie."

Awe transformed her little face as Tim grandly held his hand out to help her up. Lily watched the scene with a soft glow in her heart. Reagan hugged Tim before turning to hug Lily. Then she turned to Robbie, her entire body now straighter and more confident.

"Take good care of my mom," she told him and then wrapped her arms around his waist.

He hugged her gently, lowering his chin to his chest, and looked to be swallowing back emotion. "You take good care of Cassidy for me, Princess Pixie."

"I will," she promised, looking up, very much a young girl growing up.

"Princess Pixie, huh?" Billie closed one eye and tilted his head. "It suits you."

Yeah, it really did, Lily thought as she and Reagan shared a long smile.

Tim pointed to the house. "Come, we must tell your mother and Cassidy about your new title. Miss Pixie is no more."

She took Tim's hand, waving as they left. Lily watched them, feeling in her heart that she hadn't just fallen in love with Robbie but his family.

Billie lightly punched Robbie in the stomach. "I'll forgive

you for leaving me alone with that lunatic, two young girls, and an FBI agent if you take care of Tara."

"Don't insult me," Robbie shot back, but he nudged his brother playfully in the chest. "Maybe when I see you next, we won't be calling you Billie but Prince Blockhead."

"That's *your* name." Billie faced Lily. "Take care of Sheila. Not that she needs it, but I still don't trust that Tyler guy. Made her see God... What bullshit!"

He wandered off, muttering to himself. Robbie turned and faced her. "Thanks for your help there. I'd rather interview a kingpin than try and assure a little kid everything's going to be okay."

"I thought you did a great job." She cupped his jaw. "When you make an effort, you really are good with women. Grandpa."

He coughed out a laugh. "Some women. It's probably my old age and all the wisdom that comes with it."

Her lips twitched. "Probably. Agent Petris should be arriving any minute now. If I didn't have so many fellow agents around, I'd kiss you senseless."

"Later," he promised, grabbing her hand and squeezing it. "I should go inside and help them get everything ready to go. It would be awful if they left anything here. I mean, Cassidy can't sleep good without her teddy bear and Reagan just adores that Barbie I bought her. Oh, and before I forget. You asked for a seashell on our aborted first date. Like you said. Details."

He produced one out of his pocket and held it out to her. Her bones seemed to dissolve as she glanced at the beautiful white shell with the rust and blue-colored markings. He'd remembered that in the midst of all this? She gave in to the urge to kiss his cheek even though they were in plain view. "Somebody really is a knight in shining armor."

"Don't be giving me any titles." He shuddered like he was

shaking off a swarm of flies. "I'm fine with being Lieutenant Robbie O'Connor."

The patio door slicked open, and Billie emerged with a grinning Cassidy, who clearly wasn't interested in napping. "Hey, bro. Cassidy's got one last surprise for you before we leave."

Robbie scrunched his face suspiciously. "What is it?"

"'Cane!" she gurgled.

He heaved a giant sigh. "No f—reaking way I'm changing that diaper, Billie."

His brother lifted his chin in challenge. "You are if you're staying here. It's the only way to keep the score even."

His curse was muffled but clearly from the heart. "Dammit, it's not like I can ask Tara to do it. She's probably talking to Tyler."

"Oh, come on," Lily said, pinching his bicep. "You're a big tough man. You can handle it."

Later, when she was greeting Agent Petris, Robbie gave a girly scream that echoed throughout the house.

Lily tried to keep her face set, but Agent Petris started laughing. "That sounds like my reaction to one of my kid's dirty diapers when my wife's out shopping. I'd rather take a bullet than clean up that foul mess."

These men...her heroes.

CHAPTER TWENTY-ONE

SEEING THOSE TWO LITTLE GIRLS OFF WAS SO PAINFUL, Robbie imagined it felt like being gutshot.

He hugged Reagan tightly one last time, biting the inside of his cheek as she clung to him. When she wrenched away, Tara handed him a wide-eyed Cassidy, his cousin's face locked in a forced smile for the girls. He kissed the little girl's soft forehead, cupping her to his chest. The drool that wet his shirt felt like a badge of honor. "You have a tea party with Miss Rosie. And make Tim put that red bucket on his head and dance like the crab in *The Little Mermaid*."

Her little head shot off his chest as she stared at him, her lip wobbling. "No, you do it."

God, he actually wanted to, just to make her give that little baby laugh of hers. "Tim is funnier. I'll see you soon, okay?"

He wasn't sure what she understood exactly, but she wasn't smiling. He kissed her again before handing her to Tim, who'd finished helping Reagan into her car seat.

Tara picked up Miss Purrfect and pressed her close for a warm embrace. Robbie eyed the cat warily. Since Tara had arrived, the cat hadn't ruined any of his clothes or hissed at him naked. He'd been glad for the truce.

But when it glanced over at him with its mesmerizing green eyes, he shifted uncomfortably. There was no way he was saying goodbye to a cat. It pawed its collar, making the rhinestones glitter in the sun.

Lily gasped and clutched his arm, leaning close to his ear. "I forgot to mention it, but we put a tracking device in the cat's collar."

He drew back in shock. "When?"

"I'll tell you later," she said quietly, sending Tara a conspiratorial smile.

His mind started replaying all the times the cat had used its paw to try and pull off its collar. How Reagan had said it was new and nothing to be concerned about. Could the cat have been bothered by the tracker? Tim said they were sensitive, hadn't he? Oh shit, he couldn't believe he was going to do this...

"Tara, I know Miss Purrfect has a new collar, but do you mind if we take it off for a minute?"

Her mouth parted before she set the cat down and started unbuckling it. "Sure."

He took the collar from her and turned his body toward Lily, giving them some privacy. "Let's remove it, shall we?"

She nodded, and he watched as she extracted a tiny chip wedged inside the pink suede band. Palming it, she handed him back the collar and he returned it to Tara, who thankfully didn't ask questions as she reattached it around the cat's neck.

Cassidy gave a delighted gurgle inside the car, making him smile, but he jumped when he felt something touch his ankles. He looked down and watched in total shock as Miss Purrfect made a figure eight around his feet.

"Seems she's starting to like you," Tara commented. "I knew she'd come around."

"Come around?" He stopped himself from giving her a summation of how much shit that cat had dished out against him because the feline settled on his feet for a moment before trotting off and jumping into the Suburban.

Tim poked his head out, his shoulders shaking with repressed laughter. "Has a miracle dost appeared?"

Robbie walked over and closed the door on his brother's grinning face. "Don't say anything," he told both Tara and Lily, who were both silently laughing beside him.

Soon everyone's laughter faded as the Suburban started. Robbie watched Reagan bravely wave from the passenger window, only to hear Tara audibly sniff. He turned to see her waving frantically back, a bright but slightly forced smile on her face. He couldn't see if Cassidy was giving her little wave from her car seat and felt a pang in his chest.

Agent Petris honked the horn as they backed out of the driveway. The guy had impressed Robbie with his ability to relate to the girls—he'd been willing to puff like a dragon and had no trouble calling Reagan Princess Pixie. Still...it hurt to watch them go.

Tim gave one final wave from the car as they started down the street, and Robbie caught one last glimpse of Billie, who had his eyes face forward, like he was honing himself for the next challenge.

He wanted to call them back immediately and not let them out of his sight. Be there every moment to assure them everything was going to be okay. Instead, he lifted his hand and waved, forcing his own smile as they disappeared from view. When they were out of sight, he wanted to bend at the waist for a couple of deep breaths to release the pressure cooker inside him, but he didn't want to upset Tara. God, protecting family was going to kill him.

Brotherly love mixed in with all that other messy emotion inside him, and he felt his Adam's apple bob up and down in his throat as he tried to swallow it all down. Tara gave another loud sniff. This separation—even for a day—must be killing her if he was feeling like his body had been put in a trash compactor.

Lily put a hand to his back, a quiet reassurance that was still so new...yet so welcome. She knew when he needed a little touch here and there, and when she needed to step in. In a short time, she'd woven her way into his life, and he wanted to wrap her presence all over him. The peace she brought him, the sensation his father had told him to look for, filled his chest.

Which was a good thing, because as he turned to face Tara, she was dabbing at her eyes. The sight cut him straight to the bone. "Tara, it's going to be—"

"Don't mind me!" She laughed shakily. "Little mommy meltdown in process, but not too bad. I'm not going to let it screw up my makeup."

Sheila walked over from the edge of the garage, after giving them some privacy, and smacked his cousin gently on the back. "No worries, Tara. Tyler's only going to rub it off later."

Okay, he did *not* need to be reminded of that. He knew it was important for the agent and Tara to look cozy, but his stomach flopped when he thought about watching the staging.

"Then I'll stop worrying right now," Tara said in that same brave voice as Tyler came out of the garage, pocketing his cell phone.

"Good." Sheila shared a look with Lily. "Hey, Ty, Lily didn't give you a fake name, so what are we going to call you? Agent Hotstuff won't work obviously."

The agent was grave as he glanced toward Sheila,

thoughtful and assessing. Robbie was starting to see why Lily thought so highly of him. Agent Darren had empathy. He would connect well with people, especially ones in difficult situations. Not everyone had that ability.

Robbie wasn't sure he did, but then again, he wasn't used to bringing his emotions to the job. Lily was different. She didn't wear her heart on her sleeve so much as she did in her eyes. He thought her way was tougher. The troubles and hurts victims experienced could rip your heart out if you let it.

"I think Tara should pick my cover name," the agent finally said with a warm smile at his cousin. "If we were dating for real, what would my name be?"

The request made Tara laugh, and Robbie sent the agent an appreciative smile. Okay, distraction worked.

"Yeah, Tara," Robbie added. "I know all the names of your old boyfriends since I interviewed them all."

"Grilled, you mean," she practically scoffed, more sadness slipping from her face.

"Guilty, and I'd do it again."

Lily's warm smile eased some of the tension in his chest. "So, we have a list to crib from," she said with extra humor in her voice. "Are you going with an old classic name or something—"

"A little naughty," Sheila interrupted with a wink.

Naughty? Robbie wanted the ground to open up and swallow him whole. He also wanted to cheer Tara up.

Tara wiped her eyes with new authority, shaking off any lingering sadness, and got that familiar gleam in her eye. "How about Tom? Because Tom Brady is still my favorite fantasy, being a Pats fan, and we're going to be looking all physical in our videos. Plus, you've got those abs. Tyler, they should be illegal."

"That's why he became an FBI agent," Sheila bandied back. "It was part of his plea bargain."

Lily was fighting laughter, but Tyler only gave a wan smile. "Tom works. No need for a last name since we don't want anyone looking deeper. Also, I just got off the phone with the Charlotte office. Agents Johnson and Mathers will be here tomorrow, and they've rented the house across the street. Told the owner the false story about their little romantic getaway. She's given them the code to the back door, so we're all set."

"Terrific," Lily answered, flicking her gaze to the blue two-story with a similar architecture to the rest of the houses in the area. "The view isn't as great as ours on the beach, but it does have nice, big windows for surveillance."

Yeah, Robbie had noted that as well. Extra backup and additional surveillance were standard, but he really liked that Tyler knew the two undercover agents the Charlotte FBI office was sending down. He'd vouched for them, which had alleviated some of Robbie's ongoing stress.

Right now, he was floundering a little, treading water in the deep end of an FBI pool. Not his comfort zone. He missed his own partner, Mickey, and the other officers he usually went through doors with. But Lily's boss was working with Roland and Internal Affairs on the money laundering and the arson case in a joint task force, as they were linked, and they were seeding the story about Robbie laying low protecting his cousin and the girls, hoping the dirty cops would slip up and hang themselves.

Once the videos of Tara and her new boy toy went out tomorrow—which would coincide with another FBI agent driving his cousin to the safe house where they were taking the girls and his brothers today—all hell was supposed to break loose according to Lily's plan.

They would be ground zero for the bad guys.

He couldn't wait to get his hands on them. "Make sure the agents change the code on the back door after they arrive." Maybe he was being extra thorough, but he wanted everything tight. Who knew if the Kellys would think to rent a nearby beach house to watch their house too? And whether they'd interrogate the landlady to obtain the code...

Everyone turned to look at him, and for a moment, he wondered if he'd grown horns.

"That's standard protocol, Robbie," Tyler assured him. "No one wants a neighbor to wander in to check on the houseplants."

Robbie raised his brow, knowing Tyler had supplied that reasoning for Tara. Right. He needed to remember she didn't have the same longstanding experience with the dark side of crime that the rest of them did. His stupid criminal videos didn't show any of that. He lifted his chin at the acknowledgment. Their professional rapport was developing. If the other cops in his precinct could only see him now. Liking not just one but three Feds out of the Boston office. "Good to know. So where are we starting today?"

Sheila rubbed her hands together. "Lily, do you want to kick things off with the boating trip?"

"Maybe a little fun and speed will help everyone fall into character," Tyler agreed.

"That sounds good," Lily broke in. "Tara? What do you think? We can start there and then maybe take a few videos of you getting some sun with Tyler on the beach before we head into town for cocktails and dinner."

They had to stage a story of Tara meeting a new guy on social media, starting with posts dropping the moment Tara left tomorrow morning. Lily wasn't going to chance the Kellys coming straightaway while she was still on-site.

Lily had accounted for a few possible means of travel by the Kellys' guys. She'd ruled out the possibility of them taking a private plane since no one had ever known them to fork out that kind of money. If they went by car, it would take twelve-plus hours, but they could shorten that by flying into a local airport and renting a car. If they went that route, however, they wouldn't be able to bring their weapons and would have to either buy local or rely on a local network. They wouldn't want traceable weapons for what they planned.

That fact kept him focused.

Not only for Tara's sake, but for everyone else around him, Lily most of all. He'd been a cop for nearly twenty years but caring about her had him worrying more about something going wrong.

"I'm good with starting on the water and getting some sun." Tara cupped her arms as if chilled. "I'll just change into my new bikini."

"Let's keep the diamond earrings on," Lily said thoughtfully, putting her finger to her lips as she studied his cousin. "I want you to show off as much of the bling as possible."

Tara flicked her ears, the diamond drop earrings winking in the sunlight. "Trust me. These babies are going to sparkle. I still can't believe you have an agreement with jewelry stores for cases like this."

"We have to make the stage believable," Lily told her. "Cars, houses, clothes, jewelry. You name it. We bring it."

"Don't forget the yachts." Sheila gave a gusty sigh. "That yacht party the Colombian drug lord threw two years ago would have been pretty spectacular if I hadn't needed to spend the whole thing evading that CI's tongue. He took our undercover a little too seriously."

Robbie was a ball of tension. He hadn't thought about these women having to pretend to be some scumbag's girl-friend. He turned to Lily, who only raised a brow in his direction. Right. Better not to ask. Put it in the box labeled *the job* and don't act like a jealous boyfriend.

Boyfriend.

Jesus, he supposed that's what he was now. Was he too old to be someone's boyfriend? He shook himself. "I'll let you change while I check in with the office." Focusing on the job was going to get him through this. Plus, it helped him feel more in control.

He touched Lily's elbow before heading inside, Tara on his heels.

"Don't go all older cousin routine with me, please." She sped up and planted herself in front of him. "I'm working extra hard to put steel into my backbone."

Wanting to curse, he clenched his eyes shut for a moment. "I know, and I'm sorry."

"Just saying, especially since I know you're worrying about your new lady friend as much as me." She touched his arm, her face a combination of motherly softness and Southie toughness. "Robbie O'Connor, I love you with all my heart, so I'm going to speak plainly even though it might piss you off. If you don't put a ring on that woman's finger, I'm going to have a mass said for you and your love life. Publicly."

He cringed. They both knew what that meant. He'd have every busybody mother and desperate single woman in Southie on his ass, thinking he wanted to settle down. Women would be ringing his doorbell with pies and cakes and stalking him at the grocery store in high heels, full makeup, wafting extra hair spray. "Come on. It's early yet, Tara."

"We're Irish." She gave a comic jig. "We know when something is strong and true. And if you bring Scotty up right now, I will belt you."

Yeah, they hadn't talked about her at-large, soon-to-be ex-husband. There'd been no sightings of Scotty and his side piece, and no one knew if they were even still together. Of course, that made divorcing him more complicated.

"I'd never do that." Robbie gave a jerky nod. "Fine. I'll

admit this, but only to you. I can see Lily and me together. Forever. Even with kids, maybe. Not that I know whether she wants any." Although she clearly was terrific with Reagan and Cassidy. God, he was already missing them.

"So you talk about it." She tapped his nose like he was her kid. "I see you two together. Hard. Your family is going to go bananas. The minute I can, I'm calling your sister and telling her she needs to come back to the old neighborhood to meet your new girl."

"Tara!"

Running off in heels, she laughed all the way to the stairs.

Someone cleared their throat behind him.

Tyler held up his hands. "Sorry. I came in to change as well. I didn't mean to overhear anything."

He rubbed the back of his neck. "I'd appreciate you not saying anything. Everything is new, and the stakes are high."

"My lips are sealed." Tyler slapped him on the back as he walked by. "I meant to tell you. I've been to your brother's bar in Southie a time or two. It's one of the best Irish pubs I've been in outside of Dublin."

The thought of the rest of his family rooted him in place. He wondered how they were all doing, especially his dad in Ireland. "Good to know."

Tyler lifted a hand as he strode off. Robbie thought about going upstairs like he'd said and sending in another report to Roland Thomas, but he'd already informed his contact at Internal Affairs of their every move. He was overcompensating, and he knew it.

Besides, now Lily's boss had made contact, sending a memorandum about the cooperation between the police and the Feds on this bust, which he'd read three times over until his eyes crossed. The Feds knew their paperwork, all right, which meant everything was official now. He was going to get some flak for working with Internal Affairs *and* the Feds, but he would take it. No one would argue he'd been in an untenable situation. Of course, he'd get even more shit from the guys for dating a Fed, one he'd met while she was undercover, working on him. Thank God that hadn't made it into the internal MOU. But he could take that and more if it meant he got to be with Lily.

"How you doing there, Lieutenant?"

He was still getting used to Lily calling him that, something she did both playfully as well as to focus him back on their case.

"Fine." He rolled his tense shoulders. "Ready to get this done."

She strolled over, looking casual but professional in her cotton pants and shirt. "Then let the fun begin."

What he witnessed over the course of the rest of the day wasn't anything that qualified as fun. Tara videoed herself and her "new boyfriend, Tom," with a beauty-pageant smile on her face as the man drove the sporting boat they'd rented with the ease of a natural sailor. Both of them were naturals, and Tyler had a knack for setting up memorable shots.

To the naked eye, they looked like a couple totally in sync and hot for each other. Even Robbie was impressed by the façade.

Later, when they were lying beside each other on the beach, Tara became a little stiff while she was videoing Agent Darren putting sunscreen on her legs, so he tickled her instep, making her kick him in the chest. He'd fallen backward playfully, laughing as she'd sought her revenge, the phone soon forgotten.

As Robbie watched from his position beside Lily and Sheila, he sometimes had to remind himself they were acting. Lily watched the "show" passively while Sheila would poke Robbie in the ribs or give Tara a thumbs-up to keep everything light. One time she even fanned herself, which Tara mimicked in another video as Agent Darren rolled onto his stomach in his black swim trunks, showing off the outcome of years of strength training.

"Tara's friends are going to be so jealous of that one," Sheila said softly as Tara finished that particular video.

Robbie grimaced. "It's fake, Sheila," he responded in the same hushed voice.

She blinked repeatedly at him, making him wonder if she'd gotten sand in her eye before saying, "Honey, you clearly do not understand what I'm talking about right now."

He gave up and went inside to hammer off a brief update about their status before returning to find another wardrobe change had occurred.

As the sun went down, the couple walked on the beach, taking a selfie, the vibrant orange sun sinking into the dark blue waves behind them. They were gazing into each other's eyes as Tyler put his arm around Tara. The photo screamed they'd fallen for each other. More fodder for the Kellys, he told himself.

After that moment, they dressed for cocktails and dinner. Lily had chosen a popular restaurant at Nag's Head. Since it was the couple's first foray into a public area, Lily, Sheila, and Robbie had agreed to cover them from a distance. While Lily and Robbie watched from their post at another table, Sheila watched from the bar. Lily had instructed Tara to ask the waiter to take a photo of them, and when she did, Tyler made sure to include a portion of the menu under his hand.

Clues were essential to letting the Kellys track them, but they didn't want to be too obvious.

The final play in Lily's plan was the video Tara took of her new sports car, which Tyler had driven down. Robbie had to admit it was a honey. Not that Billie had so much as blinked an eye at it—a serious indication of his brother's predicament. Because when did Billie not go apeshit about a hot car?

And this car was hot, smoking hot, Tara said, touching the orange body of the McLaren in the video as Agent Darren flashed his killer smile and then opened the door for her after giving her a serious kiss.

Robbie winced at that one.

So far, the guy hadn't given Tara more than a few pecks and some light touches. PG movie grade. But this raised his blood pressure. Especially when Tara made a humming sound in her throat.

"Breathe," Lily whispered beside him as Sheila silently applauded the couple on her other side. "It's all for show."

"I know it is, dammit." He bit the inside of his cheek and told himself to suck it up and be a professional. "I'm not cut out for this kind of undercover shit."

"Language," Lily said merrily, making him choke on a shaft of laughter that crept up his throat.

When Tara clicked her video off and lowered her phone, Lily gave them a quick salute. "That's a wrap, folks."

He sure as hell hoped so.

The stress of this case was going to make him go completely gray.

CHAPTER TWENTY-TWO

WAITING FOR THE BAD GUYS TO SHOW UP WAS HELL.

Especially since it didn't allow her and Robbie to focus on what they really wanted—each other. Sitting next to him on the couch and trying to be professional took special skills. Because as good as she was at blocking out distractions while on a case, his scent would still wash over her and make her skin tingle. He'd told her he was going insane too, but still, he'd sat beside her on the couch. They were both gluttons for punishment, clearly.

"Pizza good tonight?" Sheila yelled from the kitchen. "I figure driving my sports car into town with my hot boy toy to go pick it up would be another perfect way to lay bread-crumbs for the guys the Kellys are sending down tomorrow. I'm glad criminals move fast when they're pissed. We only started posting two days ago, and we're having visitors."

Buck had ordered wiretaps on the Kellys after submitting joint evidence to a judge with Internal Affairs. They'd picked up chatter immediately about needing to plug a couple of holes in North Carolina, with the goons leaving tomorrow.

A few confidential informants had confirmed that

Branigan Kelly was on the rampage about Tara spending his money, especially on the McLaren. Apparently, he was ignoring his councilors, who'd advised him it could be a trap. All he wanted was *"to shut that bitch up and stop her from spending all his money."*

"I told you the spending spree was genius," Lily put in. "Plenty of incentive to hustle down here to stop her."

"You know the saying," Tyler continued, the sounds of him typing away on his laptop at the kitchen table audible. "Crime never sleeps. Good thing this boy toy doesn't object to such blatant sexism or lack of regard for his personal well-being."

"Ah, feeling a little unappreciated?" Sheila asked in a playful tone. "Come to mama."

Tyler gave a gusty laugh. "Never change, Sheila. And I'm good with pizza—and you driving around your new boy toy."

"I really hate that term," Robbie whispered for Lily's ears only, making her bite her lip to control her humor.

She knew he'd gritted his teeth plenty over the past several days, but he'd stood fast through it all. When Tara had said goodbye, he'd been a downright mountain of assurance. Not that Tara had shown one iota of worry or sadness. She'd been dry-eyed and strong, something Lily was coming to appreciate about the O'Connor clan. They stood up. No matter what.

"Pizza is fine with me too, if you really wanted my opinion, Sheila," Robbie called back.

"Are you feeling a little unappreciated too?" her partner shot back cheekily.

Robbie rolled his eyes before lowering his voice to say, "I wish I could take you out tonight, Lily."

She mirrored him rolling his eyes. "But we'd give ourselves away."

"Since we're not supposed to be here," he agreed, his voice

hushed and sexy. "Especially me. God, this is going to sound weird, but I actually miss my brothers and the girls. And Tara, of course."

"Not Miss Purrfect?" she asked, hoping to improve his mood. "Your new friend."

"That's a stretch if I ever heard it." He shuddered playfully, making her lips twitch. "It's nice not having to hide my underwear. You know, Tara coming back really changed things with the girls—not that I'd want it any other way. She's their mother and a damn good one. But it was...nice having them need me a little. God, I sound like an idiot."

If they were alone, she'd have kissed him ever so softly on the lips and then wrapped her arms around him. "I think it's sweet."

"Don't breathe a word of it to anyone." Robbie turned to face her. "Promise me. Now that we're...involved, you're going to need to remember the one cardinal rule about the O'Connors. Never show true emotion, or it will bite you in the ass."

"I promise." She winked even though she wanted to caress the hard line of his jaw. "You can trust me."

His hand grazed her arm, his eyes filled with the warmth and affection she was becoming used to. "I know, Lily. And another thing you should know about the O'Connors. When we find someone we can trust, they're ours for life."

Her heart expanded with a sweet roller coaster of emotion. "I'm the same way."

His eyes flashed with promise. With happiness. She felt her own spirits rising in her chest. God, when had she ever been this happy? And on an undercover op. She was on a teeter-totter between job excitement and a dating high. Totally crazy but oh so wonderful.

"Buck just texted us." Tyler clapped his hands, startling her. "They have eyes on the two guys the Kellys are sending down. Lily, you win the prize. They're driving down."

"I was also right about the number of guys they'd send." She smiled. "The mob does like to send people in pairs."

"They tend to be family operations, and camaraderie and chemistry are important," Robbie said dryly. "I'm glad it's only two guys. We've got them outnumbered big-time. Us four here. Agents Johnson and Mather across the street."

She knew he'd been worried about the heat coming. He'd explained that caring about her ratcheted up the stakes for him. She'd felt the personal pull as well. "Me too. We'll catch them on attempted murder, conspiracy, and a whole bunch of other offenses. Because I know they won't be abiding by local gun laws regarding bringing in weapons from another state. Oh, I can't wait! I'll split them up and work them over at the FBI office in Charlotte. They'll flip on their boss and want to turn state's evidence. It will be like Christmas in the interrogation room."

"You're sexy when you talk like that." His blue eyes twinkled. "But I hate to burst your bubble. You're going to have a hell of a time getting them to talk."

She waggled her brows. "I excel at establishing rapport with bad guys. You'd be surprised what they tell me."

"Having been hoodwinked by you, I wouldn't bet against you." He laid his hand next to hers, their fingers tangling loosely.

Sheila appeared in the doorway with a knowing look. "Hey, lovebirds. Why don't you go for a run or something? Your sexual energy is reaching all the way into the kitchen and ruining the batch of virgin margaritas I'm making."

"Yeah, go for a run," Tyler agreed, joining her in the doorway. "Buck is flying high back in Boston leading that arm of the investigation. All we're doing here is sitting around and waiting. You know how it goes."

Lily shared a look with Robbie. "Okay, only if you're sure."

"We are." Sheila jerked her finger behind her. "We've got

two more watchers across the street. Plus, the ones tailing the Kelly guys. Go."

Lily felt the pull, knowing they were covered. Agents Johnson and Mather—the undercover couple on a romantic getaway—were positioned so they had eyes on the front of the house. "You game, Grandpa?"

"Always." He pushed off the couch, extending his hand to her. She took it even though it wasn't exactly professional, but the lines were blurred.

She was trying to accept that. Plus, there was nothing unethical about them seeing each other. But she was struggling with the whole *being too obvious about it* part. Like sleeping together on an active investigation. Fortunately, Robbie had the same moral quandary, so they hadn't done more than catch a few stolen moments together. Good moments. Hot moments. Spine-tingling, toe-curling moments. Sheila had wisely not teased her about it. Much. But her partner encouraging this alone time *was* really sweet.

"I'll change and meet you outside," she told him, squeezing his hand a moment longer before taking off toward her house next door.

Inside she quickly changed, delighted to find him waiting for her at the beach's edge, stretching his calves. "I like watching you work your muscles like that," she admitted, coming closer to him and brushing his butt with the back of her hand in an *oops, I accidentally just did that* move.

He stood up, grinning. "Put your hands on me again like that, and we won't be running."

She stepped closer, feeling the heat already emanating from him. "Promises, promises. Come on, Grandpa. Let's go."

She kept her pace easy to let them both warm up. But soon he shot her a cheeky smile and sprinted ahead.

"Consider that your challenge, sweetheart," he called over his shoulder.

"Accepted!" Oh, he was so deliciously sexy, and she kept her pace easy so she could watch the hard muscles of his legs ripple along with the lats through his T-shirt. No bare chest this run. Probably wise of him. But when they got back to Boston—weather permitting—she was going to make a special request that he never run with a shirt on. Call her scandalous, but Lily Meadows was over the moon, dancing on air, and totally head over heels for Robbie O'Connor.

Punching up her speed, she enjoyed the grim look on his face when she passed him in a blur. *"Ta-ta."*

His heartfelt growl sounded on the empty beach, and she nearly laughed out loud. It was good any final renters were off having dinner, or they would have been scared by the sound.

Sand shifting under the quicksilver of her feet, she cruised to the right, following the beach out as it curved into the ocean. The blue waves were calm today, the white tips of the breakers as much of an afterthought as day-old frosting. Only a few jellyfish lay on the beach, washed up by the waves.

She filled her lungs with the salty air and savored the view. God, she was going to miss this place. Maybe they would come back for a real vacation sometime. They hadn't explored the area, and she'd love to do more surfing. She sighted a few larger waves off in the distance and noted a boater coming in hot, parting the ocean with his form of idiocy. She was glad no one else was on the water, because he was the kind of boating enthusiast who was dangerous and likely bolstered by a few beers.

Looking over her shoulder, she glanced back at Robbie. His face was clenched, his arms pumping madly as he sprinted after her. She sometimes wondered why some people were just naturally faster than others, conditioning being equal.

"You want me to slow down?" she called.

He only shook his head, his focus locked. She turned to

face forward and set about running her own race. She rather liked that he didn't mind that they ran at their own pace. Okay, he did. But he'd never ask her to slow down.

God, he was such a keeper, and she found herself thinking about meeting the rest of his family. Truth be told, she was missing the girls as well as Tim and Billie. Sure, she was closer to Tim. They got each other and had similar senses of empathy and humor. Billie was a total tough guy but still good to her. Then there was Tara, who was brave and funny and really sweet. She thought they could be good friends.

But she wondered about the rest of his family. Robbie had a sister, another adopted one of sorts, and four more brothers. Tyler said he really liked Danny, who ran the Irish pub that bore the family's last name. Goodness, there were a lot of them. She'd never had anyone really.

Then there was his father. What kind of man must Mr. O'Connor be?

"Lily!"

Robbie calling her name had her turning her head around. He was frantically pointing at something to her left on the beach. Whipping back in that direction, she noticed a solitary man jogging her way.

A ripple of shock rolled over her as she realized it was Scotty Flanagan.

Why had Tara's soon-to-be ex-husband decided to show up? They'd discussed the possibility that he might show up in the Outer Banks after Tara's posts went out, but everyone had agreed the probability was super low. Why would he show up when he had to know the Kellys were coming?

Scanning the beach, she didn't see anyone else coming from the small parking area where he'd emerged from.

Dialing down her speed, she thought the situation through. He'd obviously seen Tara's social media posts and discovered their location. Of course, they had purposely planted clues in the videos, with the curve of the beach they were running as one of them.

She studied the suspected money launderer. He was wearing a navy track suit with red stripes at the hems. His lady friend was nowhere in sight.

"It's Tara's husband," Robbie said, finally running her down.

"I know," she whispered, a plan forming quickly in her mind. "So I'm still Summer Sunshine, okay? And you've been taking care of Tara and the girls. Of course, she's been acting a little wild. But you're working on that."

"Exactly what I was thinking." He put his hand to her back protectively. "I'll lure him away by saying Tara is back at the house. You take the street back and alert Johnson and Mather. Okay, he's almost here. Let me do the talking."

They slowed to a walk, Scotty now striding rapidly to intercept them. He was clearly out of shape despite a reasonably thin body. As they grew closer, Lily studied his round, passably handsome face. He looked well rested despite the anger flushing his cheeks, and while she didn't find him attractive, she could see how others might. His brown hair curled around his forehead, making him look roguish, a little like an Irish sailor of old. He had a tan, not a sallow complexion from hiding out in a windowless room or dark circles under the eyes from trouble sleeping. God, was he stupid? The Kellys almost certainly wanted to kill him.

"I knew there was no way Tara wasn't with you," he spat the moment they reached each other. "She'd never leave the girls unprotected."

"Of course *she* wouldn't!" Robbie shot back, grabbing Scotty by the top of his track suit. "She'd die protecting her girls, but that doesn't mean she hasn't gone a little crazy over everything."

His lip curled, transforming him from roguish to downright mean. "Buying that fucking McLaren and screwing that pretty boy."

"You know Tara." Robbie shoved him backward. "It just so happens your own screwing really messed her up in the head. Along with the money—"

"Get rid of the girl." Scotty jerked his head toward Lily. "I'm not talking in front of someone who's not family."

"You're not my family, and she's just someone I've met on this 'fabulous' vacation we're on." He slid her a tight smile. "Sorry about this. Give me a moment, sweetheart, will you?"

"Sure thing, Robbie."

She walked away a few yards on the pretext of giving them privacy. With her back to them, she turned her gaze toward the sea, keeping her ears cocked. If only she'd brought her phone so she could text her partner about their visitor. Sheila would be as surprised as she was.

"Scotty, what in the hell were you thinking?" Robbie ground out.

"I was thinking we could have more, that's what!" Scotty's raised voice sounded across the beach. "It was good business and didn't hurt anyone."

"Except now it has or will. Do you have any idea the trouble Tara is in because of you, you piece of shit?"

"Of course I know! And since you're down here babysitting her with Billie and Tim, who mysteriously disappeared on the same day you did, instead of trying to resolve it as a cop, I figure you haven't figured out how to prove she didn't know what was going on."

Lily bit her lip, thinking it was interesting Scotty still referred to the nail salon as partially his.

"You're right." Robbie's tone was sharp with reproach. "I've been hoping you'd come out of hiding—"

"I am not going down for this!" Scotty cried. "I told Tara all this when she kicked me out, and I'll tell you. There's no other way to handle this other than to keep doing what I agreed to with Branigan Kelly. Tara can take me back, and everything will go back to normal. That's the only way we'll all stay out of jail and stay alive."

Lily's brows flew to her forehead, much like she imagined Robbie's had. He wanted Tara to take him back? And continue the crime? Where was Janice Brewster?

Robbie started laughing. "You've got to be fucking kidding me!"

"Look, she doesn't have to take me back as her husband— only in name. I can do my thing with Janice, and she can do her thing. Clearly, she's already started."

Asked and answered, Lily thought.

"You're unbelievable!" Robbie spat.

"Look, I can take it as long as she doesn't embarrass me. The Kellys don't care whether we're a happily married couple. All they care about is the money. Frankly, so do I. Dammit, it's not right that I've been hiding out in Maryland on a shoe-string budget while she's down here living it up in some fancy beach house with a McLaren in the driveaway. That car and everything else is mine. I did all the work."

Ah, criminals have it so hard. Lily wondered how Robbie was keeping a lid on his temper. She cut him a surreptitious glance. He was pacing, his tennis shoes digging grooves in the sand.

Scotty held out his hand, entreating. "Robbie, you've got to talk to her. Convince her."

A giant scoff sounded. "You do know I'm a sworn officer of the law, right? You're insane."

"No! Listen. You don't want Tara or the girls to end up dead or drowned in the Mystic. The only way that doesn't happen is if you stay quiet about this. Besides, the Kellys have people in your department. You can't win this one. And you're in serious hot water, being away and unavailable when there's an arson case involving your first cousin. Everyone knows you're a family first kind of guy. People are starting to suspect you already."

Lily nearly smiled. They'd laid some breadcrumbs there too, hoping Robbie's whereabouts would become the talk of the department. Interesting that Scotty was so wired in, being he was on the run and all.

"Dammit!" Robbie snarled, pacing hard as he kicked up sand. "I am not agreeing to anything."

"Fine! We'll talk it out. Lay it down from all the angles. With Tara."

Lily pretended to chew her nails as she bent over and picked up a piece of red sea glass. Scotty's pulse was pounding in his neck, and Lily imagined he reeked of flop sweat.

"Tara will have some ideas," he continued in a rush. "Once she gets over wanting to kill me."

"Good luck with that," Robbie bit out. "If I do this, and I'm not saying I will, I need to know who can fix things for me at the department. Because I'm not letting this bullshit hurt my career. I've worked too hard."

Way to sell it, Robbie. She fought a smile from her covert perch.

Scotty patted Robbie on the back, keeping a safe distance between them. "That's good thinking. They'll understand that when I introduce you. You're only looking the other way because it's family. Tara and the girls. You don't want their mom or dad to end up in prison or dead. Think of how devastated Reagan and Cassidy would be."

"If you don't shut your mouth, I'm going to do it for you. You don't deserve those kids."

"Okay, okay!" He held up his hands. "But we'd better figure out our plan, because if I can find you, so can the Kellys."

"What do you mean?" Robbie's incredulity was perfectly

pitched. "How *did* you find me? Did you talk to Tara's nail client who loves it here?"

"You don't know?" Scotty started guffawing and slapping his knee. "Tara's been posting videos and photos on social media for the past couple days about her new car and side piece to make me jealous."

"Dammit!" He gave an impressive curse. "I told her not to do that."

God, he really had a talent for undercover. She was proud of the way he was playing this.

"You know Tara. Too independent for her own good. She doesn't listen, but I knew she'd find a way to tell me where she was hiding after she realized she couldn't lay low forever. When I saw the first post, I was with Janice in Maryland at a casino my buddy told me was hot for action. I asked the table if they knew where it was and three people said the Outer Banks. It was only six hours away. Lots of people from there come down this way for vacation."

"Shit!" Robbie cursed again. "It was that easy? Jesus, we need to get to a hotel so we can talk. It's not safe here. Come on. I'll take you back to the house, but if you so much as look at Tara wrong, I'll kill you myself. Also, you aren't talking to the girls."

Gosh, her knight in shining armor did love to lay down the law.

"Fine! But they're going to hear my voice and know it's me. I'm still their father."

"They'll get over it," Robbie answered harshly. "Like Tara is. Let's go. Hey, Summer! I need to cut our run short, okay?"

She turned at his raised voice, a bright Summer Sunshine smile on her face, grateful her girl-next-door look didn't seem to have made Scotty suspicious. She didn't scream Fed. "Sure thing, Robbie. Catch you later."

She watched the two men walk back to the rental house

and started to make a beeline for the street that ran all the way to the house. She could signal to the agents across the street and have them converge on the house with her so they could arrest Scotty. She couldn't be sure whether Sheila and Tyler were still out getting the pizza, but Lily didn't want Scotty to be alone with Robbie. He'd wonder who was watching the girls and where Tim and Billie had gone. He'd start to get suspicious. That was when things turned dangerous.

As she started running, she took one more look to check their progress back to the house. They had a ways to go, seeing as she and Robbie had run all the way out to the curve in the beach. How long would it take them to walk back? Ten minutes? She glanced at the house to calculate the distance and stopped short when she saw the boat from earlier pulled up in the shallows close to their rental house.

Her gaze scanned the deck. The hotshot speed racer wasn't at the bow.

Her gut twitched. Something wasn't right. No one parked a boat in the shallows like that. First, it was illegal. Second, it could ground the boat. Third, why pull up close to their rental?

Her brain calculated the possibilities in seconds. Scotty might have brought help. But why? If he only wanted to talk to Tara and Robbie...

But maybe that wasn't his plan at all. She started jogging as she ran back through what Scotty had said. He claimed to know the names of the Kellys' dirty cops, but was that true? Why would they tell Scotty something like that? He was a low-end-of-the-chain money launderer.

And hadn't Scotty mentioned the McLaren being in the driveway? If he'd been out front already, why approach Robbie all the way out here? And where was Janice Brewster? He'd said they'd been at the casino. Together.

All Scotty wanted was for things to go back to normal, he'd said. How would he react when he found out neither Tara nor the girls were here? Had he brought along help to ensure their cooperation?

Lily picked up her speed, sprinting, arms pumping. She told herself Robbie was a smart cop. He'd see the boat and wonder at its presence. But he was still going back to the house alone, and she couldn't be sure Tyler and Sheila were there. If they entered through the back, the agents across the street wouldn't even see them.

And where *was* the guy in the boat?

She raced faster. Because when this much money was involved and people's lives were at stake, there could be any number of outcomes.

Most of them were bad.

CHAPTER TWENTY-THREE

R OBBIE HAD NEVER BEEN MORE GRATEFUL THAT LILY DIDN'T look like a Fed.

Scotty hadn't once suspected she was anything but what he'd told him. As they walked back to the house, he thought about taking Scotty into custody before they reached the house. But with that loose track suit, he couldn't be sure Scotty wasn't carrying a gun. He forced himself not to look over his shoulder for Lily. She'd be racing back to the house along the street to collect Agents Johnson and Mather. Their team would converge on him and Scotty.

Playing the various outcomes and risks through his mind, the same way he would on any operation, he almost missed the abandoned speedboat bobbing in the shallows. He'd seen the hotshot driver wreaking havoc earlier as he'd run behind Lily. But where was he and why was the boat here?

Tension worked its way through him. Scotty mentioned a friend earlier, one who'd told him about the Maryland casino. Had this guy been with him when Scotty had seen Tara's posts? Scotty wasn't known for his work ethic.

Would he have brought someone along to try and intimidate him and Tara into playing ball?

He glanced at his brother-in-law. The piece of shit was sweating. Well, he should be. But would he really have thought he could convince Tara and Robbie to go along with his half-baked plan? Dipshit wasn't the brightest bulb, but he'd managed to launder money under Tara's nose for God knows how long.

Surely he had a backup plan. Robbie fisted his hands at his sides as they closed in on the house. Were Sheila and Tyler still out getting pizza? Scotty had said he'd seen the McLaren in the driveway.

In the driveway...

Why converge on him and Lily so far from the house? Was it to give the boat's driver time to anchor and breach the house, lying in wait?

He couldn't go inside with Scotty. Especially since he didn't know whether or not he was armed. Lily wouldn't like that he wasn't waiting for her and the other agents, but he didn't feel like he had a choice. One-on-one had better odds. They were out of view of the house, so he had to make a move now.

He pretended to stumble in the sand, grabbing Scotty's arm as he started to go down, as if he were trying to catch himself. Scotty jerked in shock, but Robbie's greater weight took the man off-balance as planned. Robbie sank one knee into the sand, using his force to take Scotty down hard on his side. Whipping him onto his stomach, Robbie pressed his other knee into the man's back, ripping both arms up behind him. Sure enough, he felt the hard outline of a gun secured in the back of Scotty's pants.

"You carrying?" He pressed his knee harder into Scotty's back when the man struggled. "What were you planning, Scotty? To kill me and Tara if we didn't go along?"

"Stop it! You're hurting me."

Robbie tightened his grip. "Keep your voice down. Because I know that boat didn't just wash up onshore. You brought muscle, didn't you? Answer me!"

"You said you'd listen!" Scotty cried. "I didn't want it to go this way."

"What way?" He loosened his grip just enough and peered over the man's body until he could see Scotty's face. "You'd better tell me. Because I know something you don't. I'm here with the Feds. Tara and the girls are gone. Confess now and they might go easier on you."

"Shit!" He started bucking. "But Billie and Tim—"

"Forget about them." Robbie glanced up at the house to make certain they were alone. "That woman I was running with is a Fed, Scotty. Tell me what the plan is. Now!"

"Janice thought we needed a backup, so we brought a guy she knows from the casino." He tried to buck out of Robbie's hold. "In case you or Tara didn't go for it."

"Is Janice inside with the guy from the boat?" Robbie asked harshly. "Is he armed?"

"They're both armed." His features were clenched, face dripping with sweat. "Dammit, Robbie. You know me. I didn't want anyone to get hurt. Especially with the girls around."

"But you weren't going to stop anyone from doing what had to be done, were you?" He calculated how long it would take Lily to run back to the house. She would be there shortly. He needed to secure Scotty and intercept her. She and the agents would be walking into a trap.

Robbie transferred Scotty's wrists to one of his hands while using the other to yank out his shoelace. "I'm tying you up and leaving you here, but if you try and run, I swear it's not going to be pretty. Got me?"

"Come on, Robbie," Scotty pleaded, his eyes frantic. "We're family."

Robbie spat on the ground as he yanked out his last shoelace and started tying Scotty's hands together. "We were. You blew it the minute you put Tara and the girls in danger."

He tied a constrictor knot tightly around his wrists and then did the same to secure Scotty's ankles together, knowing the boating knot was impossible to untie when done right. He was not chancing him getting up and running. Stripping off his T-shirt, he ripped it in half.

"Open your mouth," he commanded.

Scotty's eyes went wild. "No way!"

Robbie only grabbed his jaw and forced it open, shoving half of the shirt inside and then using the other half to secure it in place. "I am not chancing you yelling for help. Now stay put."

He was up and running moments later, heading toward the yard of the third house down from them. When he reached the street, his heart jerked in response. Lily was coming out of the house across the street with the two other FBI agents. They were all dressed casually, but Robbie recognized the hunched shoulders of Feds going toward a potential crime in progress. He gave a soft birdcall and watched as their heads jerked toward him.

He held up two fingers, pointed toward their rental house, and gave the signal that the occupants were armed. Lily nodded, her face tense, her eyes flat. He started walking along the front of the house, keeping close to it, noting the McLaren wasn't in the driveway. He had a moment of relief that Scotty's partner hadn't gotten the jump on them with surprise on his side.

And then he heard the purr of a luxury sports car.

Shit.

Sheila and Tyler didn't know about the ambush.

Lily started jogging up the street, her ponytail bobbing. The other Feds made a show of going toward their SUV, popping the trunk like they were looking for something. Robbie knew they were trying to preserve their cover if Janice and her accomplice had gone to the windows to watch the sports car approach.

Robbie paused at the edge of the garage, hiding in the crevice as he watched Summer take her hair down, giving a covert signal to her partner, one she'd taught him. The McLaren passed her, slowing as it reached the house. Lily cut into the adjoining yard and started jogging back from an undetectable position toward Sheila and Tyler while Agents Johnson and Mather closed their trunk and walked across the street, acting like two prospective buyers at a car show.

When Tyler pulled into the driveway, he immediately opened the garage door with the remote. As it was lifting, he popped open his car door, reaching for the pizza and putting the three cartons on top of the vehicle. Sheila peeled out, keeping her back to the house, likely so their perpetrators wouldn't be able to see she wasn't Tara.

"Hey!" Agent Johnson called as he sauntered over in a navy T-shirt, tan shorts, and running shoes. "That's some car. Right, honey?"

"A beaut," Agent Mathers said, smiling appreciatively in her white tennis outfit. "I hope you don't think it's rude of us to ask to take a peek. I've never seen a McLaren up close."

Tyler flashed his killer smile. "Knock yourselves out, right, babe? Hey, where are you guys from?"

"Washington, DC," the man said, a husband touching his undercover wife's arm with tenderness. "We decided to take a final summer getaway."

"DC, huh?" Tyler grinned. "I went to school at George-town. How cool is that? Hey, Tara! Isn't that a coincidence?"

"It sure is," Sheila said in a pretty good imitation of his cousin's voice, fluffing her black hair. "I've never been."

"Sometimes I get a little homesick for the Beltway," Tyler continued. "Hey, you two want to grab a drink? Tara's kids and their babysitters are still at the playground, but her cousin is coming back soon from a run with his new girlfriend. We've got a ton of pizza. It would be nice to talk about my old stomping grounds. I'm Tom, by the way, and this is Tara."

Nicely played, Robbie thought. This way Janice and her accomplice would be expecting four people to come inside from the garage, but he imagined Agents Mathers and Johnson would circle around the house with Lily to take the back as Tyler and Sheila went in through the garage as expected. He wondered how Janice and her friend would react to the numbers changing. Panic? Would they start shooting? His gut gripped with worry.

"What do you say, honey?" Agent Johnson asked with a wink. "You know how much I love pizza."

Agent Mathers rested her head on his forearm. "We were actually thinking about grabbing one ourselves."

"Great!" Tyler boomed. "Come on in."

Tyler and Sheila slammed the car doors and started toward the garage, pulling out their weapons, while the other agents split off to the right side of the house, also pulling their weapons. Robbie stepped out of his hiding place as Lily sprinted across the yard from the adjoining house in a crouched position, ensuring she wouldn't be spotted from the windows. When she spied him, he saw a flash of relief in her eyes.

He motioned to her as she reached the edge of the garage. "I've got Scotty taken care of for now."

"Good, then we go in behind Tyler and Sheila," she whispered to him, pulling her weapon from the back of her running shorts. "Sorry I don't have one for you. I thought you were with Scotty. Stay behind me."

He didn't like it, but he nodded. Tyler and Sheila were talking as they approached the inner door, pretending nothing was amiss. Sheila reached for the door handle, nodding to him and Lily before opening it. Tyler went in first, going on about his time in Washington, DC, as Sheila followed.

Lily pointed her gun down and entered after them in a crouch. Unarmed, Robbie wouldn't be of much help, but he still knew how to provide backup. He swept in after her, crouching low, signaling he'd stay put while she peeled off past the laundry room, which led to the family room.

"Freeze!" Tyler shouted. "FBI."

Robbie was inside the kitchen a moment later. Janice and her muscle stood in front of the open patio door, a yard from the kitchen island. Four agents had their weapons trained on the pair.

"Shit!" The bulky dark-haired man next to her put his weapon down on the ground immediately and then crossed his hands behind his head. "What the hell are the Feds doing here? Dammit, Janice, you said this would be an easy score."

"It was supposed to be!" Janice whipped her 9mm up, her hand shaky as she tried to aim her handgun. "Stay back."

"You don't want to do that, Janice," Lily commanded in a low voice from the doorway leading from the family room, her body mostly shielded save her gun arm. "Five agents have their weapons trained on you, and we will shoot you if you discharge your weapon."

Her arm wavered, her brown eyes narrowing. "I don't understand..."

"Listen to me, Janice." Lily kept her weapon trained on the woman, staying where she was. "You're going to step away from the guy with you and lay down your weapon. Slowly."

Robbie's body tightened, knowing this is when people turned stupid. He watched as the woman cursed and then bent over, putting her gun on the floor. He breathed a sigh of relief.

"Okay, now hands behind your head like your friend here," she instructed.

Tyler and Sheila swept forward as she took the position, their weapons still drawn. Tyler picked up the guns, placing them out of reach, as Sheila kept her gun trained on them, along with the other agents.

"*Where's Scotty?*" Janice looked around and then froze when she spotted Robbie. "Hey! You were supposed to be here with Tara and the girls. Where's Tara? Where's—"

"I'm Tara today," Sheila told her in a rough voice.

"And Scotty's tied up on the beach," Robbie said, his heart still pounding in his chest. "What were you going to do, Janice? Kill me and Tara if we didn't agree to cooperate?"

"I am not talking to you, pig." She lifted her pointy chin, defiance carving her beautifully made-up face. "I told Scotty you'd never go along with it. Men! They never listen."

"And what about you?" Tyler gestured to her accomplice. "Sorry, I didn't catch your name."

A muscle ticked in his temple. "Bill Walpole."

"Well, Mr. Walpole. Did you fancy the McLaren?"

"I was hoping for a cut of it, yeah." He stared at Tyler. "What's it to you?"

"Just doing my job." Tyler glanced at Lily. "Can you get us some handcuffs?"

Agent Johnson and Mather pulled two pairs out of the deep pockets of his shorts. Lily stepped forward and took them.

"I think Robbie should do the honors," she said, holding them out. "Seeing as he likes to use them and all."

Sheila snorted, fully aware of the joke.

"By the way, Robbie," Lily asked. "What happened to your shirt?"

He looked down at his bare chest. God, he'd forgotten about that. He jerked his head toward the beach. "I secured it in Scotty's mouth so he couldn't alert his accomplices."

"Nice work, Lieutenant." Lily headed toward the back door. "Who wants to join me in arresting Scotty Flanagan? I'll let you guys take care of these two."

Robbie saw the question in her eyes. "I do." Then he went to cuff Janice and Bill.

He and Lily let themselves out as Sheila began reading Janice and her accomplice their rights. Lily brushed her body against him playfully, exhaling a long breath. "Well, after this unexpected dry run, arresting Kellys' guys tomorrow should be a piece of cake."

Spurting out a laugh, he sighted Scotty rolling like a human-sized worm across the beach, the hope of escape still in his heart apparently. "God, I hope so."

Because he was so done with this fake vacation.

CHAPTER TWENTY-FOUR

LILY'S WISH CAME TRUE, AND DAMN IF THAT DIDN'T HAVE her dancing on clouds.

The Kellys' hit men came in hot the next day like the unimaginative gangsters they were. Parking a few houses down just after dawn, they broke into the beach house, guns locked and loaded. Since the agents across the street had already alerted everyone to their presence, they were waiting for them the moment they crossed the threshold.

Fortunately, the pair didn't have a death wish. They didn't open fire when Tyler shouted, "Freeze! FBI. Lay down your weapons." Their mouths tightened as they exchanged glances before putting their weapons on the floor.

While Sheila and Tyler trained on the hit men, Lily and Robbie approached them and cuffed them together. "I'm going to cherish this moment," she told him as the lock clicked.

He gave her a playful wink as he tightened the cuffs. "Me too. I'm going to play it back on a bad day."

"Glad we could make you so happy," the one guy said in a

harsh Southie accent. "Dammit, the boss should have listened to Mo. He knew you were laying a trap."

"You talking to me?" Robbie asked, leaning closer.

"Yeah," the broad-shouldered bull of a man said, craning his neck to look at him. "You're Robbie O'Connor, and from everything we know, you're a squeaky-clean cop. Being with the Feds proves it. I don't know how you can live with yourself."

Lily fought a smile.

"It's a challenge every day." His voice was filled with irony. "But I agree with you. It's too bad for Branigan that he didn't listen to Mo this time."

Lily knew Mo referred to Maury Kelly, Branigan's first cousin and his second-in-command.

"Branigan thought your family being involved might make you think more flexibly," he said with a drawn-out sigh. "Clearly he was wrong."

She and Robbie shared a look as Agents Johnson and Mather arrived and joined them in the kitchen. "No, he wasn't. Family made this entire mess feel very personal."

A shadow passed over Robbie's face, as if he were suddenly remembering the harm the Kellys had put Tara and the girls in. These men had been sent here to kill. Maybe it wasn't personal to them, but she knew Robbie was working hard on keeping his objectivity after Scotty and company had blown it to hell yesterday. Someone in his own family had planned to hurt or possibly kill him and his family, a betrayal that cut to the bone.

Since she was in possession of one of the bad guys, she couldn't touch Robbie's arm in assurance, so she cleared her throat. He found her gaze slowly and shook himself, nodding to communicate he was all right.

She signaled to Tyler and Sheila, who were talking on their cell phones, updating their superiors about the arrests. They had made a lot of them in the past twenty-four hours and enlisted the local office for more help. "Let's get these guys up to FBI headquarters in Charlotte with the others we nabbed last night and wrap this case up."

They had a lot of interviewing to do.

Four days and a whole bunch of confessions later, Lily discovered the other benefit of dating a fellow law enforcement officer. He understood the tension a body took on from interrogation and knew exactly where to massage after she'd fallen face down on their bed in the Charlotte hotel room where their team was staying.

She lifted her shoulder as he hit a knot. "Oh, yes, right there."

His thumb dug in deeper, making her take deep breaths to glide through the release of tension. "I think you might be more knotted up than I am," he said, straddling her on the bed.

She thought about making a joke, but she went with honesty. "It might not be completely professional to mention this, but it was personal for me too. And not just because I want that promotion."

Robbie gently caressed her shoulders and kissed the top of her head before resuming his massage. "I know that. Sheila said she'd never seen you so locked and loaded in interrogation."

"We needed ironclad confessions," she said, purring when he loosened another painful knot.

"Which we got, thanks to you." His magical hands moved down along the outside of her spine. "You're right. People *do* tell you things. I'm not surprised Scotty, Janice, and their ride-along accomplice caved, but I couldn't believe you convinced the Kellys' guys to become federal prosecution witnesses against Branigan and go into Witness Protection after taking an immunity deal. The new life you painted for them in Witness Protection was almost...God, I don't want to use this word."

She leaned her head back against his hard abs. "What word?"

"Poetic." He snorted. "Timmy would have a field day if he heard it."

Laughing was not an option. The previous night he'd had a bad dream about William Shakespeare's head rolling around on the kitchen floor, spouting phrases from his works about death and betrayal and courage in the face of it all. Lily thought he was releasing internalized violence from the case in his own way.

"It was pretty poetic, I guess." She'd chosen to paint a picture of them sitting in lawn chairs by the pool, playing bridge, and each of them meeting a good woman as neither of them were married. "Sometimes people need to see a new vision for their lives. Those hit men were only in their midforties. They have a lot of life left."

"Branigan likes older, wiser guys for hits." He paused in his massage. "Says they make less mistakes than ones with young, hot blood who will shoot their way out of anything."

Lily closed her eyes as he resumed massaging her. "Bad for business all around. I'm glad you weren't upset they were offered immunity."

His hands fell away, and he lifted off her to rest on his side, so she shifted to lie facing him. "I might have to tell myself a few times it was only a job for them, but in the end, I'm practical. When little fish can help you catch big fish, you do it every time. Besides, your way got us the names of the two officers in my department on the Kellys' payroll."

She touched his face as his mouth tightened, knowing that was a second betrayal that had cut deep. "You're probably going to get a special commendation for working with Internal Affairs to bring down those cops."

"I don't want it," he bit out harshly, scrubbing his face. "I just want to get back to work and forget this ever happened."

Her heart suddenly felt all tangled up inside her chest because she knew he was hurting. "We both know that's not going to happen."

His blue eyes blazed as he cursed. "No, it's not. The other thing I tell myself—and I'm telling myself a lot of things these days—is that meeting you is one of the best things to ever happen to me. Lily Meadows, you will always be my sunshine."

She bit her lip, glad he could make a joke despite all this heaviness around them. "You're enjoying Sheila's little sunshine jokes, aren't you? She's upped her quotient because you're new to them."

Her partner was also doing her part to bolster Robbie before he had to go back to the office and face the gut-wrenching betrayal of his fellow officers head-on. He'd certainly have more to handle when they went back to Boston. Everyone agreed it would take a few more weeks to arrest Branigan and bring his organization down, given the pace of additional interrogations and further evidence collection needed to make the case airtight. Because they were not going to let his lawyer get him off on a technicality.

His gorgeous mouth tipped up in all its sexy glory. "The sunshine jokes are your Achilles' heel, and Lily, you know what I told you about letting the O'Connors discover those gems."

"So we're playing dirty now?" She slid her arm around his neck. "Did I mention I signed up for a Shakespeare quote a day email? You're going to be begging me to stop."

He shifted until he could slide deliciously over her. "That's my line," he said, kissing her swiftly as he tugged at her clothing. "By the way, after we arrest Branigan Kelly and the rest of his guys, you're going to have to meet the entire O'Connor clan. Including the Ireland contingent, who are primed to cross the pond. So prepare yourself."

She knew what he was telling her. Meeting his entire family meant they were joining forces for life big-time. "I'm ready. I figure I've got two brothers down already, plus your favorite cousins. How was everyone when you talked to them?"

He rolled them to their sides again, keeping his hands busy at the bare skin under her shirt. "Fidgety. No one likes having FBI protection, of course, but they understand the necessity. Tara was hoping you and Sheila might be the ones to shadow her and the girls once we get back to Boston."

"That's Buck's call." She kissed his jawline, loving the feel of his stubble. "But given that he's personally talked to the head of the Child Exploitation and Human Trafficking Task Force and put in for my promotion, I might be able to convince him to assign me to protection duty until the paperwork is official. Tara is an important witness in our case, after all."

She still hadn't fully taken in that her dream job was coming true. Not when she was so focused on the present case, Robbie, and living off of four hours of sleep a night.

"Tara would love that. So would Reagan and Cassidy. Fortunately, my boss is also feeling magnanimous toward me since we got the names of the dirty cops, so I might also be given some leeway to look after them. Even if it's a little unusual since we're related."

This case was filled with complications and conflicts of interests, but they would navigate them together. "If we end up looking after Tara and the girls, I'm going to insist Billie and Tim come around a lot. I couldn't imagine it any other way."

He groaned as he rose over her again. "Try. I'm begging you."

She tugged on his shirt. "Get used to those last words coming out of that gorgeous mouth of yours. Because it might be your new mantra."

Scoffing, he helped her take off his shirt. "Mantra? I don't really understand what that means. I busted a New Age bookstore four years ago for money laundering. The owner told me his mantra was world peace. I'd never heard such bullshit."

Her lips twitched. "Well, in this case, a mantra is like an intention. But we don't have to use that word. All you need to remember is the begging part."

He coughed out a laugh. "I can probably get on board with that so long as you understand you'll be begging too. But not too loudly this time, okay? Sheila is right next door, and she told me we kept her up last night."

Lily looked at the shared wall. "She did not."

His eyes sparkled with mischief. "She so did, and with great pleasure. You know her."

"Evil is her middle name," she said, groaning.

"She's only messing with you because she can," Robbie told her, grinning now. "I didn't know you blushed. Lily, it's like the first blush of sunshine—"

"Shut up." She shoved him onto his back with a quick leverage move and straddled his hips. "Or I am so getting the cuffs out."

He shifted under her, settling her more intimately against him. "Sheila mentioned those to me too. Said she was coming by tonight before she hit the hay with a special set. I believe her."

So did Lily. Her heart gave an extra knock against her ribs. "What are we going to do? Tyler's on this floor too! Oh my God! I'm going to kill her."

"We could put out the *Do Not Disturb* sign, but I don't think that would stop her."

Lily felt the urge to put her hair up and start analyzing her way out of this nightmare. "What about an APB? I've seen other guys do it as a joke."

"Do you really think that would actually work?" Robbie settled his hands on her hips, squeezing them gently. "Look, now you're all tense again. I'm going to have to dedicate some serious time to helping you relax."

"Relax?" She pushed on his chest. "How are you not embarrassed by this?"

He winced before saying, "Tyler told me I deserve props for being handcuffed to one of the most gorgeous but hands-off female FBI agents in the Bureau and coming out with a love match. It changed my perspective."

"Sheila told Tyler?" Lily started to get up, but Robbie held her in place.

"Did you really think she was going to keep it to herself?" Robbie sat up and kissed her sweetly, clearly trying to take the sting out of his words. "While we're on the subject..."

"Oh God!" She grabbed a fistful of his shirt. "Your family knows. Dammit, I'd hoped Tim—"

"No dice there." He winced. "Tim told Billie, who told Danny, and then Danny told Kathleen, and then—"

"I am in hell with a capital *H*." She flopped onto her back. "That's all there is to it. I finally meet 'the guy' for me, and I'm a joke both at work and with his family. This can't be happening."

He leaned toward the bedside table and grabbed her coconut water. "Here, drink this. And then take some deep breaths."

"Hydration and breath work is not going to fix this!" Oh, she was so embarrassed her cheeks could blister. "How can I face your family when they know about the cuffs? *Does your dad know?*"

He made a pretext of putting her coconut water carefully back in place.

"Robbie O'Connor, you answer me."

"I can't say for sure, but he has ears." He gave a full-body shiver. "You really do sound like my mother when you say that, by the way. But you're missing the point. No one in my family really cares about the cuffs. They're freaking thrilled I've found someone. Jesus, have I lost my ability to swear? I just said *freaking* without even thinking about it."

She wished she could laugh, and the fact that she couldn't had her taking those deep breaths he'd recommended.

"Also, Sheila and Tyler, but especially Sheila, are really happy for you too. Not that Tyler would gossip about us. He could tell I was upset when Sheila started quizzing me about which handcuff styles I prefer. So that's when he helped me see a different perspective."

"Wait! She quizzed you? About handcuffs? Oh, this is getting worse by the minute."

He rubbed his jaw before lying beside her. "How can I help you see this in a good way like Tyler did for me?"

Closing her eyes, she invoked a mantra of her own: *don't think about it.* "Fine. I'll deal with it. I'll remind myself I just caught some really bad guys and am getting the promotion of my life."

"Certainly something we need to celebrate." Kissing her softly, he lifted up until their eyes met. "Don't forget the part about you meeting 'the guy.' I kinda liked that part."

She did too. "I might have to do some more deep breath work and a few mantras, but I'm going to put this aside."

"Good." He kissed her more swiftly this time before pushing up off the bed. "Because Sheila's present should be arriving any minute."

She crawled off the bed and laid her hand on his arm. "You mean she gave you a time?"

He lifted his watch and tapped the face. "Yep. Ten o'clock. Said she should be able to hit the local sex store just before it closes and be back at the hotel before we—"

"Enough!" She held up a hand, wincing so hard her cheekbones hurt. "I can't take any more."

He took her hand and kissed it sweetly. "Deep breaths. Focus on your mantra."

She glared at his smiling face. "You're lucky I'm a nice person."

Taking her into his arms, he slid his hands along her back. "I'm the luckiest. I happen to be in love with the smartest, funniest, sexiest woman, who shares the same passions as I do."

She felt her heart bloom in her chest. They'd already talked about moving in together, both of them feeling the need to spend as much time together as possible while continuing to give their all to their jobs. "You mean killing their work partner?" she joked, telling herself not to think about losing Sheila as her partner—not that they wouldn't hang out in their spare time and work on cases together.

He chuckled in that low, sexy way she loved. "Funny. No, I was talking about outdoor activities like running and other competitive sports, putting bad guys behind bars, and shooting the breeze with my family. Lily, Tim, and Sheila were right to handcuff me to you. You *are* perfect for me, and whenever I look at the handcuffs she's delivering, I'm going to think about that. Hell, I might even frame them."

She was turning gooey on the inside until he got to the part about using handcuffs as a decoration motif. "You are so not. If you do, I'm going to decorate our house with inspirational sayings like *Love Lives Here* and *The Road Is Easier Because of You*."

His baby blues turned downright frosty. "You wouldn't."

"Would," she practically sang.

He huffed out an aggrieved breath before nodding. "Fine. I won't frame them. We'll put them in a nice drawer—"

"I prefer a lockbox," she said, poking a finger into his chest. "I wouldn't put it past one of your brothers to go looking for them and bring them out for show-and-tell."

His face bunched up like he'd eaten something sour. "You're right. They're totally ruthless."

A knock sounded.

"Like your partner." He kissed her quickly before going to the door. "Ready?"

She set her weight, preparing herself for the inevitable. "Open it."

Cracking it mere inches, Robbie leaned down and picked up the pink gift bag before letting the door close behind him.

"Don't think I don't see that roguish smile on your face," she accused, pointing her finger at him. "Normally I'd think it's sexy, but I'm still processing the handcuffs thing."

He wiped his face clean of emotion. "Sorry. Here. Your partner. Your gift."

"I think she means it for both of us." She flopped back onto the edge of the bed. "You open it. Since you're the one who took her handcuffs quiz. God! Do I even want to know?"

He grimaced. "All I can say is that I took one for the team." Ruffling through the tissue paper, he spurted out a laugh. And then another louder one before silencing himself.

She leaned forward, her stomach jumping. "How bad is it?" she asked, staring at the bag as if it were a ticking time bomb.

He walked over to the bed, obviously fighting a smile. "I'm in new territory here. I'm not sure how to describe it. See for yourself."

Lily took a courageous breath and reached into the gift bag after he handed it to her. Her eyes widened as she took the cuffs out and dangled them from her hand. "They have pink fur with sparkles!"

"So I see." Robbie's mouth was twitching. "I believe there's a card inside the bag."

"Oh, you are no help." She pulled out the note. *"To Lily and Robbie. The perfect pair. Like these handcuffs. I got these so no one would get hurt. They're mark-free! How cool is that? Love, Sheila."*

"It was really nice of her to pick ones that don't leave marks." Robbie came and sat next to her on the bed, nudging her shock-filled body. "I won't feel guilty about using these. I worried about marking you the first time we were cuffed together."

She turned to face him fully and held up the cuffs. "You seriously want to use these? In all their sparkly pink glory?"

He stood and pulled off his shirt, tossing it aside. "You bet I do."

Her mouth went dry at the sight of his rock-hard body. "But I thought you hated having them used on you."

He commandeered the cuffs and dangled them in the air, making the sparkles wink. "Do these look like regulation cuffs to you? Plus, they're adjustable and key free, so we don't need to worry about getting locked—"

"So they're practically childproof?" she asked as he tossed them into the center of the bed.

"I wouldn't use that term." He unzipped his slacks and peeled them down with his underwear, dispensing with his socks. "In fact, I'm going to be a real gentleman here since you look like a deer in the headlights. You can cuff me to the bed first."

Her eyes bugged. "Robbie O'Connor, you have got to be kidding! We're professionals. Law enforcement officials. We do not use furry pink handcuffs with sparkles."

He laid himself out on the bed, one gorgeous buffet of

male splendor. "You are so cute when you're embarrassed. I kinda like this side of you. It's no wonder the sweet girl-next-door cover works so well for you. You're totally her to the core."

She couldn't argue that point. "Fine. I'm going to put these on you, but I'm not entirely sold on the idea. Just because Sheila gets a wild thought in her head—"

"Doesn't mean we have to follow through," he said with a straight face. "I believe I know the age-old saying about not jumping off a bridge if someone dares you."

He was totally laughing at her, and suddenly she couldn't blame him. She hesitantly picked up the cuffs again and grimaced. The pink fur was synthetic to the touch, and the glitter was already falling onto the bed.

"Quality workmanship, obviously," he said with the snort of a laugh.

"You are having way too much fun with this," she responded, but this time with a smile. "Okay, I'm starting to see the humor too."

"About time." He put a pillow over his lap. "I was getting a little worried. Lily Meadows, will you marry me?"

"What?" she squeaked, meeting his gaze.

He lifted a shoulder, his eyes filled with love. "I wasn't sure when I was going to ask you, but I can't stop myself. Right now seems pretty damn perfect."

Her mouth dropped to the floor. "Perfect? Robbie, are you feeling all right?"

"Hear me out." He reached for her hand with a calm confidence that shocked her. "Here we both are, laughing in bed over some gag gift from your partner. Like an old married couple. I'm playing along. You're acting all hot schoolmarm."

"I am not!" She launched herself at him, the cuffs forgotten. "Don't be flippant about this. We're talking marriage—"

"I know," he said softly, his voice going deep and grave,

"and in a good marriage, people laugh over silly things. Like pink furry handcuffs. After a tough day of work."

She bit her lip as her heart swelled in her chest. She knew she would remember the way he was looking at her for the rest of her life. "Okay, go on."

His lips twitched. "Moments ago, I remembered what my mom used to say. She said when you can laugh together, you can get through anything together. That's how I feel about you. About us. So, I'm asking you again. Wait! Hang on. Jesus, I should probably pull my pants on."

Now her lips were twitching. "Seriously? We have fun pink handcuffs on the bed."

He leveled her a look. "I don't want to be hearing twenty years from now how I could have handled this more romantically."

Unexpected laughter tickled its way up her throat. "More romantic than this?"

"Oh, shit!" He pushed himself up off the bed, reaching for his pants, and then started to pull them up. "You're right. This isn't romantic at all, is it? Dammit, I don't usually give in to impulsivity or spontaneity. I should have made a plan and stuck to it."

She got up and pressed her head against his chest. "Okay, I might regret this comment, but I like you impulsive and spontaneous."

He tipped her chin up, studying her face. "You do?"

"I do." She cupped his jaw, feeling the stubble from his long day. "That's important to me too. Us laughing together. Working together. I didn't have much happiness growing up, but I've worked hard to cultivate it in my life. With you, I feel like so much more is waiting for me. Like there's all this fun and support, bliss even, available to me now. Because you are perfect for me too."

He caressed her face before cupping her cheek tenderly. "So I get a pass for proposing here? In this moment?"

She turned her head until she could kiss his palm. "Yes."

"Wait here." He crossed to the bedside stand and opened the drawer before closing it. "I'm still getting down on a knee, so prepare yourself."

She started chuckling at that determination in his voice. She was going to get some romance after all. "Should I get the handcuffs? I mean, you're bare-chested and your pants aren't zipped."

He sank to one knee and looked up, extending his hand. "But look, I have a ring."

She glanced down, all humor vanishing. Inside a black jewelry box was the brightest diamond she'd ever seen in a simple setting that suited her perfectly. "When did you go ring shopping?"

"Sheila and I went while you were talking to Buck and pushing paper," he said with a wicked grin. "I told you I had game."

She put her hand to her mouth, joy rising in her heart. "So you do. Ask me again."

She halfway expected him to roll his eyes, but his gaze held hers with love. "Lily Meadows, I love you with all my heart. Will you marry me?"

"I love you too, and you bet I will."

She tackled him—after he'd slid the ring on her finger, of course. He was laughing as he fell backward on the floor, knocking the side table against the wall.

"You just made me the happiest man ever," he said as his mouth swept in for a kiss.

A pounding sounded from the other side of the wall. "Hey! It's getting awfully rowdy over there."

Sheila!

Spurting with laughter, Robbie slid over her. "No, but it's about to."

She eyed her ring as she laid her hands on his shoulders, pulling his head down to her. Rowdy wasn't how she'd describe it.

Perfect was.

EPILOGUE

O'CONNOR'S PUB HAD SEEMED LIKE THE PERFECT PLACE FOR Lily to meet his full family for the first time.

She'd already made the rounds—first meeting his unusually emotional father, fresh back from Ireland along with the rest of the Irish contingent, and then the rest of his brothers. She'd been lifted off the ground and kissed on the cheek more times than he could count, making her soon-to-be ex-partner chortle as she was given the same treatment.

He'd told Lily he'd wanted to invite Sheila to give her another friendly face when she met his family. Of course, everyone had already wanted to meet the famous Sheila, the woman who'd duped Billie.

The moment Lily's partner had walked in, every O'Connor male had shouted out a welcome. Except for Billie. Even now, no one knew how Billie truly felt about her. Sure, he'd been jealous of Tyler, but after leaving the Outer Banks, he'd remained mostly mute on the Sheila subject. Robbie didn't plan on asking, but he knew Tara had a strategy working in that ingenious brain of hers to get to the bottom of things.

Their cousin felt she owed all of them a debt, and matchmaking Billie and Sheila might just be on her radar from the way she'd been circling those two and whispering with his brothers. Robbie only hoped no blood would be spilled. Because Billie loved to pick a fight when he was feeling cornered and emotional.

And brotherly roughhousing wasn't happening at this party if he had anything to say about it.

Although Lily had already jokingly offered to arrest them all with him if it were needed. He turned to his fiancée, relieved she was still sporting a delighted grin. From the moment they'd arrived at the pub, her happiness had been obvious. She'd told him she'd never had a family and she planned to enjoy this new part of her life. "You still good?" he asked. "Do I need to dig out one of my stupid criminal videos to keep you laughing?"

"They do make my day." She chucked him under the chin. "I'm so good that I'm ready for a dart game with one of your brothers. The new ones I've met today."

Her clarification was important because Tim and Billie were hovering around Lily, trying to ease her into the rest of their crew. There was no way they would have suggested darts, knowing the kind of mayhem that would ensue.

"Lily, since I'm kinda like your O'Connor docent, let me steer you away from accepting a dart challenge." Tim raised his pint. "Let's have a toast instead. It's safer. Watch this. *Sláinte!*"

His brother's shout was heard throughout the bar, and suddenly the whole group was raising their pints and shouting it back.

"Sláinte," she added, a little late, inciting another chorus of other toasts around the bar.

"Cool." She tapped her pint to Robbie's. "They're a friendly lot, the O'Connors."

He hoped it would stay that way, because if someone started a dart game, the O'Connor competitiveness would kick in, and things would get ugly.

"What does that word mean?" Reagan asked after running over from where she'd been standing with her mother.

Robbie ruffled her soft brown hair, avoiding the thick pink glitter headband she was wearing. Tara had tricked the two girls out in mega-bling for this party. Earlier, Tim had joked that a unicorn had barfed glitter all over them, making Cassidy peal into laughter and point to the dancing unicorns on her dress. Reagan sported a cotton dress covered in glittery butterflies decorated in a kaleidoscope of colors.

He couldn't help but smile as she looked up at him with those big baby blue O'Connor eyes. Maybe he wasn't a fan of glitter. He was still picking it off his backside after he and Lily had used Sheila's special cuffs last night. But he loved these little girls something fierce and was glad to be back in Boston where he could see them anytime he wanted. Which lately was a lot since he missed being around them.

Even Miss Purrfect seemed to look forward to seeing him, which was weird. The last time he and Lily had gone over to watch the girls with Tim and Billie, the cat had brought him a dead bird. Tim had told him it was like a feline love letter, something he hoped wouldn't become a habit. Because he really loved seeing Tara's girls in their spare time, and that was really gross.

He hoisted Reagan up because it always made her smile. "It means good health, I think, but if you want an expert opinion, go ask Kathleen and Ellie's husbands. They know the Irish language." He spied his sister sipping a ginger ale in the corner, and he savored the knowledge he was going to be an uncle. She'd even invited him to pat her belly earlier, which had made him start thinking about him and Lily having kids at some point when they were both ready.

"They talk funny," Reagan whispered as she leaned in. "I can't always understand what they're saying."

Billie threw back his head and laughed. "Neither can we, sweetheart, and I'm thinking it's for the best. One less person to listen to in this insanity."

Tim elbowed him. "Hey! You're talking about family."

"By the way, Tim," Robbie said, catching Billie's eye. "Where's your girlfriend?"

He jerked on the collar of his shirt as if someone were pulling it. "Do I look like I'm ready for you guys to make my life hell? No way I'm messing up what we've got going on with a family meet-up."

Robbie wondered how serious things were between this nurse and his brother. He shot Billie another look. His brother nodded. Yeah, they were going to find out. Even if they had to drop by Tim's retirement home on some pretext and meet this mysterious woman themselves.

"So, Lily," Billie said, putting his arm around her shoulders, "I hear you got your promotion. Way to go."

She turned absolutely radiant, making his brain short-circuit for a moment. "I hope to be starting in a few weeks now that we've arrested Branigan Kelly and a number of his associates."

"Congrats!" Tim held up his hand for a high five.

Reagan raised hers immediately after he and Lily connected. "Me too! Congrats, Lily!"

"Thanks!" Her smile lit up his heart. "I can't wait to get started."

"Mom says you rock at catching bad guys and people who make mistakes." Reagan slid out of his arms and turned to her. "Like our dad."

Robbie's throat caught. Tara had asked him and Lily what their professional opinion was about telling the girls that their father had been arrested and was likely going to jail. Sure, Scotty Flanagan had confessed, but he hadn't known enough about the Kellys' operation to receive immunity. Lily had suggested she tell them their father had made a mistake involving the law, and unfortunately, he was going to be facing the consequences.

Cassidy hadn't really understood, but Reagan had nodded slowly and said she knew he'd made her mom really mad, so mad she'd told him he couldn't live with them anymore or work at the nail salon, so it had to be bad. For the moment, the reasoning seemed to be working, but Robbie knew she'd have more questions as she got older. Whatever came, he'd promised Tara they would be there to help her answer them. Lily's background with children was going to be a big help, thank God.

Lily leaned down until she was at Reagan's eye level. "So does Robbie here, and that's a good thing, isn't it? Sometimes people who make mistakes cause a lot of trouble."

Reagan looked down at her shoes. "That's why I'm glad you and Robbie do what you do. Mom said you guys are heroes, but until I met you and Miss Morales, I didn't know girls could be that kind of hero."

Lily glanced up at Robbie and winked. "Well, there are only a few of us in the big picture, but we give it everything we've got."

"That's what Miss Morales told me," Reagan said, swinging in place. "I'm glad you guys invited her to the party. She's so funny. Did you know she arrested a man who was riding a green sheep on St. Patrick's Day? She even showed us a photo. Mom said I should do a report on you guys for school. I'm totally telling that story about the sheep."

"That would be great!" Lily straightened Reagan's head-band when it slipped in her excitement. "You should talk to my mentor too when she comes to Boston next week! She's a total rock star when it comes to catching bad guys. She's got some great stories too."

Then Lily plunged into singing the praises of women in law enforcement. Robbie caught Billie looking over with his brow furrowed as he watched Sheila talking with Danny while he manned the bar. God knew what those two were cooking up. But from the tension in Billie's face, did he think Danny was hitting on Sheila? If he did, he was an idiot, but jealousy did that to a man. He hoped his brother would wise up and ask her out.

Robbie flinched as a woman's nail poked into his side. He grabbed his cousin's hand as she laughed. "Come on, Tara! You know I hate that."

She bumped him playfully, holding a grinning Cassidy on her hip, whose drool quotient for the day had been met and then some. "It's all in good fun. Reagan, remember that question you were going to ask Billie?"

Robbie sensed danger in the air immediately. He shot Tara a warning glance.

Reagan nodded and gave a hesitant smile. "Do you miss Miss Morales being your girlfriend?"

Tim coughed loudly into his mouth.

"Blesh you," Cassidy called.

Lily bit her lip and nudged Robbie. Like he didn't know what was going on. He found he didn't mind much—nudging him in moments like this was what a good partner did. In case he was comatose or something. He cleared his throat when Billie remained silent.

A reproachful eye roll was their answer before Billie bent down to Reagan's level. "Didn't your mom tell you that Lily and Miss Morales were working for their job? You know what it means to pretend, right?"

She glanced at her mother before nodding slowly. "But Lily wasn't pretending."

The veins on the top of Billie's head were suddenly visible, and Robbie winced. This was so not good.

"Lily and Robbie had that soul thing going." He snapped his fingers. "Come on, Shakespeare. This is your area. Love and romance."

"Actually," Tim said. "Since Lily and Robbie are going to have their happily ever after, we've agreed that the standard Shakespearean tragedy doesn't really apply to them. We might even say they have a very un-Shakespeare romance. Right, Robbie?"

He thought about all the tragedy that could have happened if things hadn't gone their way. Sometimes he still had bad dreams about it, including that one with Shakespeare's head rolling around on the ground. He shuddered. "That's right. Lily and I have officially laid the whole Shakespeare thing to rest. Haven't we, babe?"

Her mouth worked before she lifted her shoulder reluctantly. "Maybe for us, but I still would miss Tim's impressions. What about you, Reagan?"

"Me too!" the little girl called.

"Me too!" Cassidy echoed, flailing her hands in the air.

Robbie leaned in to Lily. "You traitor."

She started chuckling softly, her fingers tickling the muscles of his upper thigh.

"You are so going to pay for this later," he continued in a whisper-soft voice.

She only laughed harder.

"Well, it seems we have a quorum," Tim announced, holding out his arms. "Hear ye, hear ye! The bard wishes to speak on this august occasion. Lily and Robbie, I have memorized a special verse for thee."

Reagan and Cassidy cheered and clapped as the rest of the bar grew quiet. Robbie was already grimacing.

"Speak, bard!" Lily answered in that same crazy theater accent. "We have wish to hear thy words."

"I cannot believe your girl is egging our brother on," Billie hissed.

Robbie raised a warning hand and locked his jaw.

Tim eyed the room, his Adam's apple twitching in his throat the only sign he knew the potential peril he was facing.

"Go on, Tim!" Kathleen called out with a shrill whistle.

"Yeah!" Ellie followed up with a fist in the air. "We want to hear it."

Robbie caught the gratitude in his brother's eyes before he bowed, and it hit him that it had taken courage for his little brother to take the stage, so to speak, in front of every one of his older brothers. "Go on, Tim," he finally said. "You know you can't stop yourself."

They shared a long look before his brother cleared his throat, shaking off that flash of vulnerability in his eyes.

"This verse is for my brother, who inspires great brotherly admiration, but I imagine it will also pierce the breast of both of these crime-fighting partners." He drew himself up, his stature rising. *"When the suspicious head of theft is stopped. Love's feeling is more soft and sensible than are the tender horns of cockled snails."*

Lily put her hand over her mouth, chuckling softly. "I love the theft part, Tim," she called.

"Cockled snails?" Robbie slapped a hand to his forehead. "How does that even make sense?"

"The words of Shakespeare are sometimes difficult for the layman to understand," Tim responded cheekily. "But wait, there is more."

Groans rained out across the pub amidst spurts of laughter.

"This one is for the fair and sweet Princess Lily," he said, bowing with his hand pressed to his heart.

Robbie's fiancée touched her hand to her own heart, a sheen of warmth coming into her green eyes.

"Love comforteth like sunshine after rain."

Robbie felt something claw at his throat. God, his brother... He'd nailed Lily perfectly.

"That's beautiful," Ellie's husband shouted. "We Irish understand that one, given how much rain we have. When the sunshine appears, it's like heaven's opened its own door."

Brady McGrath's comments only inspired more groans and chuckles.

"Thank you, Brady." Tim shrugged his shoulders back. "I will be silent after this, I do swear."

"You'd better," Danny called from the bar, "or we'll be using you as our dartboard later."

Robbie swung his head around to face Danny and made a slicing motion in the air. His brother lifted his hands in peace, and Robbie nodded, turning back around. Somehow, he'd become his baby brother's champion, and if he were honest, he didn't mind one bit.

Tim smiled as his eyes closed. "The final verse is this, and I hope all who hear it find it as fitting as I do. *I do love nothing in the world so well as you—is not that strange?*"

Robbie shifted until he was looking directly at Lily, whose heart was in her eyes. "Yes, I do find that strange," he said in a low voice. "What about you?"

"The strangest," she whispered, touching his arm in that connected way she had, which always wound its way around his heart.

"Well, kids," Sheila said, suddenly wrapping her arms around them, "how does it feel to be so perfect for each other and to catch the bad guys together?"

He inclined his chin to Lily. "Pretty freaking spectacular. What about you, Lily?"

Her green eyes danced. "I couldn't be happier."

"I thought so," she said, bumping them both with her hips. "Tim, your next drink is on me for making the happy couple turn all sweet and gooey like whoopie pies before our eyes."

"Thanks, Sheila." Tim crossed until he was standing in front of them. "Robbie. Lily. I wish you every happiness."

Robbie felt that strange knot in his throat again. "Oh, go off to the bar with you. You'll be lucky if Danny doesn't put something in your beer after your theatrics."

Tim's smile lit up his whole face. "It was worth it. Besides, if he does, you can bust him, right, Sheila?"

She gave a snarky laugh, taking his arm. "Poisoning is listed in section twenty-eight in the Massachusetts law—"

"Now who's showing off." Billie jerked a shoulder, clearly filled with the green-eyed monster.

There was a standoff. Sheila lifted a brow in his direction. "Is someone having a bad time at the party?"

Tara gave Billie a playful swat before he could open his mouth. "Yes, someone is. Obviously. Billie, didn't you have something you want to ask Sheila here?"

Robbie started shaking his head. Tara was so asking for a showdown, demanding a reaction like that.

Billie punched up a shit-eating grin. "Yeah, who's your mechanic?"

Robbie thought about knocking his brother out to save him from the fallout he was inviting. *"Billie."*

"It's a serious question." He stared Sheila down.

"I haven't had any car trouble so far." Sheila made a show of raising her hand and tapping something. "Knock on wood."

Billie took a step toward Sheila. "Well...if you do, Agent Morales, you bring it by to me. It will be on the house."

His very stupid brother, who had a death wish, it seemed, caressed Sheila's arm before walking past her on the way to the bar.

"Fix her car?" Lily fumed, clearly pissed since she and Sheila had been hoping for a more traditional dating request from Billie. "Robbie, I don't care if it was on the house. That's my partner he was talking to."

Sheila fisted her hands at her sides. "Like I need or want him to fix my car."

Tim touched Sheila's arm. "Let me decode that conversation for you, starting with myself. When I wanted to see if my girlfriend liked me, do you know what I did? I told her I'd come over and mow her lawn. Robbie, do you want to tell them why that's so significant?"

Robbie tucked his tongue in his cheek before saying, "Tim doesn't have a yard."

Lily and Sheila exchanged puzzled expressions.

"I had to borrow a lawnmower as well as Billie's SUV to haul it over to her house." Tim extended his hands. "Do you understand what I'm trying to tell you? Billie likes you, Sheila. Otherwise, he'd never offer to fix your car."

Tara laughed. "I have to agree. They'd rather slice off a finger than admit they have real feelings in the beginning. The first boy who liked me at school threw rocks at me to get my attention. God, I loved that kid. How's Tyler, by the way? Robbie, you should have invited him tonight."

He took Cassidy into his arms and steered Tara toward the bar. "You need another drink."

She blew him a kiss. "Just saying. I wouldn't mind seeing that fine man again even though we have never been so busy at the salons. The press after the fire was like some insane advertisement for us. Lily. Sheila. Nails on the house anytime too, but I don't like you like that."

Sheila hooted. "Too bad. You're a catch."

Tara buffed her nails on her shoulder. "I know, and I'm just starting to remember how much. Reagan, honey, you want to come with Mommy?"

"No, I'll stay with Cassidy," the little girl said, smiling up at Robbie.

There was admiration in her eyes, and he had to admit, he liked it. "You're a good big sister. Now, is everyone okay here?"

Lily glanced at Sheila, who nodded slowly. "Tim, I'm going to need CliffsNotes."

"Add me to your speed dial," his brother said, kissing her cheek, "but I think your understanding is in the top percentile already."

"Meaning I'm an idiot?" Sheila said, cocking her hip.

"Billie Speak is tough even for his brothers," Robbie said diplomatically. "Sheila, weren't you going to buy Tim a drink?"

"It's a free bar." She tagged Tim's arm. "But I'll get you a symbolic drink. Come on, Shakespeare. Maybe we can poke at your other brothers more. This girl needs some entertainment."

Tim cast her a conspiratorial glance. "It would be my pleasure."

Great. Robbie could see the blowup coming already. "Tim."

His brother looked over, a smile dancing over his lips.

"Thanks."

Inclining his chin, as if he were one of the tough O'Connor boys, Tim lifted his shoulder. "You got it."

As they left, Robbie turned to Lily, Cassidy babbling in his arms. "Well, a fight might ensue. Are you still willing to help me make some arrests if Shakespeare over there ends up causing trouble?"

She laid her hand on his back, surveying the happy crowd as Cassidy babbled to herself. "I think we can handle everyone. Besides, we have Sheila."

He looked over his shoulder. She was laughing with Tim at the bar as he talked with his hands, likely spouting more Shakespeare, if the grimace on Danny's face was any indication. He cut his gaze to Billie. His brother was propped up against one of the wooden posts in the bar, sipping a Guinness, his blue eyes downright frosty. Yeah, his brother liked Sheila. A lot.

"What are the odds Sheila will take her car over to Billie to get it fixed?" he asked.

"I have no idea." She gave her partner a quick glance. "Seems like it should be pretty fast though, huh? Got any ideas?"

He did. "Reagan, put your hands over your ears for a sec."

The little girl frowned but did as he asked.

"Are you up for a little car tampering this week? Maybe mess with the starter so she can't drive to work."

Her smile crested across her face, making him think of Tim's earlier Shakespeare quote. *Love comforteth like sunshine after rain.* God, he was really getting sappy.

"I think I can fit you in between criminal interrogations and paperwork," she quipped. "And I must say, Lieutenant O'Connor, I do like your creative strategy."

He only hoped the not-so-happy couple would too.

What would a brother do for another? A whole lot, it seemed.

"Have I become a total sap?"

She eyed him, love and happiness flashing in her beautiful eyes. "Yes, but I like it."

He did too actually. Not that he'd admit it out loud.

"How about we mingle?" He gently pulled Reagan's hands from her ears. "Good job, kiddo. You didn't need to hear that."

"Mom does that all the time now," the little girl said with a huff. "What do you think, Cassidy?"

The little girl jerked and then tensed up her face. Suddenly a burst of gunfire exploded in her diaper. Robbie grimaced and held her out midair, his nose twitching.

"Wow!" Reagan cried, laughing. "Cassidy, you had a ton of magic inside."

"'Cane," the little girl babbled, legs dangling.

"Talk about bad luck," Robbie ground out. "I'm in a sea of people and she does this with me."

Lily's mouth was twitching as she covered her nose. "Magic is an unstoppable force."

"Right," he said dryly, unwilling to interrupt Tara to change it after the time she'd been having lately. "Hey! You're my partner. How about you go with Reagan and change her diaper?"

Lily raised her brow. "You'd better not be serious."

He gave what he hoped was a persuasive smile. "You know I love you…"

"Yeah, yeah," she said dramatically. "Bribery will get you nowhere. I'm a federal officer."

She was incorruptible, and the horrible smell was rising around them. "Hey! Wasn't there something about a foul stench in Shakespeare?"

"You're resorting to quoting Shakespeare?" Lily asked with a choked laugh. "Oh, Robbie, you must be desperate."

"Desperate to be alone with you," he said, giving her a quick kiss on the mouth. "I'll be right back. I'm about to delegate."

"This I've gotta see," he heard, feeling her follow him to the bar.

Tim glanced up when they arrived beside him, pausing with his pint halfway to his mouth. Sheila's face scrunched up immediately.

"You're a lover of magic, right?" Robbie asked Tim before holding Cassidy out to him.

His baby brother held his gaze before putting down his beer. *"Be not afraid of greatness: some are born great, some achieve greatness, and some have greatness thrust upon them."*

Robbie looked at Lily. "I've got love and greatness down. The magic is all you, Tim."

"I'm good with that." Tim took Cassidy and kissed her cheek. "Princess, there is still much work to do with this clan. Come, Princess Pixie, we be the keepers of magic..."

As they walked off, Reagan skipping with them, Lily slid her arm around him. "That was a good line. Hey, Danny. Can I get two beers down here?"

His brother raised a finger in response. "Coming right up, Sunshine."

Robbie started chuckling as Lily frowned. "Your nickname is catching."

"So is the flu." She lifted the beer Danny set down moments later and waited until Robbie had his drink. "I have a toast. I agree that we have love and greatness down. But I'd say you and I both possess a special type of magic."

He leaned closer, his body brushing hers.

"We catch bad guys," she said, smiling brightly.

"To catching bad guys," he answered, lifting his glass to touch hers.

Robbie rolled his eyes, taking Lily aside. "I have one more. To love."

Because if a guy had to do without greatness and that magic stuff, Robbie would take love with Lily Meadows every time.

———

If you liked A Very Un-Shakespeare Romance, make Ava's day and leave a review.

———

Turn the page to enjoy the scene from After Indigo Irish Nights that had Robbie O'Connor becoming a favorite book boyfriend...

Everything Kathleen had told Declan about Robbie said he was the guy to approach. It sent the biggest message. He was the oldest brother, the one everyone looked up to, the one who took care of everyone. He had to speak to him. He had to convince him to let him talk to Kathleen. Maybe he could even get the man on his side.

A tall, well-muscled man appeared in the doorway. Declan saw the resemblance to Kathleen immediately in the eyes and the nose.

"Come on in and take a seat, Declan. Then you can tell me what kind of trouble you're in."

Declan sat down in the ugly brown chair in front of a battered gray desk. "I'm not in any kind of trouble."

Robbie sat behind the desk and kicked back. "You're in a police station. You look like you just got off the plane. You have bruises all over your face."

Yeah, he'd noticed people staring at him weirdly. "Can you believe no one asked why?"

He laughed. "Yeah, I can. Trust me. You're in some kind of trouble. You're the asshole who broke my sister's heart, right? I could break you into a million pieces for hurting her," Robbie finished conversationally.

His chest filled with tension, but he nodded. "I would deserve it. Robbie, I'm here to make it right. That's why I wanted to talk to you. Kathleen says you're the oldest, the one everyone looks up to."

Robbie put his hands on the top of his desk and leaned

forward. "So you figured you'd persuade me to help you with my sister. Boy, this had better be good."

As a boxer, he knew plenty of men who radiated toughness and menace. Kathleen's brother all but rolled in it. He decided the tack he would take. "How do you feel about sharing your deepest, darkest secrets, Robbie?"

He scoffed. "I fucking hate it," he said, sounding very much like Mark Wahlberg.

Declan almost smiled. "What about sharing your emotions?"

"I fucking hate that too." His eyes narrowed. "All right, so you want another shot at my baby sister. I'm thinking a public place—in case she wants to storm out or cry for help. A place where all her brothers can look out for her."

All seven, he recalled. "That sounds more than fair. I didn't want to just show up at your family's pub or ask Ellie where she was staying."

"I'm glad you didn't put Ellie in that position. She's like a sister to us. If you'd made her cry too, we'd have to kill you for sure and throw you into the bay."

Declan cleared his throat as the image rolled through his mind. It wasn't hard to imagine.

Robbie stood, cracking his neck. "I'm just kidding. Mostly."

Yeah, mostly. "You probably have a slew of ideas from your 'stupid criminal' videos on how not to dispose of the body, right? I was thinking they were amusing before, but..."

Robbie's shoulders started shaking. "So she showed them to you. You come up with the drunk leprechaun video she sent me?"

"That's right. Don't judge us Irish by his example."

He punched him in the shoulder none too lightly. "Ace, I might be starting to like you. Come on. You can sit in one of the interrogation rooms until I arrange everything with my brothers. Everyone's getting off work about now."

Inside the interrogation room, he concluded Kathleen's brother was having the time of his life trying to intimidate him. He stared at the bare walls and the two-way mirror and wondered if Robbie was observing him. In a few days, Declan hoped he'd be in a position to see all this as a bit of good *craic*.

When Robbie finally opened the door, he lifted his chin. "Let's go, tough guy. Everyone's meeting up at O'Connor's. You have one chance. Here's the rules."

He raised his brow. "There are rules?"

The man made a rude sound before saying, "One, you don't touch her. Two, if she walks away, you don't follow. Three, if you blow it, you never talk sweet to her ever again."

That was going to be hard. But it was fair, and he knew it. "Done."

"And last thing... My brothers Billie and Danny insisted on this one."

He wasn't a fearful man, but he knew this one was going to be mad.

"You make her cry, they're going to knock out your teeth and rip your limbs off. Break some bones." Robbie grinned like a jackal. "You ready to go or what?"

Declan nodded.

He didn't plan to fail.

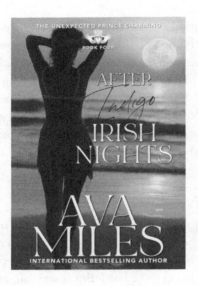

Treat yourself to After Indigo Irish Nights right this minute!

Or start at the beginning of Ava's acclaimed Unexpected Prince Charming series, set in magical Ireland, with Beside Golden Irish Fields and find more book boyfriends—all ruggedly compelling Irishmen. Wink.

THE UNEXPECTED PRINCE CHARMING

Start Ava's bestselling series, set entirely in magical Ireland.

Beside Golden Irish Fields

A stay-up-all-night story about a woman who goes to Ireland in hopes of a second chance at life and finds love in the most unexpected man.

Beneath Pearly Irish Skies

A feel-good tale about a single mom starting over in Ireland and the unexpected Prince Charming who helps her find her purpose and happiness.

Through Crimson Irish Light

A romantic classic about an artist journeying to Ireland to stand on her own, only to discover support and romance in the most surprising of men.

After Indigo Irish Nights

A heartwarming story about two jaded people who discover the power of love after letting go of the past.

Beyond Rosy Irish Twilight

A second chance at love and a first chance at happily ever after.

Over Verdant Irish Hills

A magical tale about love, family, and the power of taking risks.

Against Ebony Irish Seas

A mystical story about secrets, redemption, and the power of love.

ABOUT THE AUTHOR

Millions of readers have discovered International Bestselling Author Ava Miles and her powerful fiction and non-fiction books about love, happiness, and transformation. Her novels have received praise and accolades from *USA Today*, *Publisher's Weekly*, and *Women's World Magazine* in addition to being chosen as Best Books of the Year and Top Editor's picks. Translated into multiple languages, Ava's strongest praise comes directly from her readers, who call her books and characters unforgettable.

Ava is a former chef, worked as a long-time conflict expert rebuilding warzones to foster peaceful and prosperous communities, and has helped people live their best life as a life coach, energy healer, and self-help expert. She is never happier than when she's formulating skin care and wellness products, gardening, or creating a new work of art. Hanging with her friends and loved ones is pretty great too.

After years of residing in the States, she decided to follow her dream of living in Europe. She recently finished a magical stint in Ireland where she was inspired to write her acclaimed Unexpected Prince Charming series. Now, she's splitting her time between Paris and Provence, learning to speak French, immersing herself in cooking *à la provençal*, and planning more page-turning novels for readers to binge.

Visit Ava on social media:

 facebook.com/AuthorAvaMiles
twitter.com/authoravamiles
instagram.com/avamiles
bookbub.com/authors/ava-miles
pinterest.com/authoravamiles

DON'T FORGET...

Sign up for Ava's newsletter.

More great books? Check.
Fun facts? Check.
Recipes? Check.
General frivolity? DOUBLE CHECK.

https://avamiles.com/newsletter/

Made in the USA
Monee, IL
24 September 2024

66401471R00225